General Bounce
Or The Lady and the Locusts

by

G. J. Whyte-Melville

General Bounce
Or The Lady and the Locusts
by G. J. Whyte-Melville

Copyright © 2024

All Rights reserved.

ISBN: 978-93-61423-20-8

Published by

DOUBLE 9 BOOKS

2/13-B, Ansari Road
Daryaganj, New Delhi – 110002
info@double9books.com
www.double9books.com
Tel. 011-40042856

This book is under public domain

ABOUT THE AUTHOR

George John Whyte-Melville was a Scottish novelist who was particularly interested in field sports. He also wrote poetry. He took a hiatus in the mid-1850s to serve as an officer in Turkish irregular cavalry during the Crimean War. George John Whyte-Melville was born at Mount Melville, near St Andrews, Scotland, in 1821. He was the son of Major John Whyte-Melville and Lady Catherine Anne Sarah Osborne, as well as the 5th Duke of Leeds' grandchild on his mother's side. His father was a well-known athlete and Captain of the Royal and Ancient Golf Club of St. Andrews. When Arco Hermoso died in 1835, the marquesa was in grave financial problems, and in less than two years she married Antonio Arrom de Ayala, a much younger man. In 1849, Elizabeth Gibbs, described as "a smartly-dressed and interesting looking young woman," issued a summons for maintenance against Whyte-Melville, alleging that he was the father of her son. She reported that she had known Whyte-Melville since December 1846 and gave birth to his child on September 15, 1847. The Magistrate read other letters claimed by Gibbs to be from Whyte-Melville, in one of which the writer indicated his desire that Gibbs assign the paternity to some other person since he did not want to pay for the enjoyment of others.

CONTENTS

PREFACE

Where the rose blushes in the garden, there will the bee and the butterfly be found, humming and fluttering around. So is it in the world; the fair girl, whose sweetness is enhanced by the fictitious advantages of wealth and position, will ever have lovers and admirers enough and to spare.

Burns was no bad judge of human nature; and he has a stanza on this subject, combining the reflection of the philosopher with the *canny* discrimination of the Scot.

"Away with your follies of beauty's alarms,

The *slender* bit beauty you clasp in your arms;

But gi'e me the lass that has acres of charms,

Oh, gi'e me the lass with the *weel-plenished* farms."

Should the following pages afford such attractive young ladies matter for a few moments' reflection, the author will not have written in vain.

May he hope they will choose well and wisely; and that the withered rose, when she has lost her fragrance, may be fondly prized and gently tended by the hand that plucked her in her dewy morning prime.

CHAPTER I
MY COUSIN

Much as we think of ourselves, and with all our boasted civilisation, we Anglo-Saxons are but a half-barbarian race after all. Nomadic, decidedly nomadic in our tastes, feelings, and pursuits, it is but the moisture of our climate that keeps us in our own houses at all, and like our Scandinavian ancestors (for in turf parlance we have several crosses of the old Norse blood in our veins), we delight periodically—that is, whenever we have a fortnight's dry weather—to migrate from our dwellings, and peopling the whole of our own sea-board, push our invading hordes over the greater part of Europe, nor refrain from thrusting our outposts even into the heart of Asia, till the astonished Mussulman, aghast at our vagaries, strokes his placid beard, and with a blessing on his Prophet that he is not as we are, soothes his disgust with a sentiment, so often repeated that in the East it has become a proverb—viz. that "There is one devil, and there are many devils; but there is *no* devil like a Frank in a round hat!"

It was but last autumn that, stepping painfully into our tailor's shop—for, alas! a course of London dinners cannot be persisted in, season after season, without producing a decided tendency to gout in the extremities—hobbling, then, into our tailor's warehouse, as he calls it, we were measured by an unfledged jackanapes, whose voice we had previously heard warning his brother fractions that "an old gent was a waitin' inside," instead of that spruce foreman who, for more years than it is necessary to specify, has known our girth to an inch, and our weight to a pound. Fearful that in place of the grave habit of broadcloth which we affect as most suitable to our age and manner, we might find ourselves equipped in one of the many grotesque disguises in which young gentlemen now-a-days deem it becoming to hide themselves, and described by the jackanapes, aforesaid, who stepped round us in ill-concealed admiration of our corpulence, as "a walking coat, a riding coat, a smoking coat, or a coat *to go to the stable in!*" we ventured to inquire for "the person we usually saw," and were informed that "the gent as waited on us last year had gone for a few months' holiday to the Heast." Heavens and earth, Mr. Bobstitch was even then in Syria! What a Scandinavian! rather degenerate to be sure in size and ferocity—though Bobstitch, being a little man, is probably very terrible when roused—but yet no slight contrast to one of those gaunt, grim, russet-bearded giants that made the despot of the Lower Empire quake upon his throne. And yet Bobstitch was but obeying the instinct which he inherits from the sea-kings his ancestors, an instinct which in less adventurous souls than a tailor's fills our watering-places to overflowing, and pours the wealth, while it introduces the manners, of the capital into every bight and bay that indents the shores of Britain.

Doubtless the citizens are right. Let us, while we are in Scandinavian vein, make use of an old Norse metaphor, and pressing into our service the two Ravens of Odin, named Mind and Will, with these annihilate time and space, so as to be, like the Irish orator's bird, "in two places at once." Let us first of all take a retrospective glance at Mrs. Kettering's house in Grosvenor Square, one of the best houses, by the way, to be had in London for love or money. We recollect it well, not so many years ago, lit up for one of those great solemnities which novelists call "a rout," but which people in real life, equally martially as well as metaphorically, designate "a drum." To us creeping home along the pavement outside the *fête*, it seemed the realisation of fairyland. Row upon row, glaring carriage-lamps, like the fabulous monsters keeping watch, illuminated the square and adjoining streets, even to the public-house round the corner, that night driving a highly remunerative trade; whilst on a nearer inspection magnificent horses (horses, like ladies, look most beautiful by candle-light), gorgeous carriages—none of your Broughams and Clarences, but large, roomy, well-hung family coaches, with cartoons of heraldry on the panels—gigantic footmen, and fat coachmen, struck the beholder with admiration not totally unmixed with awe. Then the awning that was to admit the privileged to the inner realms of this earthly paradise, of which the uninitiated might know but the exterior; what a gauzy, gaudy transparency it was, no unfitting portal to that upper storey, from which the golden light was hardly veiled by jalousies and window-blinds. Ever and anon, much lashing of bay, brown, or chestnut sufferers, and the interference of a tall policeman, with a hat made on purpose to be assaulted by bludgeons, betokened the arrival of a fresh party, and angelic beings in white robes, with glossy hair, tripped daintily up the steps over a cloth, not of gold exactly, but of horse-hair, amongst a phalanx of unwashed faces, gazing half enviously at such loveliness in full dress. How beautiful we used to think these apparitions as we plodded home to our quiet chambers! but young Bareface, our connecting link with the great world, who goes to all the *best* places, through the influence of his aunt, Lady Champfront, assures us they don't look half so beautiful inside, and that he sees quite as pretty faces, and hair quite as nicely done, at the little gatherings in Russell Square and Bloomsbury, to which even we might go if we liked. A radical dog! we don't believe a word of it. Never mind, let us look at that house in the dead time of year. Without and within, from attics to basement, from the balcony facing the square to the empty bird-cage overlooking a precipice of offices at the back, Repose and Ennui reign supreme. Were it not for the knocking of the workmen next door, we might as well be in the Great Desert. There *is*, we presume, a woman in possession, but she has gone to "get the beer," and if you have ever sighed for a town-house, now is the time to be satisfied with your rustic lot, and to hug yourself that you are not paying ground-rent and taxes, church-rate, poor's-rate, and water-rate, drainage, lighting, and paving, for that ghastly palace of soot and cobwebs, dust, dreariness, and decay. There is a scaffolding up in every third house in the square; and workmen in paper caps, with foot-rules sticking out of their fustian trousers, and complexions ingrained with lime-dust, and guiltless of fresh water, seem to be the only inhabitants of this deserted region, and even they are "between earth and heaven." Brown and parched are the unfortunate shrubs in those gardens of which discontented householders "round the corner" covet so to possess a key; and the very birds, sparrows, every feather of 'em, hop about in dirty suits of plumage that can only be described as of that colour unknown to naturalists, which other people call "grimy." Who would be in London in the autumn? Not Mrs. Kettering, certainly, if she might be elsewhere; and although she had possessed this excellent and commodious family mansion, with all its boudoirs, retreats, and appurtenances, so well described in the advertisement, but a short time, and was not the giver of that "reunion of fashionables" we have depicted above (indeed, the hostess of that evening has since been economising up two pair of stairs at Antwerp); yet Mrs. Kettering having plenty of money, and being able to do what she liked, had wisely moved herself, her fancies, her imperials, and her family to the coast, where, obeying the instinct for freedom that has driven Bobstitch to the desert, she was idly inhaling the salt breezes of the Channel, and dazzling her eyes with the sun-glint that sparkled over its dancing waves.

Some few years have elapsed since the events took place which we shall endeavour to describe; but the white cliffs of our island change little with the lapse of time, though the sea does make its encroachments ever and anon when the wind has been blowing pretty steady from the south-west for a fortnight or so, and the same scene may be witnessed any fine day towards the middle of August as that which we are about to contrast with the dulness, closeness, and confinement of the great town-house in Grosvenor Square.

First, we must imagine a real summer's day, such a day as in our island we seldom enjoy till summer has well-nigh given place to autumn, but which, when it does come, is worth waiting for. Talk of climate! a real fine day in England, like a really handsome Englishwoman, beats creation. Well, we must imagine one of these bright, hot, hay-making days, almost too warm and dusty ashore, but enjoyable beyond conception on the calm and oily waves, unruffled by the breeze, and literally as smooth as glass. A sea-bird occasionally dips her wing on the surface, and then flaps lazily away, as if she too was as much inclined to go to sleep as yonder moveless fleet of lugger, brig, bark, and schooner, with their empty sails, and their heads all round the compass. There is a warm haze towards the land, and the white houses of St. Swithin's seem to glow and sparkle in the heat, whilst to seaward a modified sort of mirage would make one fancy one could plainly distinguish the distant coast of France.

Ashore, in those great houses, people are panting, and gasping, and creating thorough draughts that fill their rooms with a small white dust of a destructive tendency to all personal property. The children up-stairs are running about in linen under-garments, somewhat more troublesome than usual, with a settled flush on their little peach-like cheeks, and the shining streets are deserted, save by the perspiring pot-boy, and the fly-men drinking beer in their shirt sleeves. Only afloat is there a chance of being cool; and sailing-boat, gig, dinghy, and cobble, all are in requisition for the throng of amateur mariners, rushing like ducklings to the refreshing element.

It was on just such a day as this that Mrs. Kettering found it extremely difficult to "trim the boat." A mile or so from the shore, that boat was slowly progressing, impelled by the unequal strength of her nephew Charles, commonly called "Cousin Charlie," and its worthy proprietor, a fine specimen of the genus "seaman," who certainly had a Christian name, and probably a patronymic, but had sunk both distinctions under the sobriquet of "Hairblower," by which appellation alone he was acknowledged by gentle and simple, bold and timid, delicate ladies and bluff fishermen, along many a mile of sea-board, up and down from St. Swithin's.

"The least thing further, Master Charles," said Hairblower, ever and anon pulling the stripling's efforts round with one hand. "Don't ye disturb, madam—don't ye move, Miss Blanche; it's not *your* weight that makes her roll." And again he moistened the large, strong hand, and turned to look out ahead.

In vain Mrs. Kettering shut up her parasol, and shifted her seat; in vain she disposed her ample figure, first in one uncomfortable position, then in another; she could *not* "trim the boat," and the reason was simple enough. Mrs. Kettering's weight was that of a lady who had all her life been "a fine woman," and was now somewhat past maturity; whilst her daughter and only child, "Blanche," the occupant of the same bench, had but just arrived at that period when the girl begins to lengthen out into the woman, and the slight, lanky figure, not without a grace peculiar to itself, is nevertheless as delicate as a gossamer, and as thin as its own gauzy French bonnet.

Mother and daughter were but little alike, save in their sweet and rather languid tone of voice—no trifling charm in that sex which is somewhat prone, especially under excitement, to pitch its organ in too high a key. Mrs. Kettering was dark and brown of complexion, with sparkling black eyes, and a rich colour, much heightened by the heat. Not very tall in stature, but large and square of frame, well-filled out besides by a good appetite, a good digestion, and, though nervous and excitable, a good temper. Blanche, on the contrary, with her long violet eyes, her curving dark eyelashes, and golden-brown hair, was so slight of frame and delicate of tint as to warrant her mother's constant alarm for her health; not that there was any real cause for anxiety, but mamma loved to fidget, if not about "dear Blanche," about something belonging to her; and failing these, had a constant fund of worry in the exploits and escapades of graceless "Cousin Charlie."

"Now, Charlie, my own dear boy" (Mrs. K. was very fond of Charlie), "I know you must be over-heating yourself—nothing so bad for growing lads. Mr. Hairblower, *pray* don't let him row so hard."

"Gammon, aunt," was Charlie's irreverent reply. "Wait till we get her head round with the flood; we'll make her speak to it, won't we, Hairblower?"

"Well, Master Charles," said the jolly tar, "I think as you and me could pull her head under, pretty nigh,—howsoever, we be fairish off for time, and the day's young yet."

"Blanche, Blanche!" suddenly exclaimed Mrs. Kettering, "look at the weed just beyond that buoy—the alga, what's its name, we were reading about yesterday. Charlie, of course *you* have forgotten. I shall soon be obliged to get a finishing governess for you, Blanche."

"Oh no, dearest mamma," said the young girl, in her soft, sweet voice, which always drew Hairblower's eyes, in speechless admiration, to her gentle countenance. "I could never learn with any one but you; and then she might be cross, mamma, and I should hate her so after you!" And Blanche took her mother's plump, tightly-gloved hand between her own, and looked up in her face with such a fond, bewitching expression, that it was no wonder mamma doted on her, and Hairblower and "Cousin Charlie" too.

Mrs. Kettering was one of those people whose superabundant energy must have a certain number of objects whereon to expend itself. Though a pleasant, cheerful woman, she was decidedly *blue*—that is to say, besides being a good musician, linguist, draughtswoman, and worsted worker, she had a few ideas, not very correct, upon ancient history, a superficial knowledge of modern literature, thought Shakespeare *vulgar* and Milton *dry*, with a smattering of the 'ologies, and certain theories concerning chemistry, which, if reduced to practice, would have made her a most unsafe occupant for a ground-floor. With these advantages, and her sunny, pleasant temper, she taught Blanche *everything* herself; and if the young lady was not quite so learned as some of her associates, she had at least the advantage of a mother's companionship and tuition, and was as far removed as possible from that most amusing specimen of affectation, an English girl who has formed her manner on that of a French governess.

Mrs. Kettering had gone through her share of troubles in her youth, and being of a disposition by no means despondent, was rather happy under difficulties than otherwise. We do not suppose she married her first love: we doubt if women often do, except in novels; and the late Mr. K. was a gentleman of an exterior certainly more respectable than romantic. His manners were abrupt and commercial, but his name at the back of a bill was undeniable. The lady whom he wooed and won was old enough to know her own mind; nor have we reason to suppose but that in pleasing him she pleased herself. Many a long year they toiled and amassed, and old Kettering attended closely to business, though he never showed his books to his wife; and Mrs. Kettering exercised her diplomacy in migrating once every five years further and further towards "the West End." Their last house but one was in Tyburnia, and then old Kettering put a finishing stroke to his business, made a shot at indigo which landed him more thousands than our modest ideas can take in, and enabling him to occupy that mansion in Grosvenor Square which looked so dull in the autumn, placed Mrs. Kettering at once on the pedestal she had all her life been sighing to attain;—perhaps she was disappointed when she got there. However that may be, the enterprising merchant himself obtained little by his new residence, save a commodious vault belonging to it in a neighbouring church, in which his remains were soon after deposited, and a tablet, pure and unblemished as his own commercial fame, erected to his memory by his disconsolate widow. How disconsolate she was, poor woman! for a time, with her affectionate nature: but then her greatest treasure, Blanche, was left; and her late husband, as the most appropriate mark of his confidence and esteem, bequeathed the whole of his property, personal and otherwise, to his well-beloved wife, so the blow was to a certain degree softened, and Mrs. Kettering looked uncommonly radiant and prosperous even in her weeds.

Now, it is very pleasant and convenient to have a large property left you at your own disposal, more especially when you are blessed with a child on whom you dote, to succeed you when you have no further occasion for earthly treasure; and, in the eyes of the world, this was Mrs. Kettering's agreeable lot. The eyes of the world, as usual, could not look into the cupboard where the skeleton was; but our poor widow, or rather our rich widow, was much hampered by the shape which no one else knew to exist.

The fact is, old Mr. Kettering had a crotchet. Being a rich man, he had a right to a dozen; but he was a sensible, quiet old fellow, and he contented himself with one. Now, this crotchet was the invincible belief that he, John Kettering, was the lineal male representative of one of the oldest families in England. How he came to have lost the old Norman features and appearance, or how it happened that such a lofty descent should have merged in his own person as junior clerk to a large City counting-house, he never troubled himself to inquire; he was satisfied that the oldest blood in Europe coursed through his veins, and with the pedigree he supposed himself to possess (though its traces were unfortunately extinct), he might marry whom he pleased. As we have seen, he did marry a very personable lady; but, alas! she gave him no male heir. Under a female succession, all his toil, all his astuteness, all his money, would not raise the family name to the proud position he believed its due. He could not bear the idea of it; and he never really loved poor Blanche half so much as that engaging child deserved. When all chance of a son was hopeless, he resolved to bring up and educate his only brother's orphan child, a handsome little boy, whose open brow and aristocratic lineaments won the old man's favour from the first.

"Cousin Charlie," in consequence, became an inmate of the Kettering family, and was usually supposed by strangers to be the elder brother of pretty little Blanche.

These intentions, however, were kept a dead secret; and the children knew as little as children generally do of their future prospects, or the path chalked out for them through life. With all his fancied importance, old Kettering was a good, right-feeling man; and although it is our belief that he revoked and destroyed several testamentary documents, he ended by leaving everything to his wife, in her own power, as he worded it, "in testimony of his esteem for her character, and confidence in her affection," — previously exacting from her a solemn promise that she would eventually bequeath the bulk of her wealth to his nephew, should the lad continue to behave well, and *like a gentleman* — making a provision for Blanche at her own discretion, but not exceeding one-eighth of the whole available property.

The testator did not long survive his final arrangements. And though her promise cost his widow many a sleepless night, she never dreamed of breaking it, nor of enriching her darling child at the expense of her nephew.

Mrs. Kettering was a woman all over, and we will not say the idea of uniting the two cousins had not entered her mind; on the contrary, brought up together as they were, she constantly anticipated this consummation as a delightful release from her conflicts between duty and inclination. She was, besides, very fond of "Cousin Charlie," and looked eagerly forward to the day when she might see this "charming couple," as she called them, fairly married and settled. With all these distractions, it is no wonder that Mrs. Kettering, who, though a bustling, was an undecided woman, could never quite make up her mind to complete her will. It was a matter of the greatest importance; so first she made it, and then tore it up, and then constructed a fresh one, which she omitted to sign until things were more certain, and eventually mislaid; while, in the meantime, Blanche and "Cousin Charlie" were growing up to that age at which young people, more especially in matters of love-making, are pretty resolutely determined to have a will of their own.

The bridegroom presumptive, however, was one of those young gentlemen in whose heads or hearts the idea of marriage is only contemplated as a remote possibility, and a dreaded termination to a life of enjoyment—in much the same light as that in which the pickpocket views transportation beyond the seas. He believes it to be the common lot of mankind, but that it may be indefinitely postponed with a little circumspection, and in some cases of rare good fortune even eluded altogether.

It is curious to observe at what an early age the different instincts of the sexes develop themselves in children. Little Miss can scarcely waddle before she shoulders a doll, which she calls her baby, and on which she lavishes much maternal care, not without certain wholesome correction. From her earliest youth, the abstract idea of wife and motherhood is familiar to her mind; and to be married, though she knows not what it is, as natural and inevitable a destiny as to learn music and have a governess. Young Master, on the contrary, has no idea of being a "pater familias." His notion of being grown up is totally unconnected with housekeeping. When "he is a man, he means to be a soldier, or a sailor, or a pastry-cook—he will have a gun and hunters, and go all day to the stable, and eat as much as he chooses, and drink port wine like papa;" but to bring up children of his own, and live in one place, is the very last thing he dreams of. "Cousin Charlie" entertained the usual notions of his kind. Although an orphan, he had never known the want of a parent—uncle and aunt Kettering supplying him with as kind and indulgent a father and mother as a spoilt little boy could desire. And although he had his childish sorrows, such as parting from Blanche, going to school, being whipped according to his deserts when there, and thus smuggled through that amusing work, the Latin Grammar; yet, altogether, his life was as happy as any other child's of his own age, on whom health, and love, and plenty had shone from the day of its birth.

Of course, old John Kettering sent him to Eton, that most aristocratic of schools, where Charlie learnt to swim—no mean accomplishment; arrived at much perfection in his "wicket-keeping" and "hitting to the leg," as, indeed, he deserved, for the powers of application he evinced in the study of cricket; was taught to "feather an oar" in a method which the London watermen pronounced extremely inefficient; and acquired a knack of construing Horace into moderately bad English, with a total disregard for the ideas, habits, prejudices, and intentions of that courtly bard. Of course, too, he was destined for the army. With *his* prospects, in what other profession could he get through his allowance, and acquire gentlemanlike habits of extravagance in what is termed good society? Old Kettering wanted to make his nephew a gentleman—that was it. When asked how Charlie was getting on at Eton, and what he learnt there, the uncle invariably replied, "Learn, sir! why, he'll learn to be a gentleman."

It is a matter for conjecture whether the worthy merchant was capable of forming an opinion as to the boy's progress in this particular study, or whether he was himself a very good judge of the variety he so much admired. Our own idea is, that neither birth, nor riches, nor education, nor manner, suffice to constitute a gentleman; and that specimens are to be found at the plough, the loom, and the forge, in the ranks, and before the mast, as well as in the officers' mess-room, the learned professions, and the Upper House itself. To our fancy, a gentleman is courteous, kindly, brave, and high-principled—considerate towards the weak, and self-possessed amongst the strong. High-minded and unselfish, "he does to others as he would they should do unto him," and shrinks from the meanness of taking advantage of his neighbour, man or woman, friend or foe, as he would from the contamination of cowardice, duplicity, tyranny, or any other blackguardism. "*Sans peur et sans reproche*"—he has a "lion's courage with a woman's heart"; and such a one, be he in a peer's robes or a ploughman's smock—backing before his sovereign or delving for his bread—we deem a very Bayard for chivalry—a very Chesterfield for good breeding and good sense. We are old-fashioned though in our ideas, and doubtless our sentiments may be dubbed slow by the young, and vulgar by the great. Still, even these dissentients would, we think, have been satisfied with "Cousin Charlie's" claims to be considered a "gentleman."

Nature had been beforehand with old Kettering, and had made him one of her own mould. Not all the schools in Europe could have spoiled or improved him in that particular. And his private tutor's lady discovered this quality, with all a woman's intuitive tact, the very first evening he spent at the vicarage of that reverend Crichton, who prepared young gentlemen of fifteen years and upwards for *both* the universities and *all* the professions.

"What do you think of the new pupil, my dear?" said Mr. Nobottle to his wife—a dean's daughter, no less!—as he drew up the connubial counterpane to meet the edge of his night-cap. "He was a wild lad, I hear, at Eton. I am afraid we shall have some trouble with him."

"Not a bit of it," was the reply; "he is a gentleman every inch of him. I saw it at once by the way he helped Tim in with his portmanteau. Binks, of course, was out of the way,—and that reminds me, Mr. Nobottle, you never *will* speak to that man,—what's the use of having a butler? And then, he's such a remarkably good-looking boy—but I daresay you're half asleep already."

And, sure enough, patient Joseph Nobottle was executing a prolonged and marital snore.

Mrs. Nobottle found no occasion to recant her predictions; and Charlie was now spending his summer vacation with Mrs. Kettering at St. Swithin's.

We have left the party so long in their boat, that they have had ample time to "trim" or sink her. Neither of these events, however, took place; and after pulling round a Swedish brig, an enormous tub, very *wholesome-looking*, as Hairblower said, and holding a polyglot conversation with an individual in a red night-cap, who grinned at the ladies, and offered them "schnapps," they turned the little craft's head towards the shore, and taking "the flood," as Charlie had previously threatened, bent themselves to their work, and laid out upon their oars in a style that satisfied even the seaman, and enraptured the lad.

"What a dear boy it is!" thought Mrs. Kettering, as she looked at Charlie's open countenance, and his fair golden curls, blowing about his face, browned by the weather to a rich manly hue, and lit up with the excitement and exercise of his work. Many qualms of conscience crossed Mrs. Kettering's mind, in the transit of that mile and a half of blue water which sparkled between "the Swede" and the shore. Much she regretted her want of decision and habits of delay in not completing the important document that should at once make that handsome boy the head of his family; and firmly she resolved that not another week should pass without a proper consultation of the universal refuge, "her family man-of-business," and a further legal drawing-up of her last will and testament. Then she remembered she had left one unfinished, that would make an excellent rough draft for the future document; then she wondered where she had put it; and then she thought what a husband the handsome cousin would make for her own beautiful girl; and rapidly her ideas followed each other, till, in her mind's eye, she saw the wedding—the bridesmaids—the procession—the breakfast—and, though last, not least, the very bonnet, not too sombre, which she herself should wear on the occasion.

Not one word did Mrs. Kettering hear of a long-winded story with which Hairblower was delighting Blanche and Charlie; and which, as it seemed to create immense interest and sympathy in his young listeners, and is, besides, a further example of the general superstition of sailors as to commencing any undertaking on a Friday, we may as well give, as nearly as possible, in his own words.

"Blown, Master Charles?" said the good-humoured seaman, in answer to a question from hard-working Charlie. "Blown? Not a bit of it; nor yet tired; nor you neither. I *was* a bit bamboozled though once somewhere hereaway. It's a good many years past now; but I don't think as *I* shall ever forget it. If you'd like to hear it, Miss Blanche, I'll tell it you, as well as I can. You see, it was rather a 'circumstance' from beginning to end. Well, the fact is, I had built a smartish craft very soon after I was out of my time, and me and a man we used to call 'Downright' went partners in her, and although maybe she was a trifle crank, and noways useful for stowage, we had pretty good times with her when the mackerel was early, and the prices pretty stiffish. But there never was no real luck about her, and I'll tell ye how it was. My uncle, he promised to help me with the money for her of a Friday. She was put upon the stocks of a Friday—finished off of a Friday—sailed her first trip of a Friday—and went down of a Friday; so, as I say, Friday's the worst day, to my mind, in the whole week. Well, the *Spanking Sally*—that's what we called her, Miss—always carried a weather helm. And one day—it was a Friday, too—me and my mate was coming in with a fairish cargo—Downright he said all along she was over-deep in the water—with a light breeze from the nor'-nor'-west, and the tide about half-flood, as it might be now. I had just gone forward to look to the tackle, when the wind suddenly shifted right on the other tack, and looking out down Channel, I saw what was coming. Black, was it, Master Charlie? Not a bit; it was a white one; and I knew then we should get it *hot and heavy*. It takes something pretty cross to frighten *me*, but I own I didn't like the looks of it. Well, afore I could douse foresail the squall took her. She capsized, and down she went; and though me and Downright stood by for a start to windward, we never knew exactly how it was till we found ourselves grinning at each other over a spare oar that happened to be on board when she misbehaved, for all the world like two boys playing at see-saw with their mouths full of salt water. Downright he was an older man, and not so strong as me; so when I saw two was no company for one oar, I left it; and thinks I, if I can get off my fisherman's boots and some of my clothes, I may have a swim for it yet.

"The squall was too soon over to get up anything like a sea, and Downright he held on to his oar and struck out like a man. Well, what between floating and treading water, I got most of things clear. I was as strong as a bull then, and though it was a long swim for a man I had before me, I never lost heart noway. Downright, too, kept on close in my wake; we didn't say much, you may be sure, but I know *I* thought of his missus and four children. At last I hear him whisper quite hoarse-like, 'Hairblower, it's no use, I be goin' down now!' And when I turned on my back to look at him he was quite confused, and had let the oar cast off altogether. I couldn't see it nowhere. I tried to get alongside of him, but he was gone. I saw *the bubbles* though, and dived for him, but it was no use, and after that I held on alone. The sun was getting down too, and queer fancies began to come into my head about Downright. Sometimes I thought he was in heaven *then*, and once I'll swear I heard something whisper to me, but I couldn't tell what it said. The gulls, too, they began to stoop at me, and scream in my ears; one long-winged 'un flapped me on the cheek, and for a bit I scarcely knew whether I was dead or alive myself. At last, as I came over the tops of the rollers, I saw the spars in the harbor, and the chimneys at St. Swithin's, and for awhile I thought I should get home after all, so I turned on my side to get my breath a bit. I ought to have made a buoy, as I calculated, about this time, but seek where I would, I couldn't see it nowhere, only looking down Channel to get my bearings a little, I saw by the craft at anchor in the bay that the tide was on the turn. My heart leapt into my mouth then. I had pulled a boat often enough against the ebb hereabouts, and I knew how strong it ran, and what my chance was, swimming, and nearly done too. First I thought I'd go quietly down at once, like my mate did, and I said a bit of a prayer, just inside like, and then I felt stronger, so I thought what was best to be done; and says I, ''bout ship' now is our only chance, and maybe we shall get picked up by some fishing craft, or such like, afore we drift clean out to sea again. Well, the Lord's above all, and though I thought once or twice I was pretty nigh out of my mind, I *was* picked up at last by a Frenchman. *He'd* no call to be where he was; I think he was there special, but

I knew very little about anything else, for I was in the hospital nine weeks afore I could remember as much as I've told you. Howsoever, Friday's an unlucky day, Miss Blanche, you may take your Bible oath of it."

Hairblower did *not* tell them that half his earnings as soon as he got well went to the support of his mate's widow and her four children; perhaps it was as well he did not, for Blanche's eyes were already full of tears, and Charlie felt more than half inclined to embrace the honest seaman, but a bump against the shingle disturbed all their comments, at the same time that it broke through Mrs. Kettering's day-dreams, and Blanche had hardly got as far as "Here we are, mamma, and here's— —" when she was interrupted by Cousin Charlie's vociferous "Look alive, aunt. Hurrah! three cheers— who'd have thought it? There's Frank Hardingstone!"

CHAPTER II
THE ABIGAIL

Whilst Mr. Hardingstone offers an arm—and a good strong arm it is—to each of the ladies, and assists them slowly up the toilsome shingle, let us take advantage of Blanche's absence to peep into her pretty room, where, as it is occupied only by Gingham, the maid, we need not fear the fate of Actæon as a punishment for our curiosity.

It is indeed a sweet little retreat, with its chintz hangings and muslin curtains, its open windows looking upon the shining Channel, and all its etceteras of girlish luxury and refinement, that to us poor old bachelors seem the very essence of ladylike comfort. In one corner stands the book-case, by which we may discover the pretty proprietor's taste, at least in literature. Divers stiffish volumes on the sciences repose comfortably enough, as if they had not often been disturbed, and although scrupulously dusted, were but seldom opened; but on the sofa, near that full-length glass, a new novel lies upon its face, with a paper-cutter inserted at that critical page where the heroine refuses her lover (in blank verse), on the high-minded principle that he is not sufficiently poor to test her sincerity, or sufficiently sensible to know his own mind, or some equally valid and uncomplimentary reason—a consideration for the male sex, we may remark *en passant*, that is more common in works of fiction than in real life—while on the table a drawing-room scrap-book opens of itself at some thrilling lines addressed "To a Débutante," and commencing, "Fair girl, the priceless gems upon thy brow," by an anonymous nobleman, who betrays in the composition a wide range of fancy and a novel application of several English words. Flowers are disposed in one or two common glass vases, with a womanly taste that makes the apartment in that hired house like a home; and loose music, of the double-action pianoforte school, scatters itself about every time the door opens, in a system of fluttering disorder, which provokes Gingham to express audibly her abhorrence of a place that is "all of a litter." "She can't a-bear it—can you, Bully?" smirks the Abigail; and Blanche's pet bullfinch, the darling of her very heart, makes an enormous chest, and whistles his reply in the opening notes of "Haste to the wedding!" breaking off abruptly in the middle of the second bar. Gingham is very busy, for she is putting Blanche's "things to rights," which means that she is looking over the young lady's wardrobe with a view to discovering those colours and garments most becoming to her own rather bilious complexion, and losing no opportunity of acquainting herself with Blanche's likes, dislikes, feelings, and disposition, by reading her books, opening her letters, and peeping into her album.

Now, Gingham had been with Mrs. Kettering for many years, and was a most trustworthy person; so her mistress affirmed and thought. Certainly, with all her weaknesses and faults, she was devotedly attached to Miss Blanche; and it is our firm belief that she loved her young lady, in her heart of hearts, better than her perquisites, her tea, or even a certain Tom Blacke, whose dashing appearance and assured vulgarity had made no slight impression on her too susceptible feelings. "Every Jack has his Gill," if he and she can only find each other out at the propitious moment; and although the Gill in question *owned* to two-and-thirty, was by no means transparent in complexion, and had projecting teeth, and a saffron-coloured front, yet she was no exception to the beautiful law of nature, which provides for every variety of our species a mate of fitting degree.

When a lady confines herself studiously to the house, avoids active exercise, and partakes heartily of five meals a day, not to mention strong tea and hot buttered toast at odd times, the presumption is, that her health will suffer from the effects of such combined hardships. With patients of Gingham's class, the attack generally flies to the nerves, and the system becomes wrought up to such a pitch that nothing appears to afford the sufferer relief, except piercing screams and violent demonstrations of alarm upon slight and often imaginary occasions. Gingham would shriek as loudly to encounter a live mouse as Mrs. Kettering would have done to face a raging lion; and an unexpected meeting with any individual, even residing in the same house, was apt to produce a flutter of spirits and prostration of intellect, truly surprising to those who are unacquainted with the delicate organisation of a real lady's-maid *not* on board wages. In this critical condition, Mrs. Gingham, on the first evening of her arrival at St. Swithin's, "got a start," as she expressed it, which influenced the whole destiny of her after life. Coming down from dressing her lady, she wended her way, as usual, to "the room," that sanctum in which the etiquette of society is far more rigidly enforced than up-stairs, and to which "plush and powder" would find it far more difficult to obtain the entrée than into master's study or "missus's" boudoir. Expecting to see nothing more formidable than the butler, Gingham's alarm can be more easily imagined than described, when on entering this privileged apartment, she found its only occupant a goodish-looking, flashily-dressed young man, "taking a glass of sherry and a biscuit," and making himself very much at home.

A suppressed scream and sudden accession of faintness made it imperative on the new arrival to exert himself, and by the time they had got to "Goodness! how you frightened me, sir," and "Dear *Miss*, I beg a thousand pardings!" they became very good friends, and the timid fair one was prevailed on to sit down and partake of the refreshments hospitably provided by the butler at his mistress's expense.

Tom Blacke very soon informed the lady that "he was assistant to a professional gentleman" (in plain English an attorney's clerk), and had merely looked in to see if the house was let, to inform his employer. "I am very unhappy, miss, to have been the cause of alarming of you so, and I trust you will look over it, and may feel no ill effects from the haccident." To which Gingham, who was a lady of elaborate politeness, as became her station, and, moreover, much mollified by the constant use of the juvenile title "Miss," courteously replied that, "Indeed, it had given her *quite a turn*, but she could not regret a meeting that had introduced her to such a polite acquaintance." So they parted with many "good evenings," and an openly expressed hope that they should meet again.

Tom Blacke was a scamp of the first water, but not deficient in shrewdness, to which his professional pursuits added a certain amount of acquired cunning. He naturally reflected that the sensitive, middle-aged dame whom he had thus alarmed and soothed was probably an old and esteemed servant of the family at No. 9. The whole arrangements looked like being "well-to-do." The butler poured out sherry as if it was small beer, and probably in such an establishment the confidential maid might have saved a pretty bit of money, to which, even encumbered with the lady in question, Tom Blacke would have had no earthly objection. He was, as he said himself, "open to a match," and being a rosy, dark-whiskered fellow, with good teeth and consummate assurance, though he never looked at *you* till you had done looking at *him*, he resolved to lay siege forthwith to the heart of Mrs. Gingham. A nervous temperament is usually susceptible; and though her fingers are occupied in folding Blanche's handkerchiefs, and "putting away" her gloves, shoes, and etceteras, the Abigail's thoughts are even now far away round the corner, up two pair of stairs, in the office with Tom Blacke.

"Goodness gracious! Missus's bell!" exclaims Gingham, with a start, as if she had *not* expected that summons at its usual time—viz. when Mrs. Kettering came in to shake her feathers before luncheon—and she runs down, palpitating as if the house were on fire. Though we must not stay to see Blanche take her bonnet off and smooth those sunny ringlets, we may go and wait for her in the luncheon-room, to which she is soon heard tripping merrily down, with even brighter eyes than usual, perhaps from the excitement of meeting Cousin Charles's friend, Mr. Hardingstone, whom sly Blanche knows but very little, and with whom she is consequently extremely diffident, notwithstanding the deference of his manner, and the respectful, almost admiring tone in which he always addresses the young girl.

"Blanche, have you fed Bully? and practised your music? and read your history? Women should never neglect history. And looked for the name of that weed, whilst we think of it? and shall I give you some chicken?" said Mrs. Kettering, without waiting for an answer, as she sat down to a very comfortable repast about three o'clock in the afternoon, which she called luncheon, but which was by no means a bad imitation of a good dinner.

"No, dear mamma," said Blanche; "besides, it's too hot for lessons; but tell me, mamma, what did Mr. Hardingstone mean about a mermaid, when he whispered to 'Cousin Charlie,' and Charlie laughed?"

"A mermaid, Blanche? pooh! nonsense; there's no such animal. But that reminds me—don't forget to look over that beautiful thing of Tennyson's; girls should always be 'up' in modern literature. Do you know, Blanche, I don't quite like Mr. Hardingstone."

"O mamma," said Blanche, "such a friend of Charlie's—I'm sure we ought to like him; and I'm sure he likes *us*; what a way he came down through that horrid shingle to help you out of the boat; and did you see, mamma, what nice thin boots he had on? I think I should like him very much if we knew him better. Not so much as 'Cousin Charlie,'" added the young girl, reflectively, "or dear darling Hairblower. How shocking it was when his partner went down, mamma. Did you hear that story? But I am sure Mr. Hardingstone is very good-natured."

"That reminds me, my dear," said Mrs. Kettering, who was getting rather flushed towards the end of the chicken; "I do hope that boy has not gone to bathe: I am always afraid about water. Blanche, hand me the sherry; and, my dear, I must order some bottled porter for *you*—you are very pale in this hot weather; but I am always fidgety about Charlie when he is bathing."

From the conversation recorded above, we may gather that Mrs. Kettering, who, as we have said, was inclined to be nervous, was rapidly becoming so upon one or two important points. In the first place, with all a mother's pride in her daughter's beauty, she could not be blind to the general admiration excited thereby, nor could she divest herself of certain misgivings that Blanche would not long remain to be the solace of her widowhood, but that, to use her own expression, she was "sure to be *snapped up* before she was old enough to know her own mind." The consequence was, that Mrs. Kettering much mistrusted all her male acquaintance under the age of old-fellow-hood—a period of life which, in these days of "wonderfully young-looking men," seems indefinitely postponed; and regarded every well-dressed, well-whiskered biped as a possible subverter of her schemes, and a probable rival to "Cousin Charlie"; she kept him at bay, accordingly, with a coldness and reserve quite foreign to her own cordial and demonstrative nature. Frank Hardingstone she could not dislike, do what she would. And we are bound to confess that she was less guarded in her encouragement of that gentleman than of any other male visitor who appeared in the afternoons at No. 9, to leave a small bit of glazed pasteboard, with an inward thanksgiving for his escape from a morning visit, or to utter incontrovertible platitudes while he smoothed his hat on his coat-sleeve, and glanced ever and anon at the clock on the chimney-piece, for the earliest moment at which, with common decency, he might take his departure.

Then the safety and soundness of Blanche's heart was scarcely more a matter of anxiety than that of Charlie's body; and the boy seemed to take a ghastly delight in placing himself constantly in situations of imminent bodily peril. Active and high-spirited, he was perpetually climbing inaccessible places, shooting with dangerous guns, riding wild hacks, overheating himself in matches against time, and, greatest anxiety of all, performing aquatic feats—the principal result of his Eton education—*out of his depth,* as his aunt observed with emphasis, which were totally inexcusable as manifest temptations of fate.

He was now gone off on an expedition with his friend and senior, Hardingstone; but well did Mrs. Kettering know that yonder blue, cool-looking sea would be an irresistible temptation, and that her nephew would "bundle in," as he called it, to a moral certainty, the instant he got away from the prying gaze of the town.

"In the meantime," thought she, "it's a comfort to have Blanche safe at her studies; there is nothing like occupation for the mind to keep foolish fancies out of a young girl's head; so bring your books down here, my love," she added, aloud, "and after we have read the last act of 'Don Carlos,' you can practise your music, while I rest myself a little on the sofa."

With all its beauties, "Don Carlos" is a work of which a few pages go a long way, when translated into their own vernacular by two ladies who have but a slight acquaintance with the German language; and Blanche soon tired of the princely step-son's more than filial affection, and the guttural warmth with which it is expressed; so she drew mamma's sofa to the open window, shut the door to keep her out of the draught, and sat down to her pianoforte with an arch "Good-night, mammy; you won't hear any of my mistakes, so I shall play my lesson over as fast as ever I can."

Snore away, honest Mrs. Kettering, in the happy conviction that you have given your daughter ample occupation of mind, to say nothing of fingers, in the execution of those black-looking pages, so trying to the temper and confusing to the ear. Snore away, and believe that her thoughts and affections are as much under your control as her little body used to be, when you put her to bed with your own hands, and she said her innocent prayers on your knee. So you all think of your children; so you all deceive yourselves, and are actually surprised when symptoms of wilfulness or insubordination appear in your own families, though you have long warned your neighbours that "boys will be boys," or "girls are always thoughtless," when they have complained to you of their parental disappointments and disgusts. You think you know your children—you, who can scarce be said to know *yourself*. The bright boy at your side, who calls you by the endearing appellation of "the governor," you fondly imagine he is drinking in those words of wisdom in which you are laying down rules for his future life of frugality, usefulness, and content. Not a bit of it. He is thinking of his pony and his tick at the pie-shop, which will make a sad hole in the sovereign you will probably present to him on his return to Mr. Birch's.

You describe in well-chosen language the miseries of a "bread-and-cheese" marriage to your eldest daughter, a graceful girl, whose fair, open brow you think would well become a coronet, and she seems to listen with all attention to your maxims, and to agree cordially with "dear papa," in worldly prudence, and an abhorrence of what you call "bad style of men." When her mother, with flushed countenance and angry tones, despatches you to look for her to-night between the quadrilles, ten to one but you find her in the tea-room with Captain Clank, "that odious man without a sixpence," as your energetic spouse charitably denominates him. And yet, as child after child spreads its late-fledged wings, and forsakes the shelter of the parental nest, you go on hoping that the next, and still the next, will make amends to you for all the shortcomings of its seniors, till the youngest—the Benjamin—the darling of your old age—the treasure that was, indeed, to be your "second self"—takes flight after the rest, and you feel a dreary void at your heart, and a solemn, sad conviction that the best and holiest affections of an earthly nature are insufficient for its happiness—that there must be something better to come when everything here turns to heart-ache and disappointment.

But Blanche will not think so for many a long day yet. Though the minims and crotchets and flats and sharps were mixed up in sadly puzzling confusion, not a frown of impatience crossed that pure, open brow. Blanche's own thoughts were a panacea for all the provocations that the stiffest piece of musico-mechanism, or mechanical music, could inflict. It is a task beyond our powers to detail the vague ideas and shadowy dreams that chased each other through that glossy little head; nor have we any business to try. A young girl's brain is a page of poetry, without rhyme certainly, probably without much reason, but poetry notwithstanding. Before the world has lost its gloss of novelty, that gloss which is like the charm that dazzled the eyes of their mortal visitors, and made the fairies' straws and withered leaves and cobwebs look like purple hangings, and tapestry, and ivory, and gold — before life has borne away much to regret, and sin brought much to repent of — before the fruit has been plucked which still hangs from the Tree of Knowledge of Good and Evil, there is a positive pleasure in the mere act of thinking; and that intellectual luxury Blanche enjoyed to the utmost, whilst her fingers were tripping over the pianoforte keys, and Mrs. Kettering was snoring comfortably on the sofa.

Now, Frank Hardingstone was prime favourite and *beau idéal* with "Cousin Charlie," who, like all boys, had selected an idol a few years older than himself, and clothed him with those imaginary attributes which youth considers essential to constitute a hero. Frank was a country gentleman, in possession of his property at the early age of five-and-twenty, and, truth to tell, somewhat bored with his position. If we were to describe him, we should say he was "a man of action" rather than "a man of feeling," or "a man of business," or "a man of refinement," or "a man of pleasure," or a man of anything else. He looked energetic too, and vigorous, with his brown healthy complexion, his open forehead, clear penetrating eye, and short clustering hair and whiskers. Had he been the least thing of a coxcomb in dress or manner, the ladies would have voted him very handsome; but he was plain to simplicity in his attire, and rather abrupt in his address, so they abused him amongst themselves, but were very civil to him notwithstanding. The men, particularly the sporting ones, who are always ready with their judgments and opinions, pronounced that he "looked a good one all over," alluding, as we understand the phrase, not so much to his virtue as his corporeal powers, and capability of resisting fatigue. We are not so far removed from a state of barbarism in the present day as we are prone to flatter ourselves. When young King James called the grim old Douglas "his Graysteil," that royal heart was attached to Earl Angus for his magnificent frame, skill in feats of arms and efforts of strength, not for the giant's wisdom, which was doubtful, or his honesty, which was entirely negative; and so amongst any assemblage of young gentlemen now in the nineteenth century, the quality which excites most admiration seems to be a certain combination of activity and recklessness, which they call *hardness*. "Was Rakes in time for parade?"—"Oh yes, he drank four bottles of claret, and never went to bed—he's a deuced *hard* fellow, Rakes" (applause). "Was Captain Cropper hurt when he tumbled over that gate and broke his horse's neck?"—"Hurt? not he; you won't often see *him* hurt—there are not many fellows so *hard* as Cropper" (great applause); and thus it seems that the brain is chiefly honoured according to its capacity, not of reasoning, but of cellarage—and the head only becomes the noblest portion of the human frame when it may be fallen on with impunity. Tell these "physical force" gentlemen of a "clever horse," and every ear is erect in motionless attention—talk to them of a clever man, their shoulders are elevated in pity—of a clever woman, their mouths are drawn down in disgust. But Frank Hardingstone was, to use their favourite word, "a great card" amongst all the associates of his age and standing. Square and muscular, with temper, courage, and address, he could walk, run, leap, ride, fence, play cricket, box, and swim with the best of them, and they never suspected that this powerful frame contained a mind capable and energetic as the casket in which it was concealed.

Frank was a well-informed, well-judging man—loved mathematics, logic, and such strong intellectual food—enjoyed working out a sum or problem, or otherwise exercising his powerful mind, and would go to an iron foundry, or to see a ship built, or even to the Polytechnic, for sheer amusement. Had he been born to work for his livelihood, he would have made a capital engineer; as it was, he ought to have been in the navy, or the artillery, or anything but an idle man, living at his own place in the country. He had no relations, consequently nothing to keep him at home; people said that when alone he had no established dinner-hour—a grievous sin in our gastronomic age: he was too energetic to care very much for farming, although he did *occupy* certain acres of his own land; and too practical to be enthusiastic about field-sports, though he was a good shot, and rode right well to hounds. Altogether, Frank was out of his place in the world; and, not having arrived at that age when, if a man don't fit his destiny, he makes his destiny fit *him*, was in danger of becoming bored and careless, and a useless member of society. Luckily, Cousin Charlie's private tutor, Mr. Nobottle, held his cure close to Hardingstone Hall, and leave to course over certain grounds thereunto belonging being applied for and granted, an introduction took place between the squire and the clergyman's volatile pupil, which struck up an immediate alliance of obliger and obliged.

No two people could well be more different in disposition and appearance than were Frank and Charlie. The man—strong, sedate, practical, acute, and penetrating; the boy—light, active, hot-headed, and romantic, jumping to conclusions, averse to reasoning and reflection, acting on the impulse of the moment, and continually getting into scrapes, which his friend as continually had to get him out of. Yet after they had known each other a few months they became inseparable. Charlie went regularly, after his studies at the rectory, to pass the rest of the day at the hall; and Frank found a renewed pleasure in boating, cricket, hunting, shooting, and even fishing, from the keen enjoyment with which the "young one" entered upon these diversions. As for the "young one" himself, he thought there was nothing in the world equal to Hardingstone—so strong, so plucky, so well-read, so sagacious, with such faultless coats, and such a good seat upon a horse, he was the boy's hero (we have all had such in our day), and he worshipped him accordingly. So ill could he bear to lose sight of his Mentor, even during the sunshiny hours of the vacation, that he had begged Hardingstone to come over to St. Swithin's, no very great distance from his own place, and had promised to introduce him to the "Aunt Kettering," and "Blanche," of whom he had heard so much in the intervals of their amusements "by thicket and by stream." The promise was made and kept—and Frank was living at the Royal Hotel, disgusting the landlord by the simplicity of his habits, and the waiter by his carelessness as regarded dinner, whilst he was growing day by day in the good graces even of Mrs. Kettering, and finding, as he himself thought with great penetration, a vast deal of sound merit in the fresh, inexperienced mind of Blanche. "Your cousin looks all the better for sea-bathing, Charlie," said Hardingstone to his young companion, as they toiled slowly along the broiling parade, where every sunbeam was refracted with tenfold power from glaring houses and a scorching pavement. "It braces the system just as good head-work braces the intellect. People don't train half enough, I think—even women ought to have sound minds in sound bodies; and look what indolent, unmeaning, insipid wretches half of them are—not like your aunt. Now that's what I call a vigorous woman, Charlie; she'd do in the colonies or anywhere—she's fit to be a queen, my boy, because she's got some energy about her. As for you, young gentleman, you work hard enough out-of-doors, but you neglect your brains altogether—I don't believe now that you have opened a book since you left Nobottle's."

"Wrong again, Frank, as usual," replied Charlie; "I read for an hour this very morning, whilst I was dressing; I am very fond of reading when it's not *dry*."

"And may I ask what your early studies were, my industrious young philosopher?"

"'Parisina' and 'The Bride of Abydos'—by Jove, old fellow, it's beautiful."

Frank made a face as if he had swallowed a pill. "'Parisina' and 'The Bride of Abydos,'" he repeated, with intense disgust; "a boy of sixteen—I beg your pardon—a young *man* of your age reading Byron; why, you'll arrive at a state of mental delirium tremens before you are twenty, particularly if you smoke much at the same time. I daresay you are 'up' in 'Don Juan' as well—not that I think *he* is half so bad for you; but no man should read sentiment in such an alluring garb as Byron dressed it, till his heart is hardened and his whiskers grown. All poetry, to my mind, has a tendency to make you more or less imbecile. You should read Bacon, my boy, and Locke, and good sound reasoning Butler; but if you must have works of imagination, take to Milton."

"Hate blank verse," remarked Charlie, who opined—in which prejudice we cannot help coinciding a little—that poetry is nothing without jingle; "I can't read three pages of 'Paradise Lost.'"

"Because your brain is softening for want of proper training," interrupted Hardingstone; "if you go on like this you'll very soon be fit for Jean Jacques Rousseau, and I shall give you up altogether. No, when you go back to Nobottle's, I shall give him a hint to put you into a stiffish course of mathematics, with a few logarithms for plums, and when you are man enough to grapple with a real intellectual difficulty you will read Milton for pleasure, and like him more and more every day, for you will find——"

"Oh! bother Milton," interrupted Charlie; "Frank, I'll bet you half-a-crown you don't jump that gate without touching;" and he pointed to a high white gate leading off the dusty road into the fresh green meadows, for they were now clear of the town.

Frank was over it like a bird, ere the words were out of his admiring disciple's mouth, and their conversation, as they walked on, turned upon feats of strength and agility, and those actions of enterprise and adventure which are ever most captivating to the fancy of the young.

Charles Kettering, we need scarcely say, entertained an extraordinary fondness for all bodily exercises. Intended for the army, and "waiting for his commission," as he expressed it, he looked forward to his future profession as a career of unalloyed happiness, in which he should win fame and distinction without the slightest mental exertion—an effort to which, in truth, Charlie was always rather averse. Like most young aspirants to military honours, he had yet to learn that study, reflection, memory, and, above all, common sense, are as indispensable to the soldier's success as to that of any other professional man; and that, although physical courage and light spirits are very useful accessories in a campaign, a good deal more is required to constitute an officer, since, even in a subordinate grade, the lives of his comrades and the safety of his division may depend on his unassisted judgment alone. Charlie had good abilities, but it was a difficult matter to get him to apply them with anything like diligence; and his friend Hardingstone, whose appreciation of a favourite's good qualities never made him blind to his faults, saw this defect, and did all in his power to remedy it, both by precept and example.

Mrs. Kettering's misgivings as regarded her nephew's duck-like propensities were founded on a thorough knowledge of his taste and habits. Another mile of walking brought the pair once more to the beach, where it curved away completely out of sight of St Swithin's. The heat was intense; Charlie took his coat off, sat down upon a stone, and gazed wistfully at the sea.

"Don't it look cool?" said he; "and don't I wish, on a day like this, that I was a 'merman bold'? I say, Frank, I must have a dip—I shall bundle in."

"In with you," was the reply; "I haven't had a swim since I breasted the Mediterranean last year; only we won't stay in too long, for I promised your cousin to bring her some of that seaweed she spoke about;" and in another minute, in place of two well-dressed gentlemen standing on the beach, a couple of hats and a heap of clothes occupied the shore, whilst two white forms might be seen, ever and anon, gleaming through the blue waves as their owners dived, floated, turned upon their sides, kicked up their feet, and performed all those antics with which masterly swimmers signalise their enjoyment of their favourite element. We often hear people wishing they could fly. Now, we always think it must be exactly the same sensation as swimming; you are borne up with scarcely an effort—you seem to glide with the rapidity of a bird—you feel a consciousness of daring, and a proud superiority over nature, in thus mastering the instinctive fear man doubtless entertains of water, and bidding ocean bear you like a steed that knows its rider. The horizon appears so near that your ideas of distance become entirely confused, and the "few yards of uneven" water seem to your exulting senses like as many leagues. You dash your head beneath the green transparent wave, and shaking the salt drops from your brow, gallantly breast roller after roller as they come surging in, and with a wild, glad sense of freedom and adventure, you strike boldly out to sea. All this our two gentlemen bathers felt and enjoyed, but Frank, who had not followed this favourite diversion for a length of time, was even more delighted than his young companion with his aquatic amusements; and when the breeze freshened and the dark blue waters began to show a curl of white, he dashed away with long, vigorous strokes to such a distance from the shore as even Charlie, albeit of anything but nervous mood, thought over-venturous and enterprising. The latter was emerging from the water, when, on looking for his companion, it struck him that Frank, in the offing, was making signals of distress. Once he saw a tremendous splash, and he almost thought he heard a cry through the roar of the tide against the shingle. "By all that's fearful, he's in grief," was Charlie's mental exclamation; and whilst he thought it the gallant boy was striking out for life and death to reach his friend. What a distance it seemed! and how his knees and thighs ached with the long, convulsive springs that shot him forward! Charlie never knew before what hard work swimming might be; and now he has reached the spot he aimed at—he raises himself in the water—what is this? Merciful Heaven! Hardingstone is down! but there is a swirling circle of green and white not ten yards before him, and the lad dives deep below the surface and comes up holding his friend's motionless body by the hair; and now they are both down again, for Charlie is blown, and has not before practised the difficult feat of rescuing a man from drowning. But he comes up once more, and shakes his head, and coughs and clutches tightly to the twining hair, that even in the water has a death-like clamminess in his fingers. He is frightfully blown now, and a wave takes him sideways and turns him over—he is under Hardingstone, and this time he only comes up for an instant to go under again, with a suffocating feeling at his chest, and a painful pressure on his ears. Now he gulps at the salt water that appears to fill body, and lungs, and head; and now he seems to be whirling round and round; everything is green and giddy—there is something crooked before his face—and a feeling of pleasing languor forbids him to grasp it. The Great Uncertainty is very near—a glare of white light dazzles his eyes, and the waters settle over him, as he holds on to Hardingstone's hair with the clutch of a drowning man.

CHAPTER III
THE HANDSOME GOVERNESS

Little, indeed, do one half the world know how the other half live. Fortunate is it for us all, that we have neither the invisible cap, nor the shoes of swiftness, that did their owner such good service in the fairy tale. We might be astonished, not to say disgusted, could we follow our nearest and dearest for one short half-hour after they have left our sight; could we see them, when they think no mortal eye is upon their actions, we might smile or we might weep, according as our temperament bordered upon the sentimental or the cynical. Yet is there One that always watches. How comes it that when we hide ourselves from man, we think no shame to expose our follies to man's Creator? Will a day come when everything shall be made known? when there will be no more hypocrisy—no more respectability—no more difference between vice on the house-top and vice in the corner? There will be some strange shifting of places when that day does come—much shrinking and wincing from the general Show-up—much scarlet shame, and livid remorse, when the brow can no more be covered, nor the past undone. 'Tis a pity we should think so little of payment till the bill comes due;—in the meantime we go blindly on, deceiving and deceived—we know but little of our neighbour, and we trust in heaven our neighbour knows nothing whatever about us; so we grope about in the dark, and call it Life.

Mrs. Kettering, on the sofa, knew nothing of what Blanche was thinking about, not six feet from her—knew nothing about Charlie, struggling convulsively for life half-a-mile out at sea—knew nothing about the woman she had left to take charge of her town-house—a pattern of respectability, sobriety, and trustworthiness, then reeling out of "The Feathers," as drunk as Chloë, to use an old Eton expression, highly derogatory to the character of Horace's young and tender love, she who bounded from the bard's classical advances like a frightened kid. Our Chloë, meanwhile, was grasping a door-key, and calling for gin, regardless that she had left a tallow-candle flaring close to a heap of shavings in the back scullery, that "the airy-gate," as she called it, was "on the latch," and there was nobody to answer the front door. This last piece of carelessness was the means of inflicting an additional disappointment on one who had already in her short life known troubles and disappointments more than enough. Mary Delaval had walked up to the grim lion-headed knocker with a weary step and heavy heart; but when her summons was again and again unheeded, and the chance of finding out even Mrs. Kettering's address became hopeless, she moved away with the heavy, listless air of one who has shot the last arrow from the quiver without attaining the mark, and begins to doubt if courage and energy are indeed qualities of the slightest advantage to our welfare, and whether blind fortune is not the controller of all here below.

The sun beat fiercely upon the pavement, and there was not a breath of air to refresh those arid gardens in the parched and dusty square—yet Mary put her thick, suffocating veil down before her face and quickened her pace as she went home from her hopeless errand; for to these inconveniences she was obliged to submit, because in the freest country in the world, and the most civilised capital in Europe, she was walking on foot, without a companion or a man-servant.

"Gad, that's a good-looking woman!" said Captain Lacquers to his friend, Sir Ascot Uppercrust; "fine-ish goer, too, but tires over the pavement. If it was not so cursedly hot, 'Uppy,' we might cross over and get a look at her."

"Women rather bore me," replied Sir Ascot, who, being very young and a Body-guardsman, was of course *blasé*; "but I don't mind, to oblige you,—only promise you won't let her speak to me." So, as Captain Lacquers turned up his moustaches, Sir Ascot went through the same pantomime, for practice against the time when his own should grow; and the couple sauntered carelessly on, and, by a dexterous manœuvre, came "right across the bows" of Mary Delaval.

We may be asked what two such undeniable dandies as good-looking Lacquers, of the Lancers, and Sir Ascot Uppercrust, of the Body-guard, should be doing in London at this time of the year. We cannot tell; for love or money probably—a redundancy of the one and a deficiency of the other being the two causes that generally drive young gentlemen to the metropolis, when their confiding companions are all "faded and gone." Be it how it may, there they were, and Mary Delaval wished them anywhere else, as, following in her wake, they made sundry complimentary remarks upon her figure, ankles, and general appearance, which might have been gratifying if overheard casually, but which, under the circumstances, were doubtless extremely impertinent and reprehensible.

"I think I'll get forward, and ask her if she's going home," said Lacquers; and, curling his great black moustaches, he quickened his pace to add this crowning insult to an unprotected woman.

Mary's blood boiled in her veins—she was a soldier's daughter, and her father's spirit swelled her heart till it felt as if it would choke her—she clenched her long slender hand, and thought, almost aloud: "Oh, if I were but a man to strike the coward to the earth!—oh, if I were but a man to shoot him as he stands!" In such a mood women have shed blood ere now, but the excitement cannot last—the reaction too surely arrives; and, alas for woman's pride and woman's weakness! Mary returned the bold insolent stare with the defiant glance and the lofty carriage of a queen, and then—she burst into tears. It was too much; fatigue, anxiety, and disappointment had overcome her nerves, and she could have killed herself for the weakness, but she sobbed like a child.

Lacquers was a good-natured man, and a good fellow, as it is called, at heart—he was pained and thoroughly ashamed of himself. He took his hat off as if she had been a duchess, and with a readiness that argued this was not a first offence, and did more credit to his ingenuity than his candour, he begged her pardon, and assured her he thought she was "his cousin"— "Quite a mistake, ma'am, I assure you—pray forgive me—good-morning;" and so bowed himself off arm-in-arm with his companion, who had preserved an immovable stoicism, almost preternatural in one so young, during the whole interview.

As Mary Delaval walked on, and gradually recovered her composure, she reflected somewhat bitterly on her lot, and looked back upon her life with a feeling of discontent, that for a moment seemed almost to upbraid Providence that she had not had a fair chance. It was but for a moment— Mary had been schooled in adversity, and had profited by its lessons. In some situations of life such a temperament as hers might have been prone to grow fastidious and uncharitable. Her ideal of good would have been very high, and she would have looked down with contempt upon the grovelling spirits that constituted the mass of her fellow-creatures. But poverty and dependence had taught her many a lesson, hard to learn, but harder to forget. What had she to do with pride?—a question to be asked, if you contemplated her tall, graceful figure, with its majestic sweep and lofty gestures—her goddess-like head, set on as if the Greek had carved its proportions with his unerring chisel—her dark, deep-set grey eye, with its long lashes, veiling a world of penetration, reflection, ay, and sentiment, for the happy man who could bid it kindle into love—her faultless profile and firm determined mouth, her father's legacy, with the courage it betokened—her low, lovable brow, with its masses of thick, dark brown hair plainly braided on each side of that pale, haunting face, beautiful in the deep expression which arrives only with the maturity of womanhood; with all this she might have been a queen, yet what had she to do with pride?—a question not to be asked of a friendless, desolate woman, trudging along the streets in the dreary isolation of loneliness in London, wasting her beauty in the strife for bread, wearing her talents threadbare in the drudgery of a daily music-mistress. What a lot if there were nothing beyond! To rise early in that dingy atmosphere—to breakfast hurriedly on such a spare meal as the lady's-maid next door would deem insufficient for her mistress's poodle—to leave the dreary lodging for the scarce less dreary street; day after day to make the same round, waiting upon vulgar parents and stupid children—day after day to bend rebellious fingers over the soul-breathing chords—to dissect the harmony of heaven into "one—two—three—four," "one—two—three—four,"—and day after day to return, wearied out in body and mind, to the solitary room which cannot be called a home, and the rent of which, dear on account of *the situation*, swallows up the hard-earned coins that should decorate and supply its vacuity; with nothing to cheer, nothing to amuse, nothing to console, not even the consciousness of that beauty which is only a cause of annoyance and remark; and, above all, with nothing to love—what a lot would this be, were there not a something to look forward to—a humble hope that this is but a state of trial and probation—a humble confidence that the reward is sure to come at last!

And who was Mary Delaval? One of the many instances of a child suffering for the sins of its parents. We have said her father was a soldier, but, alas! her mother never was, properly speaking, Mrs. Delaval. Poor woman, she committed her one fault, and dearly she atoned for it. She shut the door upon herself, and her sex took good care that it should never again show a chink open to let her in. Trust them for that! she was not a proper person to be visited, and she remained outside. Captain Delaval would have married her, had he thought such a sacrifice on his part would have improved her position, for he loved her dearly; but he knew it could be of no use, in a worldly point of view, the only one in which he considered the subject, so he put it off and put it off, till too late. She never complained of the injustice done her, but it broke her heart. Rich in beauty and accomplishments, she had run away with the handsome, young artillery officer rather than be forced into a match which she detested, by a step-mother she despised. She had but one child, and on that child, it is needless to say, she doted foolishly. Delaval was a curious fellow, easy-tempered to a fault, careless of the world's opinion, and of everything but his own comfort and indulgences; a gallant soldier, notwithstanding, as brave as a lion, and a perfect authority in the code of honour adopted by his profession. Yet, for all this, he allowed the mother of his child to go upon the stage, under a feigned name, that he might live in luxury upon her earnings. Fortunately, it may be, for all parties, the artillery officer caught cold out duck-shooting, and was honoured with a military funeral some ten days afterwards. He left all he had, a small pittance, to the woman he had so deeply injured, and she retired with her daughter into a humble cottage in the West of England, where, for a time, they lived as happy as the day is long. Her whole energies were devoted to the education of her child. She taught her all she had herself learned—no mean list of acquirements—and young Mary Delaval (for, by the deceased officer's wish, they always bore his name) was skilled far beyond other girls of her age in the graceful accomplishments of womanhood, as well as in those deeper studies which strengthen the mind and form the character of youth. But Mary's girlhood had an advantage, in which her mother's was deficient. That mother, with the earnestness of one into whose soul the iron had deeply entered, impressed upon her daughter the lesson she had herself so painfully learned: "Put not your trust in man," was the substance of many a tearful entreaty, many a sage homily, from the repentant sinner to her innocent child; and, though the girl's faith was sadly shaken in the integrity of the creature, it was anchored all the more firmly in reliance on his Creator. The mother's health was but precarious. Often she thought, "What will become of Mary when I must leave her alone in the world?" and, having little else to bestow, she bequeathed to her darling that best legacy of all, the heritage of an immortal soul. Poor thing! her own constitution had been sadly broken by anxiety and disappointment, and the heart-wearing conviction that she had given up home, comfort, friends, good fame, everything, to fasten her young pure love on an unworthy object. Oh! the sickening misery of that moment, when first the idol's shrine is found to be a blank! when first the dreary misgiving dawns upon us, that the being for whom we have sacrificed our earthly all, and offered it with a smile—whom we have endued with all the attributes for which our own heart yearns—whom we have clothed with the gorgeous colouring of fancy, and decked in the false glitter of our own imagination—whom we have raised upon a pedestal, to place our neck beneath its feet, is but a stock or a stone, after all! Poor idolaters! are we not rightly punished? Have we not exalted man to be our God? and shall we worship the thing of clay with impunity? No; the very crime is made to bear its own atonement. Better that we should bow down to the dust, with crushed and empty hearts, than live on in the vain mockery of a false worship, in the degradation of a soul's homage to a mortal deity.

Poor Mrs. Delaval (for as such was the penitent lady known) bore her punishment without a murmur; but it was a sad task to leave Mary among strangers, when failing strength and wasting limbs warned her that she must soon depart. The girl was in the first lovely bloom of womanhood, bright and beautiful as if she had never known sorrow or self-denial; and must she leave her now, when most she wants a mother's care? God's will be done! There is a humble grave, in the corner of a retired churchyard, far away in the West, marked by a plain grey stone, and the initial letters of a name—nothing more; and there the spring daisies are growing over the head of one who loved not wisely—who erred, and was forgiven, but not here.

Mary Delaval was left to fight single-handed against the world. A hard battle it is for those who are not furnished with the sinews of war.

The small sum bequeathed to her by her mother's care was invested in a savings bank, *which failed*. By the way, the failure was casually mentioned in the morning papers, and trustees of savings banks, as they sipped their coffee, remarked, "Ah! another of these concerns broke: gross rascality somewhere, no doubt." We hope it proved a warning to them, to look a little carefully into affairs which they had pledged themselves to superintend, and not to grudge half-an-hour's labour, when such a trifling effort might ward off the direst calamities from their humble neighbours. What was Mary to do? Besides her beauty and the mourning on her back, she had literally nothing. And yet the girl's heart never sank for a moment; she was possessed of that invincible Anglo-Saxon resolution, for which there is no better name than the colloquial one of "pluck." Had she been a man, she would have distinguished herself; as it was, perhaps the humble part she had to play required more courage, self-command, and self-reliance than the career of many a hero. One advantage she had over many others equally indigent—her talents were brilliant, her education had been excellent, and the natural conclusion at which she arrived was, that she must be a governess or teacher in a school. The former situation there was much difficulty in attaining, qualities which are prized in a lady being considered great drawbacks to a governess; but youth and good looks are not so much out of place in the latter; and Mary, after considerable difficulty, and a voluminous correspondence, found herself installed as second assistant in one of those strongholds of innocence and propriety, termed a young ladies' seminary.

How different the life on which the orphan now embarked from all her previous experience of the world! She had been a merry little girl, in barracks, petted by officers from every regiment in the service (soldiers are all fond of children), and spoilt by papa, who thought nothing in the world equal to his little pet. She had grown into womanhood in the closest retirement of a small out-of-the-way village, associating only with her refined and cultivated mother, and preparing for a life of difficulty by study and reflection; and now she found herself the inmate of a house in which there were thirty pupils, and where she had not even a room of her own, to escape from the gossiping chatter of the girls, or the solemn platitudes of Miss Primrose, the venerable Calypso who presided over these isolated nymphs. There never was such a place for ladies' schools as the cathedral town of Bishops'-Baffler; but, as we believe all these repositories of beauty and education are conducted upon the same principles, it is needless to describe them. Health and morals are studiously attended to, and the use of the back-board inflexibly insisted on, the male sex, of course, strictly prohibited, and the arts and sciences, giving the former the preference, impartially administered. Young ladies are likewise taught to lie perfectly flat on their backs for several hours, we may say, literally, on a stretch, though of the object and intention of this feat, whether it is viewed in the light of a dreary penance, an innocent recreation, or a time-honoured institution, it does not become us, in our ignorance, to give an opinion.

But Bishops'-Baffler, with all its advantages of salubrious air, constant bell-ringing, and redundancy of ecclesiastics, has one considerable drawback to those who take upon themselves the responsible charge of young ladies in the vicinity of a cavalry barracks. The morals of a cathedral town are not very easily deteriorated; but an order from the Horse Guards, determining that a certain number of jaunty forage-caps, jingling spurs, and dyed moustaches, should be continually swaggering up and down the principal thoroughfares of any city, though it adds to the liveliness, is not supposed to conduce much to the general respectability of the place; and with all our terrors of invasion, and our admiration, as civilians, of the military character—particularly the mounted arm—we confess to a partiality for it chiefly when removed beyond flirting distance from our dwelling-house, and acknowledge with grief and shame that its vicinity, in our own experience, has invariably over-roasted our mutton, multiplied our cobwebs, and placed our female establishment generally at sixes and sevens. But if we, an independent bachelor, are thus fain to be removed from the insidious sounds of "stable-call" and "watch-setting," from the fascinating sights of "watering-order" and "guard-mounting," what must have been good Miss Primrose's care and anxiety to preserve her tender fledgelings from the roving glances of those dashing serjeant-majors, far more brilliant warriors than the very lieutenants and captains of the sober foot regiment that preceded them; or the dangerous proximity of those good-looking officers in their braided frock-coats and their well-cultivated moustaches, which serve equally as an amusement to themselves and a terror to their foes—a defence in war and an occupation in peace? Miss Primrose was a large woman; but she ought to have been a giantess to cover her brood as she would have wished, when, walking two-and-two along the pavement, they were continually encountering "the Loyal Hussars," mounted and dismounted, or entangling in the very sheep-fold of their innocence some wolf in undress uniform, who would persist in taking the wrong side of the "trottoir," and then jingling his spurs together in feigned apologies; merely, Miss Primrose well knew, as a pretext for peeping under their parasols and "uglies" at the pretty faces, blushing not in anger beneath those defences.

But what made the principal of the establishment, as she called herself, more wrathful than anything else, was to perceive that the figure on whom these warlike glances rested with the greatest marks of approval and admiration was not one of the young ladies upon whom she "lavished a mother's care, and conferred a gentlewoman's education" (see advertisement)—not one of the lady pupils for whom she felt, as she expressed it, "she was responsible, body and soul," but the majestic person, and the sweet, sad face, of the junior assistant, Mary Delaval! "Had it been myself, for instance," thought Miss Primrose, drawing up her ample frame with a proud consciousness that, twenty years ago, she, too, had a lover, "or even Miss Meagrim" (the senior assistant, a gaunt and forbidding damsel), "who certainly has a 'genteel' figure, or little Miss Dashwood, or rosy Miss Wright, I could have understood it; but the idea of that dowdy thing, with her pale face and her shabby mourning! it only shows the extraordinary tastes men have, and the unaccountable creatures they are from beginning to end."

And so poor Miss Primrose fell to ruminating on certain passages of her own early career, and a blight which nipped her young affections in the bud through the inconstancy of man.

"Have you served?" says a Frenchman to his acquaintance. "Have you suffered?" might women as well ask of each other; and there are few amongst them, we fancy, but at one time of their lives have gone through the freemasonry of sorrow.

Miss Primrose did not look like a heroine; yet she, too, had had her romance. Well, it had softened her character, for naturally she was a strong-minded woman; and the pretty gipsies over whom she presided little thought how much that austere lady sympathised with all the innocent "*espiègleries*" and girlish follies she thought it right to rebuke so severely.

Now, even Miss Primrose could not help remarking that, notwithstanding the open admiration Mary Delaval everywhere excited, no London beauty of half-a-dozen seasons could have accepted the homage due to her charms with greater coldness and carelessness than did the junior assistant. The girl seemed to live in a separate world of her own, apart from the common pleasures and foibles of her sex. She was kind and courteous to all, but she made no confidences, and had no female friend. She continued to wear her mourning-dress for years after the usual term that filial affection imposes, and with that mourning she seemed to bear about with her the continual memory, almost the companionship, of her dead mother. Even Miss Meagrim, whom she nursed through the jaundice, and who, with returning health, and a fresh accession of hideousness, confessed she owed her life to Miss Delaval's care, owned that she could not make her out; and truth to tell, both that inquisitive lady and the formidable Miss Primrose herself, were a little afraid of their stately assistant, with her classical beauty and her calm, sad face.

Years rolled on, and Mary Delaval, now in the mature bloom of womanhood, was still junior assistant at Miss Primrose's, and might have remained there till her glorious figure was bent, and her glossy braids were grey, had it not been for that order from the Horse Guards, mentioned above, which moved the head-quarters of the "Loyal Hussars" from Waterbridge to Bishops'-Baffler. Much commotion was there in the town when this regiment of "*Cupidons*" in pelisses marched in with all the honours of war; nor were the chaste retreats of our academical sanctuary entirely free from the excitement that pervaded the neighbourhood. Miss Primrose had her "front" freshly oiled, curled, and submitted to a process which, we believe, is termed "baking"; Miss Meagrim appeared with new ribbons in her cap, of a hue strangely unbecoming to her complexion; whilst a general feeling amongst the pupils in favour of "a walk," whenever the weather afforded an opportunity, argued that the attraction, whatever it might be, was decidedly out-of-doors. Mary Delaval alone seemed supremely indifferent to the movements of the military, and yet her destiny it was that the arrival of these gaudy warriors influenced in a manner she of all people could least have foreseen.

We have said that of the usual pleasures of her kind she was utterly careless; but there was one enjoyment of which Mary never wearied, and in which she lost no opportunity of indulging when she could do so without attracting observation. This was, listening to a military band. It reminded her of her childhood—it reminded her of her mother—and she could stand entranced by its sounds for hours. In the gardens where the band played there used to be a porter's lodge kept by an old fruit-woman, much patronised by the Primrose establishment, and with this ancient Pomona Mary made interest to occupy her little secluded parlour, and listen to the music, whenever her school duties permitted the indulgence. Now it happened that one sunny afternoon, when Mary, in her usual sombre attire, was snugly enjoying from her hiding-place the harmonious efforts of "the Loyals," a certain wealthy manufacturer's lady was seized with a *physical* giddiness as she promenaded in the gardens, and Captain D'Orville, *the* great card of the regiment, came clanking into the porter's lodge to get a glass of water for the dame, upon whom he was in close attendance. Mary was eager to assist in a case of distress, and the Captain, an avowed admirer of beauty, was completely staggered by the apparition he encountered in place of the grimy old woman he had expected to find within. D'Orville was a gentleman of experience, and, as became a man of war, fertile in resources. He spilt half the tumbler of water over Mary's black gown, which *coup-de-main* gave him an opportunity of excusing himself at length for his awkwardness, and prolonging his interview with the beautiful woman he had so unexpectedly fallen in with. The next day came a magnificent dress, and a note full of apologies, couched in the most respectful language, and addressed *Mrs.* Delaval. "I wonder how he found me out," thought Mary, "and why he did not put *Miss.*" There was no signature to the note, and it was impossible to send the dress back, so she folded it in her drawer, and wondered what she ought to do, and what her mother would have advised. After this, wherever Mary went, there was Captain D'Orville; at church, in her school walks, when she went out with Miss Primrose—he seemed to have an intuitive knowledge of her movements, and never to lose an opportunity of gazing at her. Mary was a woman, after all; she thought it was "very disagreeable," yet was the excitement not altogether unpleasing. Gaston D'Orville was strikingly handsome; in fact, generally considered "the best-looking fellow in the Loyals," with a peculiar charm of manner, and a thorough knowledge of the whole art, method, and practice of war as carried on against the weaker sex. What chance had the friendless teacher's heart against such a conqueror? This—there was no treachery in the citadel—there was no gratified vanity to be the enemy's best auxiliary, no trifling pique nor unworthy jealousy to make a conquest valuable merely as a conquest. Mary was one of the few women who can see things as they are, and not through the glasses of their own imagination or prejudice; and when she came to know him better, she perceived the hollow selfishness of the hardened man of the world, with a perspicuity of which he would have supposed "the handsome governess" totally incapable. That she *should* know him better he took good care, but his advances were so well timed, so respectful, and in such thoroughly good taste, that it was impossible to take umbrage at them, and Mary found herself, she scarce knew how, meeting Captain D'Orville *by accident*, walking with him as far as the end of the street, amused by his conversation, and interested in his character, before she had time to think where or how she had made his acquaintance, and in what manner such an acquaintance was likely to end. And D'Orville himself was really in love, in his own way, with "the handsome governess."

"There is no fool like an old one," he confided to his friend Lacquers, of the Lancers, in an epistle addressed to that philosopher at Brussels. "If I were a 'marrying man,' which you well know I am *not*, I should spend the rest of my life, unjust as would be the monopoly, with this glorious Mrs. Delaval. I always call her by that matronly title; it is so much more respectful, and must make her feel so much more independent. She is only a teacher, my dear fellow, a teacher in a girls' school; and yet, for dignity and grace, and real 'high-bred' manner, she might be a duchess. Such a foot and hand! I can take my oath she has good blood in her veins. Altogether, she reminds me of your old mare, Sultana—as beautiful as a star—and looks as if she would die rather than give in. I never in my life saw a woman I admired half so much; you know I am generally pretty hard-hearted, but upon my word I begin to fear I have a soft place in me somewhere. And then, my dear Lacquers, what makes the thing so exciting is this—I do not believe she cares one toss of a halfpenny for me after all, and that if I were fool enough to offer to marry her to-morrow, she would quietly balance the advantages and disadvantages of the plan, and accept, or very likely *refuse* me, with her calm, condescending dignity, extremely unflattering as it is, and without moving a muscle of her beautiful, placid countenance. Don't she wish she may have the chance? and yet, absurd as it sounds, I am horribly in love with her. You will laugh at me 'consumedly,' and sometimes I feel half inclined to laugh at myself, dodging about the stupidest of places, as deeply smitten as if I were a cornet, regretting I ever came here, and yet not man enough to leave and go on detachment, which I have the option of doing. I shall see her again this evening, and come to a decision one way or the other, for this can't go on. In the meantime, don't show me up to a soul, and believe me," etc.

That very evening, a tall, good-looking man, in undress uniform, might have been seen, as indeed he was seen, by Miss Primrose's housemaid, walking a magnificent grey charger, with its bridle over his arm, close to the foot-pavement in Crozier Street, deep in what seemed an interesting conversation with a beautiful woman in black.

"So you don't believe we unfortunates ever *are* disinterested, Mrs. Delaval? I am afraid you have a very bad opinion of the whole sex," said the gentleman, with a slight tremor in his voice, extremely unusual to him, and contrasting strangely with the steady, measured tones of his companion. "I cannot give an opinion where I have so little knowledge, Captain D'Orville," was the reply; she began to know him well now, and liked to talk *out* with him, as a woman never does with a man for whom she cares; "I can only judge by what I see. It appears to me that you all live wholly and entirely for yourselves. If you are clever, you pervert your talents to get the better of your friends in every allowable species of dishonesty; if you are brave, your courage is but made subservient to your vanity and self-aggrandisement; if you are rich, your money is devoted to your own indulgence and your own purposes. I never hear, now-a-days, of anything noble, anything disinterested, such as I have read of. But I am talking great nonsense," said Mary, checking herself, and smiling at her own enthusiasm, unconscious of the burning admiration with which the hussar's eyes were riveted on her face. Like all *fast* reckless men, there was a spice of romance about D'Orville, and he liked to bring out the latent powers of a mind somewhat akin to his own daring intellect, more particularly when that mind belonged to such a person as his companion.

"I could prove that men *may* be disinterested, even in the nineteenth century," said he, and again his voice trembled as it sank almost to a whisper—"that there *are* men who would give up station, profession, ambition, everything,—the present they enjoy, and the future they look forward to,—for the sake of one whom they esteemed—admired—in short, whom they *loved*." She would not understand him, and the calm brow was as calm as ever while she answered, "I cannot think so. I have seen quite enough as a child, for you know I am half a soldier myself, to give me no inclination to prosecute my studies in human nature. And yet I have my ideal of a hero too, but in these days there is no such character as a Leonidas, a Curtius (you know, we governesses must not forget our history), a William Tell, or a Montrose."

"I'll wear thy colours in my cap, thy picture next my heart," muttered D'Orville; and then, carried away by the impulse of the moment, and forgetful of all his worldly prudence and good resolutions, he hurried impetuously on—"Listen to me, Mrs. Delaval; I may be presumptuous to speak thus to you on such short acquaintance, but you must have seen my regard—my attention—my devotion; I cannot bear to see you wasted here, thrown away in such a place as this—you who are meant for society and brilliancy, and everything that is worth having in life. Will you rely upon *me*? will you suffer me to rescue you from this obscure lot? will you consider?" Mary stopped dead short, drew herself up, and looked her admirer full in the face: "I am so unused to this sort of language, Captain D'Orville," she observed, without a vestige of emotion, "that I do not clearly understand you. If what you have to say is fit for me to hear, pray explain yourself; if not, I wish you a good evening;" and pausing for an instant while she kept him, as it were, "chained in her eye," she turned round, and walked calmly and deliberately straight home to Miss Primrose's.

The hussar was completely taken aback by the simplicity with which his attack had been repulsed. There he stood, opposite the grey horse, utterly confounded, and not knowing whether to advance or retreat. Should he laugh the thing off, and descend to the meanness of pretending he had been in jest? He could not—no, he *dared* not meet that calm, contemptuous eye. What an eye it was, and how he felt its influence even now! Should he hurry after her, and make a *bonâ fide* proposal of marriage, such as no woman could receive but as a compliment? Psha! what! marry a governess? What would the mess say, and Lacquers, and his brother profligates? No, the good grey horse was galloped back to barracks, and D'Orville was the life and soul of the supper-party, which he returned just in time to join. What a contrast it was, with its brilliant lights, flushed countenances, noise, excitement, and revelry, to the still summer evening, and the pure, sweet face of Mary Delaval.

"She turned round and walked calmly and deliberately home."

The wealthy manufacturer's lady thought Captain D'Orville very absent and *distrait* next day in the gardens; but from that time till he went on leave he devoted himself exclusively to her service, and she never dreamed that there was such a being in the world as the handsome governess at Miss Primrose's, or the loss that establishment had sustained in its junior assistant's departure.

And now Mary had been long dragging on her weary existence as a music-mistress in London. Miss Primrose's severe comments on the impropriety of evening walks with cavalry officers led to a dignified rejoinder from her teacher, and the conversation terminated in a small arrear of salary being paid up, and Mary's wardrobe (with the exception of a certain very handsome dress, afterwards sold cheap as "returned") being packed for travelling. In London she obtained sufficient employment to keep her from starving, and that was about all. A situation as "Governess in a private family" was advertised for, and again and again she was disappointed in obtaining one, till at length hearing accidentally that Mrs. Kettering was in want of a "finishing governess" for Blanche, Mary Delaval proceeded to the town-house to make inquiries, and failing to obtain even the wished-for address, was returning in hopeless despondency, when she encountered the impertinences we have already detailed, and which were alone wanting to fill the bitter cup of dependency to overflowing. Poor Mary! hers was "a black cloud" through which it was indeed difficult to see "the silver lining."

CHAPTER IV
"LIBITINA"

To keep a gentleman waiting any length of time, either in hot water or cold, is decidedly a breach of the laws of politeness, to repair which we must return as speedily as possible to "Cousin Charlie" and his friend, lying somewhat limp and blue at the bottom of "Hairblower's" dinghy; this worthy, under Providence, having been the means of saving the rash swimmer and the gallant boy who strove to rescue him from an untimely death, which a very few seconds more of submersion would have made a certainty. That Hairblower's boat-hook should have been ready at the nick of time was one of those "circumstances," as he called them, which he designated "special," and turned upon the fact of his having started a party of amateurs in the morning on a sort of marine picnic, from which they had returned prematurely, the gala proving a failure, with no greater loss than that of a spare oar and one or two small casks belonging to the seaman. It was on the hopeless chance of picking up these "waifs and strays" as they drifted down with the tide, that "Hairblower" was paddling about in a shallow skiff, denominated "a dinghy," when his attention was arrested by an adventurous swimmer striking boldly out at a long distance from the beach. As he said himself, "There's no depending on these gentlemen, so I thought it very likely I might be wanted, and stood 'off and on' till I saw Mr. Hardingstone making signals of distress. It's no joke that cramp isn't, half-a-mile out at sea; and I might have been too late with the boat-hook if it hadn't been for Master Charles—dear, dear, there's stuff in that lad you might cut an admiral out of, and they're going to make 'a soger' of him!"

He had contrived to pull the two exhausted swimmers into his little craft; and although Charlie very soon recovered himself, his friend, who was farther gone in his salt-water potations, gave them both some uneasiness before he came thoroughly to his senses.

Whilst our hardy seaman is putting them upon their legs, and administering hot brandy-and-water in a fisherman's house near the beach, we may spare a few lines to give some account of "Hairblower," and the qualities by which he earned that peculiar designation. Born and bred a fisherman, one of that daring race with which our sea-board swarms, and from which Her Majesty's navy and the British merchant service recruit their best men, he was brought up from his very childhood to make the boat his cradle, and the wave his home. Wet or dry, calm or stormy, blow high, blow low, with a plank beneath his foot, and a few threads of canvas over his head, he was in his element; and long ere he reached the full strength of manhood he was known for the most reckless of all, even amongst those daring spirits who seem to think life by far the least valuable of their earthly possessions. Twice, as a boy, had he *volunteered* to make up the crew of a lifeboat when the oldest hands were eyeing with doubtful glances that white, seething surf through which they would have to make their way to the angry, leaden sea beyond; and the men of Deal themselves, those heroes of the deep, acknowledged, with the abrupt freemasonry of the brave, that "the lad was as tough as pin-wire, *heart* to the backbone." His carelessness of weather soon became proverbial, and his friends often expostulated with him on his rashness in remaining out at sea with a craft by no means qualified to encounter the sudden squalls of the Channel, or the heavy seas which come surging up from the Atlantic in a real Sou'-Wester. His uncle at length promised to assist him in building a lugger of somewhat heavier tonnage than the yawl he was accustomed to risk, and the *Spanking Sally*, of ill-fated memory, was the result. On the first occasion that the young skipper exultingly stamped his foot on a deck he could really call his own, he earned the nickname by which he was afterwards distinguished. His uncle expressed a hope that the owner would now be a trifle more careful in his ventures, and suggested that when it blew hard, and there was a heavy cargo on board, it was good seamanship to run for the nearest port. "Blow," repeated the gallant lad, while he passed his fingers through thick glossy curls that the breeze was even then lifting from his forehead — "Blow, uncle! you'll never catch me putting *my* helm down for weather, till it comes on stiff enough to blow every one of these hairs clean out of my figure-head!" From that hour, and ever afterwards, he was known by the *sobriquet* of Hairblower, and as such we verily believe he had almost forgotten his own original name.

Hardingstone was soon sufficiently recovered to walk back to his hotel, and with his strong frame and constitution scouted the idea of any ill effects arising from what he called "a mere ducking." Once, however, on their way home, he pressed Charlie's hand, and with a tear in his eye — strange emotion for him to betray — whispered, "Charlie, you've the pluck of the devil; you've saved my life, and I shall never forget it." We are an undemonstrative people: on the stage, or in a book, here would have been an opportunity for a perfect oration about gratitude, generosity, and eternal friendship; but not so in real life; we cannot spare more than a sentence to acknowledge our rescue from ruin or destruction, and we are so afraid of being thought "humbugs," that we make even that sentence as cold as possible.

Mrs. Kettering, though, was a lady of a different disposition. She was in a terrible taking when her nephew returned, and she observed the feverish remains of past excitement, which the boy was unable to conceal. Bit by bit she drew from him the whole history of his gallant efforts to save Hardingstone, and the narrow escape they both had of drowning; and as Charlie finished his recital, and Blanche's eyes sparkled through her tears in admiration of his heroism, Mrs. Kettering rang the bell twice for Gingham, and went off into strong hysterics.

"Dear me, miss, how providential!" said the Abigail, an hour or so afterwards, popping her head into the drawing-room, where Blanche and Charlie were awaiting news of his aunt, having left her to "keep quiet"— "Dr. Globus is down here for a holiday, and Missus bid me send for him if she wasn't any better, and now she *isn't* any better. What shall I do?"

"Send for him, I should think," said Charlie, and forthwith despatched a messenger in quest of the doctor, whilst Blanche ran up-stairs to mamma's room with a beating heart and an aching presentiment, such as often foretells too truly the worst we have to apprehend.

The curtains were drawn round Mrs. Kettering's bed, and Blanche, hoping it might only be one of the nervous attacks to which her mother was subject, put them gently aside to see if she was sleeping. Even that young, inexperienced girl was alarmed at the dark flush on the patient's face, and the heavy snorting respirations she seemed to draw with such difficulty.

"O mamma, mamma!" said she, laying her head on the pillow by her mother's side, "what is it? I beseech you to tell me! Dear mamma, what can we do to help you?"

Mrs. Kettering turned her eyes upon her daughter, but the pupils were distorted as though from some pressure on the brain, and she strove to articulate in vain. Blanche, in an agony of fear, rushed to the bell-rope, and brought Gingham and Charlie running up hardly less alarmed than herself. What could the lad do in a case like this? With the impetuosity of his character, he took his hat and hastened to Dr. Globus's house with such speed as to overtake the messenger he had previously despatched; Gingham was sent down to hunt up a prescription of that skilful physician, which had once before been beneficial; and Blanche sat her down in her mother's room, to watch, and tremble, and pray for the beloved form, stretched senseless within those white curtains.

She could scarce believe it. In that very room, not six hours ago, she had pinned her mother's shawl, and smoothed her own ringlets. Yet it seemed as if this had occurred to some one else—not to herself. With the unaccountable propensity great excitement ever has for trifling, she arranged the disordered toilet-table; she even counted the curl-papers that lay in their little triangular box; then she went down on her knees, and prayed, as those pray who feel it is the last resource. When she rose, a passion of weeping somewhat relieved her feelings, but with composure came the consciousness of the awful possibility—the separation that might be—to-night, even; and the dim, blank future, desolate, without a mother. But the familiar noises in the street brought her back to the present, and it seemed impossible that this should be the same world in which till now she had scarcely known any anxiety or affliction. Then a soothing hope stole over her that these dreadful misgivings might be groundless; that the doctor would come, and mamma would soon be better; and she would nurse her, and love her more and more, and never be wilful again; but in the midst, with a pang that almost stopped her heart, flashed across her the recollection of her father's death— the suspense, the confusion, the sickening certainty, the dreary funeral, and how, in her little black frock, she had clasped mamma's neck, and thought she had saved all, since she had not lost her. And now, must this come again? And would there be no mother to clasp when it was over? Blanche groaned aloud. But hark! the door-bell rings, there is a steady footstep on the stair, and she feels a deep sensation of relief, as though the doctor held the scales of life and death in his hands.

Gingham, in the meantime, whose composure was not proof against anything in the shape of serious illness or danger, had been wandering over the house with her mistress's keys in her hand, seeking for that prescription which she had herself put by, not three days before, but of which she had totally forgotten the hiding-place. Music, work-boxes, blotting-books were turned over and tumbled about in vain, till at length she bethought her of her mistress's writing-desk, and on opening that "sanctum," out fell a paper in her lady's hand, which ignorant Gingham herself at once perceived was meant for no such eyes as hers. She caught a glimpse, too, of her own name between its folds, and even in the hurry and emergency of the moment we are not prepared to say that female curiosity could have resisted the temptation of "just one peep," but at that instant "Cousin Charlie" and the doctor were heard at the door, and as Gingham thrust the mysterious document into her bosom, the former entered the room, and rated her soundly for prying about amongst Aunt Kettering's papers when she ought to have been up-stairs attending to herself.

Dr. Globus felt Mrs. Kettering's pulse, and turned to Blanche (who was watching his countenance as the culprit does that of the juryman who declares his fate) with a face from which it was impossible to gather hope or fear.

"Your mamma must be kept *very* quiet, Miss Blanche," said the doctor, with whom his young friend was a prime favourite. "I must turn you all out but Mrs. Gingham. I should like to remain here for a while to watch the effect of some medicine I shall give her; but we cannot have too few people in the room." And to enhance this significant hint he pointed to the door, at which Charlie was lingering with a white, anxious face.

"But tell me, *dear* doctor," implored Blanche, in an agony of suspense, "*pray* tell me, is there any danger? Will *nothing* do her any good?"

Poor girl, did you ever know a doctor that would reply to such a question?

"We must keep her quiet, my dear," was all the answer she got; and Blanche was forced to go down-stairs, much against her will, and wait in blank dismay, with her hand clasping Cousin Charlie's, and her eyes turned to the clock, on which the minutes seemed to lengthen into hours, whilst ever and anon a footstep overhead seemed to indicate there would be some news of the patient; yet no door opened, no step was heard upon the stairs. Not a word did the cousins exchange, though the boy moved at intervals restlessly in his chair. The calm, beautiful evening deepened into the purple haze of night over the Channel, the lamps began to twinkle in the street, and still the cousins sat and waited, and still nobody came.

When the door was shut, and Globus was left alone with his patient, a solemn, sagacious expression stole over the worthy doctor's face. He had long been the personal friend of Mrs. Kettering, as well as "her own medical man"; and although he would probably have felt it more had he not been called in professionally, yet it was with a heavy heart and a desponding brow that he confessed to himself there was little or no hope. He had put in practice all that skill and experience suggested—he had sent for a brother physician of high local repute, and now there was nothing more to be done save to wait for the result; so the kind-hearted man sat himself down in the chair Blanche had so lately occupied, and pondered over the many changing years, now like a dream, during which he had known that life which in yonder bed was dribbling out its few remaining sands. He remembered her the merry, black-eyed girl (once he thought her eyes brighter than those of Mrs. Globus); he saw her again the sparkling bride, the good-humoured matron, the doting mother, the not inconsolable widow. It was only yesterday he bowed to her on the parade, and thought how young she looked with her grown-up daughter; he was to have dined with them to-morrow; and the uncertainty of life looked him startlingly in the face. But the pride of science soon came to the rescue, and the practised healer forgot his private feelings in his professional reflections. And thus Dr. Globus passed his holiday—one afternoon of the precious fourteen, in which he had promised himself the fresh breezes and the out-of-doors liberty of St. Swithin's. Mrs. Globus and the children were picking up shells on the beach; his brother, whom he had not seen for ten years, was coming to dinner; but the doctor's time is the property of the suffering and the doomed, and still Globus sat and watched and calculated, and saw clearly that Mrs. Kettering must die.

The hours stole on, candles were brought into the drawing-room, and the cousins tried in vain with parched lips and choking throats to have some tea. A ring at the door-bell heralded the arrival of the other doctor, a stout man in a brown greatcoat, smelling of the night-dew. Blanche ran out to meet him—it was a relief to do something—and beckoned him silently up-stairs. She even stole into the sick-room, and caught a glimpse of her mother's figure, recumbent and covered up; but the curtains were half closed, and she could not see the dear face. Globus kindly drew her away, and shut her out, but not before the frightened girl had glanced at a dark-stained handkerchief on the floor, and sickened with the conviction that it was clotted with blood. Outside, the little housemaid was sitting on the stairs, crying as if her heart would break. Poor Blanche sat down by her in the darkness, and mingled her tears with those of the affectionate servant. She began to get hopeless now. After a while she went down again to Cousin Charlie, and was surprised to find it so late; the clock pointed to five minutes past ten; and with trembling hands she closed the windows, listening for an instant to the dash of the waves outside, with a strange, wild feeling that they never sounded so before. Then she covered up "Bully," who had been whistling ever since the lights were brought; but she had not the heart to exchange a syllable with Cousin Charlie; and that poor lad, affecting a composure that his face belied, was pretending to spell over the evening paper, of which he was vacantly staring at the advertisement sheet. Again there is a movement above, and the two doctors adjourn to another room to discuss the patient's case. Great is the deference paid by the local Esculapius to the famous London physician. What Dr. Globus recommended—what Dr. Globus said—what Dr. Globus thought—were quoted by the former ever afterwards; yet could one have witnessed the consultation of these two scientific men, it might have been instructive to observe how professional etiquette never once gave way to the urgency of the moment—how the science of curing, like that of killing, has its forms, its subordination, its ranks, its dignities, and its "customs of war in like cases." Gingham was left with the patient, and the weeping housemaid stood ready to assist, the latter showing an abundance of nerve and decision, when called upon to act, which her behaviour on the staircase would scarcely have promised. Even Gingham was less flustered than usual, now there was really something to be frightened at. Woman is never seen to such advantage as when tending the sick; the eye that quails to see a finger pricked, the hand that trembles if there is but a mouse in the room, will gaze unflinchingly on the lancet or the cupping-glass, will apply the leeches without a shudder, or pour the soothing medicament, drop by drop, into the measured wine-glass, with the steadiness and accuracy of a chemical professor. Where man with all his boasted nerve turns sick and pale, and shows himself worse than useless, woman vindicates the courage of her sex, that unselfish heroism, that passive devotion, which is ever ready to bear and be still. They seem to have a positive pleasure in alleviating the pangs of the sufferer, and taking care of the helpless. Look at a bustling matron, blessed with a large family of children, and whatever may be the opinion of the "paterfamilias," however much he may grunt and grumble (so like a *man*!) at having the quiver as full as it will hold, she, in her heart of hearts, welcomes every fresh arrival with the hospitable sentiment of "the more the merrier"; and much as she loves them all, lavishes her warmest affections on the last little uninteresting morsel of underdone humanity, which, on its first appearance, is the most helpless, as it is the least attractive, of Nature's germinating efforts; unless, indeed, she should own a dwarf, a cripple, or an idiot amongst her thriving progeny—then will that poor creature be the mother's chiefest treasure, then will woman's love and woman's tenderness hover with beautiful instinct round the head which Nature itself seems to have scouted, and the mother will press to her heart of hearts the wretched being that all else are prone to ridicule and despise. So in the sick-room, when "pain and anguish wring the brow," woman wipes the foaming lip and props the sinking head. Woman's care speeds the long doubtful recovery, and woman's prayers soothe the dying hour, when hope has spread her wings and fled away. In works like these she vindicates her angel-nature, in scenes like these she perfects that humble piety of which it appears to us she has a greater share than the stronger sex. The proud Moslem boasts there will be no women in his material paradise; let us look to ourselves, that the exclusion for us be not all the other way.

Blanche sits vacantly in the drawing-room, and thinks the doctors' consultation is to be endless, and that it is cruel to keep her so long from her mamma. Charlie puts down the paper, and drawing kindly towards his cousin, finds courage to whisper some few words of consolation, which neither of them feel to be of the slightest avail. He has been thinking that

Uncle Baldwin ought to be sent for, but he dares not excite more alarm in his companion's mind by such a suggestion, and he meditates a note to his friend Hardingstone to manage it for him. Uncle Baldwin, better known in the world as Major-General Bounce, is Mrs. Kettering's brother, and lives in the midland counties—"he should be sent for immediately," thinks Charlie, "if he is to see my aunt alive." Blanche is getting very restless, and thinks she might soon go up-stairs and see——Hush! the bedroom door opens—a rapid footstep is heard on the stairs—it is Gingham running down for the doctors—Blanche rushes to the door and intercepts her on the landing-place—the woman's face is ashy pale, and her eyes stand strangely out in the dubious light—her voice comes thick and husky. The young girl is quite composed for the instant, and every syllable thrusts straight to her heart as the maid stammers out, "O Miss Blanche! Miss Blanche! your mamma——"

The sun rose, and the waters of the Channel glittered in the morning light, but the shutters were closed at No. 9—and honest Hairblower drew his rough hand across his eyes, as he sought to get some news of "poor Miss Blanche." He met Hardingstone coming from the house, whither the "man of action" had repaired on the first intelligence of their calamity, and had made himself as useful as he could to the afflicted family. "Do she take on, poor dear?" said Hairblower, scarcely restraining the drops that coursed down his weather-beaten cheeks. "Such a young thing as that, Mr. Hardingstone, to go loose without a mother—and the poor lady, too, gone down like in a calm. They will not be leaving, sir, just yet, will 'em? I couldn't bear to think of Miss Blanche cruising about among strangers, till she begins to hold up a bit—she should come out and get the sea-air, as soon as she is able for it, and I'll have the boat covered in and ready day and night——O Mr. Hardingstone, what *can* I do, sir, for the poor young lady in her distress?" Frank shook the honest fellow's hand, and could scarcely command his own feelings enough to reply. He had done everything that was necessary in the house of death, had sent off an express for the General, sealed up Mrs. Kettering's jewel-boxes, writing-cases, etc., and performed all those offices of which the two children, for so we might almost call them, were incapable, and which, even in the presence of the Destroyer, are still hard, cold matters of business, and *must* be attended to, like the ordering dinner, and the arrangement for the funeral, though the survivors' hearts may ache, and their wounds burst out afresh, till they too wish their bodies were laid at rest beneath the sod, and their spirits were away, free and unmourning, with the loved one in those realms with which, sooner or later, we are all to be acquainted.

On the child's misery it would not become us to dwell. There are feelings over which a veil is drawn too sacred to be disturbed by mortal hand. Well might Margaret Douglas exclaim, in the old ballad—

"True lovers I may have many a one,

But a father once slain, I shall never see mair."

And when a young, affectionate girl is wailing for a parent, the voice of sorrow cannot be hushed, nor the tears dried, till grief has had its course, and time has cured the wounds now so excruciating, which ere long shall be healed over and forgotten. "Cousin Charlie," boy-like, was more easily consoled; and although at intervals his kind aunt's voice would seem to sound in his ears, and the sight of her work, her writing, or any other familiar object associated with herself would bring on a fresh accession of grief, yet in the society of Frank Hardingstone, and the anticipation of Uncle Baldwin's arrival, he found objects to divert his thoughts, and direct them to that brilliant inheritance of the young, the golden future, which never *shall* arrive. He was, besides, a lad of a sanguine, imaginative disposition, and these are the spirits over which sorrow has least power. The more elastic the spring, the more easily it regains its position; and a sensitive organisation, after the first recoil, will rise uninjured from a shock that prostrates more material souls to the very dust.

Over the rest of the household came the reaction that invariably follows the first sensations of awe inspired by sudden death. There was an excitement not altogether unpleasing in the total derangement of plans, the uncertainty as to the future created amongst the domestics by the departure of their mistress. The butler knew he should have to account for his plate, and was busied with his spoons and his inventory; the footman speculated on the next place he should get, with "a family that spent nine months of the year in London"; the very "boy in buttons" thought more of his promotion than of the kind mistress who had housed, clothed, and fed him when a parish orphan. Gingham herself, that tender damsel, was occupied and excited about Miss Blanche's mourning, and her own "breadths" of black and "depths" of crape usurped the place of unavailing regrets in a mind not calculated to contain many ideas at a time. Besides, the pleasure of "shopping," inexplicable as it may appear to man's perverted taste, is one which ravishes the female mind with an intense delight; and what with tradesmen's condolences, the interminable fund of gossip created thereby, the comparing of patterns, the injunctions on all sides "not to give way," and the visits to linen-drapers' shops, we cannot but confess that Gingham's spirits were surprisingly buoyant, considering the circumstance under which she swept those costly wares from their tempting counters. Tom Blacke, too, lost no time in assuring her of his sympathy.

"O, Miss Gingham," said wily Tom, as he insisted on carrying a huge brown-paper parcel home for her, and led the way by a circuitous route along the beach, "O, Miss Gingham, what a shock for your affectionate natur' and kindly 'eart! Yet sorrow becomes some people," added Tom, reflectively, and glancing his dark eyes into Gingham's muddy-looking face, as he offered her an arm.

"Go along with you, Mr. Blacke," replied the sorrowing damsel, forgetful of her despondency for the moment, which emboldened him to proceed.

"You ought to have a home, Miss Gingham—you ought to have some one to attach yourself to—you that attaches everybody" (he ventured a squeeze, and the maiden did not withdraw the brown thread glove which rested on his arm; so Tom mixed it a little stronger)—"a 'onest man to depend on, and a family and such like."

Tom flourished his arm along a line of imaginary olive branches, and Gingham represented that "she couldn't think of such a thing."

"Service isn't for the likes of you, miss," proceeded the tempter; "hindependence is fittest for beauty" (Tom peeped under the bonnet, and "found it," as he expressed himself, "all serene"); "a cottage and content, and a 'eart that is 'umble may 'ope for it 'ere;" with which concluding words Mr. Blacke, who was an admirer of poetry, and believed with Moore *that* would be given to song "which gold could never buy," imprinted a vigorous kiss on those not very tempting lips, and felt that the day was his own.

Ladies of mature charms are less easily taken aback by such advances than their inexperienced juniors. The position, even if new in practice, is by no means so in theory, and having often anticipated the attack, they are the more prepared to receive it when it arrives. Ere our lovers reached No. 9 he had called her by her Christian name, and "Rachel" had promised to think of it. As she closed the "area-gate" Gingham had given her heart away to a scamp. True, she was oldish, uglyish, wore brown thread gloves, and had a yellow skin; yet for all this she had a woman's heart, and, like a very woman, gave it away to Tom Blacke without a return.

In good time General Bounce arrived, and took the command from Frank Hardingstone, with many gracious acknowledgments of his kindness. The General was a man of far too great importance to be introduced at the conclusion of a chapter. It is sufficient to say, that with military promptitude and decision (which generally means a disagreeable and abrupt method of doing a simple thing) he set the household in order, arranged the sad ceremony, over which he presided with proper gravity, packed Cousin Charlie off to his private tutor's, paid the servants their wages, and settled the departure of himself and niece for his own residence.

Do we think ourselves of account in this our world?—do we think we shall be so missed and so regretted? Drop a stone into a pool, there is a momentary splash, a bubble on the surface, and circle after circle spreads, and widens and weakens, till all is still and smooth as though the water had never been disturbed; so it is with death. There is a funeral and crape and weeping, and "callings to inquire," then the intelligence gets abroad amongst mere acquaintances and utter strangers, a line in the *Times* proclaims our decease to the world. Ere it has reached the colonies we are well-nigh forgotten at home.

Mrs. Kettering was at rest in her grave; the General was full of his arrangements and his responsibilities; Charlie was back amongst his mathematics and his cricket and his Greek and Latin; the servants were looking out for fresh places; and the life that had disappeared from the surface was forgotten by all. By all save one; for still Blanche was gazing on the waters and mourning for her mother.

CHAPTER V
UNCLE BALDWIN

In an unpretending corner of the "Guyville Guide and Midland Counties' Directory" a few lines are devoted to inform the tourist that "Newton-Hollows, post-town Guyville, in the Hundred of Cow-capers, is the seat of Major-General Bounce, etc., etc., etc. The lover of the picturesque obtains, from the neighbourhood of this mansion, a magnificent view, comprising no less than seventeen churches, a vast expanse of wood and meadow-land, the distant spires of Bubbleton, and the imposing outline of the famous Castle Guy." Doubtless all these beauties might have been conspicuous had the adventurous tourist chosen to climb one of the lofty elms with which the house was surrounded; but from the altitude of his own stature he was obliged to content himself with a far less extensive landscape, seeing that the country was closely wooded, and as flat as his hand. But Newton-Hollows was one of those sweet little places, self-contained and compact, that require no distant views, no shaggy scenery, no "rough heath and rugged wood," to enhance their charm. Magnificent old timber, "the oak and the ash, and the bonny ivy tree," to say nothing of elms and chestnuts, dotted the meadows and pastures in which the mansion was snugly ensconced. People driving up, or rather along, the level approach, were at a loss to make out where the farms ended and the park began. Well-kept lawns, that looked as if they were fresh mown every morning, swept up to the drawing-room windows, opening to the ground; not a leaf was strewn on sward or gravel; not a weed, nor even a daisy, permitted to show its modest head above the surface; and as for a rake, roller, or a gardener's hat being left in a place where such instruments have no business, why, the General would have made the unfortunate delinquent eat it—rake, roller, or "wide-a-awake"—and discharged him besides on the spot. No wonder the flower-garden adjoining the conservatory, which again opened into the drawing-room, looked so trim and well-kept: "Master's" hobby was a garden, and, though utterly ignorant of the names, natures, and treatment of plants, he liked to see every variety in his possession, and spared no expense on their cultivation; and so a head gardener and five subalterns carried off all the prizes at the Bubbleton and Guyville horticulturals; and the General complained that he could never get a nosegay for his table, nor a bit of fruit for his dessert fit to eat. Yet were there worse "billets" in this working world than Newton-Hollows. The Bubbleton "swells" and county dignitaries found it often "suit their hunting arrangements" to go, over-night, and dine with "old Bounce." He would always "put up a hack for you," than which no effort of hospitality makes a man more deservedly popular in a hunting country; and his dinners, his Indian dishes, his hot pickles, his dry champagne, his wonderful claret ("not a headache in a hogshead, sir," the General would say, with a frown of defiance), were all in keeping with the snug, comfortable appearance of his dwelling, and the luxurious style which men who have served long in the army, and often been obliged to "rough it," know so well how to enjoy. Then there was no pretension about the thing whatever. The house, though it ranged over a considerable extent of ground, particularly towards the offices, was only two storeys high—"a mere cottage," its owner called it; but a cottage in which the apartments were all roomy and well-proportioned, in which enough "married couples could be put up" to furnish a very good-sized dinner-table, and the bachelors (we like to put in a word for our fellow-sufferers) were as comfortably accommodated as their more fortunate associates, who travelled with wives, imperials, cap-boxes, and ladies'-maids.

It is a bad plan to accustom unmarried gentlemen to think they can do without their comforts; it makes them hardy and independent, and altogether averse to the coddling and care and confinement with which they expect to find matrimony abound. As we go through the world, in our desolate celibacy, we see the net spread in sight of many a bird, and we generally remark, that the meshes which most surely entangle the game are those of self-indulgence and self-applause. You *must* gild the wires, and pop a lump of sugar between them too, if you would have the captive flutter willingly into the cage. When young Cœlebs comes home from hunting or shooting, and has to divest himself of his clammy leathers or dirt-encumbered gaiters in a room without a fire and with a cracked pane in the window, he takes no pleasure in his adornment, but hurries over his toilet, or perhaps begins to smoke. This should be avoided: we have known a quiet cigar do away with the whole effect of a bran-new pink bonnet. But if, on the contrary, he finds a warm, luxurious room, plenty of hot water, wax candles on the dressing-table, and a becoming looking-glass, the quarry lingers over the tie of its neckcloth with a pleasing conviction that that is not half a bad-looking fellow grinning opposite, and moreover that there is a "deuced *lovable* girl" down-stairs, who seems to be of the same opinion. So the thing works: vows are exchanged, *trousseaux* got ready, settlements drawn out, the lawyers thrive, and fools are multiplied. Had Newton-Hollows belonged to a designing matron, instead of an unmarried general officer, it might have become a perfect mart for the exchanges of beauty and valour. Hunting men are pretty usually a marrying race; whether it be from daily habits of recklessness, a bold disregard of the adage which advises "to look before you leap," or a general thick-headedness and want of circumspection, the red-coated Nimrod falls an easy prey to any fair enslaver who may think him worth the trouble of subjection; and for one alliance that has been negotiated in the stifling atmosphere of a London ball-room, twenty owe their existence to the fresh breezes, the haphazard events, and surrounding excitement of the hunting-field.

General Bounce's guests, as was natural in the country where he resided, were mostly men like mad Tom,

"Whose chiefest care

Was horse to ride and weapon wear;"

nor, like him, would they have objected to place gloves in their caps or carry any other favours which might demonstrate their own powers of fascination, and their rank in the good graces of the heiress. Yes, there was an heiress now at Newton-Hollows. Popular as had always been the General's hospitality, he was now besieged with hints, and advances, and innuendoes, having for their object an invitation to his house. What a choice of scamps might he have had, all ready and willing to marry his niece—all anxious, if possible, to obtain even a peep "of that little Miss Kettering, not yet out of the school-room, who is to have ever so many hundred thousand pounds, and over whom old Bounce keeps watch and ward like a fiery dragon."

But the passing years have little altered Blanche's sweet and simple character, though they have rounded her figure and added to her beauty. She is to "come out" next spring, and already the world is talking of her charms and her expectations. A pretty picture is so much prettier in a gilt frame, and she will probably begin life with the ball at her foot; yet is there the same soft, artless expression in her countenance that it wore at St. Swithin's ere her mother's death—the same *essence* of beauty, independent of colouring and features, which may be traced in really charming people from the cradle to the grave, which made Blanche a willing child, is now enhancing the loveliness of her womanhood, and will probably leave her a very pleasant-looking old lady.

"And Charlie comes home to-morrow," says Blanche, tripping along the gravel walk that winds through those well-kept shrubberies. "I wonder if he's at all the sort of person you fancy, and whether you will think him as perfect as I do?"

"Probably not, my dear," replied her companion, whose stately gait contrasted amusingly with Blanche's light and playful gestures. "People seldom come up to one's ideas of them; and I am sure it is not your fault if I do not expect to meet a perfect hero of romance in your cousin." We ought to know those low thrilling tones; we ought to recognise the majestic figure—the dark sweeping dress—the braided hair and classical features of that pale, serious face. Mary Delaval is still the handsome governess; and Blanche would rather part with her beauty or her bullfinch, or any of her most prized earthly possessions, than that dear duenna, who, having finished her education, is now residing with her in the dubious capacity of part chaperon, part teacher, and part friend.

"Well, dear, he *is* a hero," replied Blanche, who always warmed on *that* subject. "Let me see which of my heroes he's most like: Prince Rupert—only he's younger and better-looking" (Blanche, though a staunch little cavalier, could not help associating mature age and gravity with the flowing wigs in which most of her favourites of that period were depicted); "Claverhouse, only not so cruel,—he *is* like Claverhouse in the face, I think, Mrs. Delaval; or 'bonnie Prince Charlie'; or Ivanhoe,—yes, Ivanhoe, that's the one; he's as brave and as gentle; and Mr. Hardingstone, whose life he saved, you know, says he rides most beautifully, and will make a capital officer."

"And which of the heroes is Mr. Hardingstone, Blanche?" said her friend, in her usual measured tones. Blanche blushed.

"Oh, I can't understand Mr. Hardingstone," said she; "I think he's odd-*ish*, and quite unlike other people; then he looks through one so. Mrs. Delaval, I think it's quite rude to stare at people as if you thought they were not telling the truth. But he's good-looking, too," added the young lady, reflectively; "only not to be compared with Charlie."

"Of course not," rejoined her friend; "but it is fortunate that we are to enjoy the society of this Paladin till he joins his regiment—Lancers, are they not? Well, we must hope, Blanche, to use the language of your favourites of the middle ages, that he may prove a lamb among ladies, as he is doubtless a lion among lancers."

"Dear Charlie! how he will enjoy his winter. He is so fond of hunting; and he is to have Hyacinth, and Haphazard, and Mayfly to ride for his own—so kind of Uncle Baldwin; but I must be off to put some flowers in his room," quoth Blanche, skipping along the walk as young ladies will, when unobserved by masculine eyes; "he may arrive at any moment, he's such an uncertain boy."

"Zounds! you've broke it, you fiddle-headed brute!" exclaimed a choleric voice from the further side of a thick laurel hedge, startling the ladies most unceremoniously, and preparing them for the spectacle of a sturdy black cob trotting rebelliously down the farm road, with a fragment of his bridle dangling from his head, the remaining portion being firmly secured to a gate-post, at which the self-willed animal had been tied up in vain. Another instant brought the owner of the voice and late master of the cob into the presence of Mrs. Delaval and his niece. It was no less a person than General Bounce.

"Uncle Baldwin, Uncle Baldwin," exclaimed Blanche, who turned him round her finger as she did the rest of the establishment, "where have you been all day? You promised to drive me out—you know you did, you wicked, hard-hearted man."

"Been, my dear?" replied the General, in a tone of softness contrasting strangely with the flushed and vehement bearing of his outward man; "at that—(no, I will *not* swear)—at that doubly accursed farm. Would you believe the infernal stupidity of the people—(excuse me, Mrs. Delaval)— men with heads on their shoulders, and hair, and front teeth like other people—and they've sent the black bull to Bubbleton without winkers— without winkers, as I live by bread; but I won't be answerable for the consequences,—no, I won't make good any damages originating in such carelessness; no, not if there's law in England or justice under heaven! But, my sweet Blanche," added the General, in a tone of amiable piano, the more remarkable for the forte of his previous observations, "I'll go and get ready this instant, my darling; you shan't be disappointed; I'll order the pony-carriage forthwith. Holloa! you, sir; only let me catch you—only let me catch you, that's all; I'll trounce you as sure as my name's Bounce!" and the General, without waiting for any further explanation, darted off in pursuit of an idle village boy, whom he espied in the very act, *flagrante delicto*, of trespassing on a pathway which the lord of the manor had been several years vainly endeavouring to shut up.

General Bounce was such a medley as can only be produced by the action of a tropical sun on a vigorous, sanguine Anglo-Saxon temperament. Specimens are becoming scarcer every day. They are seldom to be met with in our conventional and well-behaved country, though here and there, flitting about a certain club celebrated for its curries, they may be discovered even in the heart of the metropolis. On board transports, men-of-war, mail-steamers, and such-like government conveyances, they are more at home; in former days they were occasionally visible inside our long coaches, where they invariably made a difficulty about the window; but in the colonies they are to be seen in their highest state of cultivation; as a general rule, the hotter the climate, the more perfect the specimen.

Our friend the General was a very phœnix of his kind. In person he was short, stout, square, and active, with black twinkling eyes and a round, clean-shaved face—small-featured and good-humoured-looking, but choleric withal. His naturally florid complexion had been baked into a deep red-brown by his Indian campaigns. If Pythagoras was right in his doctrine concerning the transmigration of souls, the General's must have previously inhabited the person of a sturdy, snappish black-and-tan terrier. In manner he was alternately marvellously winning and startlingly abrupt, the transition being instantaneous; whilst in character he was decided, energetic, and impracticable, though both rash and obstinate, with an irritable temper and an affectionate heart. He had seen service in India, and by his own account had not only experienced sundry hair-breadth 'scapes bordering on the romantic, but likewise witnessed such strange sights and vagaries as fall to the lot of few, save those whose bodily vision is assisted by that imaginative faculty denominated "the mind's eye."

The General was a great disciplinarian, and piqued himself much upon the order in which he kept the females of his establishment, Blanche especially, whose lightest word, by the way, was his law. Indeed, like many old bachelors, he entertained a reverence almost superstitious for the opposite sex, and a few tears shed at the right moment would always bear the delinquent harmless, whatever the misdemeanour for which she was taken to task. The men, indeed, found him more troublesome to deal with, and the newly-arrived were somewhat alarmed at his violent language and impetuous demeanour; but the older servants always "took the bull by the horns" fearlessly and at once, nor in the end did they ever fail to get their own way with a master who, to use their peculiar language, "was easily upset, though he soon came round again." What made the General an infinitely less disagreeable man in society than he otherwise would have been, was the fact of his having a farm, which farm served him as a safety-valve to carry off all the irritation that could not but accumulate in an easy, uneventful life, destitute of real grievances as of the stirring, active scenes to which he had been accustomed in his earlier days. If a gentleman finds it indispensable to his health that he should be continually in hot water—that he should always have something to grumble at, something to disappoint him, let him take to farming—his own land or another's, it is immaterial which; but let him "occupy," as it is called, a certain number of acres—and we will warrant him as much "worry" and "annoyance" as the most "tonic"-craving disposition can desire. Let us accompany our retired warrior to his farm-yard, whither, after an ineffectual chase, he at length followed his black pony, forgetful of Blanche and the drive, on which, in the now shortening daylight, it was already too late to embark.

In the first place, the bull was come back—he had been to Bubbleton *minus* his winkers, but no one in that salubrious town caring to purchase a bull, he had returned to his indigenous pastures and his disgusted owner—therefore must the bailiff hazard an excuse and a consolation, in which the words "poor," and "stock," and the "fair on the fifteenth," are but oil to the flame.

"Fair! he'll be as thin as a whipping-post in a week—if anybody bids five shillings for him at the fair, I'll eat him, horns and all! What weight are those sheep?" adds the General, abruptly turning to another subject, and somewhat confusing his deliberate overseer by the suddenness of the inquiry. "Now those turnips are not fit for sheep! I tell you they ought to be three times the size. Zounds, man, *will* you grow larger turnips? And have I not countermanded those infernal iron hurdles a hundred times? a thousand times!! a hundred thousand times!!! Give *me* the pail, you lop-eared buffoon—do you call *that* the way to feed a pig?" and the General, seizing the bucket from an astonished chaw-bacon, who stood aghast, as if he thought his master was mad, managed to spill the greater part of the contents over his own person and gaiters, rendering a return home absolutely indispensable. He stumped off accordingly, giving a parting direction to some of his myrmidons to catch the black cob, in as mild a tone and with as good-humoured a countenance as if he had been in this heavenly frame of mind the whole afternoon.

Now the General, when he first began to live alone, and to miss the constant interchange of ideas which a military life encourages, had acquired a habit of discoursing to himself on such subjects as were most interesting to him at the time; so as he toddled merrily along, much relieved by the bucolic blow-up, and admired his sturdy legs and swung his short arms, all the way up the long gravel-walk towards the house, his thoughts framed themselves into a string of disjointed sentences, now muttered scarcely above a whisper, now spoken boldly out in an audible tone, which would have led a stranger to suppose he was carrying on a conversation with some one on the other side of the screening Portugal laurels. "Thick-headed fellows, these bumpkins," soliloquised the General, "not like my old friends at Fool-a-pore—could make them skip about to some purpose: there's nothing like a big stick for a nigger—never mind. I'm young enough to begin again—man of iron—what an arm! what a leg! might have married a dozen peeresses, and beauties by hundreds—didn't though. Now, there's Blanche; I shall have fifty fellows all after her before Christmas—sharp dogs if they think they can weather old Bounce—Rummagee Bang couldn't. By the by, I haven't told Mrs. Delaval that story yet—clever woman, and good judgment—admires my character, I'll bet a million—an officer's daughter, too, and what a magnificent figure she has—Bounce, you're an old fool! As for Charlie, he shall stay here all the winter; there's mettle in that lad, and if I can't lick him into shape I'm a Dutchman. He'll show 'em the way with the hounds, and I'll put him up to a thing or two, the young scamp. Snaffles! Snaffles!!" roared the General, as he concluded his monologue, and passed the stables on his way to the house, "don't take any of the horses out to-morrow till you get your orders. Do you *hear* me? man alive!" And by this time, having reached home, he stumped off to dress for dinner, keeping up a running fire along the passages, as he discovered here a hearth-broom, and there a coal-scuttle, ready for him to break his shins over, and observed the usual plate and tea-cup standing sentry at each of the ladies' doors.

We may be sure that not the least comfortable of the rooms at Newton-Hollows was especially appropriated as Blanche's own, and that young lady was now sitting opposite a glass that reflected a smiling face, enduring with patience and resignation the ceremony of having "her hair done." A French maid, named "Rosine," a very pretty substitute for bilious-looking Gingham, was working away at the ivory-handled brushes, and occasionally letting fall a thick glossy ringlet athwart the snow-white cape in which the process of adornment was submitted to, whilst Mary Delaval, buried in an arm-chair drawn close to the blazing fire, and enveloped in a dressing-gown, with an open book in her hand, was quietly listening to Blanche's remarks on things in general, and her own self and prospects in particular.

That hour before dinner is the period chosen by women for their most confidential intercourse, and the enjoyment of what they call "a cozy chat." When Damon, in the small hours, smokes a cigar with Pythias, more especially if such an indulgence be treason against the rules of the house, he opens his heart to his fellow-trespasser, in a manner of which, next morning, he has but a faint recollection. He confides to him his differences with "the governor," his financial embarrassments, the unsoundness of his horses and his heart, the latter possession much damaged by certain blue eyes in the neighbourhood; he details to him the general scandal with which he is conversant, and binding him by promises of eternal secrecy, proceeds deliberately to demolish the fair fame of maid and matron who enjoy the advantage of his acquaintance; finally, he throws his cigar-end beneath the grate and betakes him "to perch," as he calls it, with an infatuated persuasion that the confidences which he has broken, will be respected by his listener, and that his debts, his difficulties, his peccadilloes, and the lameness of his bay mare, will not form the subject of conversation to-morrow night, when he, Damon, has gone back to London, and Pythias takes out his case to smoke a cigar with Dionysius. But the ladies by this time are fast asleep, dreaming, bless them, as it shall please Queen Mab—they must not wither their roses by sitting up too late, and though tolerant of smoking sometimes, they do not practise that abomination themselves, so tea-time is *their* hour of gossip, and heartily they enjoy the refreshment, both of mind and body, ere they come down demure and charming, in low evening dresses, with little or no appetite for dinner.

"Never mind Rosine," said Blanche, as that attendant concluded an elaborate plait by the insertion of an enormous hair-pin; "she can't speak a word of English. I agree with you that it is very charming to be an heiress, and I shall enjoy 'coming out,' and doing what I like; but I wish, too, sometimes, that I were a man; I feel so restrained, so useless, so incapable of doing any good. Mrs. Delaval, I think women are shamefully kept back; why shouldn't we have professions and employments? not that I should like to be a soldier or a sailor, because I am not brave, but I do feel as if I was fit for something greater than tying up flowers or puzzling through worsted work."

"There was a time when I, too, thought the same," replied Mary, "but depend upon it, my dear, that you may do an infinity of good in the station which is assigned you. I used to fancy it would be so noble to be a man, and to do something grand, and heroic, and disinterested; but look at half the men we see, Blanche, and tell me if you would like to change places with one of them. Caring only for their dress, their horses, and their dinners, they will tell you themselves, and think they are philosophers for saying so, 'that they are easy, good-tempered fellows, and if they can only get enough to eat, and lots of good hunting and good claret, they are perfectly satisfied.' Indeed, my dear, I think we have the best of it; we are more resigned, more patient, more contented; we have more to bear, and we bear it better—more to detach us from this world, and to wean us from being entirely devoted to ourselves. No, I had rather be a woman, with all her imperfections, than one of those lords of the creation, such as we generally find them."

"But still there are great men, Mrs. Delaval, even in these days. Do you think they are all selfish and egotistical, and care only for indulgences?"

"Heaven forbid, my dear; I only argue from the generality. My idea of man," said Mary, kindling as she went on in her description, "is that he should be brave, generous, and unselfish; stored with learning, which he uses not for display, but for a purpose; careless of vanity and frivolous distinction; reliant on himself and his own high motives; deep and penetrating in his mental powers, with a lofty view of the objects of existence, and the purposes for which we are here. What does it signify whether such a one is good-looking in person or taking in manner? But as I am describing a hero, I will say his frame should be robust and his habits simple, to harmonise with the vigour of his intellect and the singleness of his character."

"You have described Mr. Hardingstone exactly," exclaimed Blanche, with rising colour, and a feeling not quite of pleasure at her heart. Yet what signified it to her that Mary Delaval's Quixotic idea of a pattern man should typify so precisely her old friend Frank? Mary had never seen him; and even if she had, what was that to Blanche? Yet somehow she had taught herself from childhood to consider him her own property; probably because he was such a friend of Charlie; and she was a thorough woman—though she fancied she ought to have been born a hero—and consequently very jealous of her rights, real or imaginary. Silly Blanche! there was a sort of excitement, too, in talking about him, so she went on—"He is all that you have said, and people call him very good-looking besides, though I don't think him so;" and Blanche coloured as she spoke, and told Rosine not to pull her hair so hard.

"Well, my dear," said Mary, "then I should like to know him. But never mind the gentlemen, Blanche; there will be half-a-dozen here to dinner to-day. To return to yourself—you have a bright career before you, but never think it is traced out only for your own enjoyment. As a girl, you may in your position be an example to your equals, and a blessing to your dependents—think what a deal of good you can do even about a place like this; and then, should you marry, your influence may be the means of leading your husband and family into the right way. I have had a good deal of trouble, as you know, but I have always tried to remember, that to bear it patiently, and to do the best I could in my own path without repining, was to fulfil my destiny as nobly as if I had been a dethroned queen, or a world-famous heroine. No, my dear, this world is not a place only for dancing, and driving, and flirting, and dressing.—Good gracious! there's the dinner-bell! and my hair not 'done' yet." And away Mary rushed in the midst of her lecture, to complete those arrangements which brought her out, some ten minutes afterwards, the handsomest woman within fifty miles of Guyville.

Notwithstanding the lofty aspirations of these ladies, their contempt for the approbation of the other sex, and the short time they allowed themselves for adornment, two more tasteful and perfectly-finished toilettes have been seldom accomplished than those which at the well-lighted dinner-table enhanced the attractions of the pretty heiress and her handsome governess.

CHAPTER VI
THE BLIND BOY

Meanwhile the eventful Friday has arrived which has promoted "Cousin Charlie" to the rank of manhood. The *Gazette* of that day has announced the appointment of "Charles Kettering, Gentleman, to be Cornet in the 20th Lancers, vice Slack, who retires," and the young one, who has been cultivating the down on his upper lip for months, in anticipation of this triumph, turns up those ends, of which there is scarcely enough to take hold, and revels in the consciousness that he is a boy no longer, but an officer, a cavalry officer, and a gentleman. Old Nobottle, whom the pupil has attached to himself as an imaginative boy often does a sober old gentleman, is of the same mind, and has confided to Mr. Hardingstone his opinion of Charlie, and the bright deeds he expects from him. "The lad has all the makings of a soldier, sir," said the clergyman; "the cheerful spirits, the gallant bearing, the love of action, and the chivalrous vanity—half courageous, half coxcombical—which form the military character; and if he has a chance, he will distinguish himself. *If* he has a chance, do I say? he'll make himself a chance, sir; the boy is cut out for a recruit, and he'll learn his drill and know his men, and keep his troop-accounts smarter than any of 'em." Nobottle was waxing enthusiastic, as the old recollections stole over him, and he saw, in fancy, a certain young artillery officer, gay amongst the gayest, and brave amongst the bravest, consulted by his seniors for his science and professional knowledge, and thanked in general orders for "his distinguished gallantry" in more than one decisive action. How different from the slouching, slovenly old man, in yesterday's white neckcloth, who may now be seen budding his roses, poking about his parish, and stuffing stupid young gentlemen with as much learning as shall enable them to pass their dreaded examinations. Poor old Nobottle, you *would* marry for love, you *would* sacrifice your profession and your commission, your prospects and your all, for the red-nosed lady, then, to do her justice, a very pretty girl, who now occupies the top of your table. Like Antony, you were "all for love and the world well lost," and, after a time, you found that the exchange was against you: what you took for gold turned out to be dross,—that which was honey in the mouth became bitter as gall in the digestion; in short, you discovered Mrs. N. was a failure, and that you did not care two pins for each other. Then came poverty and recrimination and the gnawing remorse of chances thrown away, that could not possibly recur again. Fortunately for you, a classical education and Church interest enabled you to take orders and get a living, so you work on, contentedly enough, now that your sensations are deadened and yourself half torpid; and although, when your better feelings obtain the mastery, you cannot but acknowledge the superiority of the present warfare in which you are engaged over that in which you spent your gaudy youth, yet, ever and anon, that foolish old heart still pines for the marshalling of men and the tramp of steeds, "the plumed troop and the big wars, that make ambition virtue."

Hardingstone breakfasted at the rectory on the morning of Charlie's departure; he was to drive him to the station, and our young friend must indubitably have been late for the train, had he not been rescued, by a man of decision, from the prolonged farewells of the inconsolables he left behind. Binks, the butler, was overwhelmed by sorrow and strong beer; Tim, the tea-boy, who had never before seen a half-sovereign, sobbed aloud; the maids, on whom Charlie's good looks had made an impression proportionable to the softness of each damsel's heart, laughed and wept by turns; whilst Mrs. Nobottle, generally a lady of austere and inflexible disposition, weakened the very tea which she was pouring out for breakfast with her tears, and, finally, embraced Charlie with hysterical affection, and a nose redder than ever. The good rector took him aside into his study, and blessed him as a father blesses a son. "You have never given me a moment's uneasiness, my dear boy, since you came here," said the old man, with a trembling voice; "you have been a credit to me as a pupil, and a comfort as a friend; and now, perhaps, I shall never see you again. But you won't forget your old pedagogue, and if ever you are in difficulties, if ever you are in distress, remember there is a home here to which you may always apply for advice and assistance. God be with you, my boy, in the temptations of a barrack, as, if it should be your lot, in the perilous excitement of a battle. Do your duty wherever you are, and think, sometimes, of old Nobottle."

Why was it Charlie's cigar would *not* light, as he was borne away on the wheels of Frank Hardingstone's dog-cart? The tinder was quite wet, though there was not a drop of rain in the sky, and he turned away his head from his companion, and bent sedulously over the refractory tobacco. Could it be that Charlie was crying? 'Tis not improbable. Despite his recently-acquired manhood, he had a soft, affectionate heart, and if it now gave way, and came unbidden to his eyes, Frank liked him all the better for it.

And as he was whirled along on the London and North-Western, how the young soldier's thoughts ran riot in the future. Would he have changed places with any dignitary in the world, monarch, prince, or peer, or even with the heretofore much-admired Frank Hardingstone? Not he. None of these held a commission in the 20th Lancers; and were to be pitied, if not despised, accordingly. What a lot was his! Two months' leave at least, and at his time of life two months is an age, to be spent in the gaieties of Newton-Hollows, and the attenuation of Haphazard, Hyacinth, and Mayfly, the mettle of which very excellent steeds Master Charlie had fully resolved to prove. All the delights of Bubbleton and the county gaieties, with the companionship of Blanche, that more than sister, without whom, from his earliest boyhood, no enjoyment could be half enjoyed. And then the flattering pride she would feel in her officer-cousin (Charlie felt for his moustaches so perseveringly, that a short-sighted fellow-traveller thought he had a sore lip), and the request he should be in amongst the young ladies of the neighbourhood, with a romantic conviction that love was not for him, that "the sword was the soldier's bride," etc. Then the dreamer looked forward into the vistas of the future; the parade, the bivouac, and the charge; night-watches in a savage country—for the 20th were even then in Kaffirland—the trumpet alarum, the pawing troop-horses, the death-shock and the glittering blade; a certain cornet hurraing in the van, the admiration of brother officers, and the veteran colonel's applause; a *Gazette* promotion and honourable mention in dispatches; Uncle Baldwin's uproarious glee at home; and Blanche's quiet smile. Who would not be a boy again? Yet not with the stipulation we hear so often urged, of knowing as much as we do now. That knowledge would destroy it all. No, let us have boyhood once more, with its vigorous credulity and its impossible romance, with that glorious ignorance which turns everything to gold, that sanguine temperament which sheds its rosy hues even over the bleak landscape of future old age. "Poor lad! how green he is," says worldly experience, with a sneer of affected pity at those raptures it would give its very existence to feel again. "Happy fellow; he's a boy still!" says good-natured philosophy with a smile, half saddened at the thoughts of the coming clouds, which shall too surely darken that sunny horizon. But each has been through the crucible, each recognises that sparkle of the virgin gold which shall never again appear on the dead surface of the metal, beaten and stamped and fabricated into a mere conventional coin. The train whizzes on, the early evening sets in, tired post-horses grope their way up the dark avenue, wheels are heard grinding round the gravel sweep before the house, and the expected guest arrives at Newton-Hallows.

"Goodness! Charlie, how you *have* been smoking," exclaims Blanche, after their first affectionate greeting, while she shrinks a little from the cousinly embrace somewhat redolent of tobacco; "and how you're grown, dear—I suppose you don't like to be told you are grown now—and moustaches, I declare," she adds, bursting out laughing, as she catches Charlie's budding honours *en profil*; "'pon my word they're a great improvement." Charlie winced a little. There is always a degree of awkwardness even amongst the nearest and dearest, when people meet after a long absence, and the less artificial the character, the more it betrays itself; but Blanche was in great spirits and rattled on, till the General made his appearance, bustling in perfectly radiant with hospitality.

"Glad to see ye, my lad—glad to see ye; have been expecting ye this half-hour—trains always late—and always *will* be till they hang a director—I've hanged many a man for less, myself, 'up the country.' Fact, Blanche, I assure you. You'll have lots of time to dress," he observed, glancing at the clock's white face shining in the fire-light—and adding, with a playful dig of his fingers into Charlie's lean ribs, "We dine in half-an-hour, *temps militaire*, you dog! We must teach you that punctuality and good commissariat are the two first essentials for a soldier." So the General rang a peal for hand candles that might have brought a house down.

And Charlie was well acquainted with all the inmates of Newton-Hollows save Mrs. Delaval. Of her he had often heard Blanche speak as the most delightful of companions, and indulgent of governesses, but he had never set eyes on her in person; so as he effected his tie before the glass, and drew his fingers over those precious moustaches to discover if change of air had already influenced their growth, he began to speculate on the character and appearance of the lady who was to complete their family party. "A middle-aged woman," thought Charlie—for Blanche, on whom some ten years of seniority made a great impression, had always described her as such—"forty, or thereabouts—stout, jolly-looking and good-humoured, I'll be bound—I know I shall like her—wears a cap, I've no doubt, and a front, too, most probably—sits very upright, and talks like a book, till one knows her well—spectacles, I shouldn't wonder (it's no use making much of a tie for *her*)—pats Blanche on the shoulder when she gives her precedence, and keeps her hands in black lace mittens, I'll bet a hundred!" With which mental wager Master Charlie blew his candles out, and swaggered downstairs, feeling in his light evening costume, as indeed he looked, well-made, well-dressed, and extremely like a gentleman.

Mischievous Blanche was enchanted at the obvious start of astonishment with which her introduction was received by her cousin—"Mr. Kettering, Mrs. Delaval." Charlie looked positively dismayed. Was this the comfortable, round-about, good-humoured body he had expected to see?—was that tall, stately figure, dressed in the most perfect taste, with an air of more than high-breeding, almost of command, such as duchesses may be much admired without possessing—was that the dowdy middle-aged governess?—were those long, deep-set eyes, the orbs that should have glared at him through spectacles, and would black lace mittens have been an improvement on those white taper hands, beautiful in their perfect symmetry without a single ornament? Charlie bowed low to conceal the blush that overspread his countenance. The boy was completely taken aback, and, when he led her in to dinner, and heard those thrilling tones murmuring in his ear, the spell, we may be sure, lost none of its power. "She is beautiful," thought Charlie, "and nearly as tall as I am;" and he was pleased to recollect that Blanche had thought him grown. Ladies, we opine, are not so impressionable as men—at least they do not allow themselves to appear so. Either they are more cautious in their judgments, which we have heard denied by those who plume themselves on knowledge of the sex, or their hypocrisy is more perfect; certainly a young lady's education is based upon principles of the most frigid reserve, and her decorous bearing, we believe, is never laid aside, even in tea-rooms, conservatories, shaded walks, and other such resorts, fatal to the equanimity of masculine understanding; therefore Mary Delaval did by no means lose her presence of mind on being introduced to the young gentleman, of whose deeds and sentiments she had heard so much. Woman as she was, she could not but be gratified at the evident admiration her appearance created in this new acquaintance, and truth to speak, "Cousin Charlie" was a youth whose allegiance few female hearts would have entirely scorned to possess; yet there was no occasion to tell the young gentleman as much to his face.

A very good-looking face it was too, with its wide, intellectual brow, round which the brown silky hair waved in such becoming clusters—its perfect oval and delicate high-bred features, if they had a fault, too girlish in their soft, winning expression—in fact, he was as like Blanche as possible; and had his moustaches been shaved, could he indeed have submitted to the sacrifice, his stature lowered, and a bonnet and shawl put on, he might well have passed for his pretty cousin. There was nothing effeminate though about Charlie, save his countenance and his smile. That slender, graceful figure was lithe and wiry as the panther's—those symmetrical limbs could toil, those little feet could walk and run, after a Hercules would have been blown and overpowered; and when standing up to his wicket, rousing a horse, or putting him at a fence, there was a game sparkle in his eye that, to use Frank Hardingstone's expression, "meant mischief." Some of these good-looking young gentlemen are "ugly customers" enough when their blood is up, and Cousin Charlie, like the rest, had quite as much "devil" in his composition as was good for him. The "pretty page" only wanted a few years over his head, a little more beard upon his lip, to be a perfect Paladin.

But the spell went on working the whole of dinner-time; in vain the General told his most wondrous anecdotes, scolded his servants at intervals, and pressed his good cheer on the little party—Charlie *could* not get over his astonishment. Mrs. Delaval sat by him, looking like a queen, and talked in her own peculiarly winning voice and impressive manner, just enough to make him wish for more. She was one of those women who, speaking but little, seem always to mean more than they say, and on whom conscious mental superiority, and the calm subdued air worn by those who have known affliction, confer a certain mysterious charm, which makes fearful havoc in a young gentleman's heart. There is nothing enslaves a boy so completely as a spice of romance. An elderly Strephon will go on his knees to a romping schoolgirl, and the more hoydenish and unsophisticated the object, the more will the old reprobate adore her; but beardless youth loves to own superiority where it worships, loves to invest its idol with the fabulous attributes that compose its own ideal; and of all the *liaisons*, honourable and otherwise, that have bound their votaries in silken fetters, those have been the most fatal, and the most invincible, which have dated their existence from an earnest boyish heart's first devotion to a woman some years his senior, of whom the good-natured world says, "To be sure she *is* handsome, but Lor'! she's old enough to be his mother!"

Not that Charlie was as far gone as this: on the contrary, his was an imaginative poetical disposition, easily scorched enough, but almost incapable of being thoroughly *done brown*. Of such men, ladies, we would warn you to beware; the very temperament that clothes you in all the winning attributes of its own ideal can the most easily transfer those fancied attractions to a rival, inasmuch as the charm is not so much yours as his, exists not in your sweet face, but in his heated and inconstant brain. No, the real prize, depend upon it, is a sensible, phlegmatic, matter-of-fact gentleman, anything but "wax to receive," yet if you can succeed in making an impression, most assuredly "marble to retain." Such a captive clings to his affections as to his prejudices, and is properly subjected into a tame and willing Benedict in half the time it takes to guess at the intentions of the faithless rover, offering on a dozen shrines an adoration that, however brilliant, is

> Like light straw on fire,
>
> A fierce but fading flame.

Again was Charlie struck, as he swaggered off to open the door for the ladies, by the graceful movements of Mary's majestic figure. Again the half-bow with which, as she passed out, she acknowledged his courtesy, made a pleasing impression on the boy's fancy; and as he lingered for a moment, ere he shut out the rustle of their dresses and the pleasant tones of the women's voices, and returned to the arm-chair and the claret decanter, he could not help hoping "Uncle Baldwin" would be a little less profuse than usual in his hospitality, and a little less prolix in his narrative.

"The young ones drink no wine at all now-a-days," remarked the General, as Charlie a second time passed the bottle untouched, and his host filled his glass to the brim. "Fault on the right side, my lad; we used to drink too hard formerly—why, bless you, when I encountered Tortoise, of the Queen's, at the mess of the Kedjeree Irregulars, we sat for seven hours and a half to see one another out, and the two black fellows fainted who were 'told off' to bring in claret and pale ale as they were wanted. Tortoise recovered himself wonderfully about the eighth bottle; and if he hadn't been obliged to be careful on account of a wound in his head, we should have been there now. Drunk! how d'ye mean? Not the least—fact, I assure you."

Charlie got up and fidgeted about, with his back to the fire, but the General would not let him off so easily.

"Show you the farm to-morrow, my boy, you'll be delighted with my pigs—Neapolitans every hair of 'em. What? no man alive shall presume to tell me they're not the best breed! And I'll tell you what, Charlie, I've secured the handsomest short-horned bull in this country. Two hundred, you dog!—dirt cheap—and if you're fond of stock you'll be charmed with him. Poultry too—real Cochin Chinese—got three prizes at the last show; average height two feet seven inches—rare beauties. Hens and chickens in knee-breeches, and a cock in trunk-hose!" With which conclusion the chuckling old warrior permitted Charlie to wheedle him off into the drawing-room, whither they entered to find the ladies, as usual, absorbed in worsted work and sunk in solemn silence.

Pleasantly the evenings always passed at Newton-Hollows even with a small party like the present. Music, cards, cockamaroo, and the eternal racing game, of course, which gives gentle woman an insight into the two fiercest pleasures of the other sex—horse-racing and gambling—and introduces into the drawing-room the slang and confusion of the betting-ring and the hazard-table, served to while away the time. And though the General was even more diffuse than was his wont in personal recollections and autobiography, Blanche scarcely listened, so absorbed was she in her delight at having got Cousin Charlie back again, whilst that young gentleman and Mary Delaval were progressing rapidly in each other's good opinion, and exclaiming, in their respective minds, "What an agreeable person! and so *different from what I expected!*"

Blanche's birthday was always kept as a period of great rejoicing at Newton-Hollows, and a very short time after Charlie's arrival that auspicious anniversary was ushered in, as usual, by the General's appearance at the breakfast-table bearing a cotton-stuffed white and green card-box, highly suggestive of Storr and Mortimer. This was quietly placed by the side of Blanche's plate, and when the young lady made her appearance, and exclaimed, "Dear, kind Uncle Baldwin, what a love of a bracelet!" though we might have envied, we could not have grudged the General the grateful kiss bestowed on him by his affectionate niece. Uncle Baldwin's mind, however, was intent upon weightier matters than jewels and "happy returns." He was to celebrate the festival with a dinner-party; and whilst he had invited several of the *élite* of Bubbleton to celebrate his niece's birthday, he was anxious so to dispose and welcome his guests as that none should have reason to consider himself especially favoured or encouraged in the advances which all were too eager to make towards the good graces of the heiress; therefore the General held a solemn conclave, as was his wont, consisting of himself and Mrs. Delaval, who on such occasions was requested, with great pomp, to accompany him to his study, an apartment adorned with every description of weapon used in civilised or savage warfare, and to take her seat in his own huge arm-chair, while he walked up and down the room, and held forth in his usual abrupt and discursive manner.

"I have such confidence in your sound sense, Mrs. Delaval," said he, looking very insinuating, and pausing for an instant in his short, quick strides, "that I always consult you in my difficulties." This was said piano, but the forte addition immediately succeeded. "Reserving to myself the option of acting, for dictation I cannot submit to, even from you, my dear Mrs. Delaval. You are aware, I believe, of my intentions regarding Blanche. *Are* you aware of my intentions?" he interrupted himself to demand in a voice of thunder.

Mary, who was used to his manner, answered calmly, "that she was not;" and the General proceeded, in a gentle and confidential tone—

"The fact is, my dear madam, I have set my heart on a family arrangement, which I mention to you as a personal friend, and a lady for whom I entertain the greatest regard."

Mary bowed again, and could hardly suppress a smile at the manner in which the old gentleman assured her of his consideration.

"Well, though an unmarried man *as yet*, I am keenly alive to the advantages of the married state. I never told you, I think, Mrs. Delaval, of an adventure that befell me at Cheltenham—never mind now—but, believe me, I am no stranger to those tender feelings, Mrs. Delaval, to which we men of the sword—ah, ah—are *infernally* addicted. What? Well, ma'am, there's my niece now, they all want to marry her. Every scoundrel within fifty miles wants to lead Blanche to the altar. Zounds, I'll weather 'em, the villains—excuse me, Mrs. Delaval, but to proceed—I am extremely anxious to confide my intentions to you, as I hope I may calculate on your assistance. My nephew, Charlie, to be explicit, is the——Holloa! you woman, come back—come back, I say; you're carrying off the wrong coop. The dolt has mistaken my orders about the Cochin Chinas. In the afternoon, if you please, Mrs. Delaval, we'll discuss the point more at leisure."

And the General bolted through the study window, and was presently heard in violent altercation with the lady who presided over his poultry yard.

Though not very explicit, Mary had gathered enough from the General's confidences to conclude he was anxious to arrange a marriage eventually between the two cousins. Well! what was that to her? He certainly was a very taking boy, handsome, gentle, and high-spirited; nothing could be nicer for Blanche. And she was so fond of him; what a charming couple they would make. "I am so glad," thought Mary, wondering when she might congratulate the bride-elect; "so *very* glad; dear, how glad I am." Why should Mary have taken such pains to assure herself how glad she was? Why did she watch the *charming couple* with an interest she had never felt before, as she joined them on their return from their morning walk? A walk, the object of which (tell it not in Bubbleton) had been to pursue the sport of rat-hunting in a certain barn, with a favourite terrier of Charlie's, a sport that Blanche was persuaded to patronise, notwithstanding her horror both of the game and the mode of its destruction, by her affection for Charlie, and her childish habit of joining him in all his pastimes and amusements. How alike they were, with their delicate skin, their deep blue eyes sparkling with exercise and excitement, and their waving brown hair clustering round each flushed and smiling face. How alike they were, and what a nice couple they certainly did make. And Mary sighed, as again she thought how *very* glad she was!

No further interview took place that day with the General, whose many avocations scarcely permitted him time for the elaborate toilette which, partly out of respect for Blanche's birthday, partly in consideration of his dinner-party, he thought it advisable to perform. He certainly did take more pains with himself than usual; and as he fixed an order or two in an unassuming place under the breast-lap of his coat, a ray of satisfaction shot through his heart that beat beneath those clasps and medals, while the old gentleman thought aloud as usual, "Not such a bad arrangement after all! She certainly did look very queer when I talked of Blanche's marrying. No doubt she's smitten—just like the one at Cheltenham. Bounce! Bounce! you've a deal to answer for. If ever I *do*, it's time I thought of it; don't improve by keeping. 'Pon my life, I might go farther and fare worse. Zounds! there's the door-bell."

"Lady Mount Helicon!" "Captain Lacquers!" "Sir Ascot Uppercrust!" and a whole host of second-rate grandees were successively announced and ushered into the brilliantly-lighted drawing-room, to be received by the General with the *empressement* of a bachelor, who is host and hostess all in one. Blanche was too young and shy to take much part in the proceedings. Charlie, of course, was late; but Bounce was in his glory, bowing to the ladies, joking with the gentlemen, and telling anecdotes to all, till the announcement of "dinner" started him across the hall, convoying stately Lady Mount Helicon, and well-nigh lost amidst the lappets and flounces of that magnificent dame, who would not have been here at all unless she had owned an unmarried son, and a jointure entirely out of proportion to the present lord's finances. The rest of the party paired off after their illustrious leaders. Sir Ascot Uppercrust took Blanche, who was already lost in surprise at his taciturnity. Miss Deeper skilfully contrived to entangle young Cashley. Kate Carmine felt her heart beat happily against the arm of Captain Laurel, of the Bays. Mr. Gotobed made a dash at Mary Delaval, but "Cousin Charlie," who that instant entered the room, quietly interposed and led her off to the dining-room, leaving a heterogeneous mass of unappropriated gentlemen to scramble in as they best might. Mary was grateful for the rescue; she was glad to be near somebody she knew. With a flush of shame and anger she had recognised Captain Lacquers, though that worthy dipped his moustaches into his soup in happy unconsciousness that the well-dressed aristocratic woman opposite him was the same indignant damsel who would once have knocked him down if she could. With all her self-possession, Mary was not blind to the fact that her position was anomalous and ill-defined. She had found that out already by the condescending manner in which Lady Mount Helicon had bowed to her in the drawing-room. With the men she was "that handsome lady-like Mrs. Delaval"; but with the women (your true aristocrats after all) she was *only the governess*.

Dinner progressed in the weary protracted manner that the meal does when it is one of state and ceremony. The guests did not know each other well, and were dreadfully afraid (as is too often the case in good society) of being over civil or attentive to those whose position they had not exactly ascertained. It argues ill for one's stock of politeness when one cannot afford to part with ever so small a portion, save in expectation of a return. So Lady Mount Helicon was patronising and affable, and looked at everything, including the company, through her eye-glass, but was very distant notwithstanding; and the gentlemen hemmed and hawed, and voted the weather detestable—aw! and the sport with the hounds—

aw—very moderate—aw (it was d—d bad after the ladies went away); and their fair companions lisped and simpered, and ate very little, and drank as much champagne as appearances would allow; and everybody felt it an unspeakable relief when Blanche, drawing on her gloves, and blushing crimson at the responsibility, made "the move" to Lady Mount Helicon; and the muslins all sailed away, with their gloves and fans and pocket-handkerchiefs rescued from under the table by their red-faced cavaliers.

When they met again over tea and coffee, things had thawed considerably. The most solemn high-breeding is not proof against an abundance of claret, and the General's hospitality was worthy of his cellar. The men had found each other out to be "deuced good sort of fellows," and had moreover discovered mutual tastes and mutual acquaintances, which much cemented their friendships. To be sure, there was at first a partial reaction consequent upon the difficulty of breaking through a formal circle of ladies; but this feat accomplished, and the gentlemen grouped about cup-in-hand in becoming attitudes, and disposed to look favourably on the world in general, even Sir Ascot Uppercrust laid aside his usual reserve, and asked Blanche whether she had seen anything of a round game called "turning the tables," which the juvenile philosopher further confided to her he opined to be "infernal humbug." In an instant every tongue was unloosed. Drop a subject like this amongst a well-dressed crowd and it is like a cracker—here and there it bounces, and fizzes, and explodes, amongst serious exclamations and hearty laughter. Lady Mount Helicon thought it wicked—Kate Carmine thought it "fun"—Miss Deeper voted it charming—Lacquers considered it "aw—deuced scientific—aw"—and the General in high glee exclaimed, "I vote we try." No sooner said than done; a round mahogany table was deprived of its covering—a circle formed—hands joined with more energy than was absolutely indispensable—white arms laid in juxtaposition to dark coat sleeves—long ringlets bent over the polished mirror-like surface; and amidst laughing entreaties to be grave, and voluble injunctions to be silent, the incantation progressed, we are bound in truth to state, with no definite result. Perhaps the spell was broken by the bursts of laughter that greeted the pompous butler's face of consternation, as, entering the room to remove cups, etc., he found the smartly-dressed party so strangely employed. Well-bred servants never betray the slightest marks of emotion or astonishment, though we fancy their self-command is sometimes severely put to the test. But "turning the tables" was too much for the major-domo, and he was obliged to make his exit in a paroxysm of unseemly mirth. Then came a round game of forfeits—then music—then dancing, the ladies playing by turns—then somebody found out the night was pouring with rain, and the General declared it would be sure to clear in an hour or so, and nobody must go away till after supper. So supper appeared and more champagne; and even Lady Mount Helicon was ready to do anything to oblige, so, being a fine musician, she volunteered to play "The Coquette." A chair was placed in the middle of the room, and everybody danced, the General and all. Blanche laughed till she cried; and there was but one feeling of regret when the announcement of her ladyship's carriage broke up the party, just at the moment when, in accordance with the rules of the dance, Charlie sank upon one knee before the Coquette's chair, occupied by stately Mrs. Delaval. He looked like a young knight prostrate before the Queen of Beauty.

When Blanche laid her head upon her pillow, she thought over all her uncle's guests in succession, and decided not one was to be compared to Cousin Charlie; and none was half so agreeable as Mr. Hardingstone. Mary Delaval, on the contrary, scarcely gave a thought to Captain Lacquers, Sir Ascot Uppercrust, Captain Laurel, or even Mr. Gotobed, who had paid her great attention. No, even as she closed her eyes she was haunted by a young upturned face, with fair open brow and a slight moustache—do what she would, she saw it still. She was, besides, a little distracted about the loss of one of her gloves—a white one, with velvet round the wrist—what could have become of it?

CHAPTER VII
BOOT AND SADDLE

"Card of the running 'orses—*cor*-rect card! Major, dear, you always take a card of me!" pleads a weather-worn, good-looking, smart-ribboned card-woman, standing up to her ankles in mud on Guyville race-course. Poor thing! hers is a strange, hard, vagabond sort of life. This very morning she has heard mass (being an Irish-woman) seventeen miles off, and she will be on her legs the whole of the livelong day, and have a good supper and a hard bed, and be up at dawn to-morrow, ready and willing for a forty-mile tramp wherever money is to be made; so, in the meantime, she hands up half-a-dozen damp cards to Gaston D'Orville, now Major in "The Loyals," and this day principal acting-steward of "The Grand Military Steeple-Chase."

The Major is but slightly altered since we saw him last at Bishops'-Baffler. His tall figure may, perhaps, be a trifle fuller, and the lines of dissipation round his eyes and mouth a little deeper, while here and there his large whiskers and clustering hair are just sprinkled with grey; but for all this, he is still about the finest-looking man on the course, and of this fact, as of every other advantage of his position, no one is better aware than himself. Yet is he not a vain man; cool and calculating, he looks upon such "pulls in his favour," as he calls them, much as he would on "a point in the odds,"—mere chances in the game of life, to be made the most of when opportunity offers. He has just got upon a remarkably handsome white horse, to show the military equestrians "the line" over which they are to have an opportunity of breaking their necks, and is surrounded by a posse of great-coated, shawl-handkerchiefed, and goloshed individuals, mostly striplings, who are nervously ready to scan the obstacles they are destined to encounter.

There are nine starters for the great event, and professional speculators at "The Kingmakers' Arms" are even now wagering that not above three ever reach "home," so low an opinion do they entertain of "the soldiers' riding," or so ghastly do they deem the fences flagged out to prove the warriors' metal. Four miles over a stiff country, with a large brook, and a finish in front of the grand-stand, will furnish work for the horses and excitement for the ladies, whilst the adventurous jocks are even now glancing at one another aghast at the unexpected strength and height of these impediments, which, to a man on foot, look positively awful.

"I object to this fence decidedly," observes a weak, thin voice, which, under his multiplicity of wraps, we have some difficulty in identifying as the property of Sir Ascot Uppercrust. "I object in the name of all the riders—it is positively dangerous—don't you agree with me?" he adds, pointing to a formidable "double post and rail," with but little room between, and appealing to his fellow-sufferers, who all coincide with him but one.

"Nothing for a hunter," says the dissentient, who, seeing that the exploit has to be performed in full view of the ladies in the stand, would have it worse if he could. "Nothing for any horse that is properly ridden;—what do you say, major?"

"I agree with Kettering," replies the Major; for our friend "Charlie" it is, who is now surveying the country on foot, in a huge white great-coat, with a silver-mounted whip under his arm, and *no gloves*. He is quite the "gentleman-rider," and has fully made up his mind to win the steeple-chase. For this has poor Haphazard been deprived of his usual sport in the field, and trained with such severity as Mr. Snaffles has thought advisable; for this has his young master been shortening his stirrups and riding daily gallops, and running miles up-hill to keep him in wind, till there is little left of his original self save his moustaches, which have grown visibly during the winter; and for this have the ladies of the family been stitching for days at the smartest silk jacket that ever was made (orange and blue, with gold tags), only pausing in their labours to visit Haphazard in the stable, and bring him such numerous offerings in the shape of bread, apples, and lump-sugar, that had Mr. Snaffles not laid an embargo on all "tit-bits," the horse would ere this have been scarcely fit to run for a saddle!

Mrs. Delaval having been as severely bitten with the sporting mania as Blanche, they are even now sitting in the grand-stand perusing the list of the starters as if their lives depended on it—and each lady wears a blue and orange ribbon in her bonnet, the General, who escorts them, appearing in an alarming neckcloth of the same hues.

The stand is already nearly full, and Blanche, herself not the least attraction to many of the throng, has manoeuvred into a capital place with Mary by her side, and is in a state of nervous delight, partly at the gaiety of the scene, partly at the coming contest in which "Cousin Charlie" is to engage, and partly at the anticipation of the Guyville ball, her first appearance in public, to take place this very night. Row upon row the benches have been gradually filling, till the assemblage looks like a variegated parterre of flowers to those in the arena below. In that enclosed space are gathered, besides the pride of the British army, swells and dandies of every different description and calibre. Do-nothing gentlemen from London, glad to get a little fresh air and excitement so cheap. Nimrods from "the shires" come to criticise the performances, and suggest, by implication, how much better they could ride themselves. Horse-dealers, and professional "legs," of course, whose business it is to make the most of everything, and whose courteous demeanour is only equalled by the unblushing effrontery with which they offer "five points" less than the odds; nor, though last not least, must we omit to mention the *élite* of Bubbleton, who have one and all cast up from "the Spout," as that salubrious town is sometimes denominated, as they always do cast up within reach of their favourite resort. Some of all sorts there are amongst *them*. Gentlemen of family, without incumbrances—gentlemen with incumbrances and no family; some with money and no brains—some with brains and no money; some that live on the fat of the land—others that live upon their wits, and pick up a subsistence therewith, bare as might be expected from the dearth of capital on which they trade. In the midst of them we recognise Frank Hardingstone, sufficiently conspicuous in his simple manly attire, amongst the chained and velveted and bedizened tigers by whom he is surrounded. He is talking to a remarkably good-looking and particularly well-dressed man, known to nearly every one on the course as Mr. Jason, the famous steeple-chase rider, who has come partly to sell Mr. Hardingstone a horse, partly to patronise the "soldiers' performances," and partly to enjoy the gay scene which he is even now criticising. He is good enough to express his approval of the ladies in the stand, taking them *en masse*, though his fastidious taste cannot but admit that there are "some weedy-looking ones among 'em." All this, however, is lost upon Frank Hardingstone, who has ears only for a conversation going on at his elbow, in which he hears Blanche's name mentioned, our friend Lacquers being the principal speaker.

"Three hundred thousand—I give you my honour, every penny of it!" says that calculating worthy to a speculative dandy with enormous red whiskers, "and a *nice* girl too—devilish well read, you know, and all that."

"I suppose old Bounce keeps a bright look-out though, don't he?" rejoins his friend, who has all the appearance of a man that can make up his mind in a minute.

"Yeees," drawls Lacquers; "but it might be done by a fellow with some energy, you know; she *is* engaged to young Kettering, her cousin—'family pot,' you know—and she's very spooney on him; still, I've half a mind to try."

"Why, the cousin will probably break his neck in the course of the day; you can introduce me to-night at the ball. By the way, what are they betting about this young Kettering? Can he ride any?"

"Not a yard," replies Lacquers, as he turns away to light a cigar, whilst Lord Mount Helicon—for the red-bearded dandy is no less a person than that literary peer—dives into the ring to turn an honest *"pony,"* as he calls it, on its fluctuations.

"Look here, Mr. Hardingstone," exclaims the observant Jason, forcibly attracting Frank's notice to a feat which, as he keeps his eyes fixed on the stand, is going on behind him. "That's the way to put 'em at it, Major! well ridden, by the Lord Harry!" and Frank turns round in time to witness, with the shouting multitude and the half-frightened ladies, the gallant manner in which D'Orville's white horse clears the double post and rails to which Sir Ascot had objected.

The Major, it is needless to say, is a dauntless horseman, and, on being remonstrated with by Sir A. and his party on the impracticable nature of the leap which he had selected for them, and the young Mohair of the Heavies suggesting that the stewards should always be compelled to ride over the ground themselves, made no more ado, but turned the white horse at the unwelcome barrier, and by dint of a fine hand and a perfectly-broken animal, went "in and out" without touching, to the uproarious delight of the mob, and the less loudly expressed admiration of the ladies.

"That's what I call *in-and-out-clever,*" observes Mr. Jason, as the shouting subsides, thinking he could not have done it better himself; and he too elbows his way into the mass of noise, hustling, and confusion that constitutes the betting-ring.

"We ought to throw our 'bouquets' at the white horse!" says Mrs. Delaval's next neighbour, a bold-looking lady of a certain age; and Mary recognises, with mingled feelings, her military adorer and his well-known grey charger, now showing the lapse of time only by his change of colour to pure white. "I'm afraid its all very dangerous," thinks Blanche, to whom it occurs for the first time that "Cousin Charlie" may possibly break his neck; but the General at this instant touches her elbow to introduce "Major D'Orville," who, having performed his official duties, has dismounted, and works his way into the stand to make the agreeable to the ladies, and "have a look at this Miss Kettering—the very thing, by Jove, if she is tolerably lady-like."

How different is the Major's manner to that of Lacquers, Uppercrust, and half the other unmeaning dandies whom Blanche is accustomed to see fluttering round her. He *has* the least thing of a military swagger, which most women certainly like, more particularly when in their own case that lordly demeanour is laid aside for a soft deferential air, highly captivating to the weaker sex; and nobody understands this better than D'Orville. The little he says to Blanche is quiet, amusing, and to the purpose. The heiress is agreeably surprised. The implied homage of such a man is, to say the least of it, flattering; and our cavalier has the good sense to take his leave as soon as he sees he has made a favourable impression, quite satisfied with the way in which he has "opened the trenches." At the moment he did so, on turning round he encountered Mary Delaval. She looked unmoved as usual, and put out her hand to him, as if they had been in the habit of meeting every day. With a few incoherent words he bent over those long well-shaped fingers; and an observant bystander might have had the good luck to witness a somewhat unusual sight—a Major of Hussars blushing to the very tips of his moustaches. Yes; the hardened man of the world, the experienced *roué*, the dashing *militaire*, had a heart, if you could only get at it, like the veriest clown then 'squiring his red-faced Dolly to "the races" — the natural for the moment overcame the artificial—and as Gaston edged his way down through nodding comrades and smiling ladies, the feeling uppermost in his heart was, "Heavens! how I love this woman still! and what a fool I am!" But sentiment must not be indulged to the exclusion of business, and the Major too forces his way into the betting-ring.

There they are, hard at it—*Nobblers* and noblemen—grooms and gentlemen—betting-house keepers and cavalry officers—all talking at once, all intent on having the best of it, and apparently all layers and no takers. "Eight to one agin Lady Lavender," says a stout capitalist, who looks like a grazier in his best clothes. "Take ten," lisps the owner, a young gentleman, apparently about sixteen. "I'll back Sober John." "I'll take nine to two about the Fox." "I'll lay against the field *bar three*." "I'll lay five ponies to two *agin* Haphazard!" vociferates the capitalist. "Done!" cries Charlie, who is investing on his horse as if he owned the Bank of England. At this moment Frank Hardingstone pierces into the ring, and drawing Charlie towards the outskirts, begins to lecture him on the coming struggle, and to give him useful hints on the art of riding a steeple-chase; for Frank with his usual decision has resolved not to go into the stand to talk to Blanche till he has done all in his power to insure the success of her cousin. "Come and see the horse saddled, you conceited young jackanapes; don't fool away any more money; how do you know you'll win?" says Frank, taking the excited jockey by the arm and leading him away to where Haphazard, pawing and snorting, and very uneasy, is being stripped of his clothing, the centre of an admiring throng. "I know he can beat Lady Lavender," replies Charlie, whose conversation for the last week had been strictly "Newmarket"; "and he's five pounds better than the Fox; and Mohair is sure to make a mess of it with Bendigo—he owns he can't ride him; and there's nothing else has a chance except Sober John, a great half-bred brute!"

"Do you see that quiet-looking man talking to Jason there?" says Frank; "that's the man who is to ride Sober John—about the best *gentleman* in England, and he's getting a hint from the best *professional*. Do you think *you* can ride like Captain Rocket? Now, take my advice, Charlie, Haphazard is a nice-tempered horse, you *wait* on Sober John—keep close behind him—ride over him if he falls—but whatever you see Captain Rocket do, *you do the same*—don't *come* till you're safe over the last fence—and if you're not first, you'll be second!" Charlie promised faithfully to obey his friend's directions, though in his own mind he did not think it possible an *Infantry* horse could win the great event—Sober John, if he belonged to any one in particular, being the property of Lieutenant Sharpes of the Old Hundredth, who stood to win a very comfortable sum upon the veteran steeple-chaser.

"They look nervous, Tim, most on 'em," observes Captain Rocket, while with his own hands he adjusts "the tackle," as he calls it, on his horse; and his friend "Tim" giving him a "leg up," he canters Sober John past the stand, none of the ladies thinking that docile animal has the remotest chance of winning. "He seems much too quiet," says Blanche, "and he's dreadfully ugly." "Beauty is not absolutely essential in *horses*, Miss Kettering," replies a deep, quiet voice at her elbow. Major D'Orville has resumed his place by her side. Though he thinks he is paying attention to Blanche, he cannot, in reality, forbear hovering about Mrs. Delaval. That lady, meanwhile, with clasped hands, is hoping with all her heart that Captain Rocket may *not win*. If "wishes were horses," we think this young gentleman now tearing down the course upon Haphazard, throwing the dirt round him like a patent turnip-cutter, would have a good many of hers to bear him on his victorious career. By the way, Mary has never found her glove; we wonder whether that foolish boy knows anything about it. And talking of gloves, look at that dazzling pair of white kids on a level with his chin, in which "Mohair, of the Heavies," is endeavouring to control Bendigo. He has had two large glasses of sherry, yet does he still look very pale—another, and yet another, comes striding past like a whirlwind—Sir Ascot rides Lady Lavender, and Cornet Capon is to pilot the Fox. It is very difficult to know which is which amongst the variegated throng, and the ladies puzzle sadly over their cards, in which, as is usually the case at steeple-chases, the colours are all set down wrong. Each damsel, however, has one favourite at least whom she could recognise in any disguise, and we may be sure that "blue-and-orange" is not without his well-wishers in the grand-stand.

Major D'Orville is an admirable cicerone, inasmuch as besides being steward, he has a heavy book on the race, and knows the capabilities of each horse to a pound, whatever may be his uncertainty as regards the riders. "Your cousin has a very fair chance, Miss Kettering—he seems to ride uncommonly well for *such a boy*; Sir Ascot wants nerve, and Mohair can't manage his horse." "See, they've got 'em in line," exclaims the General, who is in a state of frantic excitement altogether. "Silence, pray! he's going to— ah, the blundering blockhead, it's a false start!" Major D'Orville takes out his double-glasses, and proceeds quietly without noticing the interruption, "Then the Fox has been lame, and Capon is a sad performer; nevertheless, you shall have your choice, Miss Kettering, and I'll bet you a pair of gloves on the——By Jove, they're off," and the Major puts his glasses up in scarcely veiled anxiety, whilst Mary Delaval's heart beats thick and fast, as she strains her eyes towards the fleeting tulip-coloured throng, drawing gradually out from the dark mass of spectators that have gone to witness the start.

How easy it looks to go cantering along over a nice grass country, properly flagged out so as to insure the performers from making any mistakes; and how trifling the obstacles appear over which they are following each other like a string of wild geese, more particularly when you, the spectator, are quietly ensconced in a comfortable seat, sheltered from the wind, and viewing the sports at a respectful distance. Perhaps you might not think it quite such child's play were you assisting in the pageant on the back of a headstrong, powerful horse, rendered irritable and violent by severe training (of which discipline this unfortunate class of animal gets more than enough), rasping your knuckles against his withers, and pulling your arms out of their sockets, because he, the machine, is all anxiety to get to the end, whilst you the controlling, or who ought to be the controlling power, have received strict injunctions "to wait." If your whole energies were not directed to the one object of "doing your duty" and winning your race, you might possibly have leisure to reflect on your somewhat hazardous position. "Neck-or-nothing" has just disappeared, doubling up himself and Mr. Fearless in a complicated kind of fall, at the very place over which you must necessarily follow; and should your horse, who is shaking his head furiously, as you vainly endeavour to steady him, make the slightest mistake, you shudder to think of "Frantic" running away with her rider close behind you. Nevertheless, it is impossible to decline "eternal misery on this side and certain death on the other," but *go you must*, and when safe into the next field there is nothing of any importance till you come to the brook. To be sure, the animal you are riding never would *face water*, still, your spurs are sharp, and you have a vague sort of trust that you may get over *somehow*. You really deserve to win, yet will we, albeit unused to computation of the odds, willingly bet you five to four that you are neither first nor second.

In the meantime, our friends in the stand make their running commentaries on the race. "How slow they are going," says Blanche, who, like all ladies, has a most liberal idea of "pace." "*He's over!*" mutters Mary Delaval, as "blue-and-orange" skims lightly over the first fence, undistinguished, save by *her*, amidst the rest. "One down!" says a voice, and there is a slight scream from amongst the prettiest of the bonnets. "Red-and-white cap—who is it?" and what with the distraction of watching the others, and the confusion on the cards, Bendigo has been caught and remounted ere the hapless Lieutenant Mohair can be identified. Meanwhile the string is lengthening out. "Uppy is making frightful running," says Major D'Orville, thinking how right he was to stand heavily against Lady Lavender; "however, the Fox is close upon him; and that's Haphazard, Miss Kettering, just behind Sober John." "Two—four—six—seven—nine—what a pretty sight!" says Blanche, but she turns away her head with a shudder as a party-coloured jacket goes down at the next fence, neither horse nor rider rising again. One always fancies the worst, and Mary turns pale as death, and clasps her hands tighter than ever. And now they arrive at the double post and rails, which have been erected purposely for the gratification of the ladies in the stand. The first three bound over it in their stride like so many deer. Captain Rocket pulls his horse into a trot, and Sober John goes in-and-out quite as clever as did the Major's white charger. Mr. Jason is good enough to express his approval. Charlie follows the example of his leader, and though he hits it very hard, Haphazard's fine shape saves him from a fall. Blanche thinks him the noblest hero in England, and nobody but D'Orville remarks how very pale Mrs. Delaval is getting. Mohair essays to follow the example thus set him, and succeeds in doing the first half of his task admirably, but no power on earth will induce Bendigo to jump *out* after jumping *in*, and eventually he is obliged to be ignominiously extricated by a couple of carpenters and a handsaw. His companions diverge, like a flight of wild-fowl, towards the brook. The Fox, who is now leading, refuses; and the charitable Nimrods, and dandies, and swells, and professionals, all vote that Capon's heart failed him, and "he didn't put in half enough powder." The Major knows better. The horse was once his property, and he has not laid against it without reason. The brook creates much confusion; but Sober John singles himself out from the ruck, and flies it without an effort, closely followed by Haphazard and Lady Lavender. The rest splash and struggle, and get over as they best can, with but little chance now of coming up with the first three. They all turn towards home, and the pace is visibly increasing. Captain Rocket is leading, but Charlie's horse is obviously full of running, and the boy is gradually drawing away from Lady Lavender, and nearer and nearer to the front. Already people begin to shout "Haphazard wins"; and the General is hoarse with excitement. "Charlie wins!" he exclaims, his face purple, and the ends of his blue-and-orange handkerchief floating on the breeze. "Charlie wins! I tell you. Look how he's coming up. Zounds! don't contradict *me*, sir!" he roars out to the intense dismay of his next neighbour, a meek old gentleman, who has only come to the steeple-chase in order that he may write an account of it for a magazine, and who shrinks from the General as from a raving madman. "Now, Captain Rocket," shouts the multitude, as if that unmoved man would attend to anything but the business in hand. They reach the last fence neck-and-neck, Haphazard landing slightly in advance. "Kettering wins!" "*Blast* him!" hisses D'Orville between his teeth, turning white as a sheet He stands to lose eighteen hundred by Haphazard alone, and we question whether, on reliable security, the Major could raise eighteen-pence. Nevertheless, he turns the next instant to Blanche, with a quiet, unmoved smile, to congratulate her on her cousin's probable success. "If he can only 'finish,' Miss Kettering, he can't lose," says the speculator; but he still trusts that "if" may save him the price of his commission.

What a moment for Charlie! Hot, breathless, and nearly exhausted, his brain reeling with the shouts of the populace, and the wild excitement of the struggle, one idea is uppermost in his mind—if man and horse can do it, *win he will*. Steadily has he ridden four long miles, taking the greatest pains with his horse, and restraining his own eagerness to be in front, as well as that of the gallant animal. He has kept his eye fixed on Captain Rocket, and regulated his every movement by that celebrated performer. And now he is drawing slightly in advance of him, and one hundred yards more will complete his triumph. Yet, inexperienced as he is, he cannot but feel that Haphazard is no longer the elastic, eager goer whom he has been regulating so carefully, and the truth shoots across him that his horse is beat. Well, he ought to last another hundred yards. See, the double flags are waving before him, and the shouts of his own name fall dully upon his ear. He hears Captain Rocket's whip at work, and is not aware how that judicious artist is merely plying it against his own boot to flurry the young one. Charlie begins to flog. "Sit *still*!" shouts Frank Hardingstone from the stand. Charlie works arms and legs like a windmill, upsets his horse, who would win if he were but let alone—Sober John shows his great ugly head alongside. Haphazard changes his leg—Major D'Orville draws a long breath of relief—Captain Rocket, with a grim smile, and one fierce stab with his spurs, glides slightly in advance—and Haphazard is beaten on the post by half a length, Lady Lavender a bad third, and the rest nowhere!

Blanche is dreadfully disappointed. The General thinks "the lad deserves great credit for being second in such good company;" but the tears stand in Mary Delaval's eyes—tears, we believe, of gratitude at his not being brought home on a hurdle, instead of riding into the weighing enclosure with the drooping self-satisfied air, and the arms hanging powerless down his side, which distinguish the gentleman-jockey after his exertions. The boy is scarcely disappointed. To have been so near winning, and to have run second for such an event as the "Grand Military," is a feather in his cap, of which he is in no slight degree proud; and he walks into the stand the hero of the day, for Captain Rocket is no lady's man, and is engaged to risk his neck again to-morrow a hundred miles from here. So he has put on a long great-coat and disappeared. The General accounts for Charlie's defeat on a theory peculiarly his own. "*Virtually*" says he, "my nephew won the race. How d'ye mean *beat*? It was twenty yards over the four miles. Twenty yards from home he was a length in front. If the stewards had been worth their salt, we should have won. Don't tell *me*!"

There is more racing, but the great event has come off, and our friends in the stand occupy themselves only with luncheon. Frank Hardingstone comes up to speak to Blanche, but she is so surrounded and hemmed in, that beyond shaking hands with her he might as well be back at his own place on the south coast, for any enjoyment he can have in her society. Major D'Orville is rapidly gaining ground in the good graces of all the Newton-Hollows party. He has won a great stake, and is in brilliant spirits. Even Mary thinks "what an agreeable man he is," and glances the while at a fair glowing face, eating, drinking, and laughing by turns, and discussing with Sir Ascot the different events of their exciting gallop. Lacquers, with his mouth full, is making the agreeable in his own way to the whole party. "Deuced good pie—aw—ruin me—aw—in gloves, Miss Kettering—aw—lose everything to you—aw;" and the dandy has a vague sort of notion that he might say something sweet here, but it will not shape itself into words very conveniently, so he has a large glass of sherry instead. Our friend Captain Lacquers is not so much "a man of parts," as "a man of figure." Charlie, somewhat excited, flourishes his knife and fork, and describes how he lost his race to the public in general. Gaston D'Orville, with his most deferential air, is winning golden opinions from Blanche, and thinking in his innermost soul what a traitor he is to his own heart the while; Mrs. Delaval looks very pale and subdued, and Bounce thinks she must be tired, but breaks off to something else before he has made the inquiry—still everybody seems outwardly to be enjoying him or herself to the utmost, and it is with a forced smile and an air of assumed gaiety that Frank Hardingstone takes his leave, and supposes "we shall all meet at the ball!"

Fancy Frank deliberately proposing to go to a ball! How bitterly he smiles as he walks away from the course faster and faster, as thought after thought goads him to personal exertion! Now he despises himself thoroughly for his weakness in allowing the smile of a silly girl thus to sink into a strong man's heart—now he analyses his own feelings as he would probe a corporeal wound, with a stern scientific pleasure in the examination—and anon he speculates vaguely on the arrangements of Nature, which provide us with sentimental follies for a *sauce piquante* wherewith to flavour our daily bread. Nevertheless, our man of action is by no means satisfied with himself. He takes a fierce walk over the most unfrequented fields, and returns to his solitary lodgings, to read stiff chapters of old dogmatic writers, and to work out a tough equation or two, till he can "get this nonsense out of his head." In vain, a fairy figure with long violet eyes and floating hair dances between him and his quarto, and the "unknown quantity" *plus* Blanche continually eludes his mental grasp.

We do not think Frank has enjoyed his day's pleasure, any more than Mary Delaval. How few people do, could we but peep into their heart of hearts! Here are two at least of that gay throng in whom the shaft is rankling, and all this discomfort and anxiety exists because, forsooth, people never understand each other in time. We think it is in one of Rousseau's novels that the catastrophe is continually being postponed because the heroine invariably becomes *vivement émue*, and unable to articulate, just at the critical moment when two words more would explain everything, and make her happy with her adorer. Were it not for this provoking weakness, she would be married and settled long before the end of the first volume: but then, to be sure, what would become of all the remaining pages of French sentimentality? If there were no uncertainty, there would be no romance—if we knew each other better, perhaps we should love each other less. Hopes and fears make up the game of life. Better be the germinating flower, blooming in the sunshine and cowering in the blast, than the withered branch, defiant indeed of winter's cold and summer's heat, but drinking in no dew of morning, putting forth no buds of spring, and in its dreary, barren isolation, unsusceptible of pleasure as of pain.

CHAPTER VIII
THE BALL

Bustle and confusion reign paramount at "The Kingmakers' Arms" — principal hotel and posting-house in the town of Guyville. Once a year is there a great lifting of carpets and shifting of furniture in all the rooms of that enterprising establishment. Chambermaids hurry to and fro in smart caps brought out for the occasion, and pale-faced waiters brandish their glass-cloths in despair at the variety of their duties. All the resources of the plate-basket are brought into use, and knives, forks, tumblers, wine-glasses, German silver and Britannia metal, are collected and borrowed, and furbished up, to grace the evening's entertainment with a magnificence becoming the occasion. Dust pervades the passages, and there is a hot smell of cooking and closed windows, by which the frequenters of the house are made aware that to-night is the anniversary of the Guyville Ball, a solemnity to be spoken of with reverence by the very ostler's assistant in the yard, who will tell you *"We* are very busy, sir, just now, sir, on account of *the ball."* Tea-rooms, card-rooms, supper-rooms, dancing-rooms, and cloak-rooms, leave but few apartments to be devoted to the purposes of rest; and an unwary bagman, snoring quietly in No. 5, might chance to be smothered ere morning by the heap of cloaks, shawls, polka-jackets, and other lady-like wraps, ruthlessly heaped upon the unconscious victim in his dormitory. The combined attractions of steeple-chasing and dancing bring numerous young gentlemen and their valets to increase the confusion; and, were it not that the six o'clock train takes back the Londoners and "professionals" to the metropolis, it would be out of the power of mortal functionaries to attend to so many wants, and wait upon so many customers.

That tall, pale, interesting-looking man in chains and ringlets has already created much commotion below with his insatiable demands for foot-baths and hot water. As he waits carelessly in the passage at that closed door, receiving and returning the admiring glances of passing chambermaids, you would hardly suppose, from his unassuming demeanour, that he is no less a person than Lord Mount Helicon's *gentleman.* To be sure, he is now what he calls "comparatively incog." It is only at his club in Piccadilly, or "the room" at Wassailworth, where he and the Duke's "own man" lay down the law upon racing, politics, wine, and women, that he is to be seen in his full glory. To give him his due, he is an admirable servant, as far as his own duties are concerned, and a clever fellow to boot, or he would not have picked up seven-and-thirty pounds to-day on the steeple-chase whilst he was looking after the luncheon and the carriage. We question, however, whether he could complete his toilet as expeditiously as his master, who is now stamping about his room reciting, in an audible voice, a thundering ode on which he has been some considerable time engaged, and elaborating the folds of his white neckcloth (old fifth-form tie) between the stanzas.

Lord Mount Helicon is a literary nobleman; not one of

"Your authors who's all author, fellows

In foolscap uniforms turned up with ink;"

but a sportsman as well as a scholar, a man of the world as well as a man of letters; given overmuch to betting, horse-racing, and dissipation in general, but with as keen a zest for the elegances of literature as for those beauties of the drama to which he pays fully more attention, and one who can compute you the odds as readily as he can turn a lyric or round a flowing period. Had his lordship possessed a little more common sense and a slight modicum of prudence, forethought, reflection, and such plebeian qualities, he need not have failed in any one thing he undertook. As it was, his best friends regretted he should waste his talents so unsparingly on versification; whilst his enemies (the bitter dogs) averred "Mount Helicon's rhyme was, if possible, worse than his reason." Being member for Guyville (our readers will probably call to mind how the columns of their daily paper were filled with the Guyville Election Committee's Report, and the wonderful appetite for "treating" displayed by the "free and independent" of that town during their "three glorious days")—being member, then, of course it is incumbent on him to attend the ball; so after a hurried dinner with Lacquers, Sir Ascot, Major D'Orville, and sundry other gentlemen who *live* every day of their lives, behold him curling his red whiskers and attiring his tall, gaunt form in a suit of decorous black.

"Deuced bad dinner they give one here," said his lordship to himself, still hammering away at the ode. "Wish I hadn't drunk that second bottle of claret, and smoked so much.

When the thunders of a people smite the quailing despot's ear,

And the earthquake of rebellion heaves—

No, I can't get it right. How those cursed fiddlers are scraping! and either that glass maligns me, or I look a little drunk! This life don't suit my style of beauty—something must be done. Shall I marry and pull up? Marry—will I! Bow my cultivated intellect before some savage maiden, and fatten like a tethered calf on the flat swamps of domestic respectability. Straps! go down and find out if many of the people are come."

"Several of the townspeople have arrived, my lord; but few of the county families as yet," replies Straps, whose knowledge of a member of parliament's duties would have qualified him to represent Guyville as well as his master. Lord Mount Helicon accordingly completes his toilet and proceeds to the ball-room, still mentally harping on "the thunders of a people," and "the quailing despot's ear."

The townspeople have indeed arrived in very sufficient numbers, yet is there a strong line of demarcation between their plebeian ranks and those of "the county families" huddled together at the upper end of the room. Britannia! Britannia! when will you cease to bring your coat-of-arms into society, and to smother your warm heart and sociable nature under pedigrees, and rent-rolls, and dreary conventionalities? When you do, you will enjoy yourself all the more, and be respected none the less. You will be equally efficient as a chaperon, though the trident be not always pointed on the defensive; and the lion may be an excellent watch-dog, without being trained to growl at every fellow-creature who does not happen to keep a carriage. His lordship's business, however, lies chiefly with those, so to speak, below the salt. Voters are they, or, more important still, voters' wives and daughters, and, as such, must be propitiated; for Mount Helicon, we need scarcely inform our readers, is not an English peerage, and my lord may probably require to sit again for the same incorruptible borough.

So he bows to *this* lady, and flirts with *that*, and submits to be patted on the shoulder and twaddled to by a fat little man, primed with port, but who, when not thus bemused, is an influential member of his committee, and a staunch supporter on the hustings. Nay more, with an effort that he deserves infinite credit for concealing with such good grace, he offers his arm to the red-haired daughter of his literally *warm* supporter, and leads the well-pleased damsel, blushing much, and mindful "to keep her head up," right away to the county families' quadrille at the top of the room, where she dances *vis-à-vis*—actually *vis-à-vis*—to Miss Kettering and Captain Lacquers.

That gentleman is considerably brightened up by his dinner and his potations. He has besides got his favourite boots on, and feels equal to almost any social emergency, so he is making the agreeable to the heiress with that degree of originality so peculiarly his own, and getting on, as he thinks, "like a house on fire."

"Very *wawm*, Miss Kettering," observes the dandy, holding steadily by his starboard moustache. "Guyville people always make it so hot. Charming *bouquet!*"

"Your *vis-à-vis* is dancing alone," says Blanche, cutting short her partner's interesting remarks, and sending him sprawling and swaggering across the room, only to hasten back again and proceed with his conversation.

"You know the man opposite—man with red whiskers? That's Mount Helicon. Good fellow—aw—if he could but dye his whiskers. Asked to be introduced to *you* to-day on the course. Told him—aw—I couldn't take such a liberty." Lacquers wishes to say he would like to keep her society all to himself, but, as usual, he cannot express clearly what he means, so he twirls his moustaches instead, and is presently lost in the intricacies of "La Poule." We need hardly observe that manœuvring is not our friend's forte. Blanche's eyes meanwhile are turned steadily towards the lower end of the room, and her partner's following their direction, he discovers, as he thinks, a fresh topic of conversation. "Ah! there's Hardingstone just come in—aw. Why don't he bring his wife with him, I wonder!"

"His wife!" repeated Blanche, with a start that sent the blood from her heart; "why, he's not married, is he?" she added, with more animation than she had hitherto exhibited.

"Don't know, I'm sure," replied the dandy, glancing down at his own faultless *chaussure*; "thought he was—aw—looks like a married man—aw."

"Why should you think so?" inquired Blanche, half amused in spite of herself.

"Why—aw," replied the observant reasoner, "got the married *look*, you know. Wears wide family boots—aw. Do to ride the children on, you know."

Blanche could not repress a laugh; and the quadrille being concluded, off she went with Cousin Charlie, to stagger through a breathless polka, just at the moment the "family boots" bore their owner to the upper end of the room in search of her.

Frank was out of his element, and thoroughly uncomfortable. Generally speaking, he could adapt himself to any society into which he happened to be thrown, but to-night he was restless and out of spirits; dissatisfied with Blanche, with himself for being so, and with the world in general. "What a parcel of fools these people are," thought he, as with folded arms he leant against the wall and gazed vacantly on the shifting throng; "jigging away to bad music in a hot room, and calling it pleasure. What a waste of time, and energy, and everything. Now, there's little Blanche Kettering. I *did* think that girl was superior to the common run of women. I fancied she had a heart, and a mind, and 'brains,' and was above all the petty vanities of flirting, and fiddling, and dressing, which a posse of idiots dignify with the name of society. But no; they are all alike, giddy, vain, and frivolous. There she is, dancing away with as light a heart as if 'Cousin Charlie' were not under orders for the Cape, and to start to-morrow morning. She don't care—not she! I wonder if she *will* marry him, should he ever come back. I have never liked to ask him, but everybody seems to say it's a settled thing. How changed she must be since we used to go out in the boat at St. Swithin's; and yet how little altered she is in features from the child I was so fond of. It's disappointing!" And Frank ground his teeth with subdued ferocity. "It's disgusting! She's not half good enough for Charlie. I'll never believe in one of them again!"

Well, if not "half good enough for Charlie," we mistake much whether, even at the very moment of condemnation, our philosopher did not consider her quite "good enough for Frank"; and could he but have known the young girl's thoughts while he judged her so harshly, he would have been much more in charity with the world in general, and looked upon the rational amusement of dancing in a light more becoming a sensible man—which, to do him justice, he generally was.

Blanche, even as she wound and threaded through the mazes of a crowded polka, skilfully steered by Cousin Charlie, who was a beautiful dancer, and one of whose little feet would scarcely have served to "ride a fairy," was wondering in her own mind why Mr. Hardingstone had not asked her to dance, and why he had been so distant at the steeple-chase, and speculating whether it was possible he could be married. How she hoped Mrs. Hardingstone, if there should be one, was *a nice person*, and how fond she would be of her, and yet few people were worthy of *him*. How noble and manly he looked to-night amongst all the dandies. She would rather see Mr. Hardingstone frown than any one else smile—there was nobody like him, except, perhaps, Major D'Orville; he had the same quiet voice, the same self-reliant manner; but then the Major was much older. Oh no—there was nothing equal to Frank—and how she *liked* him, he was *such* a friend of Charlie; and just as Blanche arrived at this conclusion, the skirt of her dress got entangled in Cornet Capon's spur, and Charlie laughed so (the provoking boy!) that he could not set her free, and the Cornet's apologies were so absurd, and everybody stared so, it was quite disagreeable! But a tall, manly figure interposed between her and the crowd, and Major D'Orville released her in an instant; and that deep, winning voice engaged her for the next dance, and she could not but comply, though she had rather it had been some one else. Frank saw it all, still with his arms folded, and misjudged her again, as men do those of whom they are fondest. "How well she does it, the little coquette," he thought; "it's a good piece of acting all through—now she'll flirt with D'Orville because he happens to be a great man here, and then she'll throw him over for some one else; and so they 'keep the game alive.'" Frank! Frank! you ought to be ashamed of yourself!

In the meantime, Lord Mount Helicon must not neglect a very important part of the business which has brought him to Guyville. In the pocket of his lordship's morning coat is a letter which Straps, who has taken that garment down to brush, in the natural course of things, is even now perusing. As its contents may somewhat enlighten us as well as the valet, we will take the liberty of peeping over that trusty domestic's shoulder, and joining him in his pursuit of knowledge, premising that the epistle is dated Brook Street, and is a fair specimen of maternal advice to a son. After the usual gossip regarding Mrs. Bolter's elopement, and Lady Susan Stiffneck's marriage, with the indispensable conjectures about "ministers," a body in whose precarious position ladies of a certain age take an unaccountable interest, the letter goes on to demonstrate that

> "it is needless to point out, my dear Mount, the advantages you would obtain under your peculiar circumstances by settling early in life. When I was at Bubbleton last autumn (and Globus says I have never been so well since he attended me when you were born—in fact, the spasms left me altogether), I made the acquaintance of a General Bounce, an odious, vulgar man, who had been all his life somewhere in India, but who had a niece, a quiet, amiable girl, by name Kettering, with whom I was much pleased. They have a nice place, though damp, somewhere in the neighbourhood of your borough, and I dined there once or twice before I left Bubbleton. Everything looked like *maison montée*; and from information I can rely on, I understand the girl is a great heiress. Between ourselves, Lady Champfront told me she would have from three to four hundred thousand pounds. Now, although I should be the last person to hint at your selling yourself for money, particularly with your talents and your position, yet if you should happen to see this young lady, and take a fancy to her, it would be a very nice thing, and would make you quite independent. She is prettyish in the 'Jeannette and Jeannot' style, and although her manner is not the least formed, she has no *prononcé* vulgarity, and would soon acquire our 'ways' when she came to live amongst us. Of course we should drop the General immediately; and, my dear boy, I trust you would

give up that horrid racing—young Cubbington, who has hardly left school, is already nearly ruined by it, and Lady Looby is in despair—such a mother too as she has been to him! By the by, there is a cousin in our way, but he is young enough to be in love only with himself, and appeared to me to be rather making up to the governess! Think of this, my dear Mount, and believe me,

"Your most affectionate mother,

"M. Mt. Helicon.

"P.S.—Your book is much admired. Trifles *raves* about it, and your old friend Mrs. Blacklamb assures me that *it made her quite ill.*"

Primed with such sage counsel, his lordship determined to lose no time in "opening the trenches." After enacting sundry duty-dances, by which he had gained at least one prospective "plumper," he accordingly "completed the first parallel" by obtaining an introduction to General Bounce, which ceremony Captain Lacquers performed in his usual easy off-hand style— the introducer shouting into each man's ear his listener's *own* name, and suppressing altogether that of his new acquaintance, an ingenious method of presenting people to each other without furthering their intimacy to any great extent. The General, however, and the member had known each other previously by sight as well as by name, the former having voted and spoken against the latter at the past election, with his peculiar abruptness and energy; but Mount Helicon was the last man in the world to owe an antagonist a grudge, and being keenly alive to the ridiculous, was prepared to be delighted with his political opponent, in whom he saw a fund of absurdity, out of which he promised himself much amusement.

"Glad to make your acquaintance, my Lud," said the General, standing well behind his orders and decorations, which showed to great advantage on a coat tightly buttoned across his somewhat corpulent frame—"Don't like your politics—what? never did—progress and all that, sir, not worth a row of gingerbread—don't tell *me*—why, what did Lord Hindostan say to me at Government House, when they threatened to report me at home for exceeding my orders? 'Bounce,' says his Excellency—'Bounce, *I'll see you through it*'—what? *nothing like a big stick for a nigger. Stick!* how d'ye mean?"— and the speaker, who was beginning to foam at the mouth, suddenly changed his tone to one of the sweetest politeness, as he introduced 'My niece, Miss Kettering; Lord Mount Helicon.' A second time was Frank Hardingstone forestalled; he had just made up his mind that he would dance with Blanche only *once*, sun himself yet *once* again in her sweet smile, and then think of her no more—a sensible resolution, but not very easy to carry out. Of course he laid the blame on her. "First she makes a fool of D'Orville," thought he, "a man old enough to be her father—and now she whisks away with this red-bearded radical—to make a fool of him too, unless she means to throw over Charlie; and who is the greatest fool of the three? Why, you, Frank Hardingstone, who ought to know better. I shall go home, smoke a cigar, and go to bed; the dream is over; I had no idea it would be so unpleasant to wake from it." So Frank selected his hat, pulled out his cigar-case, and trudged off, by no means in a philosophical or even a charitable frame of mind.

There was a light twinkling in the window of his lodgings over the Saddlers, some three hours afterwards, when a carriage drove rapidly by, bearing a freight of pleasure-seekers home from the ball. Inside were the General and Blanche, the former fast asleep, wrapped in the dreamless slumbers which those enjoy who have reached that time of life when the soundness of the stomach is far more attended to than that of the heart—when sentiment is of small account, but digestion of paramount importance. Age, as it widens the circle of our affections, weakens their intensity, and although proverbially "there is no fool like an old one," we question if in the present day there are many Anacreons who—

"When they behold the festive train

Of dancing youth, are young again;"

or who, however little they might object to celebrating her charms "in the bowl," would, for "soft Bathylla's sake," wreathe vine-leaves round their grizzled heads. No: Age is loth to make itself ridiculous in *that* way; and the General snored and grunted, heartwhole and comfortable, by the side of his pretty niece. How pretty she looked—a little pale from over-excitement and fatigue, but her violet eyes all the deeper and darker from the contrast, whilst none but her maid would have thought the long golden brown hair spoiled by hanging down in those rich, uncurling clusters. She was like the pale blush rose in her bouquet—more winning as it droops in half-faded loveliness than when first it bloomed, bright and crisp, in its native conservatory. The flower yields its fragrance all the sweeter from being shaken by the breeze. Who but a cousin or a brother would have gone on the box to smoke with such a girl as Blanche inside? Yet so it was. Master Charlie, who danced, as he did everything else, with his whole heart and soul, could not forego the luxury of a cigar in the cool night air, after the noise and heat and revelry of the ball. As he puffed volumes of smoke into the air, and watched the bright stars twinkling down through the clear, pure night, his thoughts wandered far—far into the future; and he, too, felt that the majesty of a sad, sweet face had impressed itself on his being—that she had been watching him to-day through his boyish exploits—and that her eye would kindle, her cheek would glow, when military honours and distinction were heaped upon him, as heaped he was resolved they should be, if ever an opportunity offered. To-morrow his career would begin! To-morrow, ay, even to-day (for it was already past midnight) he was to embark for the Cape; and scarce a thought of the bitterness of parting, perhaps for ever, shaded that bright, young imagination, as it sketched out for itself its impossible romance, worth all the material possibilities that have ever been accomplished. So Charlie smoked and pondered, and dreamed of beauty and valour. We do not think he was in very imminent danger of marrying his cousin.

Perhaps, were he inside, his flow of spirits would only disturb the quiet occupants. Blanche is not asleep, but she is dreaming nevertheless. With her large eyes fixed vacantly on the hedge-row trees and fences, that seem to be wheeling past her in the carriage lamp-light, she is living the last few hours of her life again, and seeing their past events more clearly, as she disentangles them from the excitement and confusion amongst which they actually occurred. Now she is dancing with Lacquers or Sir Ascot, and wondering, as she recalls their commonplace chatter and trite remarks, how men so insipid can belong to the same creation as "Cousin Charlie," or another gentleman, a friend of his, of whom, for the first time in her life, she feels a little afraid. Now she laughs to herself as she recollects Cornet Capon's agony of shyness, and the burning blushes with which that diffident young officer apologised for tearing her dress. Anon she sees Major D'Orville's commanding figure and handsome, manly face, while the low musical voice is still ringing in her ear, and the quiet deferential manner, softened by a protective air of kindness, has lost none of its charm. Blanche is not the first young lady, by a good many, who has gone home from a ball with a flattered consciousness that a certain gallant officer thinks her a "very superior person," and that the good opinion of such a man is indeed worth having. The Major was "a dangerous man"; he betrayed no coxcombry to mar the effect of his warlike beauty and chivalrous bearing. He never "sank" the profession, but always spoke of himself as a "mere soldier," whilst his manner was that of a "finished gentleman." He had distinguished himself, too, on more than one occasion; and the men all had a great opinion of him. Woman is an imitative animal; and a high reputation, especially for courage, amongst the gentlemen, goes a long way in the good graces of the ladies. Add to these the crowning advantage, that the Major, except in one instance of which we know the facts, came into the unequal contest with a heart perfectly invulnerable and case-hardened by intercourse with the world, and a selfishness less the result of nature than education. When a man, himself untouched, makes up his mind that a woman *shall* love him, the odds are fearfully in his favour. Blanche *liked* him already; but if "in the multitude of counsellors there is safety," no less is there security in the multitude of admirers; and ere the Major's image had time to make more than a transient impression, that of Lord Mount Helicon chased it away in the mental magic-lantern of our fair young dreamer. He had taken her in to supper; and how pleasant he was! so odd, but so agreeable—such a command of language, and such a quaint, absurd way of saying commonplace things. Not so bad-looking either, in spite of his red whiskers; and such a beautiful title! How well it would sound! and Blanche smiled at herself as the idea came across her. But a handsome, manly fellow leaning against the wall was looking at her with a stern, forbidding expression she had never seen before on that open brow, and Blanche's heart ached at the vision. Mr. Hardingstone was surely very much changed; he who used to be so frank, and kind, and good-humoured, and to lose no opportunity of petting and praising the girl he had known from a child; and to-night he had never so much as asked her to dance, and scarcely spoken to her. "What right had he to look so cross at me?" thought the girl, with the subdued irritation of wounded feelings; "what had I done to offend him, or why should I care whether I offend him or not? Poor fellow, perhaps he is in low spirits about Cousin Charlie's going away so soon." And Blanche's eyes filled with tears—tears that she persuaded herself were but due to her cousin's early departure.

Like the rising generation in general, Charlie was a great smoker. His ideas of "campaigning" were considerably mixed up with tobacco, and he lost no opportunity of qualifying for the bivouac by a sedulous consumption of cigars. He dashed the last bit of "burning comfort" from his lips as the carriage drove into the avenue at Newton-Hollows. Protracted yawns prevented much conversation during the serving-out of hand-candlesticks. Good-nights were exchanged; "We shall all see you to-morrow before you go, dear," said Blanche, as she disappeared into her room; and soon the sighing of the night wind was the only sound to disturb the silence of that long range of buildings, where all were sunk in slumber and repose—all save one.

At an open window, looking steadfastly forth into the darkness, sat Mary Delaval. She had not stirred for hours, and she might have been asleep, so moveless was her attitude, had it not been for the fixed, earnest expression of her dark grey eye. One round white arm rested on the window-ledge, and her long black hair fell in loose masses over the snowy garments, which, constituting a lady's *déshabillé*, reveal her beauties far less liberally than the costume she more inaptly terms "full dress." Mary is reasoning with herself—generally an unsatisfactory process, and one that seldom leads to any definite conclusion; sadly, soberly, and painfully, she is recalling her past life, her selfish father, her injured mother, the hardships and trials of her youth, and the ray of sunshine that has tinged the last few weeks with its golden light. She never thought to entertain folly, madness, such as this; yet would she not have had it otherwise for worlds. Bitter are the dregs, but verily the poison is more than sweet. And now he is going away, and she will never, never see him again; that fair young face will never more greet her with its thrilling smile, those kindly joyous tones never more make music for her ear. To-morrow he will be gone. Perhaps he may fall in action—the beautiful brow gashed—the too well-known features cold and fixed in death: not if prayers can avert such a fate. Perhaps he will return distinguished and triumphant; but in either case what more will the poor governess have to do with the young hero, save to love him still? Yes, she may love him *now*—love him with all her heart and soul, without restraint, without self-reproach, for she will *never* see him again. On that she is determined; their paths lie in different directions, like two ships that meet upon the waters and rejoice in each other's companionship, and part, and know each other no more. It was foolish to sit up for him to-night; but it is the last, *last* time, and she could not resist the temptation to wait and watch even for the very wheels that bore him home; and now it is over—all over— he will never know it; but she will always think of him and pray for him, and watch over Blanche for *his* sake, and love him, adore him dotingly— madly—to the last; and cold, haughty, passionless Mary Delaval leant her head upon her two white arms, and sobbed like a broken-hearted child.

We wonder if any man that walks the earth is worthy of the whole idolatrous devotion of a woman's heart. Charlie was snoring sound asleep, whilst she who loved him wept and prayed and suffered. Go to sleep too, foolish Mary, and pleasant dreams to you: "Sorrow has your young days shaded;" it is but fair that your nights should glow in the rosy, fancy- brightened hues of joy.

CHAPTER IX
WANT

As you walk jauntily along any of the great thoroughfares of London, you arrive, ever and anon, at one of those narrow offshoots of which you would scarcely discover the existence, were it not for the paved crossing over which you daintily pick your way on the points of your jetty boots. All the attention you can spare from passing events is devoted to the preservation of your *chaussure*, and you do not probably think it worth while to bestow even a casual peep down that close, winding alley, in which love and hate, and hopes and fears, and human joys and miseries and sympathies, are all packed together, just as they are in your own house in Belgravia, Tyburnia, or Mayfair, only considerably more cramped for room, and a good deal worse off for fresh air. That noble animal, the horse, generally occupies the ground-floor of such tenements as compose these narrow streets, whilst the dirty children of those bipeds who look after his well-being, embryo coachmen, and helpers, and stablemen, play and fight and vociferate in the gutter, with considerable energy and no little noise, munching their dinners *al fresco* the while, with an appetite that makes dry bread a very palatable sustenance. A strong "smell of stables" pervades the atmosphere, attributable perhaps to the accumulation of that agricultural wealth which, in its *right* place, produces golden harvests; and the ring of harness and stamp of steeds, varied by an occasional snort, nearly drown the plaintive street organ, grinding away, fainter and fainter, round the corner. Shirts, stockings, and garments of which we neither know the names nor natures, hang, like Macbeth's banners, "on the outward walls." Washing appears to be the staple commerce, while porter seems the principal support, of these busy regions; and as the snowy water-lily rises from the stagnant marsh, so does the dazzling shirt-front, in which you will to-day appear at dinner, owe its purity to that stream of soapy starch-stained liquid now pouring its filthy volume down the gutter. Dirty, drowsy-looking men clatter about with pails and other apparatus for the cleansing of carriages, whilst here and there an urchin is pounced upon and carried off by some maternal hawk, with bare arms and disordered tresses, either to return with a smeared mouth and a festive slice of bread and treacle, or to admonish its companions, by piercing cries, that it is undergoing summary punishment not undeserved. The shrill organ of female volubility, we need hardly say, is in the ascendant; and we may add that the faces generally met with, all dirty and careworn though they be, are gilded by an honest expression of contentment peculiar to those who fulfil their destiny by working for their daily bread.

In one of the worst lodgings in such a mews as we have faintly endeavoured to describe, in a dirty, comfortless room, bare of furniture, and to which laborious access is obtained by a dilapidated wooden staircase, sits our old acquaintance Gingham, now Mrs. Blacke, but who will never be known to "the families in which she lived" by any other than her maiden patronymic. Though in her best days a lady of no fascinating exterior, she is decidedly altered for the worse since we saw her at St. Swithin's, and is now, without question, a hard-featured and repulsive-looking woman. She has lost the "well-to-do" air, which sits more easily on those who live at "housekeeping" than on those "who find themselves," and everything about her betrays a degree of poverty, if not of actual want, sadly repugnant to the habits of an orderly upper-servant in a well-regulated establishment.

Of all those who sink to hardships after having "seen better days," none bear privation so ill as this particular rank. They have neither the determination and energy of "the gentle," nor the happy carelessness and bodily vigour of the labouring class. It is lamentable to watch the gradual sinking of a once respectable man, who has been tempted, by the very natural desire of becoming independent, to leave "service" and set up on his own account. From his boyhood he has been fed, housed, and clothed, without a thought or care of his own, till he has spread into the portly, grave, ponderous official, whom not even his master's guests would think of addressing save by the respectful title of "Mister." He has saved a "pretty bit o' money"; and on giving warning, announces his long-concealed marriage to the housekeeper, who has perhaps saved a little more. Between them they muster a *very* few hundred pounds; and on this inexhaustible capital they determine to set up for themselves. If he takes a public-house, it is needless to dwell on the almost inevitable catastrophe. But whatever the trade or speculation on which he embarks, he has everything to learn; education cannot be had without paying for it; business connections cannot be made—they must *grow*. Those are positive hardships to *him*, which could scarcely be felt as wants by others of his own sphere, who had not always lived, as he has, on the fat of the land. Discontent and recrimination creep into the household. The wife makes home uncomfortable, and "the husband goes to the beer-shop." The money dwindles—the business fails—fortunate if the family do not increase. "Trade *never* was so bad," and it soon becomes a question of assignees and ten shillings in the pound. The man himself is honest, and it cuts him to the heart. Only great speculators can rise, like the Phœnix, in gaudier plumage after every fresh insolvency; and hunger begins to stare our once portly acquaintance in the face. At last he is completely "sold up," and if too old to go again into service, he will probably think himself well off to finish in the workhouse. And this is the career of two-thirds of those who leave comfortable homes for the vague future of a shadowy independence, and embark upon speculations of which they neither understand the nature nor count the cost.

But we must return to Gingham, bending her thin, worn figure over some dirty needlework, and rocking with her foot a wooden cradle, in which, covered by a scanty rug not over-clean, sleeps a little pinched-up atom of a child, contrasting sadly with those vigorous, brawling urchins out of doors. There is a scanty morsel of fire in the grate, though the day is hot and sultry, for a "bit of dinner" has to be kept warm for "father"; and very meagre fare it is, between its two delf plates. A thin-bladed knife and two-pronged fork lie ready for him on the rough deal table, guiltless of a cloth; and Gingham wonders what is keeping him, for he promised faithfully to come back to dinner, and the poor woman sighs as she stitches and rocks the child, and counts the quarters told out by the neighbouring clock, and ponders sadly on old times, than which there is no surer sign of a heart ill at ease. Well-to-do, thriving people are continually looking forward, and scheming and living in the Future; it is only your worn, dejected, hopeless sufferer that recalls the long-faded sunshine of the Past.

Gingham's marriage took place at St. Swithin's as soon after Mrs. Kettering's death as appearances would allow, and was conducted with the usual solemnities observed on such occasions in her rank of life. There was a new shawl, and a gorgeous bonnet, and a cake, with a large consumption of tea, not to mention excisable commodities. Tom Blacke looked very smart in a white hat and trousers to match, whilst Hairblower signalised the event by the performance of an intricate and unparalleled hornpipe, such as is never seen now-a-days off the stage. Blanche made the bride a handsome present, which was acknowledged with many blessings and a shower of tears. Gingham's great difficulty was, how ever she should part with Miss Blanche! and "all went merry as a marriage bell." But they had not long been man and wife ere Tom began to show the cloven foot. First he would take his blushing bride to tea-gardens and such places of convivial resort, where, whilst she partook of the "cup that cheers but not inebriates," he would sip consolatory measures of that which does both. After a time he preferred such expeditions as she could not well accompany him on, and would come home with glazed eyes, a pale face, and the tie of his neckcloth under his ear. The truth will out. Tom was a drunken dog. There was no question about it. Then came dismissal from his employer, the attorney. Still, as long as Gingham's money lasted, all went on comparatively well. But a lady's-maid's savings are not inexhaustible, and people who live on their capital are apt to get through it wonderfully fast. So they came down from three well-furnished rooms to a kitchen and parlour, and from that to one miserable apartment, serving all purposes at once. Then they moved to London to look for employment; and Tom Blacke, a handy fellow enough when sober, obtained a series of situations, all of which he lost owing to his convivial failing. Now they paid two shillings a week for the wretched room in which we find them, and a hard matter it often was to raise money for the rent, and their own living, and Tom's score at "The Feathers," just round the corner. But Gingham worked for the whole family, as a woman will when put to it, and seemed to love her husband the better the worse he used her, as is constantly the case with that long-suffering sex. "Poor fellow," she would say, when Tom reeled home to swear at her in drunken ferocity, or kiss her in maudlin kindness, "it's trouble that's drove him to it; but there's good in Tom yet—look how fond he is of baby." And with all his faults, there is no doubt little Miss Blacke possessed a considerable share of her father's heart, such as it was.

But even gentle woman's temper is not proof against being kept waiting, that most irritating of all trials; and Gingham, who in her more prosperous days had been a lady of considerable asperity, could "pluck up a spirit," as she called it, even now, when she was "*raised*,"—so, surmounting the coffee-coloured front with a dingy bonnet, and folding her bare arms in a faded shawl, she locked baby in, trusting devoutly the child might not wake during her absence, and marched stoutly off to "The Feathers," where she was sure to find her good-for-nothing husband.

There he was, sure enough, just as she expected, his old black coat glazed and torn, his pinched-up hat pressed down over his pale, sunken features, his whole appearance dirty and emaciated. None but his wife could have recognised the dapper Tom Blacke, of St. Swithin's, in that shaky, scowling, dissipated sot. Alas! she knew him in his present character too well. There he was, playing skittles with a ponderous ruffian, in a linen jacket and high-lows, who looked like a showman of a travelling menagerie, only not so respectable; and a little Jew pedlar, with a hawk eye and an expression of countenance that defied Mephistopheles himself to overreach him. There was her husband, betting pots of beer and "goes" of gin, though the cupboard was bare at home and the child crying for food—marking his game with a trembling hand, cheating when he won, and blaspheming when he lost, like the very blackguard to which he was rapidly descending.

Gingham shook a little as she advanced, twirling the door-key nervously round her finger; but she determined to try the *suaviter in modo* first, so she began, "Tom! Tom Blacke! dinner's ready, ain't you coming home?"

"Home! Home be — —! and you, too, Mrs. Blacke; we won't go home till mornin'—shall us, Mr. Fibbes?" Mr. Fibbes, although appearances were much against him, in his linen jacket and high-lows, was a man of politeness where the fair were concerned, so he took a straw out of his mouth, and replied, "Not to cross the missus, when sich is by no means necessary; finish the game first, and then we'll hargue the pint—that's what *I* say."

"O Tom, *pray* come away," said poor Gingham, who had caught sight of the chalked-up score, and knew, by sad experience, what havoc it would make with the weekly earnings. "I durstn't leave the child not a minute longer; I've kept your bit of dinner all hot for you—come away, there's a dear!"

"Not I," said Tom, poising his wooden bowl for a fresh effort, and, irritated by his failure, bursting forth upon his wife. "How *can* I leave these gentlemen in their game to attend to you? Come, let's have no nonsense; be off! *be off!*" he repeated, clenching his fist, and raising his voice to a pitch that called forth from the large man the admonitory remark that "*easy does it,*" whilst the little Jew's eyes glittered at the prospect of winning his game.

But Gingham was roused, and she went at him fiercely and at once: "Shame—shame on ye!" she exclaimed, in a low, hoarse voice, gradually rising, as she got more excited, and her pale features worked with passion, "with the child cryin' at home, and me obliged to come and look for you in such a place as this; me that slaves and toils, and works my fingers to the bone," holding up her needle-scarred hands to the by-standers, who were already collecting, as they always do when there is a prospect of *a row*. "Call yourself a man!—*a man*, indeed!—and let your wife and child starve whilst you are taking your diversion, and enjoying of yourself here? And you too," she added, attacking the large man and the Jew with a suddenness which much startled the former, "*you* ought to be ashamed of yourselves, you ought; keeping of him here, and making of him as bad as yourselves—though perhaps *you're* not husbands and fathers, and don't know no better. Ay, do, you coward! strike a woman if you dare! Was it for this I left my place and my missus? Oh dear, oh dear, whatever shall I do?" and Gingham, throwing her apron over her head, sank upon a bench in a passion of weeping, supported by a phalanx of matrons who had already collected, and who took part in the altercation, as being to all intents and purposes a Government question.

Tom Blacke was furious, of course. Had it not been for the large man, he would have struck his wife to the ground—alas! not the first time, we fear, that she had felt the weight of a coward's arm; but that ponderous champion interposed his massive person, and recommended his friend strongly "not to cross the missus." Truth to tell, Mr. Fibbes had a little shrew of a black-eyed wife at home, who ruled the roast, and kept her great husband in entire subjection; besides which, like most square, powerful men, he was a good-natured fellow, though not very respectable; and having won as much beer as he wanted from Tom, willingly lent his good offices to solder up the quarrel, which ended, as such disturbances generally do, in a sort of half-sulky reconciliation, and the wife marching off in triumph with her captured husband. The women, as usual, had formed the majority of the crowd, and of course sided with the injured lady; so Tom Blacke, after a few ineffectual threats, and an oath or two, left the ground with his still sobbing wife, promising himself an ample revenge if she should dare to cross him at home, when there was no one by to take her part.

When they arrived at the desolate room which served them for home, "baby" was awake, and crying piteously to find its little self alone. On what trifles do the moods and tempers of the human mind depend! The child set up a crow of delight to see its father, instead of the hideous howl in which it had been indulging, and stretched out its little arms with a welcome that went straight to the drunkard's heart. In another moment he was dancing the little thing up and down in perfect good humour; and poor Gingham, thoroughly overcome, was leaning her head against his shoulder in a paroxysm of reconciled affection, and going through that process of relief known to ladies by the expressive term of "having a good cry."

How many a matrimonial bicker has been interrupted and ended by the innocent smile of "one of these little ones"! How many an ill-assorted couple have been kept from separation by the homely consideration of "what should be done with the children"! How many an evil desire, how many an unkind thought, has been quenched at its very birth by the pure, open gaze of a guileless child! The stern, severe man, disgusted with the world, and disappointed in his best affections, has a corner in his heart for those whom he prizes as his own flesh and blood; the passionate, impetuous woman, yearning for the love she seeks in vain at home, her mind filled with an image of which it is sin even to think, and beset by the hundred temptations to which those are exposed who pass their lives in wedded misery, pauses on the very threshold, and is saved from guilt when she thinks of her darlings. Sunshine and music do they make in a house, with their bright, happy faces, the patter of their little feet, and the ringing echoes of their merry laugh. Grudge not to have the quiver full of them. Love and prize them whilst you may; for the hour will come at last, and your life will be weary and your hearth desolate when they take wing and fly away.

So Tom Blacke and his wife are reconciled for the time, and would be comparatively happy, were it not for the grinding anxiety ever present to their minds of how to "make both ends meet"—that consideration which poisons the comfort of many a homely dwelling, and which in their case is doubtless their own fault, or at least the fault of the "pater familias," but none the less bitter on that account.

"There is the baker to pay, and the rent," sighed Gingham, enumerating them on her fingers; "and the butcher called this morning with his account; to be sure it is but little, and little there is to meet it with. I shall be paid to-day for the plain-work, and I got a bit of washing yesterday, that brought me in sevenpence-halfpenny," she proceeded, immersed in calculation; "and then we shall be three-and-eightpence short—three-and-eight-pence! and where to get it I don't know, if I was to drop down dead this minute!"

"I *must* have a little money to-day, too, missus," said Tom, in a hoarse, dogged voice; "can't ye put the screw on a little tighter? A man may as well be starved to death as worried to death; and I can't face 'The Feathers' again without wiping off a bit of the score, ye know." Gingham's eye glanced at the Sunday gown, hanging on a nail behind the door—a black silk one, of voluminous folds and formidable rustle, the last remnant of respectability left—and she thought *that*, too, must follow the rest to the pawnbroker's, to that receptacle of usury with which, alas! she was too familiar, and from which even now she possessed sundry mocking duplicates, representing many a once-prized article of clothing and furniture.

Tom saw and interpreted the hopeless glance. "No, no," said he, relenting, "not quite so bad as that, neither; I wouldn't strip the gown off your back, Rachel, not if it was ever so; I couldn't bear to see you, that was once so respectable, going about all in rags. We *might* get on, too," added he, brightening up, with an expression of desperate cunning in his bad eye—"we might get money—ay, plenty of it—if you were only like the rest: you're too mealy-mouthed, Mrs. Blacke, that's where it is."

"O Tom, what would you have me do?" exclaimed his wife, bursting afresh into tears; "we've been honest as yet through it all, and I've borne and borne because we *were* honest. I'd work upon my bare knees for you and the child—I'd starve and never complain *myself*, if I hadn't a morsel in the cupboard; but I'd keep my honesty, Tom, I'd keep my honesty, for when *that's* gone, all's gone together."

"Will your honesty put decent clothes on your back, missus?" rejoined Tom, who did not see that the article in question was by any means so indispensable; "will your honesty put a joint down before the fire, such as we used to sit down to every day, when we was first man and wife, and lived respectable? Will your honesty furnish a bellyful for this poor little beggar, that's whining now on my knee for a bit to eat?" Gingham began to relent at this consideration, and Tom pursued his advantage: "Besides, it's not as if it was to do anybody any harm; there's Miss Blanche got more than she knows what to do with, and the young gentleman—he's away at the wars. *Honesty*, indeed! if honesty's the game, you've a right to your share, what Mrs. Kettering intended you should have. I think I ought to know the law; and the law's on our side, and the justice too. Ah! Rachel, you used not to be so difficult to come round once," concluded Tom, trying the *tender* tack, when he had exhausted all his other arguments; and recalling to his wife's mind, as he intended it should do, their early days of courtship, and the carriage of a certain brown-paper parcel by the sea-shore.

But Gingham felt she had right on her side; and when we can indulge the spirit of contradiction never dormant in our natures, and fight under the banner of truth at the same time, it is too great a luxury for mortal man, or especially mortal woman, to forego, so Gingham was game to the last. "No, Tom, *no!*" she said, steadily and with emphasis, "I *won't* do it, so don't ask me, and there's an end of it!"

Her husband put the child down in disgust, banged his hat upon his head, as if to go back to "The Feathers," and was leaving the room, when a fresh idea struck him. If he could but break down his wife's self-respect he might afterwards mould her more easily to his purpose, and the course he proposed to adopt might, at any rate, furnish him in the meantime with a little money for his dissipation; so he turned round coaxingly to poor Gingham, and asked for his bit of dinner, and put the infant once more upon his knee, ere he began to sound her on the propriety of applying for a little assistance to her darling Miss Blanche. "You ought to go and see your young lady, Rachel," said he, quite good-humouredly, and with the old keeping-company-days' smile; "it's only proper respect, now she's grown to be a great lady, and come to London. I'll mind the child at home; it likes to be left with its daddy—a deary—and you brush yourself up a bit, and put on your Sunday gown there, and take a bit of a holiday; you needn't hurry back, you know, if they ask you to stay tea in the room, and I'll be here till you come home; or if I'm not, I'll get one of the neighbours to look in. So now go, there's a good wench."

Mrs. Blacke had not heard such endearing language since the sea-side walks at St. Swithin's—she felt almost happy again, and nearly forgot the "three-and-eightpence" wanting for the week's account. Sundry feminine misgivings had she, as to her personal appearance being sufficiently fine to face the new servants, in the exalted character of Miss Blanche's late lady's-maid; but women, even ugly ones, have a wonderful knack of adorning themselves on very insufficient materials, and Tom assured her the black silk looked as good as new, and that bonnet always *did* become her, and always *would*—so she gave the child a parting kiss, and her husband many injunctions to take care of the treasure, and started in wonderfully good spirits; Tom's last injunction to her as she departed being to this effect—"If Miss Blanche should ask you how we're getting on, Rachel, you put your pride in your pocket—mind that—put your pride in your pocket, do you understand?" So the drunkard was left alone with his child.

We have already said Tom was fond of the little thing—in fact, it was the only being on earth that had found its way to his heart. Man must love *something*, and Tom Blacke, the attorney's clerk, who had married for money as if he had been a ruined peer of the realm, cared just as little for his wife as any impoverished nobleman might for the peeress with whom his income was necessarily encumbered; but the more indifferent he was to the mother, the fonder he was of the child; and with all his liking for skittles and vulgar dissipation (the whist and claret of higher circles), he thought it no hardship to spend the rest of the afternoon with an infant that was just beginning to talk. He fully intended, as he had promised, to remain at home till his wife returned, but a drunkard can have no will of his own. When a man gives himself up to strong drink he chooses a mistress who will take no denial, for whom appetite grows too fiercely by what it feeds on, whose beck and call he must be ever ready to obey, for she will punish his neglect by the infliction of such horrors as we may fancy pictured in the imagination of the doomed—till he fly for relief back to the enchantress that has maddened him; and whilst the poison begets thirst as the thirst craves for the poison, the liquid fire poured upon the smouldering flame eats, and saps, and scorches, till it expires in drivelling idiocy, or blazes out in raving, riotous madness. Mr. Blacke was tolerably cheerful up to a certain point, when he arrived at that state which we once heard graphically described by the sergeant of a barrack-guard, on whom the duty had devolved of placing an inebriated warrior in solitary confinement—"Was he drunk, sergeant?" said the orderly officer. "No, sir." "Was he sober, then?" "No, sir." "How? neither drunk nor sober! what d'ye mean?" "Well, sir, the man had been drinking, no doubt, *but the liquor was just dying out in him.*"

So with Tom Blacke—after an hour or so the liquor began to *die out in him*, and then came the ghastly reaction. First he thought the room was gloomy and solitary, and he got nearer the child's cradle for company—the little thing was again asleep, and he adjusted its coverlet more comfortably—ah! that slimy, crawling creature! what is it? so near the infant's head—he brushed it away with his hand, but swarms of the same loathsome insects came climbing over the cradle, chairs, and furniture. Now they settled on his legs and clothes, and he beat them down and flung them from him by hundreds, shuddering with horror the while; then he looked into the corners of the room, and put his hands before his eyes after each startled glance, for hideous faces grinned and gibbered at him, starting out from the very walls, and mopping and mowing, shifted their forms and places, so that it was impossible to identify them. He could have borne these, but worse still, there was a Shape in the room with him, of whose presence he was fearfully conscious, though whenever he manned himself to look steadily at it, it was gone. He could not bear to have this visitant *behind* him, so he backed his chair hard against the wall. In vain—still on the side from which he turned his head the grim Shape sat and cowered and blinked at him. He knew it—he felt it—mortal nerves could bear it no longer. He grew desperate, as a man does in a dream. Should he take the child and run for it? No! he would meet It on the narrow stairs, and he could not get by there. Ha! the window! bounding into the air, child and all, he might escape. He was mad now—he was capable of anything. Come along, little one!—they are blocking up the room—they cover the room in myriads—the Shape is waving them on—light and freedom without, the devil and all his legions within—Hurrah!

Fortunate was it for the hope of the Blacke family that Mrs. Crimp was at this instant returning to her lodgings above, accompanied by several promising young Crimps, with whom, as she toiled up the common staircase, she kept up a running fire of objurgation and entreaty. The homely sounds, the familiar voices, brought Tom Blacke to himself. The vicinity of such a material dame as Mrs. Crimp was sufficient to destroy the ideal in the most brandy-sodden brain, and the horrors left their victim for the time. But he dared not remain to encounter a second attack. He could not answer for the consequences of another hour in that room alone with the child; so he asked his neighbour, a kind, motherly woman, and as fond of a baby as if she had not nursed a dozen of her own, to keep an eye upon his little one, and betook himself straight to "The Feathers," to raise the accursed remedy to his lips with a trembling hand, and borrow half-an-hour's callousness at a frightful sacrifice. Tom thought he knew what was good for his complaint, and "clung to the hand that smote him" with the confirmed infatuation of a sot. So we leave him at the bar, with a glazed eye, a haggard smile, and the worm that never dies eating into his very vitals.

In the meantime, Gingham, with the dingy bonnet somewhat cocked up behind, and her bony fingers peeping through the worn thread gloves, is making her way along the sunny pavement in the direction of Grosvenor

Square. The old black silk gown looks worse than she expected in that searching light, and she feels nervous and shy at revisiting her former haunts; nor does she like leaving home for many hours at a time. But as she walks on, the exercise does her good. The moving objects on all sides, and the gaudy bustle of London in the height of the season, have an exhilarating effect on her spirits. It is so seldom she has *an outing*; moped up for days together in that mews, the very change is enjoyment; and the shops, with their cheap dresses and seductive ribbons, are perfect palaces of delight. She cannot tear herself from one window, where an excellent silk for her own wear, and a frock "fit to dress an angel," as she thinks, for baby, are to be sold, in tempting juxtaposition, respectively for a mere nothing. If she was sure the colour of the silk would *stand*, she would try and scrape the money together to buy it; but a pang shoots through her as she recalls the fatal "three-and-eightpence," so she walks on with a heavy sigh, and though she knows she never can possess it, yet she feels all the better for having seen such a dress as *that*.

And these, and such as these, are the pleasures of the poor in our great metropolis. Continual self-denial, continual self-restraint, continual self-abasement—like Tantalus, to be whelmed in the waters of enjoyment which must never touch the lip. In the country the poor man can at least revel in its freshest and purest delights. We have been told that "the meek shall inherit the earth"; and the day-labourer, mending "my lord's" park fence, has often far more enjoyment in that wilderness of beauty than its high-born proprietor. While the latter is in bed, the former breathes the sweet morning air and the scent of a thousand wild flowers, whose fragrance will be scorched up ere noon. The glad song of birds makes music to his ear—the whole landscape, smiling in the sunlight, is spread out for the delight of his eye. Not only the park, and the waving woods, and the placid lake, are his property for the time, but the cheerful homesteads, and the scattered herds, and the hazy distance stretching away as far as those blue hills that melt into the sky. He can admire the shadow of each giant elm without disturbing himself as to which of them must be marked for the axe; he can watch the bounding deer without caring which is the fattest to furnish a haunch for solemn dinners and political entertainments, where people eat because they are weary, and drink because they are dull. The distant view he looks upon is to him a breathing, sparkling world, full of light and life and hope—not a mere county, subdivided into votes and freeholds, and support and interest. His frame is attempered by toil to the enjoyment of natural pleasures and natural beauties. The wild breeze fans his brow—the daisies spring beneath his feet—the glorious summer sky is spread above—and the presence of his Maker pervades the atmosphere about him. For the time the man is happy—

happier, perhaps, than he is himself aware of. To be sure he is mortal, and in the midst of all he sighs for beer; yet is his lot one not unmixed with many pure and thrilling pleasures; and if he can only get plenty of work, there are many states of existence far worse than that of an English field-labourer.

Not so with the sons of toil in town—there, all enjoyment is artificial, all pleasure must be paid for—the air they breathe will support life, but its odours are far different from those of the wild flower. If their eyes are ever gladdened by beauty, it is but the pomp and splendour of their fellow-creatures, on which they gaze with sneering admiration—half envy, half contempt. If their ears are ever ravished by music, there is a tempting demon wafting sin into their hearts upon the sounds—there is a mocking voice of ribaldry and vulgar revelry accompanying the very concord of heaven. What pleasure *can* they have but those of the senses? Where have they to go for relaxation but to the gin-shop? What inducement have they to raise themselves above the level of "the beasts which perish"?

Honour to those who are working to provide intellectual amusements for the masses, and that education of the soul which places man *above* the circumstances by which he is surrounded! Much has been done, and much is still left to do. Those waves must be taught to leap ever upwards, to fling their separate crests towards the sky; for if the tempest should arise, and they should come surging on in one gigantic volume, they will make a clear breach wherever the embankment happens to be weakest; and who shall withstand their force?

Can we wonder to find the lower classes sometimes discontented, when we think of their privations and their toils? Shall a man starve with but half-an-inch of plate-glass betwixt his dry white lips and the reeking abundance of luxurious gluttony? and shall he turn away without a murmur, die, and make no sign? Shall a fellow-creature drag on an existence of perpetual labour, with no pleasures, no relaxations, almost no repose; and shall we expect this dreary, blighted being to be always contented, always cheerful, always respectful to his superiors? Is it to be all one way here below? shall it be all joy, and mirth, and comfort, and superfluity with the one; and all want, and misery, and grim despair with the other? Forbid it, Heaven! Let us, every man, put his shoulder to the wheel—let each, in his own circle, be it small or great, do all in his power for those beneath him—beneath him but in the accident of station, brothers in all besides—live and let live—stretch a helping hand to all who need it—treat every man as one who has an immortal soul—and though "they shall never cease out of the land," yet will their wants be known and their hardships alleviated, and the fairest spirit of heaven—angelic Charity—shall spread her wings widest and warmest in London for the poor.

CHAPTER X
SUPERFLUITY

London for the rich, though, is a different thing altogether. "Money cannot purchase happiness," said the philosopher. "No," replied a celebrated wit, himself well skilled in circulating the much-esteemed dross, "but it can purchase a very good imitation of it;" and none can gainsay the truth of his distinction. What can it do for us in the great Babylon? It can buy us airy houses—cool rooms—fragrant flowers—the best of everything to eat and drink—carriages—horses—excitement—music—friends—everything but a good appetite and content. London for the rich man is indeed a palace of delights. See him at the window of his club, in faultless attire, surrounded by worshippers who perform their part of the mutual contract most religiously, by finding conversation and company, both of the pleasantest, for him who provides drag and dinner, equally of the best. Though they bow before a calf, is it not a golden one? though they "eat dirt," is it not dressed by a French cook? See him cantering in the Park—an animal so well broke as that would make John Gilpin himself appear a fine horseman. What envious glances follow him from the humble pedestrian—what sunny smiles shine on him from lips and eyes surmounting the most graceful shapes, the most becoming neck-ribbons! No, admiring stranger! You are not in the Bazaar at Constantinople—you are amidst England's high-born beauties in the most moral country on earth; yet even here, with sorrow be it said, there is many a fair girl ready to barter love, and hope, and self-respect, for a box at the opera and an *adequate* settlement—only it must be large enough. Within fifty yards of this spot may Tattersall's voice be heard any Monday or Thursday proclaiming, hammer in hand, his mercenary ultimatum, "The best blood in England, and she is to be sold." Brain-sick moralists would read a lesson from the animal's fate. Our men of the world are satisfied to take things as they are. Meanwhile the calf has shown himself long enough to his idolaters; he dines *early* to-day—a quarter past eight—therefore he canters home to dress. Man has no right to insult such a cook as his by being hungry, so he trifles over a repast that Apicius would have envied, and borrows half-an-hour's fictitious spirits from a golden vintage that has well-nigh cost its weight in gold. What an evening is before him! All that can enchant the eye, all that can ravish the ear—beauties of earth and sounds of heaven—the very revelry of the intellect, and "the best box in the house" from which to see, hear, and enjoy. The calf is indeed pasturing in the Elysian fields, and we need follow him no longer. Can he be otherwise than happy? Can there be lips on which such fruits as these turn to ashes? Are beauty, and luxury, and society, and song, nothing after all but "a bore"? Nature is a more impartial mother than we are prone to believe, and the rich man need not always be such an object of envy only because he *is* rich.

But pretty Blanche Kettering enjoyed the glitter and the excitement, and the pleasures of her London life, even as the opening flower enjoys the sunshine and the breeze. It requires a season or two to take the edge off a fresh, healthy appetite, and *ennui* scowls in vain upon the *very* young. Gingham thought her young lady had never looked so well as she did to-day, of all days in the year the one in which Blanche was to *be presented*. Yes—it was the day of the Drawing-room, and our former Abigail forgot the supercilious manners of the new porter, and the high and mighty ways of the General's gentleman, and even her own faded black silk, in a paroxysm of motherly affection and professional enthusiasm, brought on by the beauty of her darling, and the surpassing magnificence of her costume. Blanche was nearly dressed when she arrived, standing like a little princess amongst her many attendants—this one smoothing a fold, that one adjusting a curl, and a third holding the pincushion aloft, having transferred the greater portion of its contents to her own mouth.

Would that we had power to describe the young lady's dress; would that we could delight bright eyes, should bright eyes condescend to glance upon our page, with a critical and correct account of the materials and the fashion that were capable of constituting so attractive a *tout ensemble*—how the gown was brocade, and the train was silk, and the trimmings were gossamer, to the best of our belief!—how pearls were braided in that soft brown hair, and feathers nodded over that graceful little head, though to our mind it would have been even better without these accessories—and how the dear girl looked altogether like a fairy queen, smiling through a wreath of mist, and glittering with the dewdrops of the morning.

"Lor', miss, you do look splendid!" said Gingham, lost in admiration, partly at the richness of the materials, partly at the improvement in her old charge. Blanche was a very pretty girl, certainly, even in a court dress, trying as is that costume to all save the dark, tall beauties, who do indeed look magnificent in trains and feathers; but then the Anglo-Saxon *blonde* has her revenge next morning in her simple *déshabillé* at breakfast—a period at which the black-eyed sultana is apt to betray a slight yellowness of skin, and a drowsy, listless air, not above half awake. Well, they are all very charming in all dresses—it's lucky they are so unconscious of their own attractions.

Blanche was anything but a vain girl; but of course it takes a long time to dress for a Drawing-room, and when mirrors are properly arranged for self-inspection, it requires a good many glances to satisfy ladies as to the correct disposition of "front, flanks, and rear"; so several minutes elapse ere Gingham can be favoured with a private interview, and she passes that period in admiring her young lady, and scanning, with a criticism that borders on disapprobation, the ministering efforts of Rosine, the French maid.

A few weeks of London dissipation have not yet taken the first fresh bloom off Blanche's young brow; there is not a single line to herald the "battered look" that will, too surely, follow a very few years of late hours, and nightly excitement, and disappointments. The girl is all *girl* still— bright, and simple, and lovely. With all our prejudices in her favour, and our awe-struck admiration of her dress, we cannot help thinking she would look yet lovelier in a plain morning gown, with no ornament but a rose or two; and that Mary Delaval's stately beauty and commanding figure would be more in character with those splendid robes of state. But Mary is only a governess, and Blanche is an heiress; so the one remains up-stairs, and the other goes to Court. What else would you have?

It is difficult for an inferior at any time to obtain an interview with a superior, and nowhere more so than in London. Gingham was secure of Blanche's sympathy as of her assistance; but although the latter was forthcoming the very instant there was the slightest hesitation perceived in her answer to the natural question, "How are you getting on?" Gingham was deprived of her share of the former by a thundering double-knock, that shook even the massive house in Grosvenor Square to its foundation, and the announcement that Lady Mount Helicon had arrived, and was even then waiting in the carriage for Miss Kettering.

"Good-bye, good-bye, Gingham," said Blanche, hurrying off in a state of nervous trepidation, she scarcely knew why; "I mustn't keep Lady Mount Helicon waiting, and of course she won't get out in her train—come again soon—good-bye;" and in another moment the steps were up, the door closed with a bang, and Blanche, spread well out so as not to get "creased," by the side of stately Lady Mount Helicon, in a magnificent family coach, rich in state-liveried coachman and Patagonian footmen, to which Cinderella's equipage in the fairy tale was a mere costermonger's cart.

As the stout official on the box hammer-cloth, whose driving, concealed as he is behind an enormous nosegay, is the admiration of all beholders, will take some little time to reach the "string," and when placed in that lingering procession, will move at a snail's pace the whole way to St. James's, we may as well fill up the interval by introducing to the reader a lady with whom Blanche is rapidly becoming intimate, and who takes a warm—shall we say a *maternal?*—interest in the movements of our young heiress.

Lady Mount Helicon, then, is one of those characters which the metropolis of this great and happy country can alone bring to perfection. That she was once a merry, single-hearted child, is more than probable, but so many years have elapsed since that innocent period—so many "seasons," with their ever-recurring duties of card-leaving, dinner-receiving, ball-haunting, and keeping up her acquaintance, have been softening her brain and hardening her heart, that there is little left of the child in her world-worn nature, and not a great deal of the woman, save her attachment to her son. She is as fond of him as it is possible for her to be of anything. She is proud of his talents, his appearance, his acquirements, and in her heart of hearts of his wildness. Altogether, she thinks him a great improvement on the old lord, and would sacrifice anything for him in the world, save her position in society. That position, such as it is, she has all her life been struggling to retain. She would improve it if she could, but she will never get any farther. She belongs to the mass of good society, and receives cards for all the "best places" and most magnificent entertainments; but is as far removed as a curate's wife in Cornwall from the inner circle of those "bright particular stars" with whom she would give her coronet to associate.

Lady Long-Acre *bows* to her, but she never *nods*. Lady Dinadam invites her to the great ball, which that exemplary peeress annually endures with the constancy of a martyr; but as for the little dinners, for which her gastronomic lord is so justly renowned, it is needless to think of them. She might just as well expect to be asked to Wassailworth. And although the Duke is hand-and-glove with her son, she well knows she has as much chance of visiting the Emperor of Morocco. Even tiny Mrs. Dreadnought alternately snubs and patronises her. Why that artificial woman, who has no rank and very little character, should be one of "the great people" is totally inexplicable; however, there she *is*, and Lady Mount Helicon looks up to her accordingly. Well, there are gradations in all ranks, even to the very steps before the throne. In her ladyship's immediate circle are the Ormolus, and the Veneers, and the Blacklambs, with whom she is on terms of the most perfect equality; while below her again are the Duffles, and the Marchpanes, and the Featherheads, and a whole host of inferiors. If Lady Long-Acre is distant with *her*, can she not be condescending in her turn to Lady Tadpole? If Dinadam, who uses somewhat coarse language for a nobleman, says he "can't stand that *something* vulgar woman," cannot Lady

Mount Helicon cut young Deadlock unblushingly in the street, and turn the very coldest part of her broad shoulder on Sir Timothy and Lady Turnstile? "City people, my dear," as she explains for the edification of Blanche, who is somewhat aghast at the uncourteous manœuvre. Has she not a grand object to pursue for eighteen hours out of every twenty-four? Must she not keep alive the recollections of her existence in the memories of some two or three hundred people, who would not care a straw if she were dead and buried before to-morrow morning? Is it not a noble ambition to arrive at terms of apparent intimacy with this shaky grandee, or that superannuated duchess, because they *are* duchesses and grandees? Can horses and carriages be better employed than in carrying cards about for judicious distribution? Is not that a delightful night of which two-thirds are spent blocked up in the "string," and the remainder suffocated on the staircase? In short, can money be better lavished, or time and energy better applied, than in "keeping up one's acquaintance"?

This is the noble aim of "all the world." This it is which brings country families to London when their strawberries are ripe, and their roses in full bloom. The Hall looks beautiful when its old trees are in foliage, and its sunny meadows rippled with the fresh-mown hay. But, dear! who would be out of London in June? except, of course, during Ascot week. No, the gardener and the steward are left to enjoy one of the sweetest places in England, and the family hug themselves in the exchange of their roomy chambers, and old oak wainscoting, and fresh country air, for a small, close, ill-constructed house, redolent of those mysterious perfumes which are attributed to drains, and grimy with many a year's accumulation of soot and other impurities, but happy, thrice happy in its *situation*—not a quarter of a mile from St. James's Street, and within a stone's throw of Berkeley Square! Year after year the exodus goes on. Year after year has the squire sworn stoutly that he will enjoy *this* summer at home, and perjured himself, as a man invariably does when he attests by oath an opinion in defiance of his wife. While there are daughters to marry off, and sons to get commissions for, we can account in a measure for the migratory movement, though based, we conceive, on fallacious principles. But when John has got his appointment, through the *county* member after all, and Lucy has married the young rector of the adjoining parish, who fell in love with her at the *county* archery meeting, why the two poor old folks should make their annual struggle, and endure discomfort, is only to be explained by the tenacity with which English people cling to their national superstitions and their national absurdities.

Even little Blanche, living in one of the best houses in Grosvenor Square, and going to Court under a peeress's "wing," sighed while she thought of

Newton-Hollows and its shrubberies, and her garden just blooming into summer luxuriance. As they toiled slowly down St. James's Street, envying the privileged grandees with the *entrée* through St. James's Park, our pretty heiress would fain have been back in her garden-bonnet, tying up her roses, and watching her carnations, and idling about in the deep shades of her leafy paradise. Not so the chaperon. She was full of the important occasion. It was her pleasure to *present* Miss Kettering, and her business to arrange how that maidenly patronymic should be merged in the title of Mount Helicon: for this she was herself prepared to lapse into a *dowager*. Who but a mother would be capable of such a sacrifice? Yet it must be; none knew better than her ladyship—excepting, perhaps, the late lord's man of business, and certain citizens of the Hebrew persuasion, collectors of noblemen's and gentlemen's autographs—how impossible it was for "Mount" to go on much longer. His book on the Derby was a far deeper affair than his "Broadsides from the Baltic"—where the publisher lost shillings on the latter, the author paid away hundreds on the former—and the literary sportsman confessed, with his usual devil-may-care candour, that "between black-legs and blue-stockings he was pretty nearly told-out!"—therefore must an heiress be supplied from *the canaille* to prop the noble house of Mount Helicon—therefore have the Mount Helicon arms, and the Mount Helicon liveries, and the Mount Helicon carriage, been seen day after day waiting in Grosvenor Square—therefore does their diplomatic proprietress speak in all societies of "*her* charming Miss Kettering," and "*her* sweet Blanche," and therefore are they even now arriving in company at St. James's, followed by the General in his brougham, who has come to pay his respects to his sovereign in *the tightest* uniform that ever threatened an apoplectic warrior with convulsions. "My dear, you look exquisite," says the chaperon, "only mind how you get out, and don't dirty your train, and recollect your feathers; when you curtsey to the Queen, whatever you do, don't let them bob in her Majesty's face." Blanche, albeit somewhat frightened, could not help laughing, and looked so fresh and radiant as she alighted, that the very mob, assembled for purposes of criticism, scarcely forbore from telling her as much to her face. "Don't be nervous, my dear," and "*Pray* don't let us get separated," said the two ladies simultaneously, as they entered the palace; and Blanche felt her knees tremble and her heart beat as she followed her conductress up the stately, well-lined staircase, between rows of magnificent-looking gentlemen-officials, all in full dress. The kettle-drums of the Life Guards booming from without did not serve to reassure her half so much as the jolly faces of the beef-eaters, every one of whom seems to be cut out to exactly the same pattern, and, inexplicable as it may appear, is a living impersonation of Henry VIII.; but she took courage after a time, seeing that nobody was the least frightened except herself, and that young Brosier of the Guards, one of her dancing-partners, and to-day on duty at St. James's, was swaggering about as much at home as if he had been brought up in the palace instead of his father's humble-looking parsonage. Blanche would have liked it better, though, had the staircase and corridor been a little more crowded; as it was, she felt too conspicuous, and fancied people looked at her as if they knew she was clutching those two tickets, with her name and her chaperon's legibly inscribed thereon, for the information of an exalted office-bearer, because this was her first appearance at Court, and she was going *to be presented.* Innocent Blanche! The gentlemen in uniform are busy with their collars (the collar of a uniform is positive strangulation for everything but a *bonâ fide* soldier), whilst those in civil vestures are absorbed in the contemplation of their own legs, which, in the unusual attire of silk stockings and "shorts," look worse to the owner than to any one else, and that is saying a good deal. The General is close behind his niece, and struts with an ardour which yesterday's levee in that same tight coat has been unable to cool. The plot thickens, and they add their tickets to a table already covered by cards inscribed with the names of England's noblest and fairest, for the information of the grand vizier, and—shall we confess it?—the gentlemen of the press! Lady Mount Helicon bows right and left with stately courtesy: Blanche seizes a moment to arrange her train and a stray curl unobserved; and the General, between gold lace and excitement, breaks out into an obvious perspiration. Blanche's partners gather round her as they would at a ball, though she scarcely recognises some in their military disguises. And those who have not been introduced whisper to each other, "*That's* Miss Kettering," and depreciate her, and call her "very pretty *for an heiress.*" Captain Lacquers is magnificent; he has exchanged into the "Loyal Hussars," chiefly on account of the uniform, and thinks that in "hessians" and a "pelisse" he ought not to *be bought* under half-a-million. He breakfasted with "Uppy" this morning, and rallied that suitor playfully on his advantage in attending the Drawing-room, whereas Sir Ascot was to be on duty, and is even now lost in jack-boots and a helmet, on a pawing black charger, outside. D'Orville is there too, with his stately figure and grave, handsome face. His hussar uniform sits none the worse for those two medals on his breast; and his beauty is none the less commanding for a tinge of brown caught from an Indian sun. He is listening to the General, and bending his winning eyes on Blanche. The girl thinks he is certainly the *nicest* person *here.* By a singular association of ideas, the whole thing reminds the General of the cavalry action at Gorewallah, and his energetic reminiscences of that brilliant affair are by no means lost on the bystanders.

"Blanche, my dear, there's Sir Roger Rearsby—most distinguished officer. What?—I was his brigade-major at Chutney, and we—D'Orville, *you* know that man—how d'ye mean?—why, it's Colonel Chuffins. I pulled him from under his horse in the famous charge of the Kedjerees, and stood across him for two hours—*two hours,* by the god of war!—till I'd rallied the Kedjerees, and we swept everything before us. I suppose you'll allow Gorewallah was the best thing of the war. Zounds! I don't believe the Sepoys have done talking of it yet! Look ye here: Marsh Mofussil occupied the heights, and Bahawdar Bang was detached to make a demonstration in our rear. Well, sir——"

At this critical juncture, and ere the General had time to explain the strategy by which Bahawdar Bang's manœuvre was defeated, he and his party had been swept onward with the tide to where a doorway stemmed the crowd into a mass of struggling confusion. Lappets and feathers waved to and fro like a grove of poplars in a breeze; fans were broken, and soft cheeks scratched against epaulettes and such accoutrements of war; here and there a pair of moustaches towered above the surface, like the yards of some tall bark in a storm; whilst ever and anon a heavy dowager, like some plunging seventy-four that answers not her helm, came surging through the mass with the sheer force of that specific gravity which is not to be denied. As the state-rooms are reached, the crowd becomes more dense and the heat insufferable. A red cord, stretched tightly the whole length of the room, offers an insuperable barrier to the impetuous, and compels the panting company to defile in due order of precedence—"first come first served" being here, as elsewhere, the prevailing maxim. And now, people being obliged to stand still, make the best of it, and begin to talk, their remarks being as original and interesting as those of a well-dressed crowd usually are. "Wawt a crush—aw"—says Captain Lacquers, skilfully warding off from Blanche the whole person of a stout naval officer, and sighing to think of the tarnish his beloved hessians have sustained by being trodden on— "there's Lady Crane and the Miss Cranes—that's Rebecca, the youngest, she's going to be presented, poor girl!—aw—she's painfully ugly, Miss Kettering—aw—makes me ill to look at her." Poor Rebecca! she's not pretty, at least in a court dress, and is dreadfully frightened besides. She knows the rich Miss Kettering by sight, and admires her honestly, and envies her too, and would give anything to change places with her now, for she has a slight *tendresse* for good-looking, unmeaning Lacquers. Take comfort, Rebecca, you will hardly condescend to speak to him, when you go through the same dread ordeal next year, in this very place, as Marchioness Ermindale. The Marquis is looking out for a young wife, and has seen you already, walking early, in shabby gloves, with your governess, and has made up his mind, and will marry you out of hand before the end of the season. So you will be the richest peeress in England, and have a good-looking, good-humoured, honest-hearted husband, very little over forty; and you will do pretty much what you like, and never go with your back to the horses any more; only you don't know it, nor has it anything to do with our story, except to prove that the lottery is not, invariably, "all blanks and no prizes"—that a quiet, unassuming, lady-like girl has fully as good a chance of winning the game as any of your fashionable beauties—your dashing young ladies, with their pictures in print-books, and their names in the clubs, and their engagements a dozen deep, and their heart-broken lovers in scores—men who can well afford to be *lovers*, seeing that their resources will not admit of their becoming husbands. Such a suitor is Captain Lacquers to the generality of his lady-loves, though he means honestly enough as regards Blanche, and would like to marry her and her Three per Cents, to-morrow. Misguided dandy! what chance has he against such a rival as D'Orville? Even if there were no Frank Hardingstone, and Cousin Charlie were never to come back, he is but on a par with Sir Ascot, Lord Mount Helicon, and a hundred others— there is not a toss of a halfpenny for choice between them. Nevertheless, he has great confidence in his own fascinations, and not being troubled with diffidence, is only waiting for an opportunity to lay himself, his uniform, and his debts at the heiress's feet.

The Major, meanwhile, whom Lady Mount Helicon thinks "charming," and of whom she is persuaded *she* has made a conquest, pioneers a way for Blanche and her chaperon through the glittering throng. "It *is* very formidable, Miss Kettering," says he, pitying the obvious nervousness of the young girl, "but it's soon over, like a visit to the dentist. You know what to do, and the Queen is so kind and so gracious, it's not half so alarming when you are really before her; now, go on; that's the grand vizier; keep close to Lady Mount Helicon; and mind, don't turn your back to any of the royalties. I shall be in the gallery to get your carriage after it's over. I shall be so anxious to know how you get through it."

"Thank you, Major D'Orville," replied poor Blanche, with an upward glance of gratitude that made her violet eyes look deeper and lovelier than ever; and she sailed on, with a very respectable assumption of fortitude, but inwardly wishing that she could sink into the earth, or, at least, remain with kind, protecting Major D'Orville and Uncle Baldwin, and those gentlemen whose duty did not bring them into the immediate presence of their sovereign.

These worthies, having nothing better to do, began to beguile the time by admiring each other's uniforms, criticising the appearance of the company, and such vague impertinences as go by the name of general conversation. Lacquers, who had just caught the turn of his hessians at a favourable point of view, was more than usually communicative. "Heard of Bolter?" says he, addressing the public in general, and amongst others a first cousin of that injured man. "Taken his wife back again—aw—soft, I should say—fact is, she and Fopples couldn't get on; Frank kicked at the poodle directly he got to the railway station; he swore he would only take the parrot, and they quarrelled there. I don't believe they went abroad at all, at least not together. Seen the poodle? Nice dog; they've got him in Green Street; very like Frank; believe he was jealous of him!" A general laugh greeted the hussar's witticism, and the cousin being, as usual, not on the best of terms with his relation, enjoyed the joke more than any one else. Major D'Orville alone has neither listened to the story nor caught the point. Blanche's pleading, grateful eyes haunt him still. He feels that the more he likes her, the less he would wish to marry her. "She is worthy of a better fate," he thinks, "than to be linked to a broken-down *roué*." And as is often the case, the charm of beauty in another brings forcibly to his mind the only face he ever really loved; and the Major sighs as he wishes he could begin life again, on totally different principles from those he has all along adopted. Well, it is too late now. The game must be played out, and he proceeds to cement his alliance with the General by asking him to lunch with him at his club "after this thing's over."

"We'll all go together," exclaimed Lacquers, who had been meditating the very same move against his prospective uncle-in-law, only he couldn't hit the right pronunciation of a *déjeuner à la fourchette*, the term in which he was anxious to couch his invitation.

"Not a member, sir," says the General, with a well-pleased smile at the invitation; "cross-questioned by the waiter, kicked out by the committee—what?—only belong to 'The Chelsea and Noodles'—don't approve of clubs in the abstract—all very well whilst one's a bachelor—eh? D—d selfish and all that—wife moping in a two-storied house at Bayswater—husband swaggering in a Louis Quatorze drawing-room in Pall Mall. Can't dine at home to-day, my love; where's the latch-key? Promised to have a mutton-chop at the club with an old brother-officer. Wife dines on chicken broth with her children, and has a poached egg at her tea. Husband begins with oysters and ends with a pint of claret, by himself too—we all know who the old brother-officer is—lives in the Edgeware Road!—how d'ye mean?" Lacquers goes off with a horse-laugh; he enjoys the joke amazingly; it is just suited to his comprehension. "Then we'll meet in an hour from now," says he, as the crowd, surging in, breaks up their little conclave; "should like to show you our pictures—aw—fond of high art, you know—and our staircase, Arabian, you know, with the ornaments quite Mosaic. *A-diavolo!*" And pleased with what he believes to be his real Spanish farewell, our dandy-linguist elbows his way up to Lady Ormolu, and gladdens that panting peeress with the pearls and rubies of his intellectual conversation.

All this time Blanche is nearing the ordeal. If she thought the crowd too dense before, what would she not give now to bury herself in its sheltering ranks? An ample duchess is before her with a red-haired daughter, but everywhere around her there is room to breathe, and walk, and *to be seen*. Through an open door she catches a glimpse of the Presence and the stately circle before whom she must pass. Good-natured royalties, of both sexes, stand smiling and bowing, and striving to put frightened subjects at their ease, and carrying their kind hearts on their handsome open countenances; but they are all whirling round and round to Blanche, and she cannot tell uniforms from satin gowns, epaulettes from ostrich plumes, old from young. It strikes her that there is something ridiculous in the way that a central figure performs its backward movement, and the horrid conviction comes upon her that she will have to go through the same ceremony before all those royal eyes, and think of her train, her feathers, her curtsey, and her escape, all at one and the same agonising moment. A foreign diplomatist makes a complimentary remark in French, addressed to his neighbour, a tall, soldier-like German with nankeen moustaches. The German unbends for an instant that frigid air of military reserve which has of late years usurped the place of what we used to consider foreign volubility and politeness—he stoops to reply in a whisper, but soon recovers himself, stiffer and straighter than before.

Neither the compliment nor its reception serves to reassure Blanche. In vain she endeavours to peep past the duchess's ample figure, and see how the red-haired daughter pulls through. The duchess rejoices in substantial materials, both of dress and fabric, so Blanche can see nothing. Another moment, and she hears her own name and Lady Mount Helicon's pronounced in a whisper, every syllable of which thrills upon her nerves like a musket-shot. She reaches the door—she catches a glimpse of a tall, handsome young man with a blue ribbon, and a formidable-looking phalanx of princes, princesses, foreign ambassadors, and English courtiers, in a receding circle, of which she feels she is about to become the centre. Blanche would like to cry, but she is in the Presence now, and we follow her no farther. It would not become us to enlarge upon the majesty which commands reverence for the queen, or the beauty which wins homage for the woman; to speak of her as do her servants, her household, her nobility, or all who are personally known to her, would entail such language of devoted affection as in our case might be termed flattery and adulation. To hurrah and throw our hats up for her, with the fervent loyalty of an English mob—to cheer with the whole impulse of every stout English heart, and the energy of good English lungs, is more in accordance with our position and our habits, and so "Hip, hip, hip—God save the Queen."

"Oh, dear! if I'd only known," said Blanche, some two hours afterwards, as Rosine was brushing her hair, and taking out the costly ostrich plumes and the string of pearls, "I needn't have been so frightened after all! So good, so kind, so considerate, I shouldn't the least mind being presented every day!"

CHAPTER XI
CAMPAIGNING ABROAD

In the "good old times" when railways were not, and the *nec plus ultra* of speed was, after all, but ten miles an hour, he who would take in hand to construct a tale, a poem, or a drama, was much hampered by certain material conditions of time and place, termed by critics the unities, and the observance of which effectually prevented all glaring vagaries of plot, and many a *deus ex machinâ* whose unaccountable presence would have saved an infinity of trouble to author as well as reader. But we have changed all this now-a-days. When Puck undertook to girdle the earth in "forty minutes," it was no doubt esteemed a "sporting offer," not that Oberon seems to have been man enough to "book it"; but we, who back Electra, should vote such a forty minutes "dead slow"—"no pace at all!" Ours are the screw-propeller and the flying-express—ours the thrilling wire that rings a bell at Paris, even while we touch the handle in London—ours the greatest possible hurry on the least possible provocation—we ride at speed, we drive at speed—eat, drink, sleep, smoke, talk, and deliberate, still at full speed—make fortunes, and spend them—fall in love, and out of it—are married, divorced, robbed, ruined, and enriched, all *ventre à terre!* nay, time seems to be grudged even for the last journey to our long home. 'Twas but the other day we saw a hearse clattering along at an honest twelve miles an hour! Well, forward! is the word—like the French grenadier's account of the strategy by which his emperor invariably out-manœuvred the enemy. There were but two words of command, said he, ever heard in the grand army—the one was "*En avant! sacr-r-ré ventre-bleu!*" the other, "*Sacr-r-ré ventre-bleu! en avant!*" So forward be it! and we will not apologise for shifting the scene some thousands of miles, and taking a peep at our friend Cousin Charlie, fulfilling his destiny in that heaven-forsaken country called Kaffirland. When it rains in South Africa it rains to some purpose, pelting down even sheets of water, to which a thunderstorm at home is but as the trickling of a gutter to the Falls of Niagara—Nature endues her whole person in that same leaden-coloured garment, and the world assumes a desolate appearance of the most torpid misery. The greasy savage, almost naked, crouching and coiling like a snake wherever covert is to be obtained, bears his ducking philosophically enough;

he can but be wet to the skin at the worst, and is dry again almost before the leaves are; but the British soldier, with his clothing and accoutrements, his pouches, haversacks, biscuits, and ammunition—not to mention Brown Bess, his mainstay and dependence—nothing punishes him so much as wet. Tropical heat he bears without a murmur, and a vertical sun but elicits sundry jocose allusions to beer. Canadian cold is met with a jest biting as its own frost, and a hearty laugh that rings through the clear atmosphere with a twang of home; but he hates water—drench him thoroughly and you put him to the proof; albeit he never fails, yet, like Mark Tapley, he *does* deserve credit for being *jolly* under such adverse circumstances.

Look at that encampment—a detached position, in which two companies of a British regiment, with a handful of Hottentots, are stationed to hold in check some thousands of savages: the old story—outnumbered a hundred to one, and wresting laurels even from such fearful odds. Look at one of the heroes—the only one visible indeed—as he paces to and fro to keep himself warm. A short beat truly, for he is within shot of yonder hill, and the Kaffirs have muskets as well as "assagais." No shelter or sentry-box is there here, and our warrior at twelvepence a day has "reversed arms" to keep his firelock dry, and covers his person as well as he can with a much-patched weather-worn grey great-coat, once spruce and smart, of the regimental pattern, but now scarcely distinguishable as a uniform. To and fro he walks—wet, weary, hungry, and liable to be shot at a moment's notice. He has not slept in a bed for months, and has almost forgotten the taste of pure water, not to mention beer; yet is there a charm in soldiering, and through it all the man is contented and cheerful—even happy. A slight movement in his rear makes him turn half-round; between him and his comrades stands a tent somewhat less uncomfortable-looking than the rest, and from beneath its folds comes out a hand, followed by a young, bronzed face, which we recognise as Cousin Charlie's ere the whole figure emerges from its shelter and gives itself a hearty shake and stretch. It is indeed Charlie, "growed out of knowledge," as Mrs. Gamp says, and with his moustaches visibly and tangibly increased to a very warlike volume. The weather is clearing, as in that country it often does towards sundown; and Charlie, like an old campaigner, is easing the tent-ropes, already strained with wet. "I wish I knew the orders," says the young lancer to some one inside, "or how I'm to get back to head-quarters—not but what you fellows have treated me like an alderman." "You should have been here yesterday, my boy," said a voice from within, apparently between the puffs of a short, wheezing pipe. "We only finished the biscuit this morning, and I could have given you a mouthful of brandy from the bottom of my flask—it is dry enough now, at all events. The baccy 'll soon be done too, and we shall be floored altogether if we stay here much longer." "Why the whole front don't advance I can't think," replied Charlie, with the ready criticism of a young soldier. "If they'd only let us get *at* these black beggars, we'd astonish them!" "Heaven knows," answered the voice, evidently getting drowsy, "our fellows are all tired of waiting——By Jove," he added, brightening up in an instant, "here comes 'Old Swipes'; I'll lay my life we shall be engaged before daybreak, the old boy looks so jolly!"—and even as he spoke, a hale, grey-headed man, with a rosy countenance and a merry, dark eye, was seen returning the sentry's salute as he advanced to the tent which had sheltered these young officers, and passing on with a good-humoured nod to Charlie, entered upon an eager whispered conversation with the gentleman inside, whose drowsiness seemed to have entirely forsaken him. "Old Swipes," as he was irreverently called (a nickname of which, as of most military sobriquets, the origin had long been forgotten), was the senior captain of the regiment, one of those gallant fellows who fight their way up without purchase, serving in every climate under heaven, and invariably becoming grey of head long ere they lose the greenness and freshness of heart which in the Service alone outlive the cares and disappointments that wait on middle age.

Now, Charlie had been sent to "Old Swipes" with dispatches from head-quarters. One of the general's *aides-de-camp* was wounded, another sick, an *extra* already ordered on a *particular service*; and Charlie, with the dash and gallantry which had distinguished him from boyhood, volunteered to carry the important missives nearly a hundred miles through a country not a yard of which he knew, and threading whole hordes of the enemy with no arms but his sabre and pistols, no guide but a little unintelligible Hottentot. From the Kat River frontier to the defenceless portals of Fort Beaufort, the whole district was covered with swarms of predatory savages; and but that Fortune proverbially favours the brave, our young lancer might have found himself in a very unpleasant predicament. Fifty miles finished the lad's charger, and he had accomplished the remainder of his journey walking and riding turn-about with his guide on the hardy little animal of the latter. No wonder our dismounted dragoon was weary—no wonder the rations of tough beef and muddy water which they gave him when he arrived elicited the compliment we have already mentioned to the good cheer of "The Fighting Light-Bobs," as the regiment to which "Old Swipes" and his detachment belonged was affectionately nicknamed in the division. The great thing, however, was accomplished—wet, weary, and exhausted, Charlie and his guide arrived at their destination by daybreak of the second day. The young lancer delivered his dispatches to the officer in command, was received like a brother into a subaltern's tent, already containing two inhabitants, and slept soundly through the day, till awakened at sunset by a strong appetite for supper, and the absolute necessity for slackening the tent-ropes recorded above.

"Kettering, you must join our council of war," said the cheery voice of the old captain from within; "there's no man better entitled than yourself to know the contents of my dispatches. Come in, my boy; I can give you a pipe, if nothing else."

Charlie lifted the wet sailcloth and crept in—the conclave did not look so very uncomfortable after all. Certainly there was but little room, but no men pack so close as soldiers. The old captain was sitting cross-legged on a folded blanket in the centre, clad in a russet-coloured coat that had once been scarlet, with gold lace tarnished down to the splendour of rusty copper. A pair of regimental trousers, plentifully patched and strapped with leather, adorned his lower man, and on his head he wore a once-burnished shako, much gashed and damaged by a Kaffir's assagai. He puffed forth volumes of smoke from a short black pipe, and appeared in the most exuberant spirits, notwithstanding the deficiencies of his exterior; the real proprietor of the tent, a swarthy, handsome fellow, with a lightning eye and huge black beard and whiskers, was leaning against the centre support of his domicile, in a blue frock-coat and buckskin trousers, looking very handsome and very like a gentleman (indeed, he is a peer's younger son), though no "old clothes man" would have given him eighteenpence for the whole of his costume. He had hospitably vacated his seat on a battered portmanteau, "warranted solid leather," with the maker's name, in the Strand—it seemed so odd to see it there—and was likewise smoking furiously, as he listened to the orders of his commander. A small tin basin, a canister of tobacco, nearly finished, a silver hunting-flask—alas! quite empty—and a heap of cloaks, with an old blanket in the corner, completed the furniture of this warlike palace. It was very like Charlie's own tent at head-quarters, save that his cavalry accoutrements gave an air of finish to that dwelling, of which he was justly proud. So he felt quite at home as he took his seat on the portmanteau and filled his pipe. "Just the orders I wanted," said the old captain, between his whiffs; "we've been here long enough, and to-morrow we are to advance at daybreak. I am directed to move upon that 'Kloof' we have reconnoitred every day since we came, and after forming a junction with the Rifles, we are to get possession of the heights."

"The river will be out after this rain," interrupted the handsome lieutenant; "but that's no odds; our fellows can all swim—'gad, they want washing!"

"Steady, my lad," said the veteran, "we'll have none of that; I've got a Fingo at the quarter-guard here that'll take us over dry-shod. I've explained to him what I mean, and if he don't understand it now he will to-morrow morning. A 'Light-Bob' on each side, with his arms sloped, directly the water comes in at the rent in these old boots," holding up at the same time a much-damaged pair of Wellingtons, "down goes the Fingo, poor devil, and out go my skirmishers, till we reach the cattle-ford at Vandryburgh."

"I don't think the beggar *will* throw us over," replied the subaltern. "I suppose I'd better get them under arms before daybreak; the nights are infernally dark, though, in this beastly country, but my fellows all turn out smartest now when they've no light."

"Before daybreak, certainly," replied "Old Swipes"; "no whist *here*, Kettering, to keep us up very late. Well," he added, resuming his directions to his subaltern, "we'll have the detachment under arms by four. Take Sergeant Macintosh and the best of the 'flankers' to form an advanced guard. Bid him make every yard of ground good, particularly where there's *bush*; but on no account to fire unless he's attacked. We'll advance in column of sections—*mind that*—they're handier that way for the ground; and Harry—where's Harry?" "Here, sir!" said a voice, and a pale, sickly-looking boy, apparently about seventeen years of age, emerged from under the cloaks and blankets in the corner, where he had been lying half asleep, and thoroughly exhausted with the hardships of a life which it requires the constitution of manhood to undergo. Poor Harry! with what sickening eagerness his mother, the clergyman's widow, grasps at the daily paper, when the African mail is due. How she shudders to see the great black capitals, with "Important News from the Cape!" What a hero his sisters think Harry! and how mamma alone turns pale at the very name of war, and prays for him night and morning on her knees till the pale face and wasted form of her darling stand betwixt her and her Maker. And Harry, too, thinks sometimes of his mother; but oh! how different is the child's divided affection from the all-engrossing tenderness of the mother's love! The boy is fond of "soldiering," and his heart swells as "Old Swipes" gives him his orders in a paternal tone of kindness. "Harry, I shall entrust you with the rear-guard, and you must keep up your communications with the sergeant's guard I shall leave here. He will probably be relieved by the Rifles, and you can then join us in the front. If they don't show before twelve o'clock, fall back here; pack up the baggage, right-about-face, and join 'the levies,' they're exactly five miles in our rear; if you're in difficulties, ask Sergeant File what is best to be done, only don't club 'em, my boy, as you did at Limerick."

"Well, sir," said the handsome lieutenant, "we've all got our orders now, except Kettering; what are we to do with him?"

"Give him some supper first," replied the jolly commandant; "but how to get him back I don't know; we've had a fine stud of oxen for the last ten days, but as for a horse, I have not seen one since I left Cape Town."

"We're doing nothing at head-quarters, sir," exclaimed Charlie, with flashing eyes; "will you allow me to join the attack to-morrow, with your people?"

The three officers looked at him approvingly, and the ensign muttered, "By gad, he's a trump, and no mistake!" but "Old Swipes" shook his grey head with a half-melancholy smile as he scanned the boy's handsome face and shapely figure, set off by his blue lancer uniform, muddy and travel-stained as it was. "I've seen many a fine fellow go down," thought the veteran, "and I like it less and less—this lad's too good for the Kaffirs; d—n me, I shall never get used to it;" however, he did not quite know how to refuse so soldier-like a request, so he only coughed, and said, "Well—I don't approve of *volunteering*—we old soldiers go where we're ordered, but we *never volunteer*. Still, I suppose you won't stay here, with fighting in the front. 'Gad, you *shall* go—you're a *real* good one, and I *like* you for it." So the fine old fellow seized Charlie's hand and wrung it hard, with the tears in his eyes.

And now our three friends prepared to make themselves comfortable. The old captain's tent was the largest, but it was not water-tight, and consequently stood in a swamp. His supper, therefore, was added to the joint stock, and the four gentlemen who, at the best club in London, would have turned up their noses at turtle because it was *thick*, or champagne because it was sweet, sat down quite contentedly to half-raw lumps of stringy beef and a tin mug only half filled with the muddiest of water, glad to get even that.

How they laughed and chatted and joked about their fare! To have heard them talk one would have supposed that they were at dinner within a day's march of Pall Mall, London—the opera, the turf, the ring, each and all had their turn; and when the sergeant on duty came to report the "lights out," said lights consisting of two lanterns for the whole detachment, Charlie had just proposed "fox-hunting" as a toast with which to finish the last sip of brandy, and treated his entertainers to a "view-holloa" *in a whisper*, that he might not alarm the camp, which, save for the lowing of certain oxen in the rear, was ere long hushed in the most profound repose.

Now, these oxen were a constant source of confusion and annoyance to the "old captain" and his myrmidons, whose orderly, soldier-like habits were continually broken through by their perverse charge. Of all the contradictory, self-willed, hair-brained brutes on the face of the earth, commend us to an ox in Kaffirland. He is troublesome enough when first driven off by his black despoilers, but when recaptured by British troops he is worse than ever, as though he brought back with him, from his sojourn in the bush, some of the devilry of his temporary owners, and was determined to resent upon his preservers all the injuries he had undergone during his unwilling peregrinations. Fortunately, those now remaining with the detachment were but a small number, destined to become most execrable beef, large herds retaken from the savages having already been sent to the rear; but even this handful were perpetually running riot, breaking out of their "kraal" on the most causeless and imaginary alarms when in the camp, and on the march making a point of "knocking up" invariably at the most critical moment. Imagine the difficulties of a commander when, in addition to ground of which he knows comparatively nothing, of an enemy outnumbering him hundreds to one, lurking besides in an impenetrable bush, where he can neither be reached nor seen—of an extended line of operation in a country where the roads are either impassable or there are none at all—and, above all, of a trying climate, with a sad deficiency of water—he has to weaken his already small force by furnishing a cattle-guard, and to prepare himself for the contingency of some thousands of frantic animals breaking loose (which they assuredly will should his position be forced), and the inevitable confusion which must be the result of such an untoward liberation. The Kaffirs have a knack of driving these refractory brutes in a manner which seems unattainable to a white man. It is an interesting sight to watch a couple of tall, dark savages, almost naked, and with long staves in their hands, manœuvring several hundred head of cattle with apparently but little trouble. Even the Hottentots seem to have a certain mysterious influence over the horned troop; but for an English soldier, although goaded by his bayonet, they appear to entertain the most profound contempt.

Charlie, however, cared little for ox or Kaffir; the lowing of the one no more disturbed him than the proximity of the other. Was he not at last in front of the enemy? Should he not to-morrow begin his career of glory? The boy felt his very life-blood thrill in his veins as the fighting propensity—the spirit of Cain, never quite dormant within us—rose to his heart. There he lay in a corner of the dark tent, dressed and ready for the morrow, with his sword and pistols at his head, covered with a blanket and a large cloak, his whereabout only discernible by the red glow from his last pipe before going to sleep; the handsome lieutenant was already wrapped in slumber and an enormous rough great-coat (not strictly regulation); the ensign was far away in dreamland; and Charlie had watched the light die out from their respective pipes with drowsy eyes, while the regular step of the sentry outside smote less and less distinctly on his ear. He had gone through two very severe days, and had not been in a bed for weeks. Gradually his limbs relaxed and tingled with delightful languor of rest after *real* fatigue. Once or twice he woke up with a start as Fancy played her usual tricks with the weary, then his head declined, his jaw dropped, the pipe fell to the ground, and Charlie was fast asleep.

Far, far away on a mountain in Inverness the wild stag is *belling* to the distant corries, and snuffing the keen north air as he stamps ever and anon with lightning hoof that cuts the heather tendrils asunder and flings them on the breeze. Is he not the great master-hart of the parcel? and shall he not be circumvented and stretched on the moor ere the fading twilight darkens into night? Verily, he must be stalked warily, cautiously, for the wind has shifted and the lake is already ruffling into pointed, white-crested waves, rising as in anger, while their spray, hurried before the tempest, drifts in long-continuous wreaths athwart the surface. Fitful gusts, the pent-up sobs of rising fury, that must burst or be released, chase the filmy scud across that pale moon, which is but veiled and not obscured; while among the ferns and alders that skirt the water's edge the wind moans and shrieks like an imprisoned demon wailing for his freedom. Mists are rising around the hazy forms of the deer; cold, chilling vapours through which the mighty stag looms like some gigantic phantom, and still he swells in defiance, and *bells* abroad his trumpet-note of war. Charlie's finger is on the trigger; Uncle Baldwin, disguised as a Highlander, whispers in his ear the thrilling caution, "Take time!" The wind howls hideously, and phantom shapes, floating in the moonlight, mock and gibber and toss their long, lean arms, and wave their silver hair. No, the rifle is *not* cocked; that stubborn lock defies the force of human fingers—the mist is thickening and the stag moves. Charlie implores Uncle Baldwin to assist him, and drops upon his knees to cover the retiring quarry with his useless weapon. The phantoms gather round; their mist-wreaths turn to muslin dresses, and their silver hair to glossy locks of mortal hues. The roaring tempest softens to an old familiar strain. Mary Delaval is before him. Her pale, sweet face is bent upon the kneeling boy with looks of unutterable love, and her white hand passes over his brow with an almost imperceptible caress. Her face sinks gradually to his—her breath is on his temples—his lips cling to hers—and he starts with horror at the kiss of love, striking cold and clammy from a grinning skull! Horror! the rifleman, whose skeleton he shuddered to find beneath his horse's feet not eight-and-forty hours ago! What does he here in the drawing-room at home? *Home*—yes, he is at home, at last. It must have been fancy—the recollections of his African campaign! They are all gone to bed. He hears the General's well-known tramp dying away along the passage; and he takes his candle to cross the spacious hall, dark and gloomy in that flickering light. Ha! seated on the stairs as on a throne frowns a presence that he dare not pass. A tall, dark figure, in the shape of a man, yet with angel beauty—no angel form of good—glorious in the grandeur of despair—magnificent in the pomp and glare of hell—those lineaments awful in their very beauty—those deep, unfathomable eyes, with their eternity of suffering, defiance, remorse, all but repentance or submission! Could mortal look and not quail? Could man front and not be blasted at the sight? On his lofty forehead sits a diadem, and on the centre of his brow, burned in and scorched, as it were, to the very bone, behold the seal of the Destroyer—the single imprint of a finger.

The boy stands paralysed with affright. The Principle of Evil waves him on and on, even to the very hem of his garment; but a prayer rises to the sleeper's lips; with a convulsive effort he speaks it forth aloud, and the spell is broken. The mortal is engaged with a mortal enemy. Those waving robes turn to a leopard-skin *kaross*, the glorious figure to an athletic savage, and the immortal beauty to the grinning, chattering lineaments of a hideous Kaffir. Charlie bounds at him like a tiger—they fight—they close—and he is locked in the desperate embrace of life or death with his ghastly foe. Charlie is undermost! His enemy's eyes are starting from their sockets—his white teeth glare with cannibal-like ferocity—and his hand is on the boy's throat with a grip of iron. One fearful wrench to get free—one last superhuman effort of despair, and.... Charlie wakes in the struggle!—wakes to find it all a dream; and the cold air, the chilling harbinger of dawn, stealing into the tent to refresh and invigorate the half-suffocated sleepers. He felt little inclination to resume his slumbers; his position had been a sufficiently uncomfortable one—his head having slipped from the pistol-holsters on which it had rested, and the clasp of his cloak-fastening at the throat having well-nigh strangled him in his sleep. The handsome lieutenant's matter-of-fact yawn on waking would have dispelled more horrid dreams than Charlie's, and the real business of the coming day soon chased from his mind all recollections of his imaginary struggle. Breakfast was like the supper of the preceding night—half-raw beef, eaten cold, and a whiff from a short pipe. Ere Charlie had finished his ration, dark though it was, the men had fallen in; the advanced guard had started; Ensign Harry had received his final instructions, and "Old Swipes" gave the word of command in a low, guarded tone—"Slope arms! By your left—Quick march!"

Day dawned on a spirit-stirring scene. With the swinging, easy step of those accustomed to long and toilsome marches the detachment moved rapidly forward, now lessening its front as it arrived at some narrow defile, now "marking time" to allow of its rear coming up, without effort, into the proper place. Bronzed, bold faces theirs, with the bluff, good-humoured air of the English soldier, who takes warfare as it comes, with an oath and a jest. Reckless of strategy as of hardship, he neither knows nor cares what his enemy may be about, nor what dispositions may be made by his own officers. If his flank be turned he fights on with equal unconcern, "it is no business of his"; if his ammunition be exhausted he betakes himself to the bayonet, and swears "the beggars may take their change out of that!"

The advanced guard, led by the handsome subaltern, was several hundred paces in front. The Hottentots brought up the rear, and the "Fighting Light-Bobs," commanded by their grey-headed captain, formed the column. With them marched Charlie, conspicuous in his blue lancer uniform, now respectfully addressing his superior officer, now jesting good-humouredly with his temporary comrades. The sun rose on a jovial, light-hearted company; when next his beams shall gild the same arid plains, the same twining *mimosas*, the same glorious landscape, shut in by the jagged peaks of the Anatola mountains, they will glance back from many a firelock lying ownerless on the sand; they will deepen the clammy hue of death on many a bold forehead; they will fail to warm many a gallant heart, cold and motionless for ever. But the men go on all the same, laughing and jesting merrily, as they "march at ease," and beguile the way with mirth and song.

"We'll get a sup o' brandy to-night, anyhow, won't us, Bill?" says a weather-beaten "Light-Bob" to his front-rank man, a thirsty old soldier as was ever "confined to barracks."

"Ay," replies Bill, "them black beggars has got plenty of lush—more's the pity; and they doesn't give none to their wives—more's their sense. Ax your pardon, sir," he adds, turning to Charlie, "but we shall advance right upon their centre, now, anyways, shan't us?"

Ere Charlie could reply he was interrupted by Bill's comrade, who seemed to have rather a *penchant* for Kaffir ladies. "Likely young women they be, too, Bill, those niggers' wives; why, every Kaffir has a dozen at least, and we've only three to a company; wouldn't I like to be a Kaffir?"

"*Black!*" replied Bill, in a tone of intense disgust.

"What's the odds?" urged the matrimonial champion, "a black wife's a sight better than none at all;" and straightway he began to hum a military ditty, of which fate only permitted him to complete the first two stanzas:—

> "They're sounding the charge for a brush, my boys!
> And we'll carry their camp with a rush, my boys!
> When we've driven them out, I make no doubt
> We'll find they've got plenty of lush, my boys!

For the beggars delight

To sit soaking all night,

Black although they be.

And when we get liquor so cheap, my boys!

We'll do nothing but guzzle and sleep, my boys!

And sit on the grass with a Kaffir lass,

Though smutty the wench as a sweep, my boys!

For the Light Brigade

Are the lads for a maid,

Black although she may be."

"Come, stow that!" interrupted Bill, as the *ping* of a ball whistled over their heads, followed by the sharp report of a musket; "here's music for your singing, and dancing too, faith," he added, as the rear files of the advanced guard came running in; and "Old Swipes" exclaimed, "By Jove! they're engaged. Attention! steady, men!—close up—close up"—and, throwing out a handful of skirmishers to clear the bush immediately in his front and support his advanced guard, he moved the column forward at "the double," gained some rising ground, behind which he halted them, and himself ran on to reconnoitre. A sharp fire had by this time commenced on the right, and Charlie's heart beat painfully whilst he remained inactive, covered by a position from which he could see nothing. It was not, however, for long. The "Light-Bobs" were speedily ordered to advance, and as they gained the crest of the hill a magnificent view of the conflict opened at once upon their eyes.

The Rifles had been beforehand with them, and were already engaged; their dark forms, hurrying to and fro as they ran from covert to covert, were only to be distinguished from the savages by the rapidity with which their thin white lines of smoke emerged from bush and brake, and the regularity with which they forced position after position, compared with the tumultuous gestures and desultory movements of the enemy. Already the Kaffirs were forced across the ford of which we have spoken, and, though they mustered in great numbers on the opposite bank, swarming like bees along the rising ground, they appeared to waver in their manœuvres, and to be inclined to retire. A mounted officer gallops up, and says a few words to the grey-headed captain. The "Light-Bobs" are formed into column of sections, and plunge gallantly into the ford. Charlie's right-hand man falls pierced by an assagai, and as his head declines beneath the bubbling water, and his blood mingles with the stream, our volunteer feels "the devil" rising rapidly to his heart. Charlie's teeth are set tight, though he is scarce aware of his own sensations, and the boy is dangerous, with his pale face and flashing eyes.

The "Light-Bobs" deploy into line on the opposite bank, covered by an effective fire from the Rifles, and advance as if they were on parade. "Old Swipes" feels his heart leap for joy. On they march like one man, and the dark masses of the enemy fly before them. "Well done, my lads!" says the old captain, as, from their flank, he marks the regularity of their movement. They are his very children now, and he is not thinking of the little blue-eyed girl far away at home. A belt of *mimosas* is in their front, and it must be carried with the bayonet! The "Light-Bobs" charge with a wild hurrah; and a withering volley, very creditable to the savages, well-nigh staggers them as they approach. "Old Swipes" runs forward, waving them on, his shako off, and his grey locks streaming in the breeze—down he goes! with a musket-ball crashing through his forehead. Charlie could yell with rage, and a fierce longing for blood. There is a calm, matronly woman tending flowers, some thousand miles off, in a small garden in the north of England, and a little girl sitting wistfully at her lessons by her mother's side. They are a widow and an orphan—but the handsome lieutenant will get his promotion without purchase; death-vacancies invariably go in the regiment, and even now he takes the command.

"Kettering," says he, cool and composed, as if he were but giving orders at a common field-day, "take a sub-division and clear that ravine; when you are once across you can turn his flank. Forward, my lads! and if they've any nonsense *give 'em the bayonet!*"

Charlie now finds himself actually in command—ay, and in something more than a skirmish—something that begins to look uncommonly like a general action. Waving the men on with his sword he dashes into the ravine, and in another instant is hand-to-hand with the enemy. What a moment of noise, smoke, and confusion it is! Crashing blows, fearful oaths, the Kaffir war-cry, and the soldiers' death-groan mingle in the very discord of hell. A wounded Kaffir seizes Charlie by the legs, and a "Light-Bob" runs the savage through the body, the ghastly weapon flashing out between the Kaffir's ribs.

"You've got it *now*, you black beggar!" says the soldier, as he coolly wipes his dripping bayonet on a tuft of burnt-up grass. While yet he speaks he is writhing in his death-pang, his jaws transfixed by a quivering assagai. A Kaffir chief, of athletic frame and sinewy proportions, distinguished by the grotesque character of his arms and his tiger-skin *kaross*, springs at the young lancer like a wild-cat. The boy's sword gleams through that dusky body even in mid-air.

"Well done, blue 'un!" shout the men, and again there is a wild hurrah! The young one never felt like this before.

Hand-to-hand the savages have been beaten from their defences, and they are in full retreat. One little band has forced the ravine, and gained the opposite bank. With a thrilling cheer they scale its rugged surface, Charlie waving his sword and leading them gallantly on. The old privates swear he is a good 'un. "Forward, lads! Hurrah! for *blue 'un!*"

The boy has all but reached the brink; his hand is stretched to grasp a bush that overhangs the steep, but his step totters, his limbs collapse — down, down he goes, rolling over and over amongst the brushwood, and the blue lancer uniform lies a tumbled heap at the bottom of the ravine, whilst the cheer of the pursuing "Light-Bobs" dies fainter and fainter on the sultry air as the chase rolls farther and farther into the desert fastnesses of Kaffirland.

CHAPTER XII
CAMPAIGNING AT HOME

In a neat, well-appointed barouche, with clever, high-stepping brown horses and everything complete, a party of three well-dressed persons are gliding easily out of town, sniffing by anticipation the breezes of the country, and greeting every morsel of verdure with a rapture only known to those who have been for several weeks in London. Past the barracks at Knightsbridge, where the windows are occupied by a race of giants in moustaches and shirt-sleeves, and the officers in front of their quarters are educating a poodle; past the gate at Kensington, with its smartest of light-dragoon sentries, and the gardens with their fine old trees disguised in soot; past dead walls overtopped with waving branches; on through a continuous line of streets that will apparently reach to Bath; past public-houses innumerable, and grocery-shops without end; past Hammersmith, with its multiplicity of academies, and Turnham Green, and Chiswick, and suburban terraces with almost fabulous names, and detached houses with the scaffolding still up; past market-gardens and rosaries, till Brentford is reached, where the disappointed traveller, pining for the country, almost deems himself transported back again east of Temple Bar. But Brentford is soon left behind, and a glimpse of the "silver Thames" rejoices eyes that have been aching for something farther afield than the Serpentine, and prepares them for the unbounded views and free, fresh landscape afforded by Hounslow Heath. "This is really the country," says Blanche, inhaling the pure air with a sigh of positive delight, while the General exclaims, at the same instant, with his accustomed vigour, "Zounds! the blockhead's missed the turn to the barracks, after all."

The ladies are very smart; and even Mary Delaval (the third occupant of the carriage), albeit quieter and more dignified than ever, has dressed in gaudier plumage than is her wont, as is the practice of her sex when they are about to attend what they are pleased to term "a breakfast." As for Blanche, she is too charming—such a little, gossamer bonnet stuck at the very back of that glossy little head, so that the beholder knows not whether to be most fascinated by the ethereal beauty of the fabric, or wonder-struck at the dexterity with which it is kept on. Then the dresses of the pair are like the hues of the morning, though of their texture, as of their "trimmings," it becomes us not to hazard an opinion. Talk of beauty unadorned, and all that! Take the handsomest figure that ever inspired a statuary—dress her, or rather undress her to the costume of the Three Graces, or the Nine Muses, or any of those *dowdies* immortalised by ancient art, and place her alongside of a moderately good-looking Frenchwoman, with dark eyes and small feet, who has been permitted to dress *herself*: why, the one is a mere corporeal mass of shapely humanity, the other a sparkling emanation of light and smiles and "tulle" (or whatever they call it) and coquetry and all that is most irresistible. Blanche and Mary, with the assistance of good taste and good milliners, were almost perfect types of their different styles of feminine beauty. The General, too, was wondrously attired. Retaining the predilections of his youth, he shone in a variety of under-waistcoats, each more gorgeous than its predecessor, surmounting the whole by a blue coat of unexampled brilliancy and peculiar construction. Like most men who are not in the habit of "getting themselves up" every day, he was always irritable when thus clothed in "his best," and was now peculiarly fidgety as to the right turn by which his carriage should reach the barracks where the "Loyal Hussars," under the temporary command of Major D'Orville, were about to give a breakfast of unspeakable splendour and hospitality.

"That way—no—the other way, you blockhead!—straight on, and short to the right!" vociferated the General to his bewildered coachman, as they drew up at the barrack-gate; and Blanche timidly suggested they should ask "that officer," alluding to a dashing, handsome individual guarding the entrance from behind an enormous pair of dark moustaches.

"That's only the sentry, Blanche," remarked Mary Delaval, whose early military experience made her more at home here than her companion.

"Dear," replied Blanche, colouring a little at her mistake, "I thought he was a captain, at least—*he's very good-looking*."

But the barouche rolls on to the mess-room door, and although the ladies are somewhat disappointed to find their entertainers in plain clothes (a woman's idea of a hussar being that he should live and die *en grande tenue*), yet the said plain clothes are so well put on, and the moustaches and whiskers so carefully arranged, and the fair ones themselves received with such *empressement*, as to make full amends for any deficiency of warlike costume. Besides, the surrounding atmosphere is so thoroughly military. A rough-rider is bringing a young horse from the school; a trumpet is sounding in the barrack-yard; troopers lounging about in picturesque undress are sedulously saluting their officers; all is suggestive of the show and glitter which makes a soldier's life so fascinating to woman.

Major D'Orville is ready to hand them out of the carriage. Lacquers is stationed on the door steps. Captain Clank and Cornet Capon are in attendance to receive their cloaks. Even Sir Ascot Uppercrust, who is here as a guest, lays aside his usual *nonchalance*, and actually "hopes Miss Kettering didn't catch cold yesterday getting home from Chiswick." Clank whispers to Capon that he thinks "Uppy is making strong running"; and Capon strokes his nascent moustaches, and oracularly replies, "The divil doubt him."

No wonder ladies like a military entertainment. It certainly is the fashion among soldiers, as among their seafaring brethren, to profess far greater devotion and exhibit more *empressement* in their manner to the fair sex than is customary in this age with civilians.

The latter, more particularly that maligned class, "the young men of the present day," are not prone to put themselves much out of their way for any one, and treat you, fair daughters of England, with a mixture of patronage and carelessness which is far from complimentary. How different you find it when you visit a barrack or are shown over a man-of-war! Respectful deference waits on your every expression, admiring eyes watch your charming movements, and stalwart arms are proffered to assist your delicate steps. Handsome, sunburnt countenances explain to you how the biscuit is served out; or moustaches of incalculable volume wait your answer as to "what polka you choose their band to perform." You make conquests all around you, and wherever you go your foot is on their necks; but do not for this think that your image never *can* be effaced from these warlike hearts. A good many of them, even the best-looking ones, have got wives and children at home; and the others, unencumbered though they be, save by their debts, are apt to entertain highly anti-matrimonial sentiments, and to frame their conduct on sundry aphorisms of a very faithless tendency, purporting that "blue water is a certain cure for heart-ache"; that judicious hussars are entitled "to love and to ride away"; with other maxims of a like inconstant nature. Nay, in both services there is a favourite air of inspiriting melody, the burden and title of which, monstrous as it may appear, are these unfeeling words, "The girls we leave behind us!" It is *always* played on marching out of a town.

But however ill our "captain bold" of the present day may behave to "the girl he leaves behind him," the lady in his front has small cause to complain of remissness or inattention. The mess-room at Hounslow is fitted up with an especial view to the approbation of the fair sex. The band outside ravishes their ears with its enchanting harmony; the officers and male guests dispose themselves in groups with those whose society they most affect; and Blanche finds herself the centre of attraction to sundry dashing warriors, not one of whom would hesitate for an instant to abandon his visions of military distinction, and link himself, his debts, and his moustaches, to the fortunes of the pretty heiress.

Now, Sir Ascot Uppercrust has resolved this day to do or die—"to be a man or a mouse," as he calls it. Of this young gentleman we have as yet said but little, inasmuch as he is one of that modern school which, abounding in specimens through the higher ranks of society, is best described by a series of negatives. He was *not* good-looking—he was *not* clever—he was *not* well-educated; but, on the other hand, he was not to be intimidated—not to be excited—and *not* to be taken in. Coolness of mind and body were his principal characteristics; no one ever saw "Uppy" in a hurry, or a dilemma, or what is called "taken aback"; he would have gone into the ring and laid the odds to an archbishop without a vestige of astonishment, and with a carelessness of demeanour bordering upon contempt; or he would have addressed the House of Commons, had he thought fit to honour that formidable assemblage by his presence, with an equanimity and *insouciance* but little removed from impertinence. A quaint boy at Eton, *cool hand* at Oxford, a deep card in the regiment, man or woman never yet had the best of "Uppy"; but to-day he felt, for once, nervous and dispirited, and wished "the thing was over," and settled one way or the other. He was an only son, and not used to be contradicted. His mother had confided to him her own opinion of his attractions, and striven hard to persuade her darling that he had but to see and conquer; nevertheless, the young gentleman was not at all sanguine of success. Accustomed to view things with an impartial and by no means a charitable eye, he formed a dispassionate idea of his own attractions, and extended no more indulgence to himself than to his friends. "Plain, but neat," he soliloquised that very morning, as he thought over his proceedings whilst dressing; "not much of a talker, but a *devil to think*—good position—certain rank—she'll be a *lady*, though rather a *Brummagem* one—house in Lowndes Street—place in the West—family diamonds—and a fairish rent-roll (when the mortgages are paid)—that's what she would get. Now, what should I get? Nice girl—'gad, she *is* a nice girl, with her 'sun-bright hair' as some fellow says—good temper—good action—*and* three hundred thousand pounds. The exchange is *rather* in my favour; but then all girls want to be married, and that squares it, perhaps. If she says 'Yes,' sell out—give up hunting—drive her about in a phaeton, and buy a yacht. If she says 'No,' get *second leave*—go to Melton in November—and hang on with the regiment, which ain't a bad sort of life, after all. So it's hedged both ways. Six to one and half-a-dozen to the other. Very well; to-day we'll settle it."

With these sentiments it is needless to remark that Sir Ascot was none of your sighing, despairing, fire-eating adorers, whose violence frightens a woman into a not unwilling consent; but a cautious, quiet lover, on whom perhaps a civil refusal might be the greatest favour she could confer. Nevertheless, he liked Blanche, too, in his own way.

Well, the band played, and the luncheon was discussed, and the room was cleared for an impromptu dance (meditated for a fortnight); and some waltzed, and some flirted, and some walked about and peeped into the troop-stables and inspected the riding-school, and Blanche found herself, rather to her surprise, walking *tête-à-tête* with Sir Ascot from the latter dusty emporium, lingering a little behind the rest of the party, and separated altogether from the General and Mary Delaval. Sir Ascot having skilfully detached Lacquers, by informing him that he had made a fatal impression on Miss Spanker, who was searching everywhere for the credulous hussar; and having thus possessed himself of Blanche's ear, now stopped dead-short, looked the astonished girl full in the face, and without moving a muscle of his own countenance, carelessly remarked, "Miss Kettering, would you like to marry me?" Blanche thought he was joking, and although it struck her as an ill-timed piece of pleasantry, she strove to keep up the jest, and replied, with a laugh and low curtsey, "Sir Ascot Uppercrust, you do me too much honour."

"No, but will you, Miss Kettering?" said Sir Ascot, getting quite warm (for him). "Plain fellow—do what I can—make you happy—and all that."

"'Sir Ascot Uppercrust, you do me too much honour.'"

Poor Blanche blushed crimson up to her eyes. Good heavens! then the man was in earnest after all! What had she done—she, the pet of "Cousin Charlie," and the *protégée* of Frank Hardingstone—that such a creature as this should presume to ask her such a question? She hesitated—felt very angry—half inclined to laugh and half inclined to cry; and Sir Ascot went on, "Silence gives consent, Miss Kettering—'pon my soul, I'm immensely flattered—can't express what I feel—no poet, and that sort of thing—but I really am—eh!—very—eh!" It was getting too absurd; if she did not take some decisive step, here was a dandy quite prepared to affiance her against her will, and what to say or how to say it, poor little Blanche, who was totally unused to this sort of thing, and tormented, moreover, with an invincible desire to laugh, knew no more than the man in the moon.

"You misunderstand, Sir Ascot," at last she stammered out; "I didn't mean—that is—I meant, or rather I intended—to—to—to—decline—or, I should say—in short, *I couldn't for the world!*" With which unequivocal declaration Blanche blushed once more up to her eyes, and to her inexpressible relief, put her arm within Major D'Orville's, that officer coming up opportunely at that moment; and seeing the girl's obvious confusion and annoyance, extricating her, as he seemed always to do, from her unpleasant dilemma and her matter-of-fact swain.

And this was Blanche's first proposal. Nothing so alarming in it, young ladies, after all. We fear you may be disappointed at the blunt manner in which so momentous a question can be put. Here was no language of flowers—no giving of roses and receiving of carnations—no hoarding of locks of hair, or secreting of bracelets, or kidnapping of gloves—none of the petty larceny of courtship—none of the dubious, half-expressed, sentimental flummery which *may* signify all that mortal heart can bestow, or *may* be the mere coquetry of conventional gallantry. When *he* comes to the point, let us hope his meaning may be equally plain, whether it is couched in a wish that he might "be *always* helping you over stiles," or a request that you will "give him a *right* to walk with you by moonlight without being scolded by mamma," or an inquiry as to whether you "can live in the country, and *only* come to London for three months during the season," or any other roundabout method of asking a straightforward question. Let us hope, moreover, that the applicant may be *the right one*, and that you may experience, to the extent of actual impossibility, the proverbial difficulty of saying—No.

Now, it fell out that Major D'Orville arrived in the nick of time to save Blanche from further embarrassment, in consequence of his inability, in common with the rest of his fellow-creatures, "to know his own mind." The Major had got up the *fête* entirely, as he imagined, with the idea of prosecuting his views against the heiress, and hardly allowed to himself that, in his innermost soul, there lurked a hope that Mrs. Delaval might accompany her former charge, and he might see her *just once more*. Had D'Orville been thoroughly *bad*, he would have been a successful man; as it was, there gleamed ever and anon upon his worldly heart a ray of that higher nature, that nobler instinct, which spoils the villain, while it makes the hero. Mary had pierced the coat-of-mail in which the *roué* was encased; probably her very indifference was her most fatal weapon. D'Orville really loved her—yes, though he despised himself for the weakness (since weakness it is deemed in creeds such as his), though he would grind his teeth and stamp his foot in solitude, while he muttered, "Fool! fool! to bow down before a woman!" yet the spell was on him, and the chain was eating into his heart. In the watches of the night *her image* sank into his brain and tortured him with its calm, indifferent smile. In his dreams *she* bent over him, and her drooping hair swept across his forehead, till the strong man woke, and yearned like a child for a fellow-mortal's love. But not for him the childlike trust that can repose on human affection. Gaston had eaten of the tree of knowledge, the knowledge of good and evil; much did the evil predominate over the good, and still the galling thought goaded him almost to madness. "Suppose I should gain this woman's affections—suppose I should sacrifice my every hope to that sweet face, and find her, after all, like the rest of them! Suppose *I*, too, should weary, as I have wearied before of faces well-nigh as fair—hearts even far more kind—is there no green branch on earth? Am I to wander for ever seeking rest and finding none? Am I to be cursed, like a lost spirit, with longings for that happiness which my very nature will not permit me to enjoy? Oh that I were wholly good, or wholly bad! that I could loathe the false excitement and the dazzling charms of vice, or steep my better feelings in the petrifying waters of perdition! I *will* conquer my weakness. What should I care for this stone-cold governess? I *will* be free, and this Mrs. Delaval shall discover that *I* too can be as careless, and as faithless, and as hard-hearted as—*a woman!*" With which laudable and manly resolution our dashing Major proceeded to make the agreeable to his guests, and to lose no opportunity of exchanging glances and mixing in conversation with the very lady he had sworn so stoutly to avoid. But with all his tactics, all his military proficiency in manœuvring, he found it impossible to detach Mary from her party, or to engage her in a *tête-à-tête* with himself. True-hearted and dignified, with her pure affection fixed upon another, she was not a person to descend to coquetry for the mere pleasure of a conquest, and she clung to the General for the purpose of avoiding the Major, till old Bounce became convinced that she was to add another name to the list of victims who had already succumbed before his many fascinations. The idea had been some time nascent in his mind, and as it now grew and spread, and developed itself into a certainty, his old heart warmed with a thrill he had not felt since the reign of the widow at Cheltenham, and he made the agreeable in his own way by pointing out to Mary all the peculiarities and arrangements of a barrack-yard, interspersed with many abrupt exclamations and voluminous personal anecdotes. Major D'Orville hovered round them the while, and perhaps the very difficulty of addressing his former love enhanced the charm of her presence and the fascination against which he struggled. It is amusing to see a thorough man of the world, one accustomed to conquer and enslave where he is himself indifferent, awkward as the veriest schoolboy, timid and hesitating as a girl, where he is *really* touched—though woman—

> "Born to be controlled,
>
> Stoop to the forward and the bold."

She thereby gauges with a false measure the devotion for which she pines. Would she know her real power, would she learn where she is truly loved, let her take note of the averted eye, the haunting step, ever hovering near, seldom daring to approach, the commonplace remark that shrinks from the one cherished topic, and above all the quivering voice, which, steady and commanding to the world beside, fails only when it speaks to her. Mary Delaval might have noted this had her heart not been in Kaffirland, or had the General allowed her leisure to attend to anything but himself. "Look ye, my dear Mrs. Delaval, our stables in India were ventilated quite differently. Climate? how d'ye mean? climate makes no difference—why, I've had the Kedjerees picketed in thousands round my tent. What? D'Orville, you've been on the Sutlej—'gad, sir, your fellows would have been astonished if I'd dropped among you there."

"And justly so," quietly remarked the Major; "if I remember right, you were in cantonments more than three thousand miles off."

"Well, at any rate, I taught those black fellows how to look after their nags," replied the General. "I left them the best-mounted corps in the Presidency, and six weeks after my back was turned they weren't *worth a row of pins*. Zounds, don't tell me! jobbing—jobbing—nothing but jobbing! What? No *sore backs* whilst I commanded them—at least among *the horses*," added our disciplinarian, reflectively; "can't say as much with regard to the *men*. But there is nothing like a big stick for a nigger—so let's go and see the riding-school."

"I have still got the grey charger, Mrs. Delaval," interposed the Major, wishing old Bounce and his Kedjerees in a hotter climate than India; "poor fellow, he's quite white now, but as great a favourite still as he was in 'the merry days,'" and the Major's voice shook a little. "Would you like to see him?"

Mary understood the allusion, but her calm affirmative was as indifferent as ever, and the trio were proceeding to the Major's stables, that officer going on before to find his groom, when he met Blanche, as we have already said, and divining intuitively what had taken place by her flushed countenance and embarrassed manner, offered his arm to conduct her back to her party, thereby earning her eternal gratitude, no less than that of Sir Ascot, who, as he afterwards confided to an intimate friend, "was *completely in the hole,* and didn't the least know what the devil to do next."

And now D'Orville practically demonstrated the advantage in the game of flirtation possessed by an untouched heart. With the governess he had been diffident, hesitating, almost awkward; with the pupil he was eloquent and winning as usual. His good taste told him it would be absurd to ignore Blanche's obvious trepidation, and his knowledge of the sex taught him that the "soothing system," with a mixture of lover-like respect and paternal kindness, might produce important results. So he begged Blanche to lean on his arm and compose her nerves, and talked kindly to her in his soft, deep voice. "I can see you have been annoyed, Miss Kettering— you know the interest I take in you, and I trust you will not consider me presumptuous in wishing to extricate you from further embarrassment. I am an old fellow now," and the Major smiled his own winning smile, "and therefore a fit chaperon for young ladies. I have nobody to care for" (D'Orville, D'Orville! you would shoot a man who called you a liar), "and I have watched you as if you were a sister or a child of my own. Pray do not tell me more than if I can be of any service to you; and if I can, my dear Miss Kettering, command me to the utmost extent of my powers!" What could Blanche do but thank him warmly? and who shall blame the girl for feeling gratified by the interest of such a man, or for entertaining a vague sort of satisfaction that after all she was neither his sister nor his daughter. Had he been ten years older she would have thrown her arms round his neck, and kissed him in childlike confidence; as it was, she pressed closer to his side, and felt her heart warm to the kind, considerate protector. The Major saw his advantage, and proceeded—"I am alone in the world, you know, and seldom have an opportunity of doing any one a kindness. We soldiers lead a sadly unsatisfactory, desultory sort of life. Till you 'came out' this year, I had no one to care for, no one to interest myself about; but since I have seen you every day, and watched you enjoying yourself, and admired and sought after, I have felt like a different man. I have a great deal to thank you for, Miss Kettering; I was rapidly growing into a selfish, heartless old gentleman, but you have renewed my youthful feelings and freshened up my better nature, till I sometimes think I am almost happy. How can I repay you but by watching over your career, and should you ever require it, placing my whole existence at your disposal? It would break my heart to see you thrown away—no; believe me, Miss Kettering, you have no truer friend than myself, none that admires or loves you better than your old chaperon;" and as the Major spoke he looked so kindly and sincerely into the girl's face, that albeit his language might bear the interpretation of actual love, and was, as Hairblower would have said, "uncommon near the wind," it seemed the most natural thing in the world under the circumstances, and Blanche leaned on his arm, and talked and laughed, and told him to get the carriage, and otherwise ordered him about with a strangely-mixed feeling of childlike confidence and gratified vanity. The party broke up at an early hour, many of them having dinner-engagements in London; and as D'Orville handed Blanche into her carriage, he felt that he had to-day made a prodigious stride towards the great object in view. He had gained the girl's confidence, no injudicious movement towards gaining her heart *and* her fortune. He pressed her hand as she wished him good-bye; and while he did so, shuddered at the consciousness of his meanness. Too well he knew he loved another—a word, a look from Mary Delaval, would have saved him even now; but her farewell was cold and short as common courtesy would admit of, and he ground his teeth as he thought those feet would spurn him, at which he would give his very life to fall. The worst passions of his nature were aroused. He swore, some day, to humble that proud heart in the dust, but the first step at all events must be to win the heiress. This morning he could have given up all for Mary, but *now* he was himself again, and the Major walked moodily back to barracks, a wiser (as the world would opine), but certainly not a better man.

Care, however, although, as Horace tells us, "she sits behind the horseman," is a guest whose visits are but little encouraged by the light dragoon. Our gallant hussars were not inclined to mope down at Hounslow after their guests had returned to town, and the last carriage had scarcely driven off with its fair freight, ere phaeton, buggy, riding-horse, and curricle were put in requisition, to take their military owners back to the metropolis; that victim of discipline, the orderly officer, being alone left to console himself in his solitude, as he best might, with his own reflections and the society of a water-spaniel. To-morrow morning they must be again on the road, to reach head-quarters in time for parade; but to-morrow morning is a long way off from gentlemen who live every hour of their lives; so away they go, each on his own devices, but one and all resolved to make the most of the present, and glitter, whilst they may, in the sunshine of their too brief noon.

St. George's clock tolls one, and Blanche has been asleep for hours in her quiet room at the back of the house in Grosvenor Square. Pure thoughts and pleasant dreams have hovered round the young girl's pillow, and the last image present to her eyes has been the kind, handsome face of Major D'Orville—the hero who, commanding to all besides, is so gentle, so considerate, so tender with her alone. "Perhaps," thought she, as the midnight rain beat against her window-panes, "he is even now going his bleak rounds at Hounslow" (Blanche had a vague idea that the hussars spent the night in patrolling the heath), "wrapped in his cloak, on that dear white horse, very likely thinking of *me*. How such a man is thrown away, with his kindly feelings, and his noble mind, and his courageous heart. 'Nobody to care for,' he said; 'alone in the world';" and little Blanche sighed a sigh of that pity which is akin to a softer feeling, and experienced for an instant that startling throb with which love knocks at the door, like some unwelcome visitor, ere habit has emboldened him to walk up-stairs, unbidden, and make himself at home.

Let us see how right the maiden was in her conjectures, and follow the Major through his bleak rounds, and his night of military hardships.

As we perambulate London at our loitering leisure, and stare about us in the desultory, wandering manner of those who have nothing to do, now admiring an edifice, now peeping into a print-shop, we are often brought up, "all standing," in one of the great thoroughfares, by the magnificent proportions, the architectural splendour, of a building which our peaceful calling debars us from entering. Nevertheless we may gaze and gape at the stately outside; we may admire the lofty windows, with their florid ornaments, and marvel for what purpose are intended the upper casements, which seem to us like the bull's-eyes let into the deck of a three-decker, magnified to a gigantic uselessness; we may stare till the nape of our neck warns us to desist, at the classic ornaments raised in high relief around the roof, where strange mythological devices, unknown to Lemprière, mystify alike the antiquarian and the naturalist,—centaurs, terminating in salmon-trout, career around the cornices, more grotesque than the mermaid, more inexplicable than the sphinx. In vain we cudgel our brains to ask of what faith, what principle these monsters may be the symbols. Can they represent the *insignia* of that corps so strangely omitted in the *Army List*—known to a grateful country as the horse marines? Are they a glorious emanation of modern art? or are they, as the Irish gentleman suggested of our martello towers, only intended to puzzle posterity? Splendid, however, as may be the outward magnificence of this military palace, it is nothing compared with the luxury that reigns within, and the heroes of both services enjoy a delightful contrast to the hardships of war, in the spacious saloons and exquisite repasts provided for its members by the "Peace and Plenty Club."

"Waiter—two large cigars and another sherry-cobbler," lisps a voice which, although somewhat thicker than usual, we have no difficulty in recognising as the property of Captain Lacquers. That officer has dined "severely," as he calls it, and is slightly inebriated. He is reclining on three chairs, in a large, lofty apartment, devoid of furniture, and surrounded by ottomans. From its airy situation, general appearance, and pervading odour, we have no difficulty in identifying it as the smoking-room of the establishment. At our friend's elbow stands a small table, with empty glasses, and opposite him, with his heels above the level of his head, and a cigar of "*sesquipedalian*" length in his mouth, sits Sir Ascot Uppercrust. Gaston D'Orville is by his side, veiling his handsome face in clouds of smoke, and they are all three talking about the heiress. Yes; these are the Major's *rounds*, these are the hardships innocent Blanche sighed to think of. It is lucky that ladies can neither hear nor see us in our masculine retreats.

"So she refused you, Uppy; refused you point blank, did she? 'Gad, I like her for it," said Lacquers, the romance of whose disposition was much enhanced by his potations.

"Deuced impertinent, I call it," replied the repulsed; "won't have such a chance again. After all, she's not *half* a nice girl."

"Don't say that," vociferated Lacquers, "don't say that. She's *perfect*, my dear boy; she's enchanting—she's got *mind*, and that—what's a woman without intellect?—without the what-d'ye-call-it spark?—a—a—you recollect the quotation."

"A pudding without plums," said Sir Ascot, who was a bit of a wag in a quiet way; and "A fiddle without strings," suggested the Major at the same moment.

"Exactly," replied Lacquers, quite satisfied; "well, my dear fellow, I'm a man that adores all that sort of thing. 'Gad, I can't do without talent, and music, and so on. Do I ever miss an opera? Didn't I half ruin myself for Pastorelli, because she could dance? Now, I'll tell you what"—and the speaker, lighting a fresh cigar, forgot what he was going to say.

"Then *you're* rather smitten with Miss Kettering, too," observed D'Orville, who, as usual, was determined not to throw a chance away. "I thought a man of your many successes was *blasé* with that sort of thing;" and the Major smiled at Sir Ascot, whilst Lacquers went off again at score.

"To be sure, I've gone very deep into the thing, old fellow, as you know; and I think I *understand* women. You may depend upon it they like a fellow with brains. But I ought to settle; I 'flushed' a grey hair yesterday in my whiskers, and this is just the girl to suit. It's not her money I care for; I've got plenty—at least I can get plenty at seven per cent. No, it is her intellect, and her refusing Uppy, that I like. What did you say, my boy? how did you begin?" he added, thinking he might as well get a hint. "Did you tip her any poetry? Tommy Moore, and that other fellow, little What's-his-name?" Lacquers was beginning to speak very thick, and did not wait for an answer. "I'll show you how to settle these matters to-morrow after parade. First I'll go to——Who's that fellow just come in? 'Gad, it's Clank—good fellow, Clank. I say, Clank, will you come to my wedding? Recollect I asked you to-night; be very particular about the date. Let me see; to-morrow's the second Sunday after Ascot. I'll lay any man three to two the match comes off before Goodwood."

D'Orville smiles calmly. He hears the woman whom he intends to make his wife talked of thus lightly, yet no feeling of bitterness rises in his mind against the drunken dandy. Would he not resent such mention of another name? But his finances will not admit of such a chance as the present wager being neglected; so he draws out his betting-book, and turning over its well-filled leaves for a clear place, quietly observes, "I'll take it—three to two, what in?"

"Pounds, ponies, or hundreds," vociferates Lacquers, now decidedly uproarious; "thousands if you like. Fortune favours the brave. Vogue la thingumbob! Waiter! brandy-and-water! Clank, you're a trump: shake hands, Clank. We won't go home till morning. Yonder he goes: tally-ho!" And while the Major, who is a man of conscience, satisfies himself with betting his friend's bet in hundreds, Lacquers vainly endeavours to make a corresponding memorandum; and finding his fingers refuse their office, gives himself up to his fate, and with an abortive attempt to embrace the astonished Clank, subsides into a sitting posture on the floor.

The rest adjourn to whist in the drawing-room; and Gaston D'Orville concludes his rounds by losing three hundred to Sir Ascot; "Uppy" congratulating himself on not having made such a bad day's work after all.

As the Major walks home to his lodgings in the first pure flush of the summer's morning, how he loathes that man whose fresh unsullied boyhood he remembers so well. What is he now? Nothing to rest on; nothing to hope for—loving one—deceiving another. If he gain his object, what is it but a bitter perjury? Gambler—traitor—profligate—turn which way he will, there is nothing but ruin, misery, and sin.

CHAPTER XIII
THE WORLD

"Can't do it, my lord—your lordship must consider—overwritten yourself sadly of late—your 'Broadsides from the Baltic' were excellent— telling, clever, and eloquent; but you'll excuse me—you were incorrect in your statistics and mistaken in your facts. Then your last novel, 'Captain Flash; or, the Modern Grandison,' was a dead loss to us—lively work—well reviewed—but it *didn't sell*. In these days people don't care to go behind the scenes for a peep at aristocratic ruffians and chivalrous black-legs—no, what we want is something original—hot and strong, my lord, and lots of nature. Now, these translations"—and the publisher, for a publisher it was who spoke, waved his sword of office, a huge ivory paper-cutter, towards a bundle of manuscripts—"these translations from the 'Medea' are admirably done—elegant language—profound scholarship—great merit—but the public won't look at them; and even with your lordship's name to help them off, we cannot say more than three hundred—in point of fact, I think we are hardly justified in going as far as that;" and the publisher crossed his legs and sat back in his arm-chair, like a man who had made up his mind.

We have almost lost sight of Lord Mount Helicon since the Guyville ball, but he now turns up, attending to business, as he calls it, and is sitting in Mr. Bracketts' back-room, driving as hard a bargain as he can for the barter of his intellectual produce, and conducting the sale in his usual careless, good-humoured manner, although he has a bill coming due to-morrow, and ready money is a most important consideration. The little back-room is perfectly lined with newspapers, magazines, prospectuses, books, proof-sheets, and manuscripts, whilst the aristocracy of talent frown in engravings from the walls—faces generally not so remarkable for their beauty as for a dishevelled, untidy expression, consequent on disordered hair pushed back from off the temples, and producing the unbecoming effect of having been recently exposed to a gale of wind; nevertheless, the illegible autographs beneath symbolise names which fill the world.

Mr. Bracketts, the presiding genius of the place, is a remarkable man; his broad, high brow and deep-set flashing eyes betray at once the man of intellect, the champion whose weapon is the brain, whilst his spare, bent frame is attenuated by that mental labour which produces results precisely the converse of healthy physical exertion. Mr. Bracketts might have been a great poet, a successful author, or a scientific explorer; but, like the grocer's apprentice who is clogged with sweets till he loathes the very name of sugar, our publisher has been surfeited with talent till he almost pines to be a boor, to exchange the constant intellectual excitement which wears him to shreds for placid ignorance, a good appetite, and fresh air. How can he find time to embody his own thoughts who is continually perusing, rejecting, perhaps licking into shape those of others? How can he but be disgusted with the puny efforts of the scribbler's wing, when he himself feels capable of flights that would soar far out of the ken of that every-day average authorship of which his soul is sick?—so beyond an occasional slashing review, written in no forbearing spirit, he seldom puts pen to paper, save to score and interline and correct; yet is he, with all his conscious superiority, not above our national prejudices in favour of what we playfully term *good* society. We fear he had rather go to a "crush" at Lady Dinadam's than sup with Boz. He is an Englishman, and his heart warms to a peer—so he lets Lord Mount Helicon down very easy, and offers him three hundred for his manuscript.

"Hang it, Bracketts," said his lordship, "it's worth more than that—look what it cost me; if it hadn't been for that cursed 'Sea-breeze' chorus I should have been at Newmarket, when 'Bowse-and-Bit' won 'The Column'—and I should have landed '*a Thou*' *at least*. But I was so busy at it I was late for the train. Come, Bracketts, spring a point, and I'll put you 'on' about 'Sennacherib' for the Goodwood Cup."

"We should wish to be as liberal as possible, my lord," replied Mr. Bracketts, shaking his head with a smile, "but we have other interests to consult—if I was the only person concerned it would be different—but, in short, I have already rather exceeded my powers, and I can go no farther!"

"Very well," said Lord Mount Helicon, looking at his watch, and seeing it was time for him to be at Tattersall's; "only if it goes through another edition, we'll have a fresh arrangement. It's time for me to be off. Any news among the fraternity? Anything *good* coming out soon?"

"Nothing but a novel by a lady of rank," returned Mr. Bracketts, with a meaning smile; "and we all know what that is likely to be. Capital title, though: 'Blue-bell; or, the Double Infidelity'—the name will sell it. Good-morning; good-morning, my lord. Pray look in again, when you are this way." And the publisher, having bowed out his noble guest, returned to his never-ending labours, whilst Lord Mount Helicon whisked into the street, with five hundred things to do, and, as usual, a dozen appointments to keep, all at the same time.

Let us follow him down to Tattersall's, whither, on the principle of "business first and pleasure afterwards," he betakes himself at once, treading as it were upon air, his busy imagination teeming with a thousand schemes, and his spirits rising with that self-distilled elixir which is only known to the poetic temperament, and which, though springing to a certain extent from constitutional recklessness, owes its chief potency to the self-confidence of mental superiority—the reflection that, when all externals are swept away, when ruin and misfortune have done their wickedest, the productive treasure, the germ of future success, is still untouched within.

"If the worst comes to the worst," thinks his lordship, "if 'Sennacherib' breaks down, and Blanche Kettering fights shy, and the sons of Judah thunder at the door of the ungodly, and 'the pot boils over,' and the world says 'it's all up with Mount,' have I not still got something to fall back upon? Shall not my very difficulties point the way to overcome them? and when I am driven into a corner, *won't* I come out and astonish them all? I've got it *in* me—I know I have. And the reviewers—pshaw! I defy them! Let them but lay a finger on my 'Medea,' and I'll give them such a roasting as they haven't had since the days of the 'Dunciad.' Byron did it: why shouldn't I? If I could only settle down—and I *could* settle down if I was regularly cleaned out—I think I am man enough to succeed. Bring out a work that would shake the Ministry, and scatter the moderate party—then for Progress, Improvement, Enfranchisement, and the March with the Times (rogue's march though it be), and Mount Helicon, at the head of an invincible phalanx, in the House, with unbounded popularity out of doors, an English peerage—fewer points to the coronet—a seat in the Cabinet—why not? But here we are at Tattersall's;" and the future statesman is infernally in want of a few hundreds, so now for "good information, long odds, a safe man, and a shot at the favourite!"

As he walked down the narrow passage out of Grosvenor Place, now bowing to a peer, now nodding to a trainer, now indulging in quaint *badinage*, which the vulgar call "chaff," with a dog-stealer, who would have suspected the rattling, agreeable, off-hand Mount Helicon of deep-laid schemes and daring ambition? Nobody saw through him but old Barabbas, the Leg; and he once confided to a confederate on Newmarket Heath, "There's not one of the young ones as knows his alphabet, 'cept the Lively Lord; and take my word for it, Plunder, he's a deep 'un."

If a foreigner would have a comprehensive view of our system of English society all at one glance, let him go into the yard at Tattersall's any crowded "comparing day," before one of our great events on the turf. There will he see, in its highest perfection, the apparent anomaly of aristocratic opinions and democratic habits, the social contradiction by which the peer reconciles his familiarity with the Leg, and his *hauteur* towards those almost his equals in rank, who do not happen to be "of his own set." There he may behold Privy Councillors rubbing shoulders with convicted swindlers, noblemen of unstained lineage, themselves the "mirror of honour," passing their jests for the time, on terms of the most perfect equality, with individuals whose only merit is success; and that indescribable immunity some persons are allowed to enjoy, by which, according to the proverb, "one man is entitled to steal a horse, when another may not even look at a halter." But this apparent equality can only flourish in the stifling atmosphere of the ring, or the free breezes of Newmarket Heath. Directly the book is shut my lord is a very different man, and Tom This or Dick That would find it another story altogether were he to expect the same familiarity in the county-rooms or the hunting-field which he has enjoyed in that vortex of speculation, where, after all, he merely represents a "given quantity," as a layer of the odds, and where his money is as good as another man's, or, at least, is so considered. Nay, the very crossing which divides Grosvenor Place from the Park is a line of demarcation quite sufficient to convert the knowing, off-hand nod of our lordly speculator into the stiff, cold bow and studiously polite greeting of the "Grand Seigneur." Verily, would-be gentlemen, who take to racing as a means of "getting into society," must often find themselves grievously deceived. But Lord Mount Helicon is in the thick of it. Tattersall greets him with that respectful air which his good taste never permits him to lay aside, whether he is discussing a matter of thousands with Sir Peter Plenipo, or arranging the sale of a forty-pound hack for an ensign in the Guards; therefore is he himself respected by all. "*You* should have bought two of the yearlings, my lord," says he, in his quiet, pleasant voice; "Colonel Cavesson never sent us up such a lot in his life before."

"Ha! Mount!" exclaims Lord Middle Mile, with a hearty smack on his friend's shoulders, "the very man I wanted to see," and straightway he draws him aside, and plunges into an earnest conversation, in which, ever and anon, the whispered words—"Carry the weight," "Stay the distance," and "Stand *a cracker* on Sennacherib," are distinctly audible.

"I can afford to lay your lordship seven to one," observes an extra-polite individual, who seems to consider the laying and taking the odds as the normal condition of man, and whose superabundant courtesy is only equalled by the deliberate carefulness of his every movement, masking, as it does, the lightning perception of the hawk, and, shall we add, the insatiable rapacity of that bird of prey? Mount Helicon moves from one group to another, intent on the business in hand. He invests largely against "Nesselrode" (not the diplomatist nor the pudding, but the race-horse of that name), and backs "Sennacherib" heavily for the Goodwood Cup. He takes the odds to a hundred pounds, besides, from his polite friend, "who regrets he cannot offer him a point or two more," and, on looking over the well-filled pages of his book, hugs himself with the self-satisfied feeling of a man who has done a good day's work, and effected the crowning stroke to a flourishing speculation.

As he walks up the yard a quick step follows close upon him, a hand is laid upon his shoulder, and a well-known voice greets him in drawling tones, which he recognises as the property of our military Adonis, the irresistible Captain Lacquers. "Going to the Park, Mount?" says the hussar, with more animation than he usually betrays. "If you've a mind for a turn, I'll send my cab away;" and the peer, who cultivates Lacquers, as he himself says, "for amusement, just as he goes to see Keeley," replying in the affirmative, a tiny child, in top-boots and a cockade, is with difficulty woke, and dismissed, in company with a gigantic chestnut horse, towards his own stables. How that urchin, who, being deprived of his natural rest at night, constantly sleeps whilst driving by day, is to steer through the omnibuses in Piccadilly, is a matter of speculation for those who love "horrid accidents"; but it is fortunate that the magnificent animal knows his own way home, and will only stop once, at a door in Park Lane, where he is used to being pulled up, and where, we are concerned to add, his master has no business, although he is sufficiently welcome. "The fact is, I want to consult you, Mount, about a deuced ticklish affair," proceeded the dandy, as he linked his arm in his companion's, and wended his way leisurely towards the Park.

"Not going to call anybody out, are you?" rejoined Mount, with a quaint expression of countenance. "'Pon my soul, if you are, I'll put you up with your back to a tree, or along a furrow, or get you shot somehow, and then no one will ever ask me to be a 'friend' again."

"Worse than that," replied Lacquers, looking very grave; "I'm in a regular fix—*up a tree*, by Jove. Fact is, I'm thinking of marrying—marrying, you know; devilish bad business, isn't it?"

"Why, that depends," said his confidant; "of course you'll be a great loss, and all that; break so many hearts too; but then, think—the duty you owe your country. The breed of such men must not be allowed to become extinct. No; I should say you ought to make the sacrifice."

Lacquers looked immensely comforted, and went on—"Well, I've made arrangements—that's to say, I've ordered some of the things—dressing-case, set of phaeton-harness, large chest of cigars—but, of course, it's no use getting everything till it's all settled. Now, *you* know, Mount, I'm a deuced domestic fellow, likely to make a girl happy. I'm not one of your tearing dogs that require constant excitement; I could live in the country quite contentedly part of the year. I've got resources within myself—I'm fond of hunting and shooting and—no, I can't stand fishing, but still, don't you think I'm just the man to settle?"

"Certainly; it's all you're fit for," replied his friend.

"Well, now to the point. I've not asked the girl yet, you know, but I don't anticipate much difficulty there," and the suitor smoothed his moustaches with a self-satisfied smile; "but, of course, the relations will make a bother about settlements, 'love light as air,' you know, and 'human flies,' and that; still we must provide for everything. Well, *my* lawyer informs me that I can't settle anything during my brother's lifetime, and he's just a year older than myself—that's what I call 'a stopper.' Now, Mount, you're a sharp fellow—man of intellect, you know—'gad, I wouldn't give a pin for a fellow without brains—what do you advise me to do?"

This was rather a poser, even for a gentleman of Lord Mount Helicon's fertile resources; but he was never long at a loss, so as he took off his hat to a very pretty woman in a barouche, he replied, in his off-hand way, "Do? why, elope, my good fellow—run away with her—carry her off like a Sabine bride, only let her take all her clothes with her—save you a *trousseau*. Has she money?"

"Plenty, I fancy; from what I hear, I should think Miss Kettering can't have less than——"

"The devil!" interrupted Lord Mount Helicon, in a tone that would have made most men start. "You don't mean to say *you* want to marry Miss Kettering?"

"Well, I think *she* wants to marry *me*," rejoined Lacquers, perfectly unmoved; "and you know one can't refuse a lady; but it's only fair to say she hasn't actually *asked* me."

Lord Mount Helicon felt for a moment intensely disgusted. Blanche's beauty, and her simple, pretty manner, had touched him, as far as a man could be touched who had so many irons in the fire as his lordship, but the impulse for *fun*, the delight he experienced in quizzing his unsuspecting friend, soon overcame all other feelings, and he proceeded to egg Lacquers on, and assure him of his undoubted success, for the express purpose of amusing himself with the hussar's method of courtship. "Besides," thought he, "such a flat as this hanging about her will keep the other fellows off; and with a girl like *her*, I shall have little difficulty in 'cutting *him* out.'"

So he advised his friend to take time, and "allow her to get accustomed to his society, and gradually entangled in his fascinations; and then, my dear fellow," he added, "when she finds she can't live without you—when she has got used to your engaging ways, as she is to her poodle's—when she can no more bear to be parted from you than from her bullfinch, then speak up like a man—bring all your science into play—come with a rush—and win cleverly at the finish!"

"Ay, that's all very well," mused the captain, "that's just my idea; but in the meantime some fellow might cut me out. Now, there's our Major—D'Orville, you know ('gad, how hot it is! let's lean over the rails)—D'Orville seems to be always in Grosvenor Square. He's an old fellow, too, but he has a deuced taking way with women. I don't know what they see in him either. To be sure he *was* good-looking; but he's a man of no education" (Lacquers himself could scarcely spell his own name), "and he must be forty, if he's a day. Look at this fellow on the black cob. By Jove! it's old Bounce, and talk of the devil—there's D'Orville riding with Miss Kettering next the rails. This *is* a go."

Now, the little guileless conversation we have here related was hardly more worthy of record than the hundred and one nothings by the interchange of which gentlemen of the present day veil their want of ideas from each other, save for the fact of its being overheard by ears into which it sank like molten lead, creating an effect far out of proportion to its own triviality. Frank Hardingstone was walking close behind the speakers, and unwittingly heard their whole dialogue, even to the concluding remark with which Lacquers, as he leaned his elbows on the rails, and passed the frequenters of "the Ride" in review before him, expressed his disapprobation of the terms on which Major D'Orville stood with Blanche Kettering. Poor Frank! How often a casual word, dropped perhaps in jest from a coxcomb's lips, has power to wring an honest, manly heart to very agony! Our man of action had been endeavouring, ever since the Guyville ball, to drive Blanche's image from his thoughts, with an energy worthy of better success than it obtained. He had busied himself at his country place with his farm and his library and his tenants and his poor, and had found it all in vain. The fact is, he was absurdly in love with Blanche—that was the long and short of it—and after months of self-restraint and self-denial and discomfort, he resolved to do what he had better have done at first, to go to London, mingle in society, and enter the lists for his lady-love on equal terms with his rivals. And this was the encouragement he received on his appearance in the metropolis. He had a great mind to go straight home again, so he resolved to call on the morrow in Grosvenor Square, to ascertain with his own eyes the utter hopelessness of his affection, and then—why, then make up his mind to the worst, and bear his destiny like a man, though the world would be a lonely world to him for evermore. Frank was still young, and would have repelled indignantly the consolation, had such been offered him, of brighter eyes and a happier future. No, at his age there is but one woman in the universe. Seared, callous hearts, that have sustained many a campaign, know better; but verily in this respect we hold that ignorance is bliss. Frank, too, leaned against the rails when Mount Helicon and Lacquers passed on, and gazed upon the sunshiny, gaudy scene around him with a wistful eye and an aching heart.

CHAPTER XIV
TO PERSONS ABOUT TO MARRY

It was high noon in the great world of London—that is to say, it was about half-past five p.m.—and the children of Mammon were in full dress. In the streets, gay, glittering, well-appointed carriages were bowling smoothly along, with sleek horses stepping proudly together, and turning, as coachmen say, on a sixpence, guided by skilful pilots who could drive to an inch. Inside, shaded by parasols of the most gorgeous hues, sat fair delicate women, dressed to the utmost perfection of the art, with aërial bonnets at the very back of their glossy hair and dainty heads, bent down as they reclined upon their cushions till every upward glance shot from beneath those sweeping eyelashes bore a tenfold shaft of conquest against the world. Anon taper fingers in white kid gloves were kissed to a dandy on the pavement, and the fortunate dandy bowed, and sprang erect again, a taller man by an inch. 'Tis always judicious to *appear* on the best of terms with smart ladies in coroneted carriages. Bond Street was in a state of siege— "Redmayne's" looked like a beehive—"Hunt and Roskell's" resembled a flower-show—country cousins were bewildered and overcome—quiet old gentlemen like ourselves were pining for their strawberries and their roses—wearied servants meditated on the charms of beer—the narrow strip of sky overhead smiled blue as the Mediterranean, and the tide of carriages in Piccadilly was like the roar of the ocean. In the Park, though the space was greater, yet did the crowd appear no less—double lines of carriages blocked up the drive by the Serpentine, and unassuming broughams with provokingly pretty faces inside halted perforce amongst the matronage of England, defiant in the liveries and escutcheons of their lawful lords. In the Ride the plot was thickening still, and half a country seemed to be gathering on "the broad road"—we speak literally, not metaphorically—mounted on steeds worth a prince's ransom, we ought to say, but here our conscientious regard for verity compels us to stop short, and to remark that although every now and then our eye may be gladdened by that most beautiful of all spectacles, a handsome woman on a fine horse, yet in many sorry instances the gentlemen of England, who "sit at home at ease," effectually prevent their wives and daughters from enjoying a like sedentary composure, by mounting them on the veriest *"rips"* that ever disgraced a side-saddle. "He'll do to carry a lady," they say of some wretch that has neither pace nor strength nor action for themselves, and forthwith gentle woman, blest in her ignorance, tittups along, nothing doubting, upon this tottering skeleton. Fortune favours her own sex, but *if* anything happens a woman is almost sure to be hurt. No—to carry a lady a horse ought to be as near perfection as it is possible for that animal to arrive—strong, fast, well-shaped, handsome, and fine-tempered, his good qualities and his value should correspond with the treasure and the charms which are confided to his charge. But we have said there are exceptions, and Blanche's bay horse, "Water King," was a bright particular star among his equine fellows. Humble pedestrians stopped to gaze open-mouthed on that shapely form—the marble crest, the silky mane, the small quivering ear, the wide proud nostril, and the game wild eye—the round powerful frame, hard and smooth and well-defined as sculptured marble, showing on the "off-side" its whole lengthy proportions uninterrupted save by girth and saddle-flap, and the little edge of cambric handkerchief peeping from the latter. High-couraged as he was gentle, few horses could canter up the Ride like "Water King," and as he bent himself to his mistress's hand, snorting in his pride, his thin black tail swishing in the air, and his glossy skin flecked with foam, many a smart philosopher of the *"nil admirari"* school turned upon his saddle to approve, and drawled to his brother idler, "'Gad, that's a monstrous clever horse, and *rather* a pretty girl riding him." Major D'Orville thought they were a charming couple as he accompanied Miss Kettering and her steed with the careful air of proprietorship seldom assumed save by an accepted suitor. The Major was a delightful companion for the Park. He knew everybody, and everybody knew him. He had the knack of making that sort of quiet disjointed conversation which accords so well with an equestrian *tête-à-tête*. Defend us at all times from a long story, but especially on horse-back! The Major's remarks, however, were seldom too diffuse. "You see that man on the cream-coloured horse," he would say; "that's Discount, the famous money-lender. He gave a dinner yesterday to ten people that cost a hundred pounds, and he is telling everybody to-day all the particulars of the 'carte' and the 'bill.' Do you know that lady with the dark eyes and a netting all over her horse?—that's Lady Legerdemain—she keeps a legion of spirits, as she says, and will raise the dead for you any night you like to go to her house in Tyburnia proper." "How shocking!" Blanche replies, with a look of incredulity. "Fact, I assure you," returns the Major. "Sir Roger Rearsby asked to see an old brother-officer who was killed at Toulouse, and they showed him his own French cook! but Lady Legerdemain says the spirits are fallible, just like ourselves. Who is this in uniform?—why, it's 'Uppy'—he don't look very disconsolate, does he, Miss Kettering?" and the Major smiled a meaning smile, and Blanche looked down and blushed. "Some men would not 'wear the willow' so contentedly," proceeded D'Orville, lowering his voice to half-melancholy tone—"it's setting too much upon a cast to ask a question when a negative is to swamp one's happiness for life. I honour the man that has the courage to do it, but for my part I confess I have *not*." "I never knew you were deficient in that particular," replied Blanche, looking down again, and blushing deeper than before. Blanche! Blanche! you little coquette, you are indeed coming on in the atmosphere of London—you like the Major very much, but you do not like him well enough to marry him— yet you would be unhappy to lose him, you spoilt child!—and so you lead him on like this, and look more bewitching than ever with those downcast eyes and long, silky lashes. Notwithstanding their difference of years, our pair are playing a game very common in society, called "Diamond cut diamond." "I am a thorough coward in some things," returned D'Orville, not without a flush of conscious pride, as he remembered how his spirit used to rise with the tide of battle; "like all other cowards, nothing would make me bold but the certainty of success." He pressed closer to "Water King's" side, and sank his voice almost to a whisper as he added—"Could I but hope for *that*, I could dare anything. Could I but think that my devotion, my idolatry, was not entirely thrown away, I should be——" The Major stopped short, for Blanche turned pale as death, and her head drooped as if she must have fallen from her horse.

What made the girl start and sicken as though an adder had stung her to the quick? What made her lean her little hand for support on "Water King's" strong, firm neck? Because her brain was reeling, and everything— joy—sunshine—existence—seemed to be passing away. Was it for the mute reproach conveyed by that pale face amongst the crowd—was it for the calm, broad eye, bent on her "more in sorrow than in anger," and seeming, as it gazed, to bid her an eternal farewell?

Frank Hardingstone had seen it all. Unobserved himself among the pedestrians that thronged the footway, he had marked Blanche and her cavalier as they paced slowly down the Ride, had marked the girl's flush of triumph as her admirer drew closer and closer to her side, had marked that nameless "something" between the pair which people can never entirely conceal when they "understand each other," and had drawn his own conclusions from the sight. But the decencies of society must be preserved, though the heart is breaking, and Frank drew himself up and took his hat off with a bow that did honour to his qualities as an actor. The old gentleman in gaiters and the tall boy from Eton on either side of him never guessed the amount of mental agony undergone by a fellow-creature whom they actually touched! Civilisation has its tortures as well as barbarism. Blanche, too, returned the courtly gesture, but her weaker nature was scarcely equal to the effort, and had it not been that Uncle Baldwin had fidgeted up, on the instant, in more than his usual hurry to get home, she was conscious that her strength must have given way, and—feel for her, beautiful and daring Amazons who frequent the Ride!—that she must have burst into tears, and made a scene in the Park!

Now old Bounce, albeit a gentleman of extremely punctual habits, as is often the case with those who have nothing to do, and, moreover, a man of healthy appetite and a strong regard for the dinner-hour, had never before betrayed such a morbid anxiety to get home and dress as on the occasion in question. The fact is, he, too, was restless and excited, although the sensation had its own peculiar charms for the veteran, who entertained at sixty a spice of that romance which is often erroneously considered peculiar to sixteen. Yes, "the boy with the bow" no more disdained to take a shot at Bounce than at Falstaff, and our old friend was even now balancing on the brink of that eventful plunge which, if not made before "the grand climacteric," it is generally thought advisable to postpone *sine die*. Mary Delaval had made an unconscious conquest. The feeling had been gradually but surely developed, and the constant presence of such a woman had been too much, even for a heart hardened by more than forty years of soldiering, baked by an Indian sun, and further defended by triple plies of flannel, worn for chronic rheumatism, and usually esteemed as effective a rampart against the assaults of love as the "æs triplex" of Horace itself. First the General thought, "This Mrs. Delaval was a very nice creature. Zounds! it's lucky for her I'm not a younger man!" then he arrived at "*Beautiful* woman, begad. *Zounds!* it's lucky for *me* she's not half aware of her attractions!" and from that the transition was easy and natural to "Sensible person; such manners, such dignity; fit for any position in the world. Zounds! I'll make her Mrs. Bounce—do as I like—my own commanding-officer, nobody else to consult—of course *she* won't throw such a chance away." This latter consideration, however, although he repeated it to himself twenty times a day, had hitherto prevented the General from making any decided attack.

When a man, even an old one, *really* cares for a woman, he is always somewhat diffident of success, and Mary's sexagenarian suitor, though bold as brass in theory, was like any other lover in practice. But the breakfast at the barracks had wonderfully encouraged the General. He found Mrs. Delaval constantly at his side. He knew nothing of her previous acquaintance with D'Orville, still less could he guess at the secret which lay buried in her heart, and which was fading her beauty and deepening her expression day by day. How could he tell whose tears they were that blistered the newspaper on that "African Mail" column?—so the natural conclusion at which he arrived was, that the same charms which had done such execution in India, and had driven the Cheltenham widow to the verge of despair, were again at their old tricks; and that, having succeeded in attaching the most adorable of her sex, it only remained for him, in common humanity, to present her with all that was left of his fascinating self. And now began in earnest the General's qualms and misgivings. It was a tremendous step; he had never done it before; though often on the brink, he had always drawn back in time, and yet many of his old friends had got through it. Mulligatawney had married a widow—by the by, was Mrs. Delaval a widow? he never thought of asking—perhaps her husband was alive! At any rate this state of uncertainty was not to be borne, and after consulting one or two of his old cronies, and getting their opinions, he would take some decided step—that he would—ask the question, and stand the shot like a man. The General agreed with Montrose—

"He either fears his fate too much,

Or his deserts are small,

Who dares not put it to the touch,

To win or lose it all."

In pursuance of this doughty resolution, our veteran warrior took advantage of his niece's long *tête-à-tête* with Major D'Orville to drop behind on the black cob, and sound his two old friends, Mulligatawney of the Civil Service, and Sir Bloomer Buttercup of no service at all, save that of the ladies, on the important step which he meditated taking.

"Lonely place, London," said the General, reining in the cob, and settling himself into what he considered a becoming attitude, "at least for a bachelor. No solitude like that of a crowd.—What?"

"Better be alone than bothered to death by women," growled Mulligatawney, a thin, withered, sour-looking individual, with a long yellow face. "I *like* London, *en garçon*, only Mrs. Mulligatawney always *will* come up whenever I do. Egad, you bachelors don't know when you're well off."

"Poor bachelors," simpered Sir Bloomer Buttercup, riding up with his best air, he having dropped behind (a young rogue!) to make eyes at a very smart lady on the *trottoir*. "Poor fellows, nobody lets us alone, Bounce, and yet we're perfectly harmless—innocent as doves. I wish I was married, though, too; it fixes one, eh? keeps the butterfly constant to the rose;" and Sir Bloomer heaved his padded chest with an admirably got-up sigh, still shooting *œillades* at the nowise disconcerted lady on the *trottoir*. You would hardly have guessed Sir Bloomer to be sixty-five; at least, not as he appeared before the world on that cantering grey horse. To be sure, he had his riding costume on; riding hat, riding wig, riding coat, trousers, boots, and padding; not to mention a belt, the loosening of which let the whole fabric fall to pieces. They say he is lifted on his horse; we have reason to believe he could not *walk* five yards in that dress to save his life. Perhaps if we saw him, as his valet does, divested of his beautiful white teeth, his dark hair and whiskers, his florid healthy colour, and that stalwart deep-chested figure of buckram and wadding which encases the real man within, we might not be disposed to question the accuracy of Burke's "Peerage and Baronetage" in point of dates. But as he sits now, on his high broke horse, in his well-stuffed saddle, the very youngest of the shavelings who aspire to dandyism call him "Buttercup" to his face, and plume themselves on his notice, and quote him, and look up to him, not as a beacon, but an example.

"You're *right*, sir," says the General, with his accustomed energy, in a tone that makes the black cob start beneath him. "Don't tell me—should have married forty years ago. Never mind; better late than never. Now, I'll tell you, I've thought of it. We're not to live entirely for ourselves. How d'ye mean? I've thought of it, I tell you!"

"*Thought* of it, have you?" rejoined Mulligatawney, with a grim smile; "then at *your* time of life, Bounce, I should recommend you to confine yourself to *thinking* of it."

"Not at all, my dear fellow," lisps Sir Bloomer. "Bounce, I congratulate you. Introduce me, *pray*. Is she charming? young? beautiful? graceful? Happy Bounce—lucky dog—irresistible warrior!" The General feels three inches taller, and resolves to settle the matter the instant he gets home. But Mulligatawney interposes with his sardonic grin. "No fool like an old one. You'll excuse me, but if you ask my advice, I'll give it you in three words, 'Do and Repent'; you'll never regret it but once—*experto crede*." The General turns from one to the other, like the Wild Huntsman between his ghostly advisers, the Radiant Spirit on his white charger, and the Mocking Demon on his steed from hell—he feels quite incapable of making up his mind.

"Delightful state," says Sir Bloomer;—"Always in hot water," growls Mulligatawney. "Lovely woman; affectionate nurse; take care of you when you're ill," pleads the one;—"Cross as two sticks; open carriage in an east wind; give a ball when you've got the gout," urges the other. "Interchange of sentiment; linked in rosy chains; heaven upon earth," lisps the ancient dandy;—"Always quarrelling; Kilkenny cats; if you *must* go to the devil, go your own way, but not in double harness," grunts the world-worn cynic: and the General turns his cob's head and accompanies his niece home, more perplexed than ever, as is usually the case with a man when, bethinking him that "in the multitude of counsellors there is safety," he has been led into the hopeless labyrinth of "talking the matter over with a few friends."

CHAPTER XV
PENELOPE AND HER SUITORS

"Look who it is, Rosine!" exclaimed Blanche, as her maid rushed to the window of her dressing-room, commanding as it did a view of Grosvenor Square, and a peep at every visitor who came to that front door, which was even now reverberating from a knock applied by no feeble hand.

"Il n'y a pas de voiture, mademoiselle," replied Rosine; "ce n'est qu'un monsieur à pied—mais il n'est pas mal, lui, je trouve." The latter observation escaped Rosine more as a private reflection of her own than a remark for her lady's ear, and was indeed no more than due to the general appearance of Frank Hardingstone, as he stood at that well-known door, his strong heart beating like a girl's.

"Run, and say I'll be down directly, Rosine, if it's any one for me," said Blanche, her colour rising as she thought *who* it was likely to be, and wondered why he had not called before, and determined to punish him and keep him waiting, and be very cold when they *did* meet, and so show him that she did not choose to be accountable to *him* indeed for her actions, and would ride in the Park with whom she pleased, and was utterly indifferent to his good opinion, and independent of him altogether—and thus resolving, our consistent young lady looked at herself in the glass, and was pleased to see that her eyes were bright and her hair smooth, and that she should confront Frank armed with her best looks, which proves how entirely careless she was of that gentleman's admiration.

In the meantime the object of all this severity was kicking his heels in the spacious drawing-room appropriated to morning visitors, whither he had been conducted by an elaborately polite footman, who after informing him that "the General was *hout*, and Miss Kettering at '*ome*," made a precipitate retreat, leaving him to his own thoughts and the contemplation of his well-dressed figure in some half-dozen mirrors. Frank soon tired of these resources, and found himself driven to the table for amusement, where he found the usual litter of handsomely-bound books, costly work-boxes, grotesque paper-cutters, and miniatures painted in all the glowing colours of the rainbow. He was nervous (for him)—very nervous, and though he took one up after another, and examined them most minutely, he would have been sorely puzzled to explain what he was looking at. Nor did a contemplation of Blanche's portrait in ivory serve to restore the visitor's composure, albeit representing that young lady smiling with all her might under a heavy crimson curtain. He shut up the case with a savage *snap*, and replaced it with a bitter sneer. But if the representation of Miss Kettering's outward semblance met with so little favour, neither did her album, which we may presume was the index of her mind, seem to afford greater satisfaction to this discontented young man. It opened unfortunately at some lines by Lord Mount Helicon, "addressed to B— — on being asked whether the disfigurement of the object was not a certain cure for any man's love," and was entitled—

"THE FADED FLOWER.

"I spied a sweet Moss-rose my garden adorning,
With a blush at her core like the pink of a shell,
And I wrung from her petals the dewdrop of morning,
And gathered her gently and tended her well.
For the bee and the butterfly round her were humming,
To whisper their flattering love-tale, and fly;
And too surely I knew that the season was coming,
When the flower must fade and the insect must die.

So deep in the shade of my chamber I brought her,
And sheltered her safe from the wind and the sun,
And cared for her kindly and dipped her in water,
And vowed to preserve her when summer was done.
Though dark was my dwelling, this darling of Flora,
Like a spirit of beauty, enlivened the gloom;
Yet more than I loved her I seemed to adore her,
Less fond of her fragrance than proud of her bloom.

But long ere the brightness of summer was shaded,
My Moss-rose was drooping and withering away;
Her perfume had perished, her freshness had faded—
The very condition of life is decay.
And now more than ever I cherish and prize her,
For love shall not falter though beauty depart;
And far dearer to me, because others despise her,

That Moss-rose, all withered, lies next to my heart."

"Rubbish," growled Frank; "that any man in his senses should write such infernal nonsense, and then have the face to put his name to it! *His* moss-rose, indeed! and this is what women like. These are the coxcombs they prefer to a plain, sensible, true-hearted gentleman—put wisdom, talent, courage, faith, and truth in one scale, and weigh them against a soft voice, a large pair of whiskers, and varnished boots in the other—why, the boots have it twenty to one! and it is for this thoughtless, ungrateful, unfeeling, volatile, ill-judging sex that we are all prepared to go through fire and water, sacrifice friends, country, fame, position, honour itself! Blanche! Blanche is as bad as the rest, but *I* at least will no longer be such a fool. I have no idea of becoming a *pis-aller*—a substitute—a stop-gap—if this hair-brained peer should change his mind, and that warlike *roué* find some one he likes better than Miss Kettering. O Blanche! Blanche! that I had never known you, or having known you, could rate you at your real value, and give you up without a struggle!"

"How do you do, Miss Kettering? What a beautiful day!" Only the last sentence of the foregoing, be it observed, was spoken aloud; Frank had just schooled himself to the point of separation for ever, when the door opened and Blanche entered, looking so exactly as she used, with the same graceful gestures, and the same kind smile, that her empire was, for the moment, completely re-established; and although she, too, had meant to be very reserved and very distant, she could not forbear greeting her old admirer with all the cordiality of bygone days. These young people loved one another very much; each would have given the world to pour forth hopes, and fears, and misgivings, and vows, and reproaches, and pardons, into the other's ear, but the lip *will* tremble when the heart is full, and they got no further than "How do you do?" and "What a beautiful day!" Blanche was the first to regain her composure, as is generally the case with a lady, perhaps from her being more habituated to losing it—perhaps from her whole training being one of readier hypocrisy than that of man. Be this how it may, the deeper water, when stirred, is longer in smoothing its ruffled surface; and whilst the lover's lip shook, and his heart beat, the girl's voice was steady and tranquil, though she dared not trust herself, save with the commonplace topics and every-day conversation of society. They tried Chiswick—the new singer—the Drawing-room—Lady Ormolu's ball—the opera—and the Park; this last was tender ground, and Blanche coloured to the temples when Frank hesitated and stammered out (so different from his usual manly, open address) that he "*thought* he had seen her yesterday, and her horse was looking remarkably well. By the by, was she not riding with——"

"Major D'Orville," announced the polite footman, with the utmost stateliness; and our handsome hussar made his appearance, and paid his respects to Miss Kettering in his usual self-possessed and dignified manner, contrasting favourably with poor Frank's obvious embarrassment and annoyance, now heightened by the intrusion of so unwelcome a visitor at such an unlucky moment. A few seconds more might have produced an explanation, a reconciliation—possibly a scene—but that cursed door-knocker could not be still, even for so short a space; and Mr. Hardingstone was once more at a dead-lock.

And now began another game at cross purposes, which, though not uncommon amongst ladies and gentlemen who are of opinion that "two form pleasanter company than three," is, nevertheless, a dull and dreary recreation when persisted in for any length of time. It is termed "sitting each other out," and was now performed by Frank Hardingstone and the Major in its highest perfection. But here again the man of war had an advantage over the civilian. Besides the occupation afforded him by his moustaches, of which ornaments even D'Orville acknowledged the value in a case like the present, he was thoroughly at his ease, and consequently good-humoured, lively, and agreeable; whereas Frank was restless, preoccupied, almost morose. He had never before appeared to such disadvantage in Blanche's eyes. But if he hoped to obtain her ear by dint of patient assiduity, and an obvious intention to remain where he was till dinner-time, he must have been grievously disappointed, for again a thundering knock shook the house to its foundations, and "Lord Mount Helicon" was announced by the polite footman, with an extra flourish on account of the title. His lordship greeted Blanche with the greatest *empressement*, nodded to the gentlemen with the most hearty cordiality, as though rivalry was a word unknown in his vocabulary, and settled himself in an arm-chair by the lady's side with a good-natured assurance peculiarly his own.

"Do you ride to-day, Miss Kettering?" said he, with the most matter-of-course air. "I promised the General to show him my famous pony, so I have ordered 'Trictrac' (that's his name) to be here at five—perhaps you'll allow me to accompany you."

Frank looked intensely disgusted: he had brought no hacks to town, and if he had, would never have proposed to ride with his lady-love in such an off-hand way. Even the Major opened his eyes wider than usual, and gave an extra twirl to his moustaches; but "Mount" rattled on, nothing daunted: "We shall have Lacquers here directly. I met him as I drove up Bond Street, coming out of Storr and Mortimer's, and I taxed him on the spot with the accusation that he was going to be married. He couldn't stand the test, Miss Kettering! he blushed—actually blushed—and tried to get rid of me by an assurance that he was very busy, and that we should meet again in the Park. But I know better; he's coming here, I can take my oath of it. His hair is curled in five rows, and he never wears more than four, save for particular occasions. He is very fidgety about his 'chevelure,' '*his* chevalier,' he calls it; and went the other night to hear 'The Barbiere,' as he himself acknowledged, 'to get a wrinkle, you know, about dressing and shaving and all that.'"

Blanche laughed in spite of herself; and Frank, seizing his hat in ill-concealed vexation, bade her a hurried farewell, and rushed out of the house, just as the redoubtable Lacquers made his appearance, "got up," as Lord Mount Helicon had observed, with the greatest magnificence, and fully resolved in his own mind to push the siege briskly with the heiress, and at least to lose no ground in her good graces for want of attention to the duties, or rather, we should say, the pleasures of the toilette.

Poor Frank was very wretched as he stalked down the sunshiny street, and almost vowed he would never enter *that* house again. He felt a void at his heart that quite startled him. He had no idea he was so far gone. For a time he believed himself really and utterly miserable; nor did the reflection that such a feeling was a bitter satire on his boasted strength of mind—on that intellectual training of which he was so proud—serve to administer much consolation. Like the ruined gamester, who

"Damned the poor link-boy that called him a duke,"

Frank felt inclined to quarrel with the world in general, and buttoned his coat with savage energy when the poor crossing-sweeper held out her toil-worn hand for a penny. He relented too, and gave her money, and felt ashamed that he should have thought for an instant of visiting his own afflictions on that hard-working creature, the more so as a sailor-looking man in front of him had evidently given a trifle to the poor industrious woman.

Frank thought he recognised those broad shoulders, that large, loose frame and rolling gait; in another moment he was alongside Hairblower, and clasping the delighted seaman's hand with a warmth and cordiality by no means less vigorously returned.

"The last person as I ever expected to come across hereaway," said Hairblower, his broad, honest face wrinkling with pleasure. "I little thought when I came cruising about this here place as I should fall in with friends at every corner; and pretty friends they've showed theirselves, some on 'em."

As the seaman spoke these last words in bitter and desponding tones, Frank remarked that he looked pale and haggard; and though his clear eye and good-humoured smile were the same as ever, he had lost the well-to-do air and jovial manner which used to distinguish him at St. Swithin's. Frank asked if there was anything wrong: "You know I'm an old friend, Hairblower; I can see something has happened—can I assist you? At any rate, tell me what is the matter."

The tears stood in Hairblower's eyes, and again he wrung Frank's hand with a grasp like a vice, and his voice came hoarse and thick as he replied, "God bless you, Mr. Hardingstone, you're a real gentleman, *you* are, and though I'm a plain man and poor—*poor*, I haven't five shillings left in the world—you think it no shame to be seen walking and talking with the likes of me in the broad daylight, and that's what I call *manly*, sir: no more didn't Master Charlie—poor lad! he's far enough now; many's the time he's said to me, 'Hairblower,' says he—but that's neither here nor there. Well, Mr. Hardingstone, things has gone cross with me now for a goodish bit: the fishin' 's not what it used to be, nor the place neither. Bless ye, I've seen the day when I could take and put my ten-pound note on the old table at home, ay, and another to the back of that! but times is altered now, betterer for some, worserer for others. I've had my share, mayhap, but I've been drifting to leeward a long while back, and I've had a deal of way to fetch up. Well, sir, I'm pretty stiff and strong yet, and the Lord's above all, so I thought I might just get things together a bit, and streak up here to London town, and so look out for a berth in some of these here ships a-going foreign. I've neither chick nor child to care for me at home, and I reckoned as a voyage wouldn't hurt me no worse now than five-and-twenty years ago. Well, sir, to make a long story short, I got a bit o' money together, as much as would buy me an outfit and chest, and such like, for I meant to ship as second mate at the worst, and I always liked to be respectable; and when I'd got that I'd got *all*, but I didn't owe no man a farthing, and so would be ready to clear out with a clean breast. Lord, sir, what a place this here town is for sights: go where I would there was something to be seen. To be sure I hadn't many shillings to throw away, and I just looked straight afore me, and I never so much as winked at the mammon horse, nor the stuffed sea-serpent, nor the biggest man in Europe, nor the fattest woman, nor the world turned upside down, nor none on 'em, till I was brought up all standing by a board, where they offered to show me some True-blue Kaffirs, all alive and as dark as natur'. Well, sir, I knew a very respectable Kaffir family once, on the coast of Africa, where we used to land a boat's crew, at odd times, for fresh water and such like; and, thinks I, I'll just go and have a peep at the True-blues, and see if they remind me of my old friends. There they was, Mr. Hardingstone, sure enough. Old True-blue was a stampin', and yellin', and hissin', and makin' of such a disturbance as he never got leave to do at home, and his wives, five or six on 'em, was yowlin', and cryin', and kickin' up the devil's delight, as *I* never see them when they was living decently in the bush. Well, sir, when the True-blues held on for a while to have their beer, the company was invited to go and inspect 'em closer, and pat 'em, and feel 'em, and I made no doubt they was Ingines myself, when I got the wind of 'em; but just as I was castin' about to see if I could fish up an odd word or two of their language, only to be civil, you know, to strangers, True-blue's wife—she comes up and lays hold of me by the whiskers, and grins, and smiles, and points, and pulls at 'em like grim Death; and old True-blue himself—he comes up and has a haul, too, and grins, and chatters, and looks desperation fierce, and so they holds me amongst 'em. You see, Mr. Hardingstone, they're not used to beards, 'cos it's not their natur', nor whiskers neither. Well, I looked uncommon foolish, and the company all began to laugh; and I heard a voice behind me say, 'Why, it's Hairblower!' and I turns round, and who should I see but an old friend of mine, by name Blacke, as was a lawyer's clerk at St. Swithin's: *friend*, is he?" and Hairblower ground his teeth, and doubled a most formidable-looking fist, as he added, "if ever I catch him I'll give him his allowance; *friend*, indeed! I'll teach him who his friends are."

For a while the seaman's indignation was too strong for him, and he walked on several paces without saying a word, forgetful apparently of his companion and his situation, and all but his anger at the unworthy treatment to which he had been subjected. As he cooled down, however, he resumed: "Well, Mr. Hardingstone, in course we went out together, and we turned into a Tom-and-Jerry shop to have some beer, and spin a bit of a yarn about old times; and I asked him about his missus, and he remembered all the ins-and-outs of the old place, and I liked to talk to him all about it, 'specially as I shouldn't see it again for a goodish while; and we had some grog and pipes, and was quite comfortable. After a time, a chap came in—a big chap, in a white jacket and ankle-boots—and he took no notice of us, but began braggin' and chaffin' about his strength, and his liftin' weights and playin' skittles and such like; and Blacke whispers to me, 'Hairblower,' says he, 'you're a strong chap; put this noisy fellow down a bit, and perhaps he'll keep quiet.' Well, he kept eggin' of me on, and at last I makes a match, stupid like, to lift a heavier weight than the noisy one. So the landlord, he brings in half-a-dozen fifty-sixes, and I beats him all to rubbish. So he was somethin' mad at that, and offered to play me at skittles for five pounds, or ten pounds, or twenty pounds; and I said it was foolish to risk so much money for amusement, but I'd play him for a sovereign, 'cos, ye see, my blood was up, and I wasn't a-goin' to knock under to such a land-lubber as this here. 'Sovereign!' says he, 'I don't believe as you've got a sovereign,' and he pulls out a handful of notes and silver, and such like; and, says he, 'Afore

I stake,' says he, 'let me see my money covered; it's my belief that this here's a plant.' 'You ought to be ashamed of yourself,' says Blacke, the first time he spoke to him; '*my* friend's a gen'l'man, and can show *the ready* against all you've got—coin for coin, and shillin' for shillin'.' With that I pulls out my purse and counts my money down on the table—eleven golden sovereigns and a five-pound note. So we gets to skittles quite contented, and I puts my purse back in my jacket pocket, and gives it to Blacke to hold. Well, sir, I polished him off at skittles, too, and he paid his wager up like a man, and treated us all round, and behaved quite sociable-like; so we got drinkin' again—him and me and Blacke—at the same table. After a time my head began to get bad—I never felt it so afore—and the mixture I was drinkin' of—gin it was and beer—seemed to taste queerish, somehow, but I thought nothing of it, and drank on, thinking as the stuff would soon settle itself; but it didn't though; for in a little while the room and the tables and the chairs seemed to be heavin' and turnin' and pitchin', and I felt all manner of ways myself, and broke out into a cold sweat, and says I, 'I think I'll go out into the fresh air a bit, for I'm taken bad,' says I, 'someway; but don't ye disturb yourselves, I'll soon be back again.' So Blacke he helped me out, and directly I got into the yard where the skittles was, I see the place all green-like, and after that I remember no more till I found myself on the landlord's bed upstairs; and by that time it was ten o'clock at night, so I up and asked what was become of my friend; and the landlord he told me both the gentlemen was gone, and that they had said I didn't ought to be disturbed, and that I was *often so*; and they was goin' away without payin' the score, but the landlord was a deep cove, and he wouldn't let them off without settling, so they paid it all, and so walked away. Well, I got my jacket and walked away too; and all in a moment I thought I'd *heard* of such things, and I'd feel in my pocket to see if my purse was safe. There was *the purse* sure enough, but the *money* was gone, every groat of it—there wasn't a rap left to jingle for luck, Mr. Hardingstone. Well, sir, it all came across me at once—I'd been hocussed, no doubt—they drugged my lush, the thieves, and then they robbed me—and my old friend Tom Blacke, as I've known from a boy, was at the bottom of it. The landlord, he thought so too; but he was in a terrible takin' himself for the character of his house, and he gave me half-a-crown, and begged I'd say nothin' about it; and that half-crown, all but sixpence I gave just now to a poor creatur' that wanted it more nor me, is the whole of my fortun', Mr. Hardingstone. But it's not the money I care for—thank God, I can work and get more—it's the meanness of a man I once thought well of. That's where it is, sir, and I can't bear it. Blacke by name, and black by natur'—he must be a rank bad 'un; and I'm ashamed of him, that I am!"

Hairblower got better after making a clean breast of it. He had no friends in London—none to confide in, none to advise him; and his chance meeting with Frank Hardingstone "did him a sight of good," as he said himself, and "made a man of him again." Nor was the rencontre less beneficial to Frank. When a man is suffering from that imaginary malady (none the less painful for being imaginary) which originates in the frown of a pretty girl, there is nothing so likely to do him good as a stirring piece of real business, to which he must devote all his energies of body and mind. Byron recommends a sea-voyage, with its accompanying sea-sickness; the latter he esteems a more perfect cure than "purgatives," or "the application of hot towels." Not but that these unromantic remedies may be extremely effective; but, failing such counter-irritants, we question whether a visit to Scotland-yard, and an interview with those courteous and matter-of-fact gentlemen who preside over our well-organised metropolitan police force, be not as good a method of cauterising the wound as any other, more particularly when such a visit is undertaken for the express purpose of seeing a friend through an awkward scrape. Frank soon had Hairblower into a cab, and off on his way to the head-quarters of that detective justice which is anything but blind; where the seaman, having again told his unvarnished tale, and been assured that his grievances should meet with the promptest attention, was dismissed, not a little comforted, though at the same time most completely puzzled. Frank's assistance to his humble friend, however, did not stop here. He *liked* Hairblower, partly, it must be confessed, because the seaman was so strong and plucky, and possessed such physical advantages as no man despises, though he who shares them himself often rates them higher than the rest of the world. Frank enjoyed associating with men of all sorts, but more especially he relished the society of such daring spirits as are accustomed to look death in the face day by day, in the earning of their very subsistence, and to trust their own cool heads and strong hands amidst all the turmoil of the deep, "blow high, blow low." Many a wild night had he been out in the Channel with his sailor friend, when an inch or two more canvas, or a moment's neglect of the helm, would have made the reckless couple food for those fishes after which they laboured so assiduously; and our two friends, for so we must call them, notwithstanding their difference of station, had learned to depend on each other, and to admire reciprocally the frame that labour could not subdue, the nerves that danger could not daunt. So now the gentleman talked the sailor's affairs over with him as if he had been a brother. He gave him the best advice in his power; he recommended him to go back to St. Swithin's to prosecute the fishing trade once more, and with the same delicacy which he would have thought due to one of his own rank, he offered to *lend* him such a sum of money as would enable him to begin the world again, and expressly stipulated that he should be repaid by instalments varying with the price of mackerel and the success of the fishing.

"If once you get your head above water, I know you can swim like a duck," said Frank, grasping the honest fellow's hand, "so say no more about it. We'll have rare times in the yawl before the summer's quite done with; and till then, God bless you, old friend, and good luck to you!" As Hairblower himself expressed it, "you might have knocked him down with a feather."

How different the world looked to Frank when he parted with his old companion from what it had seemed some few hours before, as he left the great house in Grosvenor Square. There is an infallible recipe for lowness of spirits, nervousness, causeless misery, and mental irritation, which beats all Dr. Willis's restorative nostrums, and emancipates the sufferer more rapidly than even the famous "Ha! ha! Cured in an instant!" remedy. When oppressed with *ennui*, the poet says—

"Throw but a stone, the giant dies!"

and so, when the bright sky above seems leaden to your eyes—when the song of birds, the prattle of children, or the gush of waters, fall dully upon your ear—when the outward world is all vanity of vanities and existence seems a burden, and, as Thackeray says, "Life is a mistake"—go and do a kindly action, no matter how or where or to whom; but, at any sacrifice, at any inconvenience, go and do it—and take an old man's word for it, you will not repent. Straightway the fairy comes down the kitchen chimney, and touches your whole being with her wand. Straightway the sun bursts out with a brilliant smile, the birds take up a joyous carol, the children's voices are like the morning hymn of a seraph choir, and the babbling of the stream woos your entranced ear with the silver notes of Nature's own melody. Those are now steeds from Araby which seemed but rats and mice an hour or two ago. That is a glittering equipage which you had scouted as a huge, unsightly pumpkin. You yourself, no longer crouching in dust and ashes, start upright, with your face to heaven, attired in the only robe that preserves eternal freshness, the only garment you shall take away with you when you have done with all the rest—the web of charity, that cloak which covers a multitude of sins. You have, besides, this advantage over Cinderella—that whereas her glass slippers and corresponding splendour must be laid aside before midnight, your enchantment shall outlast the morrow; your fairy's wand can reach from earth to heaven; your kindly action is entered in a book from which there is no erasure, whereof the pages shall be read before men and angels, and shall endure from everlasting to everlasting.

CHAPTER XVI
FORGERY

In the meantime, whilst the higher characters of our drama are fluttering their gaudy hour in the bright sunshine of fashionable life, whilst the General and Blanche and Mary, and Mount Helicon and D'Orville and Lacquers, and all of that class are driving and dining, and dressing and flirting, and otherwise improving their time, grim Want is eating into the very existence of some amongst our humbler friends, and Vice, too often the handmaid of Penury, is shedding her poison even on the scanty morsel they wrest from the very jaws of danger and detection.

Tom Blacke, as we have already seen, has overleapt the narrow boundary which separates dissipation from crime; and poor Gingham knows too well that opportunity alone is wanting to confer on him a notoriety infamous as that which is boasted of by his more daring associates. He is out now at all hours, chiefly, however, during the night, and obtains supplies of money for which she cannot account, and about which she has been taught it is better not to question him. He drinks, too, with more circumspection than was his wont, and has dreadful fits of despondency, during which he trembles like a child, and from which nothing seems to arouse him save the prattle of his infant. He is very diligent, too, in making inquiries as to the sailing of divers ships for the United States; and, being a sharp fellow, has acquainted himself thoroughly with the geography of that country, and the amount of capital requisite to enable a man to set up for himself under the star-spangled banner. He has already hinted to his wife that if he could but get hold of a little money he should certainly emigrate; and by dint of talking the matter over, Gingham, although she has a dreadful horror of the sea, contracted at St. Swithin's, is not entirely unfavourable to the plan. Poor woman! she has not much to regret in leaving England. Let us take a peep at their establishment in the Mews, as they sit by the light of a solitary tallow candle, the mother stitching as usual, though her eyes often fill with tears, whilst ever and anon she glances cautiously towards the cradle, to see if the child is asleep, and listening to its heavy, regular breathing, applies herself to the needle more diligently than before. This is the hour at which Tom usually goes out; but to-night he shows no signs of departure, sitting moodily with his chair resting against the wall, and his eyes fixed on vacancy. At length he rouses himself with an effort, and bids Rachel make him some tea.

"I'm glad you're not going out to-night, Tom," says his wife; "I feel poorly, somehow, and its lonesome when you're away for long."

"I'd never go out o' nights, lass," replies Tom—"never, if I wasn't drove to it. But what's a man to do?—this isn't a country for a poor man to live in—there's no liberty here. Ah, Rachel, you're made for something better than this; stitching away day after day, and not a gown or a bonnet fit to put on. You're losing your looks too—you that used to be so genteel every way." Mrs. Blacke smiles through her tears; he has not spoken to her so kindly for many a long day. "There's a country we might go to," he adds, looking sideways at her, to watch the effect of his arguments, "where a man as is a man, and knows his right hand from his left, needn't want a good house to cover him, nor good clothes to his back. We'd be there in six weeks at the farthest—what's that?—why, it's nothing; and the child all the better for the sea air. There's a ship to start next Thursday, first class, and all regular. In two months from this day we might be in America; and they don't *keep* a man down there because he is down. Rachel, I'd like to see you dressed as you used to be; I'd like to bring up the little one to be as good as its parents, at least. I'd like to be there now; why, the dollars come in by handfuls, and silk's as cheap as calico."

How could woman resist such an El Dorado? How could such an inducement fail to have its due weight? His wife feels that she could start forthwith, but there is one insuperable difficulty, and she rejoins—

"Ah, that's all very well, Tom, and we might get our heads above water over there, it's likely enough. But how are we to get to America?—people can't travel nor do anything else without money; and where is it to come from?"

"*You know,*" replied Tom, with a meaning smile on his pale, anxious face; and while he speaks the clock of a neighbouring church strikes ten.

"Any way but *that*, Tom," says his wife, with a shudder. "I'd do anything, and bear anything for you; but not *that*, Tom—not *that*, as you've a soul to be saved!"

"It must be that way, or no way at all, missus," Tom hisses between his teeth, keeping down his anger and a rising oath with a strong effort. "I've done all I can; it's time for *you* to take your share. Why, look ye here, Rachel; a hundred pound's a vast of money—a hundred pounds is five hundred dollars. Oh, I'm not going blindly to work, you may depend. If we could begin life with half that, over the water, it would be the making of us. I'd leave off drinking—so help me heaven, I would!—take the pledge, and work like a new one. You'd have a house of your own, Rachel, instead of such a dog-hole as this; and I'd like to see one of them that would take the shine out of my wife on Sundays, when she was tidied up and dressed. Then we'd put the little one to school, when she's old enough, and we'd keep ourselves respectable, and attend to business, and be a sight happier than we've ever been in this miserable country. And all just for the scratch of a pen; Rachel, d'ye think I'd refuse *you* a trifle like that, if you was to ask me?"

"O Tom, I never could do it," says his wife; "good never would come of such a sin as that."

"Well, Rachel," rejoins her husband, "there's some men would make ye. Well, you needn't draw up so; I'm not going to come it so strong as all that. Let's talk it over peaceably, any way. And first, where's the harm? There's Master Charlie, if ever he comes back from the wars, isn't he to marry Miss Blanche? And so it's six to one, and half-a-dozen to the other. And what's a hundred pounds out of all their thousands? Besides, didn't the old lady mean to leave you as much as that? and didn't you deserve it? And if she had lived, wouldn't she have signed her own name; and where's the harm of your doing it for her? You can write like your old mistress, Rachel," adds the tempter, with a ghastly smile; "there's pen and ink yonder on the mantelpiece. Come!" Rachel wavers; but education and good principles are still too strong within her, and she assumes an air of resolution she does not feel, as she takes up her work, and replies—

"Never, Tom, never!—not if you was to go down upon your bended knees. O Tom, Tom! don't ask me, and don't look at me so, Tom. I've been a good wife to you; don't ask me to do such a thing, Tom; don't."

Her husband pauses for a moment, as though nerving himself for a strong effort, and answers, speaking every word distinctly, and as if in acute physical pain—

"Then it must come out, wife; you must know it all, sooner or later; and why not now? Rachel, *I'm wanted*—they're looking for me, the bloodhounds—it's my belief they were after me this very morning. If I don't cross the seas on my own account, the beaks will send me fast enough on theirs."

"O Tom, Tom! what have you done?" interrupts his wife, clasping her hands, and straining her eyes, dilated with horror, upon her husband's working features. "It's not—— Tom, I can't bring myself to say it. You haven't lifted your hand against another?"

"No, no, Rachel," says he; "not so bad as that, lass, not so bad as that; but it's fourteen years, anyhow, if they bring it home to me. *I* must cut and run, whatever happens. Now, there's some men would be off single-handed, and never stop to say good-bye; but I'm not one of that sort. I couldn't bear to leave you and the child; and I won't neither. Rachel, do you mind the time when we sat on the beach at St. Swithin's, and what you said to me there? Well, dear, that's past and gone, now; but you're not changed, anyhow. Will you do it, Rachel, for *my sake*?"

The poor woman wavers more and more; she is white as a sheet, and the perspiration stands in beads on her lip and forehead. Tom produces a pen and ink, and a certain document we recognise as having lain in Mrs. Kettering's writing-case the night she died at St. Swithin's. But his wife shrinks from the pen as from a serpent, and he has to force it into her fingers.

"It's the *last time*, Rachel," he pleads; "I'll never ask you to do such a thing again. It's the *last time* I'll do wrong myself, as I stand here. It's but a word, and it will be the saving of us both; ay, and the little one yonder, too—think what she'd be growing up to, in such a place as this. You sign, dear, and I'll witness—I can write my own name, and my old master's too; he's dead and gone now, but he didn't teach me law for nothing."

She does not hear him; her whole being is absorbed in the contemplation of her crime. But she *does* it. Pale, scared, and breathless, she leans over the coarse deal table; and though the dazzling sheet is dancing beneath her eyes, and her hands are icy cold, and her frame shakes like a leaf, every letter grows distinct and careful beneath her fingers, and burns itself into her brain, the very facsimile of her old mistress's signature. The clock strikes eleven; and at the first clang she starts with the throb of newly-awakened guilt, and drops the pen from her failing grasp. But the deed is done. From that hour the once respectable woman is a felon; and she feels it. To-morrow morning, for the first time in her life, she will awake with the leaden, stupefying, soul-oppressive weight of actual law-breaking guilt; and from this night she will never sleep as soundly again.

Tom prided himself, above all things, on being "up to trap," as he expressed it. He thought his own cunning more than a match for all the difficulties of his situation and the vengeance of the law. He was considered "a knowing hand" amongst his disreputable associates, and had the character of a man who was safe to keep his own neck out of the noose, whatever became of his comrades'. But, though a bold schemer, he was a very coward in action, and his nerves were now so shattered by hard drinking that he was almost afraid of his own shadow. A bad conscience is always the worst of company, but to a man not naturally brave it is a

continual bugbear—a fiend that dogs his victim, sleeping or waking—
sits with him at his meals, pledges him in his cups, and grins at him on
his pillow. Tom possessed this familiar to perfection. Like all "suspected
persons," he conceived his movements to be of more importance in the eyes
of Justice than they really were; and although the "hocussing" and robbery
of Hairblower richly deserved condign punishment, he was suffering from
causeless alarm when he informed his wife that he was "wanted" on that
score. The truth is, the police were on a wrong scent. The landlord either
could not, or would not, give them any actual information as to his guests;
he "remembered the circumstance of the gentleman being taken ill—did
not know the parties with whom he was drinking—thought they were
friends of the gentleman—the parties paid for their liquor, and went away,
leaving the other party asleep—it was no business of his—had never been
in trouble before, he could swear—commiserated the party who had got
drunk, and gave him half-a-crown out of sheer humanity—had known
what it was to want half-a-crown himself, and to get drunk too—was doing
an honest business now, and thought publicans could not be too particular."
So the blue-coated myrmidons of Scotland Yard got but little information
from Boniface; and for once were completely at fault, more especially as
Hairblower, *more suorum*, did not know the number of the note he had lost—
could swear it was for five pounds, but was not quite clear as to its being
Bank of England. Under these circumstances, Tom, had he only known it,
might have walked abroad in the light of day, and put in immediate practice
any schemes he had on hand. Instead of this he chose to lie in hiding, and
only emerged in the evening, to take his indispensable stimulants at one
or other of the low haunts which he frequented. Men cannot live without
society; the most depraved must have friends, or such as they deem friends,
on whom to repose their trust; and Tom Blacke, in an unguarded moment
of gin and confidence, let out the whole story of the will (though he was
cunning enough to omit the forgery) and boasted what an engine he could
make of it to extort money from Miss Blanche's guardian, and how he was
certain of getting *at least* a hundred pounds, and detailed the proposed
plan of emigration, and, in short, explained the general tenor of his future
life and present fortunes to Mr. Fibbes; of all which matters, though by no
means a gentleman of acute perception, that worthy did by degrees arrive
at the meaning, quickening his intellects the while with many pipes and
a prodigious quantity of beer. Now, Mr. Fibbes had been concerned in
his earlier youth in a business from which his size and his stupidity had
gradually emancipated him, but which, compared with his present trade,
might almost be called an innocent and virtuous calling. It consisted in
ascertaining by diligent and clandestine vigilance the relative merits of race-
horses as demonstrated by their *private trials*, and is termed in the vernacular

"touting." What may be the *moral* guilt of such forbidden peeps we are not sufficient casuists to explain, but it is scarcely considered amongst the least particular classes a *respectable* way of obtaining a livelihood. Nor did the association gain additional lustre from the adhesion of Mr. Fibbes, who, until his great frame grew too large to be concealed, and his hard head too obtuse to make the best of his information, was the most presuming, as he was least to be depended on, of the whole brotherhood. In this capacity, however, he had made the acquaintance of Major D'Orville, a man who liked to have tools ready to his hand for whatever purpose he had in view; and Mr. Fibbes had been careful to keep up the connection, by respectful bows whenever they met in the streets, or at races, or such gatherings as bring together sporting gentlemen of all ranks. On these occasions Mr. Fibbes would make tender inquiries after the Major's health, and his luck on the turf, and the well-being of his white charger, and sundry other ingratiating topics; or would inform him confidentially of certain rats in his possession which could be produced at half-an-hour's notice, without fail— of terriers, almost imperceptible in weight, which could be backed to kill the rats aforesaid in an incredibly short space of time—of toy-dogs surpassing in beauty and discreet in behaviour—or of the pending match against time which "The Copenhagen Antelope" meant to *square* by running *a cross*, or, in other words, losing it on purpose to play booty. Primed with such conversation he amused the Major, who liked to study human nature in all its phases, and they seldom met without a lengthened dialogue and the transfer of a half-crown from the warrior's pocket into Mr. Fibbes' hand; the latter accordingly lost no opportunity of coming across his generous patron.

Now, Mr. Fibbes had observed, by hanging about Grosvenor Square and making use of his early education, that Major D'Orville was a constant visitant at a certain house in that locality; indeed, on more than one occasion he had held the white horse at the very door which was honoured by the egress and ingress of Blanche Kettering herself. We may be sure he lost no time in discovering the name of the owner, and mastering such particulars of her fortune, position, general habits, and appearance as were attainable through the all-powerful influence of beer; so when Tom Blacke made his ill-advised confidences to his boon companion, omitting neither names, facts, nor dates, Mr. Fibbes, who, to use his own words, was "not such a fool as he looked," put *that* and *that* together quite satisfactorily enough, to be sure he had some information well worth a good round douceur, for the ear of his friend the Major. And he waylaid him in consequence, the first sunshiny afternoon on which, according to his wont, D'Orville appeared in the neighbourhood of his lady-love's domicile.

"Want yer horse held, Major?" said he, leaning his huge, dirty hand on the white charger's mane. "Haven't seen your honour since we won so cleverly at Hampton—no offence, Major!"

"None whatever, my good fellow," said the Major, who, by the way, was never in a hurry, though few men loved going *fast* better; "none whatever; but I'm busy now, I've no time to stop. Good-day to you."

"Well, but, Major, see," pleaded Mr. Fibbes, still smoothing the white horse's mane, "I've got something at my place you *would* like to look at— she's a *real* beauty, she is—I refused five sovereigns for her this blessed mornin'; for I said, says I, no, says I, not till the Major has seen her, 'cause she *is* a rare one—not that you care for such in a general way, Major, but if once you clapped eyes on 'Jessie,' you'd never rest till you got her down at the barracks. I never see such a one."

"Such a what?" inquired D'Orville, gradually waxing curious about such manifold perfections.

"Why, such an out-an'-outer," retorted Mr. Fibbes, half angrily; "none of your *brindles*—I can't abide a brindle—they may be good, but they look so *wulgar*. No, no, Jessie's none of your brindles."

"Well, but *what* is she, my good fellow?" said the Major; "I can't stay here all day."

"*Bul,*" replied Mr. Fibbes, throwing into the monosyllable an expression of mingled anger and contempt, which, having given the Major sufficient time to digest, he followed up by the real topic on which he was anxious to enlarge. "No offence, Major," he repeated, "but I've got something else to say—you'll excuse me, sir—but you've stood a friend to me, and I won't see you put upon. Major, there's a screw loose here—it's not *on the square,* you understand."

"What do you mean?" said the Major, amused in spite of himself, at the ungainly nods and winks with which Mr. Fibbes eked out his mysterious communication.

"Well, Major," replied his informant, "what I mean is this here. Some men would hold out in my place, and I've seen the day when my information was worth as much as my neighbours'; but when I've to do with a real gent, why, I trusts to him, and he gives *what he pleases.* Now, Major, look at that there house—it's a good house up-stairs and down, fixtures and furniture all complete, I make no doubt—Major, there's *a man of straw* in that house." Mr. Fibbes paused, having delivered himself of this oracular piece of information; but, finding his listener less interested in the discovery of the artificial stranger than he had reason to expect, he proceeded in his own way to clear up his metaphor. "What I says is this—a bargain's a bargain; now the young woman as owns that house has got *the boot on the other leg*—my information's *good*, Major, you may depend on it; there's another horse in the stable, sir—there's a young gent as owns all the property they keep such a talk about; I won't ask ye to believe my naked word, Major" (such a request, indeed, would have been superfluous), "but what should you say if I was to tell you—I've spoke to the party as has *seen the will*?"

"Why, I should say that if you have any information that is really well-authenticated, I'll pay you fairly for it, as I always have done," replied D'Orville, unmoved as usual, though in his innermost heart a tide of doubts and hopes and fears was swelling up, in strange tumultuous confusion.

"Well, Major," whispered his informant, "as far as I can learn, for I ain't no scholar, you know—but *as* far as I can learn, there's been a will found, and by that will the young lady as owns this here house don't own it by rights, and can't keep it much longer. There's a old gentleman as lives here, rayther a crusty old gentleman, so my mate tells *me*, and he knows *nothing* good or bad; but it stands just as I've said, you may depend; and instead of Miss Kettering, if that's her name, being such a grand lady, why she's no better off than I am, and that's *where* it is. My mate wouldn't deceive *me* no more than I'm deceivin' you. Thank ye, Major, you always was a real gentleman; thank you, sir, and good-day to you. You won't come up and take a look at Jessie?" So saying, Mr. Fibbes put his dirty hand, not quite empty, however, into his pocket, and with a snatch at his rough hat, and an awkward obeisance, took his departure, his linen jacket and ankle-boots fading gradually in the direction of the nearest public-house, whither he proceeded incontinently to "wet his luck," after the manner of his kind.

D'Orville laid the rein on his favourite's neck, and paced along at a slow, thoughtful walk, the white horse wondering, doubtless, at his master's unusual fit of equestrian meditation. And what were the suitor's feelings as he pondered over the news he had just received, the downfall of his golden castles in the air, the blow which would surely fall heavy on that bright, happy girl, whom he had been endeavouring to attach to himself day by day? Did he mourn over his withered hopes of wealth and ease? did he regret the melting of the vision, and pine for the domestic future, now impossible, which he had contemplated so often of late? or did he chivalrously resolve to give his hand to a penniless bride where he had been wooing a wealthy heiress, and to love her even more in her misfortunes than he had admired her in her prosperity? Alas! far from it. Some fifteen years ago, indeed, young Gaston D'Orville would have sacrificed his all to a woman, almost to any woman, and been well pleased to throw his heart into the bargain; but fifteen years of the world have more effect on the inner than the outward man, and the boy of five-and-twenty thinks that a glory and a romance which the man who is getting on for forty deems a folly and a bore. The Major was not prepared to give up *everything*, at least for *Blanche*, and his first sensations were those of relief, almost of satisfaction, as he thought he was again free—for of course this arrangement couldn't go on; it would be madness to talk of it now: no, he would make his bow while it was yet time: how lucky he had never positively committed himself: nobody could say *he* had behaved ill. Of course he would take proper measures to ascertain the truth of that rascal's report; and if it had foundation, why, he was once again at liberty. He had his sword and his debts, but India was open to him, as it had been before, and a vision stole over him (the hardened man of the world could scarce repress a smile at his own folly)—a vision stole over him of military distinction, active service, a return to England—and Mary Delaval. So the Major drew his rein through his fingers, pressed his good horse's sides, and cantered off, but did not, *that* afternoon, pay his usual visit in Grosvenor Square.

CHAPTER XVII
CLUB LAW

"Who the deuce ever heard of 'military duty' interfering with dinner? and what's the use of being one's own commanding-officer if one can't give oneself leave?—What?—read that, Blanche!" We need hardly observe that it was General Bounce who spoke, as he tossed a note across the luncheon-table to his niece, and proceeded to bury himself in his other dispatches. The General was none of your dawdling, half-torpid, dressing-gown and slipper gentlemen, who consider London a fit place in which to spend the greater part of the day in *déshabillé*—not a bit of it. The General was up, shaved, and rosy and breakfasted, and prepared to fuss through his day, every morning punctually at eight. On the one in question he had reviewed a battalion of Guards who were at drill in the Park, utterly unconscious of their inspection by such a martinet, and had been good enough to express his disapprobation of their dress, method, and general efficiency, to a quiet, unassuming bystander whom he had never set eyes on before, but who happened to be a peer of the realm, and whose son, indeed, commanded the very regiment under discussion. The peer was quite alarmed at the denunciations of a casual acquaintance, so fierce of demeanour and of such warlike costume, the General never stirring abroad, for these morning excursions, save in a military surtout, buttoned very tight, a stiff black stock and buckskin gloves, armed moreover with a bamboo walking-stick, which he brandished with great impartiality. After his strictures on the sovereign's body-guard he proceeded into the City by a hansom cab; there was no cab-rebellion in those days, but, nevertheless, Bounce succeeded in having a violent altercation with his driver, which resulted in that observer of human nature setting him down for a madman, and his own discomfiture on referring the dispute to an impartial policeman. From thence he visited his stables, and instructed divers helpers belonging to the adjoining mews in the proper method of washing a carriage, a lesson received by those worthies with much covert derision. The General was by this time ready for "tiffin," as he still called it—a meal at which, for the first time in the day, he met the ladies of his establishment, read his notes, letters, etc., and arranged with Blanche the details of the gay life they were every day leading. That young lady, in a very pretty morning-gown, now occupied the head of the table; Mary was up-stairs with a headache—she was very subject to them of late—yet a skilful practitioner might have guessed the malady lay elsewhere; and whilst the General, with his eyebrows rising into his very forehead, perused a dirty, ill-conditioned-looking missive, which seemed to afford him great astonishment, his niece glanced over her military suitor's excuse for not dining with them, in which he expressed his regret that duty and the absolute necessity of his presence in barracks would prevent his having that pleasure, but did not as usual suggest any fresh arrangements for rides, drives, or walks, which should insure him the charms of her society. Blanche was a little hurt and more than a little offended; yet, had she closely examined her own feelings, she would probably have been surprised to find how little she *really* cared whether he came or not. "Well, Uncle Baldwin," she said, with her usual merry smile, "you and I will dine *tête-à-tête*, for I don't think poor Mrs. Delaval will be able to come down. We shall not quarrel, I fancy—shall we?" The General was dumb. His whole soul seemed absorbed in the missive which hid his face, but, judging from the red swollen forehead peeping above, indignation appeared to be the prevailing feeling inspired by its contents. It was not badly written, though in an unsteady hand, nor was it incorrectly spelt; it bore no signature, and was to the following effect—

"General Bounce,

"Sir,—This from a friend.—Seeing that you would probably be averse to an exposure of family matters, in which Miss Blanche's name must necessarily appear, a well-wisher sends these few lines to warn you that *all has been discovered*. The late Mrs. K.'s will has been found, in which she devises everything, with the exception of certain legacies, to C——. The writer has seen it, and knows where it is to be found. His own interests prompt him to make *everything* public, but his regard for the family would induce him to listen to terms, could he himself be guaranteed from loss. General, time is everything: to-morrow may be too late. If you should be unwilling to disturb muddy water, an advertisement to X. Y., in the second column of the *Times*, or a line addressed to P. Q., care of Mr. John Stripes, Bear and Bagpipes, corner of Goat Street, Tiler's Road, Lambeth, would meet with prompt attention. Be wise."

We regret to state that the General's exclamation, on arriving at the conclusion of this mysterious document, was of a profane fervour, inexcusable under any provocation, and very properly amenable to a fine of five shillings by the laws of this well-regulated country. It was repeated, moreover, oftener than once; and without deigning to explain to his astonished niece the cause of his evident discomposure, was followed by his immediate departure to his own private snuggery—by the way, the very worst and darkest room in the house, whither our discomfited warrior made a tremulous retreat, banging every door after him with a shock that caused the very window-frames to quiver again.

"Zounds! I won't believe it!—it's impossible—it's a forgery—it's a lie— it's an artifice of the devil! Why, it's written in a clerk's hand. 'Gad, if I thought there was a word of truth in it, I'd go to bed for a month!" burst out the General, as soon as he was safe in his own sanctuary, choking with passion, and tugging at the black stock and tight frock-coat as if to put his threat of retiring into immediate execution. It was one of his peculiarities, which we have omitted to mention, to adopt this method of avoiding the common annoyances and irritations of life. When anything went wrong in the household, the General made no more ado but incontinently proceeded to *strip and turn in*. When there was an *émeute* below stairs, and Newton-Hollows was in a "state of siege"—a calamity which occurred about once in two years—the proprietor used to go to bed till the disturbance had completely blown over. When the news arrived of Mrs. Kettering's death, her brother gave vent to his feelings between the sheets, although he was obliged to get up within a few hours and travel post-haste to join the afflicted family at St. Swithin's; nay, it is related of him that, on one occasion, when an alarming fire happened to break out in a country-house where he was staying on a visit, nothing but the personal exertions of his friends, who hurried after him, and carried him off by force from his chamber, where he was rapidly undressing, prevented his being burnt alive in his nightcap. At the present crisis the General had already divested himself of coat, waistcoat, etc., ere the sight of a clean change of apparel, laid out ready for his afternoon wear, altered the current of his ideas, and he bethought him that it would be wiser to walk down to his club, amuse himself as usual in his habitual resorts, and thus drive this impertinent "attempt at extortion," for so he did not hesitate to call it, entirely from his mind, than place himself at once *hors de combat* amongst the blankets. So, instead of his night-gear, the General struggled into a stiffer black stock and a tighter frock-coat even than those which he had discarded, and arming himself with his formidable bamboo (how he wished the head and shoulders of his unknown correspondent were within its range), strutted off to Noodles', feeling, as he cocked his chin up, and threw his chest out, and struck his cane against the sunny pavement, that he was still young and *débonnaire*, as in the *beaux jours* at Cheltenham twenty, ay, thirty years ago.

No place makes a man forget his years so much as London. In the great city, one unit of that circling population rapidly loses his individuality. There nothing seems extraordinary—nothing seems out of the common course of events—there, it is proverbial, people of all pretensions immediately find their own level. If a man thinks he is wiser, or better, or cleverer, or handsomer, or stronger, or more famous than his neighbours, in London he will be sure to meet those who can equal, if not excel him, in all for which he gives himself credit; and so if an elderly gentleman begins to feel at his country-place that all around him speaks of maturity, not to say decay— that his young trees, and his old buildings, and his missing contemporaries, and the boy to whom he gave apples standing for the county, and the village he remembers a hamlet growing into a town, and all such progressive arrangements of Father Time, hint rather personally at old-fellowhood—let him come to London, and take his diversion amongst a crowd of fools more ancient than himself: he will feel a boy again—Regent Street will not appear altered to his enchanted eye, though they *have* taken down the colonnade in that well-remembered thoroughfare. Pall Mall is as much Pall Mall to him as it was when he trod it in considerably tighter boots, never mind how many years ago. At his club the same waiter (waiters never die) will bring him the paper, and stir the fire for him, just as he used to do when the Reform Bill was a thing unheard of, and he can contemplate his bald head in the very same mirror that once reflected locks of Hyacinthine cluster. He meets an old crony, and he is shocked (though but for the moment) to find him so dreadfully altered—it is possible the old crony, in his heart of hearts, may return the compliment, but in all human probability he will greet the friend of his boyhood as if he had seen him the day before yesterday. If a very demonstrative man, and it should be before two o'clock in the day—for in the afternoon our English manners are all squared to the same pattern— the old crony may perhaps exclaim, with languid rapture, "Why, I haven't seen you *for ages*; I don't think you were in London *all* last season!" Why should our gentleman from the country undeceive him, and tell him they have not met for more than twenty years, and remind him with mellowing heart of boyhood's sunny hours and joyous escapades? The old crony will only think him *a twaddle* and *a bore*, and thank his stars that he has stuck to London and the world, and his gods, such as they are, and is a much *younger* man of his age than his rustic friend. And so our country mouse will find in a day or two that the artificial sits quite as easily upon *him*. When he has visited two or three of his old haunts he will feel as if he had never left them. He will go, perhaps, to some well-remembered palace of revelry, and find there, it may be, one contemporary out of a hundred with whom he once drank deep of dissipation and amusement, but he forgets the other ninety-nine. He feels as if the world had gone along with him, and that threescore years and odd were, after all, as the French king's courtiers said, *L'âge de tout le monde*; so he lifts the cup of pleasure once more with shaking hands to his poor, dry old lips, and pours its flood, erst so luscious, over a palate, alas! deadened to all but the intoxication of the draught. Why is it that we so sedulously strive to deceive ourselves about the lapse of time? Why do we so wilfully close our eyes to that certainty that every passing moment brings an instant nearer? It must come! Why will we not look the shape steadily in the face? We are not afraid to front our fellow-man in the struggle for life and death; why should we shrink from the shadowy foe, from whom there is no escape? Perhaps, like all other distant horrors, it will lose half its terrors when it does approach—perhaps it will turn out a friend after all. Man lives in the future; can he not carry his future a little beyond life? Will it be such a bereavement to lose a poor, old, worn-out frame, with its gout and its rheumatism, and its hundred aches and pains, and burdens dragging it day by day towards the earth from whence it sprung? But where will the disembodied self find shelter? "Ay, there's the rub," and so "conscience doth make cowards of us all."

Well, young or old, boys will be boys, whether at one score or three, and all the sermonising in the world will not empty St. James's Street towards four o'clock on a summer's afternoon, or prevent one nose being flattened against those club-windows from which the *terrarum domini* of the present day look upon the world with a mixture of good-humoured satire and careless contempt. Stoics are they in manners and principles, Epicureans in tastes and practice, and Philosophers of the Porch on the clear bright evenings—or rather midnights—when they assemble to smoke in gossiping brotherhood. But now, in the afternoon, laws human and divine would vote it "bad style" to have anything in their mouths save the tops of their canes and riding-whips, and these are scarcely removed to make a passing remark on the unconscious General as, having accomplished the crossing of Piccadilly, he sweeps under the guns of battery No 1, on his way to his own resort, where he too will stand at a window and make comments on the passers-by. Talking of these batteries, we can recollect, old as we are, when we preferred to thread the press of Piccadilly, and so dodging down Bury Street to bring up eventually opposite Arlington Street, rather than face the ordeal of passing under those great guns. Yet was our cab well hung and well painted, our tiger a pocket-Apollo, and our horse well-actioned and in good condition, while no one but ourselves and the dealer who sold him to us could be aware of his broken knee. What strategy wasted! What skill in charioteering thrown away! How should we then, in our shy and sensitive boyhood, have winced from the truth, that no one probably in that dreaded window would have thought it worth while to waste a single monosyllable on anything so insignificant as ourselves. Verily, *mauvaise honte* is a contradictory foible; but of this weakness the General, like most men who have arrived at his time of life, has but a small leaven. He toddles boldly down, under the battery, masked as it is by the *Times* newspaper, and nods familiarly to a well-brushed hat and luxuriant pair of grey whiskers just peering above the broadsheet. The whiskers return the salutation, and a stout gentleman at the fireplace, where he has been standing for the last three-quarters of an hour, hatted, gloved, and umbrellaed, as though prepared for instant departure, carelessly remarks, "Old Bounce is getting devilish shaky;" to which the grey whiskers reply, "No wonder; he's an oldish fellow now. Why, Bounce'll be a lieutenant-general next brevet. By the by, when *are* we to have a brevet?" the whiskers forgetting, as after the lapse of so many years it is natural they should, that they were at school with "the oldish fellow," who was then a "younger fellow" than themselves. However, they have talked about him quite long enough, and pass on to a fresh topic by the time the General himself arrives at Noodles'.

This very excellent and exclusive club seems to bear to institutions of a like nature much the same relation that Greenwich and Chelsea Hospitals do to the crews and battalions of our forces by land and sea. Should the warrior who enlists under the banner of Fashion have the good fortune to escape the various casualties common in his profession, such as absenteeism, imprisonment, marriage, or any other sort of ruin, he is pretty safe to anchor at Noodles' at last. There he brings up, after all his perils and all his triumphs, amongst a shattered remnant of those who set sail with him in the morning of life, when every wind was fair and every channel practicable. Many have been lured by the siren on to sunken rocks, and gone down "all standing"—many have lost their reckoning and drifted clean away, till they can "fetch up" no more—many have been captured by crafts trim and flaunting as themselves, and towed away as prizes into different havens, where they ride in somewhat wearisome monotony—and of many there is no account, save that which shall be rendered when the sea gives up its dead. Yet a few crazy old barks have made the haven at last—worn, leaky, and sea-worthless, with bulging ribs and warped spars, and tackle strained, yet are they still just buoyant enough to float—can still drift with the tide, and, above all, are still disposed to take in cargo on every available opportunity. As London is now constituted, you can almost tell a man's age by the clubs he frequents. "Tell me your associates, and I will tell you your character," says the ancient philosopher. "Tell me your club, and I will tell you your age," says the modern "ingenious youth," as that sporting Falstaff Mr. Jorrocks calls him, who begins with huge cigars, gin and soda-water, and billiards, much bemused, at Trappe's. Anon, as his collars get higher, and the down upon his cheek begins to justify a nobler ambition, he aspires to the science of numbers, and lays the odds to more experienced calculators at "The Short-Grass." But our youth is becoming a man-about-town, or thinks he is, and must have the *entrée* to more than one of these luxurious republics; so according to his rank, his profession, or his pretensions, he affects another afternoon club, esteeming it, whichever it may be, the best and *most select* in London. Here he has a plentiful choice. If a professional or a politician, he will find associations purposely established for those of his own practice or opinions; and here they are looming like a city of palaces — the Conflagrative, the Anarchic, the Regency, the Hat-and-Umbrella, the Chelsea, and the Peace and Plenty. Is there not the Megatherium for the literary, and the Munchausen for the travelled? But peradventure our youth is fast, and aspires to be a man of figure; so shall his carriage be seen waiting at the Godiva, or himself shall face the ballot at Blight's. For a time all goes on smooth and sunny; but the young ones keep growing up, and they rather jostle him in his chair, and "people let in such boys now-a-days"; so in disgust he abdicates a sovereignty conferred by years, and retreats to quieter resorts, where the cutlet is equally well dressed and the wine a thought better. So we find him presiding over house-dinners at Alfred's, or winning the odd trick after a quiet *parti carré* at Snookes's. But even from these celestial seats he must be ousted at last. Still that pressure from below keeps increasing year by year, "and the young men of the present day are so slangy, and so noisy, and so disagreeable," that he can stand it no longer, and puts his name down for the first vacancy in that last refuge recommended by his old friend Sapless. Behold him at length shouldered into the harbour, and safely landed at Noodles'.

Thither we have likewise brought the General, and given him ample time to spell through the papers, and reconnoitre his acquaintance as they pass up and down St. James's Street. But the General is ill at ease — he cannot get that infernal anonymous letter out of his head; do what he will, he cannot prevent himself from glancing at the second column of the *Times*, and poring over a map of London in search of Goat Street, Tiler's Road, Lambeth. He fancies, too, as a man is apt to do when self-conscious of anything peculiar, that people look at him strangely; and if two men happen to whisper in a window, he cannot help thinking they must be talking about him. At last he gets nervous, and determines to take counsel of a friend; nor is he long in selecting a recipient for his sorrows, inasmuch as the most remarkable object in the room is Sir Bloomer Buttercup, who is standing in an attitude near the fireplace (Sir Bloomer, for certain mechanical reasons, cannot sit down in that particular pair of trousers), and to him the General resolves to confide his annoyances, and by his advice determines to abide.

Although, probably, no man in this world ever managed his own affairs so badly as Sir Bloomer Buttercup—partly, it must be owned, in consequence of his having the most generous heart that ever beat under three inches of padding—yet in all matters unconnected with self, his judgment was as sound as his penetration was remarkable. No man had got his friends out of so many scrapes, no man had given such good counsel, and no man had probably done so many foolish things as kind, good-natured Sir Bloomer; and when he minced after the General into an empty room on those poor, gouty, shiny toes, he really felt as ready as he expressed himself, to "see his old friend through it, whatever it was."

"I'll tell you what, Bounce," lisped the old beau, as the General concluded his tale with that most puzzling of questions, "What would you advise me to do?"—"I'll tell you what. I think I know a fellow that can sift this for us to the bottom. You know, my dear boy, that I have occasionally been in slight difficulties—merely temporary, of course, and entirely owing to circumstances over which I had no control" (Sir B. had spent two fortunes, and was now living on the recollection of them, and the possible reversion of a third)—"but still difficulties—eh?—a ten-knot breeze was always more to my fancy than a calm. Well, I've been brought in contact with all kinds of fellows, and I do know one man, a sort of a lawyer, that's in with every rogue in London. He could get to the rights of this in twenty-four hours if we made it worth his while. He's a clever fellow," added Bloomer reflectively, "a very clever fellow; in fact, a most consummate rascal. Shall I take you to him?"

"This instant," burst out the General, with a terrific snatch at the bell; "I'll send for my brougham—what?—it'll be here in five minutes. Zounds! not go in a brougham? Why not?"

Sir Bloomer had frightful misgivings as to the effects on his costume of the necessary attitude in which carriage exercise must be taken; but in the cause of friendship he was prepared to hazard even a rupture of the most important ties, and he replied heroically, "I'll see you through it, Bounce; what o'clock is it? Ah! I promised—never mind—they must be disappointed sometimes; and for the sake of your charming niece, I'd go through fire and water a good deal farther than the City. Bounce, Bounce, what an angel that girl is! She mustn't be told a syllable of this—not a syllable; with me, of course, it's secret as the grave." So the pair started, firmly persuaded that not a soul in London, save their two selves, knew a word about the letter, or the will, or the dethronement of poor little Blanche from her pedestal as an heiress.

CHAPTER XVIII
THE STRICTEST CONFIDENCE

You must be an individual of an equally sanguine temperament and confiding disposition, if you believe that what you impart to your neighbour in the modern Babylon under seal of the strictest secrecy, might not as well be published in the leading article of the *Times* newspaper. How "things get about" is one of those inexplicable mysteries for which nobody is able or willing to account. Some people lay it to servants—some to the amiable generosity in imparting information for which the fair sex are so remarkable; the latter, again, say that "every bit of scandal in London originates at those horrid clubs!" but few will allow that Rumour owes a large portion of her ubiquity to that organisation of mankind which makes a secret utterly valueless unless shared with another. What is the use of knowing something we must not tell? In the strictest confidence, of course, it was told us under promise that we would not breathe a syllable to a single soul—we only make an exception in your favour under the same solemn obligation. You, of course, in mysterious conclave with Tom, will bear in mind our prohibition, and, acting as we have done, Tom shall become a party to the treason. Still upon oath, it will not be long, we think, before Jack and Harry are empowered to join chorus, and whilst our cherished mystery becomes patent to the world in general, we ourselves feel completely absolved from the consequences of our breach of trust. In the whole of Lady Mount Helicon's crowded rooms to-night, we believe Blanche herself is the only person that is not aware of her own precarious position; and the girl, happy in her ignorance, looks brighter and more blooming than usual, though *the world* will admire her less on this occasion than it has ever done before. Yes, this is one of Lady Mount Helicon's "At Homes," with a small italicised "*Dancing*" in the corner; and a very brilliant affair it is, as the hostess herself is fully persuaded:—the front and back drawing-room, and the boudoir beyond that, are thrown open and lighted with dazzling brilliancy, whilst a softer lustre shed upon the conservatory and balcony, craftily covered in for the purpose, lures to those irresistible man-traps without betraying their insidious design. Below stairs, libraries and school-rooms and other resorts, devoted in every-day life to far more practical uses, are now cleared and emptied for the reception of shawls, cloaks, and coverings, and the production of countless cups of tea and glasses of lemonade. Lady Mount Helicon's own maid, in a toilette of gorgeous magnificence, presides over this department, casting the while glances of covert scorn and envy at a younger and prettier assistant in a more becoming cap, on whom the dandies, as they enter, impress with unnecessary circumlocution the propriety of taking great care of their gregos, paletôts, and other sheep's-clothing. In the dining-room preparations are making for a "stand-up supper" of unparalleled luxury, but we think it right to warn the champagne-drinking guests, that on passing the door in the morning we spied several hampers of that popular fluid, labelled with the *maker's name*, and much as we admire its chemical preparation and laudable cheapness, we are concerned to admit that "the splendid sparkling of that house at 45s." always disarranges our internal economy for several days after an indulgence in its delights. Mount Helicon himself never drinks his mother's champagne, and to his abstinence he attributes his own unfailing health. At Dinadam's, or Lord Long-Acre's, or Wassailworth, he does not by any means practise the same self-denial. Still it is doubtless good enough for a ball, and what with the young ladies, and the old gentlemen, and the servants, will experience a very fair consumption. A bearded band meanwhile is in waiting up-stairs, elaborately dressed, and from the conductor in white kid gloves to *the Piccolo* in a chin-tuft, rejoicing in boots of jetty brilliancy, and neckcloths dazzling with starch. The whole establishment is so utterly at variance with its usual routine, and the house looks so entirely changed when thus stripped and lighted for reception, that if the old lord, who never permitted these *bouleversements*, could but come back, he would scarcely recognise his former home, and would unquestionably be glad to return to the quiet of his family vault. The presiding genius of the scene, the hostess herself, is already at her post. A very capital dressmaker, an abundance of well-selected jewellery, and a mysterious compound much enhancing the beauty of the human hair, have turned her out a very personable dame, and as she stands in the middle of her ball-room, as yet "monarch of all she surveys," and spreads her rustling folds, and buttons her well-fitting gloves, the possibility of her marrying again seems no such absurdity after all, nor does she herself look upon such an event as by any means a remote contingency. But soon the knocker is at work, the chariot wheels are clattering in the street, and stentorian voices, louder in proportion to their indistinctness, announce the fast-arriving guests. Unlike a country ball, the feathers of the ladies require but little shaking after a short drive from the next street, nor, fresh from their own impartial mirrors, need they hazard the opinion of perhaps an unbecoming reflector; so they troop up-stairs with small delay, their glossy locks, white shoulders, and gossamer draperies showing to the greatest advantage in the well-lighted ball-room. The earliest arrivals of course receive the most affectionate greeting, proportionately decreased as the plot thickens, till the shake by both hands, and graceful little compliment about "looking so well," subsides into a stately courtesy and the coldest welcome good-breeding, not hospitality, will admit. At last all individual figures are well-nigh lost in the crush. A mass of charming dresses and well-made coats are swaying and struggling in the doorways, the band is pealing forth a melody of Paradise, and the votaries of the quadrille are striving to adhere to their superstitious evolutions by treading on each other's toes, entangling each other's dresses, begging each other's pardon, and generally complaining of the heat of the atmosphere and crowded state of the room. It is at this juncture that "General Bounce" and "Miss Kettering" make their appearance, the General having placed a guard upon his lips, and neither during the dinner nor the drive hinted at his misgivings and inner discomfiture. "Poor Blanche!" he mutters, as he follows her up the wide, stately staircase; "she'll know it soon enough, if it's true—zounds! a girl like that would be a prize without a penny—the young fellows now-a-days are not like what *we* used to be." And as the General arrived at this conclusion he bowed his bald head nearly into Lady Mount Helicon's bosom, in return for her stately, measured greeting. That greeting, both to himself and Blanche, was colder than usual; the girl, frank and unconscious, did not perceive the change, but her uncle caught himself saying, almost aloud, "Zounds! is it possible that this old cat knows it too?" The music ceased, the dancers walked about, the wrongly-paired ones looking for "mamma," or "my aunt," inwardly longing to get rid of each other, and glancing in every direction for their own particular vanities, the more fortunate couples likewise keeping a sharp look-out for the chaperons, but this in order to avoid them, and hinting that "It's much cooler on the staircase," or "Have you seen the conservatory?" to prolong the delicious interview. The tea-room begins to fill, and incautious youth presses that domestic beverage on beauty nothing loth, nor reflects that charming as are those ringlets drooping over the cup, and rosy as are the lips that whisper their soft affirmative, it would be as well that he should distinctly know his own mind as to whether he would like this celestial being to make tea for him during the rest of his life, and whether it would be always as sweet as it is now. For the first time in her experience of a London season Blanche, begins to think it a "stupid ball." She has not yet been asked to dance; and spoilt by her previous successes, she feels hurt at the neglect. "The best men," as they are called, have not yet, indeed, arrived—if, as is somewhat uncertain, they will come at all, for they sometimes throw Lady Mount Helicon over; and "Mount" himself is still detained at the "House." But there are plenty of beardless dandies and gay young guardsmen, who are far more prone to dance; and yet they all seem to keep aloof. To be sure, whenever they *have* asked her formerly she has always been "engaged"; but she would like to stand up now, even with young Deadlock, if it was only for "the look of the thing." However, she hangs contentedly on the General's arm, and "bides her time." It is not long coming. A tall, good-looking man, with features expressive only of a kind disposition and a general air of self-satisfaction, bows and sidles and screws himself towards Blanche and her chaperon, receiving as his natural homage the smiles of the old ladies on whose toes he is treading, and regardless of the imploring looks of the young ones who hope he is going to ask them to dance. His glossy hair is curled distinctly in five rows, which, according to Lord Mount Helicon's account, betokens weighty intentions; and it is no other than our friend Captain Lacquers, who has dined temperately, abjured his usual cigar, and come here for the especial purpose of meeting Miss Kettering. A bow, an indistinct murmur about "not engaged," and "honour," and "delighted," and the couple are off, tripping gracefully round amongst the whirling confusion of the *Valse des Fantassins*, truly "a mighty maze, but not without a plan."

To explain the intentions of our rotatory hussar, we must take the liberty of putting the clock back a few hours—an impossibility only permitted to the novelist—and record a conversation which took place between Lacquers and his friend Sir Ascot that very afternoon, in a secluded window of the Godiva Club.

"Well out of this business about Miss Kettering," said the latter, who was becoming more communicative since he had found so little difficulty in speaking his mind to Blanche on a previous occasion. "You've heard of the smash? Not a penny, after all. Downright swindling, I call it—that old Bounce must be a deep one. They tell me that, except the life-interest of the house in Grosvenor Square, she hasn't a brass farthing. It's frightful to think of," added the old head on young shoulders, scanning with rigid attention his companion's face, in which concern was more apparent than surprise.

"Poor thing, poor thing" rejoined Lacquers; "I had no idea it was so bad as that. They told me she was sure to have Newton-Hollows, at any rate. She must feel it sadly, poor girl; I wonder how she looks since it all came out."

"Oh, I fancy very few people know it as yet," suggested Sir Ascot, who was somewhat uncharitable in his conclusions. "I daresay they'll try to brazen it out, at least till the end of the season. They may if they like, for all I care. I never knew any good come of these *half-bred* ones, and *I'll* have nothing more to do with them!"

Lacquers heard as though he heard him not. He was trying to think, and his well-cut features were gathered into an expression of hopeless perplexity, at which his companion could scarce forbear laughing outright. At last he had recourse to the never-failing moustache; and drawing inspiration from its touch, he began —

"Uppy, you're a safe fellow — eh? — wouldn't throw a fellow over, and put him in the hole, you know. You've got some brains, too — made a capital book on the Ascot Stakes. Now you understand finance and arithmetic, and that — what should *you* say a married fellow could live upon? Of course he wouldn't require so many luxuries as a single one; but what do you think, now, a fellow like *me*, for instance, could do with?"

Sir Ascot looked completely taken aback. "Why, you'd never be such a fool as to think of — —"

"That's neither here nor there, old boy," interrupted Lacquers; "of course if I *do* you shall have the earliest intelligence. But come, here's a book and a pencil; let's see how the thing would work with good management and strict economy. *Strict economy*, you know, of course." Lacquers had a great idea, *in theory*, of strict economy. So the young man sat down, and went deep into the various items of rent, and stable expenses, and opera-boxes and pin-money, and cigars and travelling; Sir Ascot arriving at the conclusion that a quiet couple might manage to exist upon something over two thousand a year; whilst Lacquers thought it was to be done, with *strict economy*, of course, for about five hundred less; but as they both entirely overlooked an indispensable item termed "housekeeping," we think it needless to record their calculations for the benefit of the inexperienced.

"Well," said Lacquers, when he had finished his arithmetic and put his betting-book once more into his pocket, "I think it can be done — I believe a fellow *ought* to marry, you know; what does Shakespeare say about 'Solitude being born a twin'? it certainly sobers him" —(Sir Ascot smiled as he admitted that was undoubtedly a strong argument)— "and altogether married fellows get into more respectable habits. Look at a breakfast in a country-house; you see all the married ones up and dressed with the lark, while the single men come dawdling down at all hours. Yes, there's a good deal to be said on both sides, like a Chancery lawsuit; but I'll think it over,

Uppy, my boy, I'll think it over." And Lacquers did think it over, and arrived at a conclusion as honourable to his heart as it was antagonistic to that worldly wisdom by which all with whom he associated thought it right to regulate their every action. Here was a man spoilt by the accident of personal beauty and good birth and position. From his earliest boyhood he had never been taught that there was any ulterior object in life save to shine in society, if not intellectually, why, physically, with a handsome person and fine clothes—a far more effectual passport than all the talents to the good graces of the world. What wonder that the tree grew up as it had been bent? what wonder that the hussar had scarcely two ideas beyond his uniform and his betting-book, and his seat upon a horse? that he looked on the world at large as the butterfly on the sunny square enclosed by the garden wall—a mere stage for display, a mere hot-bed for physical enjoyment, to be got the most out of during the bright, gaudy hours of noon; and afterwards—why, afterwards, when the sun goes down and the chill dews of evening clog his fading wings—the butterfly must do the best he can, and perish as he may. With such an education, the sole manly quality left was courage, and it was only the touchstone of a gentle face like Blanche's that brought out the latent generosity of a character overlaid with faults, for which its training was more to blame than its organisation. We are obliged to confess that Lacquers was vain, thoughtless, self-opinionated, frivolous, ignorant, and empty-headed, but there *was* some good in him, and it was brought out, as it always will be when it exists at all, by a woman's smile, and, above all, by a woman's misfortunes.

Lacquers made up his mind that he would marry Blanche Kettering without a sixpence. The young lady's consent he rather prematurely counted on as a matter of course, but in making this resolution he deserves some credit for the readiness with which he was prepared to sacrifice all that to him was precious in life, at the feet of his lady-love. He was a younger brother, and, it is needless to add, considerably involved—of course he must bid farewell to all those amusements and pursuits which have hitherto constituted his actual existence. No more Derbys and Hamptons, and Richmond breakfasts, and Greenwich dinners, all vanities enticing enough in their way—no more stalls at the opera, and supper-parties in the suburbs, likewise vanities of a more dangerous tendency—no more hunting in Leicestershire and deer-stalking in Scotland, yachting at Cowes and philandering at Paris—all these must be given up; and worse than all, the profession he delights in, the regiment he is devoted to, must be offered at the shrine of domestic respectability. That these would be privations no man could feel more keenly than Lacquers, yet was he prepared to go through with it, and had it been necessary, we firmly believe he would have cut off his very moustaches and laid them at the feet of Blanche Kettering! Therefore it was that he appeared on the evening in question at Lady Mount Helicon's ball; therefore it was that his manner had assumed a softness and diffidence which made Blanche confess to herself, as she leaned on his arm in the intervals of the dance, that he was "really very much improved"; and therefore it was that he suggested the old excuse of "looking at the flowers in the conservatory," and skilfully availing himself of a general rush downstairs connected with supper, managed to entice his partner into a secluded corner of that love-making retreat, which had indeed been already occupied by several pairs for the same purpose, and having furnished her with a cup of tea, and himself with an ice to keep them both quiet, he entered with much circumlocution on one of those embarrassing interviews such as, we are quite sure, no lady who condescends to glance over these pages but must have experienced at least *once* before she had been out two seasons.

"That's a case," said Mrs. Blacklamb, as she swept down to supper on Lord Mount Helicon's arm, her dark, haughty features writhing with something between a smile and a sneer, while she caught a glimpse of Blanche's well-cut profile, and one of Lacquers's faultless boots in a mirror opposite their retreat. "Will it *be*, do you think?" she added with a softening expression, for all women warm towards a love-affair, and even Mrs. Blacklamb, with her many faults, was a very woman, perhaps rather too much so, in her heart of hearts.

"I hope not," replied Mount, with a smile into his companion's face. "I'm very much in love with her myself. If it hadn't been for 'the Division' I should have been where Lacquers is at this moment. Look what my patriotism has cost me, but I don't regret it *now*," and he emphasised the monosyllable with an almost imperceptible pressure of the arm that hung upon his own, a movement that had little effect on Mrs. Blacklamb, with whom flirtation (whatever that comprehensive word may mean) was the daily business of life.

"Why, you know you would have married her, and too happy if she had only been the catch you all thought she was," replied the lady. "I must say I could not help being delighted, though I was sorry for *her*, poor girl, to see you all 'getting out' just as you do when some racehorse breaks down, trying which could be first to pull himself clear of the scrape, and leave his neighbours in the lurch. Major D'Orville behaved *shamefully*, and you still worse, for she really was fond of *you*."

"Mount's" imperturbable good-humour was proof against quizzing, so the sneer fell harmless, and he replied carelessly, "Fond? of course she was, but not so *very* fond—no. Mrs. Blacklamb, I'm easily imposed on by ladies. I think it's my diffidence that stands so much in my way; even where my affections are most irrevocably engaged, where I worship is hopeless constancy, and I feel my heart breaking, and my—my—my hair coming out of curl, I dare not ask my enslaver more than whether she will have a glass of wine. Give Mrs. Blacklamb some champagne, and I'll have a little sherry, if you please;" so the pair went on jesting and philandering and making fools of each other and of themselves, but they troubled their heads no more about the couple in the conservatory; and when "Mount" deserted his fair companion and returned into the ball-room, as he said, "to dance just once with Miss Kettering, in common decency," he sought her in vain, for she was gone.

"Uncle Baldwin," said Blanche, when they reached home, and lingered a moment in the drawing-room before retiring—"Uncle Baldwin, I've got something to say to you." Blanche blushed and hesitated, and looked at the little white satin shoe she was resting on the fender in every possible point of view. "To-night at the ball, I—that's to say, Captain Lacquers—in short, I dare say you remarked—in the conservatory, you know—Oh, Uncle Baldwin, *he proposed* to me," and Blanche, half-laughing, half-crying, and blushing over her neck and shoulders, hid her face on the breast of the General's coat, as she used to do when she had been a naughty little girl and repented, ten years ago.

"Zounds! Blanche, what did you say?" burst out the General, in a terrible taking, as he thought now everything must come out. "Yes or No, my darling, don't keep me in suspense—which is it, heads or tails? in or out? I mean, Yes or No?"

"No!" whispered Blanche, to the General's inexpressible relief, who cooled down into a prolonged *whew*, like the escape of steam from a safety-valve; but it was rather difficult to say it, he seemed so sorry and so patient and considerate. "Do you know, Uncle Baldwin, I never thought so highly of Captain Lacquers as I do to-night."

"Probably not, my dear," grunted the General, "you never knew before he thought so highly of you. But, Blanche, as we are here, and—and it's not very late—zounds! they've put that clock on again—well, dear, I too have got something to tell you; but mine, I am sorry to say, is bad news. Prepare yourself, my dear Blanche. I'm sure you will bear it well, my little pet, and as long as I have a roof over my head you will have a home; but, in short, it's no use mincing the matter, Blanche, you're not an heiress after all—you won't have a sixpence beyond what I can leave you, and that's little enough, heaven knows. They've found your mother's will, my dear, and a most unfair and unreasonable will it is; but still, my pretty Blanche, it makes you a penniless young lady, after all!"

"Is that the worst?" answered Blanche, looking up with an air of immense relief, though she had turned deadly pale; "is that all, Uncle Baldwin? dear me, I'm not worse off than half the other girls I know. We shall leave this house, I suppose," she added, looking round at the ample room and its stately furniture, jumping at once to conclusions, as young ladies will do, "and we shall live entirely at Newton-Hollows, and I shall be there all the time my garden looks most beautiful; but we shan't have to send away Mrs. Delaval, shall we?" (The General winced.) "And when will it all be settled? and when shall we go?"

"Blanche, you're a diamond," said the General, his eyes filling with tears; "you've the pluck of ten women. You ought to have commanded the Kedjerees. Go to bed now, my dear, and to-morrow we'll look things boldly in the face, and see what is best to be done." So the General stumped off with his bed-candle, more than ever doating on his niece, more than ever persuaded that she inherited her sterling qualities from his side of the house, and not from that "poor, foolish old Kettering," as he called him, and more than ever indignant with all the young men of his acquaintance, except Lacquers, for not being on their knees to Blanche. "They've no energy; they've no devotion; zounds! they've no chivalry amongst 'em—none whatever! If I was such a fellow as any one of these, 'gad, I'd go to bed and never get up again;" with which soliloquy the General proceeded to divest himself of his ball-going attire, and prepared for his refuge from all the ills of life.

To those who are conversant with the habits of ladies, it is needless to mention that Blanche did not, by any means, follow her uncle's excellent advice and example, in betaking herself to immediate repose. The fair sex will easily comprehend how she sought Mrs. Delaval's room, and how the two ladies sat up in "their wrappers" and consoled each other, and talked it all over, backwards and forwards, and came to no very logical conclusions; and, above all, how the proposal and its reception were quite as engrossing a topic, and were quite as much dwelt on as the loss of Blanche's fine fortune; nor will it escape their observation that Mary's greater worldly experience would clearly foresee the substitution of one cousin for another in this revolution amongst the Kettering possessions, and how a marriage between the two was the only plan to make everything right; and how the fair young face, with its kind eyes, that had haunted her so long, was farther from her now than ever. She knew, of course, long ago, that it was hopeless and impossible—that must surely have been a great consolation! When a child cries for the moon, and a cloud comes and covers up the coveted bauble, and hides it away, the urchin has small comfort in being told that it is just as near the object of its desires as when it could see it, and look, and long, and stretch its tiny hands. When the beggar-maiden sets her affections on King Cophetua, without a hope, in these days, of the famous fabulous *mésalliance* being perpetrated, the fact that it does not, in reality, remove him one iota farther than before from her humble self, helps but little to assuage the pang inflicted on her infatuated heart by his Majesty's nuptials with one of his own degree. The impossible may be increased in love, if not in logic, and Mary was lying awake and desponding, long after Blanche had forgotten all the excitement and changes of the evening in happy, dreamless slumbers.

CHAPTER XIX
DISPATCHES

Mary Delaval, in London, was one of the many flowers born to "waste their sweetness on the desert air," for London is, indeed, a desert to those who are in it and not of it, whose destiny seems to have been warped into a strange unfitness in the great, struggling, noisy, pompous town; whose proper place would seem to be in some quiet, secluded nook, the ornament and the joy of a peaceful home, instead of the ever-shifting surface of that seething tide which drifts them here and there in aimless restlessness. Verily, Fortune does sometimes shuffle the pack in most inexplicable confusion—*Ludum insolentem, ludere pertinax*—she seems to take a perverse pleasure in smuggling the court-cards into all sorts of incongruous places, and to carry out the Latin poet's metaphor, *trans-mutat incertos honores*, or, in plain English, palms the trumps, with dexterous sleight-of-hand, where they seem utterly valueless to influence the result of the game. As society is constituted, such a woman as Mary, with her queenly dignity, her charming manner, her striking beauty, and, above all, her noble, well-cultivated mind, was just as thoroughly *tabooed* and excluded from the circle of her so-called superiors as if she had been a quadroon in the United States, whose very beauty owes its brilliance to that African stain which, in the Land of Freedom and Equality, makes a shade of colouring the badge that entitles man to lord it over his brother more despotically than over the beasts of the field. Thank God for it, we have no slavery in England; and the time cannot be very far distant when slavery shall be a word without a meaning in the dictionary of every language on the face of the globe. Already, from East to West, the trumpet-note has sounded, and those stir in their sleep who have drugged themselves into insensibility, and stopped their ears against the voice of the charmer, but cannot smother the still small whisper within. Scarcely has its last peal died away beneath the blushing Western wave, ere its echoes are caught up in the very heart of the Morning Land, and even now, while we write, a barbarian despot is quailing on his celestial throne, and the voice of Liberty—real Liberty, Civilisation, and Christianity—is thundering in the ears of millions and millions of immortal beings, hitherto held in thraldom, throughout that mysterious empire, which for ages has been a sealed book to all other nations upon earth. Shall not England still be in the van, as she has always been? Never yet has she failed in the good cause, and never will she. Has she not ever struck for Freedom and the Cross? inseparable watchwords, that the experience of the world has taught us must go hand in hand, or not at all; and where she strikes, good faith, she drives well home. Has she not ever been the first assailant in the breach? stood the outmost bulwark in the gap? and will she fail now? Believe it not. Her destiny would seem the brightest that Providence has yet ordained for any nation since the world began. Formidable and glorious without, she is setting her house in order within. Steadily and gradually the good cause—the universal brotherhood of the soul—is progressing everywhere; through wars and rumours of wars, through political clouds and private disappointments, there seems to be in all men's minds a settled conviction that "the good time's coming"; and if, as we firmly believe, England shall bear the glorious banner in the van, why, night and morning will we go down upon our knees and thank God that we are Englishmen! But what has all this to do with a penniless governess, sitting up two pair of stairs in Grosvenor Square? Thus much, as we think: our social system is yet a long way from perfection—there is yet much to be improved and much prejudice to be taken away—we have too much class-feeling and class-isolation, and, perhaps, on no people do these shortcomings in our charity fall so heavily as on those to whom we entrust the education of our children. What is it in which we are so superior to them that entitles us to hold ourselves thus aloof, and, for all the courtesy of our wayfaring salutation, virtually "to pass by on the other side"? What is it that constitutes the talismanic qualification for what we modestly term *good* society? Is it birth, that accident on which we so rationally plume ourselves? They generally possess even that negative advantage. Is it education, intellect, cultivation of mind? We do not entrust our darlings to their care because they are *inferior* to us in attainments, or we should teach the pupils ourselves. Is it manner? We do not quarrel with a peer for being gross, or a millionaire for being vulgar—and those of whom we are speaking generally show no want at least of decorum in their demeanour and conversation. Is it money? God forbid! Is it then mere frivolity and assumption in which we excel? For shame! No; the truth must out; there is a leaven still left in us of the very essence of vulgarity, the feeling that we are ill at ease with a so-called inferior, or the domineering spirit which every schoolboy knows too well, prompting us to exult in every chance advantage we may possess over a fellow-creature. Of these amiable causes we may take our choice; but one or other it is which leaves the governess to pine up-stairs in her school-room, while revelry and pleasure and good-fellowship are laughing below.

Now, Mary had, indeed, little of this sort of neglect to complain of; yet was she lonely and sad during the London season which Blanche enjoyed so much. She could not, of course, accompany her to all the balls and "At Homes" which were fast becoming the business of the girl's life; if she had, we think the worshipful body of chaperons would have lost nothing in dignity, and gained a good deal in grace, beauty, and good-humour by her adhesion. So she felt she was too much separated from Blanche, whom she dearly loved; and it was with a sensation almost of satisfaction, for which she was, nevertheless, quite angry with herself, that she heard of the entire disturbance of all the family arrangements, and the loss of fortune sustained by the young heiress. "Ah," thought Mary, "perhaps I may be of some use to her now in her distress; at any rate, I can give her good counsel and practical instruction how to *bear*—none better;" and had it not been for a certain marriage, which seemed more than ever indispensable, Mary would have been ashamed to confess to herself how glad she was.

The General, it is needless to say, was a man of vigorous execution when he had once made up his mind. He had ascertained, as he believed, the validity of the will, had paid Gingham her legacy, with a gratuity over and above on his own account, and now held a council of war with the two ladies, before breakfast, in which he discloses his plans with a degree of meekness nothing could ever have brought him to, save a misfortune affecting his beloved Blanche.

"No going abroad this year, my dear," said the General, looking the while less warlike than usual; "glad of it—what? A German watering-place—bah! an association of blackguards in an overgrown village, robbing the public to soft music in the open air. No, my dear, we'll get to Newton-Hollows before the strawberries are done—and I'm glad of it. We'll let this great house—you're tired of it, Blanche, and so am I; what's the use of a house all up and down-stairs? You should have seen my bungalow at Simlah—a man could get about in that and hear himself speak. Well, we'll put down two of the carriages and one of the footmen—that pompous one. Zounds, if he had stayed a week longer I must have bastinadoed him—and we'll start Poulard: confound him, he never gives one a dinner fit to eat, and wouldn't dress a cutlet for Mrs. Delaval, only the day before yesterday, because we dined out—I'll trounce him before he goes. Then, my dear, we'll keep your scrubby pony for the little carriage, and 'Water King' can go down home with the others, and you'll ride a deal more there than in London, Blanche. Manage? I'll manage—how d'ye mean? I'm only a steward till Charlie comes back. I must write to Charlie by this mail, and we'll have him safe and sound from the Kaffirs—and rejoicings when he comes home, and a—who knows what?"—(Mary Delaval got up at this juncture, went to fetch her work, and sat majestically down to it, as the General went on.)—"Yes, we'll make it all right when Charlie comes back. Let me see, we ought to have a mail to-day. Zounds, these servants they read all the news—money market, foreign intelligence, every one of their own cursed advertisements for places they won't keep six months—and then, if I ask whether the paper's come, 'Please, sir, it's not ironed.' Ironed! 'Gad, I'll iron them—wish I'd my Kitmugar here—bamboozle them well on the soles of their feet—there's no liberty in this country. Blanche, ring the bell, there's a dear—oh, here it comes;" and the General's further strictures were cut short by the entrance of his old, pompous servant, who laid the paper out for his master's perusal with a strange air of mingled pity and concern. The General put on his spectacles, deliberately unfolded the sheet, and after a glance at the money market, in which consols had, as usual, fluctuated the fraction of a fraction, he turned to the well-known column in which the budget of the African mail was likely to be detailed; Blanche leaning over his shoulder the while, and Mary watching them with an eager glance that seemed almost prescient of evil. Suddenly the General's face flushed up to a purple hue. "Engagement with the Kaffirs," he muttered; "gallant repulse of the enemy—capture—loss—strong position—brilliant success of the Light Brigade—O my boy! my boy!" And, forgetful of all around, the old man leaned his head upon the table and gave way to a passion of grief that was frightful to contemplate. There it was, sure enough, in distinct, choicely-printed types—there was no mistaking the name, or the regiment, or the authenticity of the report, and Blanche, with bloodless lips and stony eyes, could see nothing but that one line of hopeless import—"Missing, Cornet Kettering, of the 20th Lancers." Yes, she had skimmed through killed and wounded, with the agonising fear of seeing her cousin returned in that awful list, and a deep sigh of relief was rising to her lips as she recognised no beloved name among the sufferers, when it was frozen back again by the startling truth. And there she stood, utterly colourless, her hair pushed back from her temples, and her eyes staring wildly and vacantly, as she kept her finger pressed on the dreadful line, of which she too well comprehended the meaning.

The General rocked to and fro in an agony of grief, his broken exclamations of childish despair strangely mingled with those warlike sentiments of honour and resignation which become second nature in the soldier's character.

"My boy, my boy! my gallant, handsome, light-hearted Charlie! I might have known it must be so—I've seen it a hundred times—the youngest, the fairest, the happiest, go down at the first shot. That pale, tender lad at the sortie from Bayonne—my subaltern at Quatre Bras—my *aide-de-camp* in the Deccan, always the brightest and the most hopeful—and now my boy, my

Charlie! Why did I let him go? a soldier's fate, poor lad. Well, well, every bullet has its billet—but, oh, he need never have gone to that savage country. O my boy, my boy! you were more than a son to me, and now you're lying mangled and rotting in the bush below the Anatolas."

Mary alone preserved her presence of mind. Utter despair is the most powerful of sedatives; and she walked deliberately across the room, took the paper from Blanche's unresisting hands, and satisfied herself of the worst. A special paragraph of nearly six lines was devoted to the fate of "this gallant and promising young officer, who was last seen waving his men on in a brilliant attack which he led against a numerous horde of savages; the enemy were driven from their defences at all points; but we regret to learn Cornet Kettering was reported missing at nightfall, and we have reason to fear, from the barbarous and ferocious character of Kaffir warfare, it will be almost impossible to recover or identify his remains."

And was this the end of all? Was this the fate of the bright, happy, beloved boy, whose image, as she last saw him, radiant in health and hope, had never since left her mind?—mangled—defaced—butchered—dead!—that awful word comprised everything—never to see him more, never to hear his voice; to feel as if it was all a dream, as if it had never been; as if there was no Past, and there would be no Future—that the deadening, heavy, soul-sickening Present was to be all! But she could not give him up like this: the report was dated immediately previous to the departure of the mail, and there might be a possibility of error. Steadily, calmly, closely, like a heroine as she was, Mary read through the whole official account of the engagement, word for word, and line for line; how "the Brigadier had received information of the enemy's movements, and had held himself in readiness, and had given such and such orders, and executed such and such movements," all detailed in the happy, self-satisfied style which characterises official accounts of the game of death; how in a previous report his Excellency had been apprised of the capture of so many head of cattle, and the submission of so many chiefs with hard names; and how the Brigadier had great pleasure in informing his Excellency of the further capture of several thousand oxen, and the discomfiture of more chiefs, and all with a loss of life trifling compared to the important results of this brilliant *coup-de-main*. How the troops, and the levies, and the Hottentots, had each and all reaped their share of laurels, by their gallantry in attack, their steadiness under fire, and general cheerfulness and good discipline through long, toilsome marches and harassing privations; and how the Brigadier's own thanks were due to officers commanding regiments, and officers commanding companies, and his *aides-de-camp*, and his quartermaster, and his medical staff, and all the brave fellows who had won their share in the triumph of the hour; and the report concluded with a few feeling words of manly regret for those who had earned a soldier's grave, amongst whom poor "Old Swipes," shot down as he led his men so gallantly to the attack, was not forgotten; whilst a line of concern for the uncertainty attending Cornet Kettering's fate (otherwise honourably mentioned in the dispatch) wound up the whole. All this Mary read with a painful distinctness that seemed to burn every word into her brain, and from it she gathered, indeed, small hope and small consolation. Truly, war is a fine thing in the abstract! The martial music, the flaunting colours, the steady tramp of bold, bronzed men, exulting in their freemasonry of danger, the enthusiasm of the spectators, the professional charlatanry (we use the word with no disrespectful meaning) which pervades the brotherhood,—all this is taking enough when the engine is in repose; and then the joys of a campaign, the continual change of scene, the never-flagging excitement, the little luxuries of the bivouac, the rough good-fellowship of the march, and the boiling, thrilling excitement of the encounter—all these doubtless have their charms when the machine is put into action; but there is a sad reverse to the picture, and those who read with the military enthusiasm of ignorance such captivating accounts of brilliant strategy and daring heroism, should recollect that the same Gazette which makes captains and colonels, makes also widows and orphans; that eyes are gushing and hearts breaking over those very lines that bid the uninterested peruser thrill with warlike ardour and half-envious pride in the deeds of arms of his countrymen. The greatest hero of the age has recorded his opinion of those scenes in which he reaped his own immortal laurels, when he said, "he prayed God he might never again see so frightful a calamity as a national war;" and his opinion has been often quoted, to the effect that a battle won was the next most horrible sight to a battle lost. Far and wide spreads the crop of misery that springs from that iron shower. Its effects are not confined to wasted fields and blackened houses, and devoted ranks stretched where they fell in all the ghastly distortions of violent death. Far, far away, in happy homes and peaceful families, women and children must wail and pine in vain for him whom they will never see again on earth; and the ounce of lead that carries death into that loyal, kind heart, scatters misery and grief, and penury, perhaps, and ruin, over the gentle dependents here at home in England, that have none to trust to, none to care for them, save him who lies cold and stiff upon the field of glory. Glory! when will men learn the right meaning of the word?

Well, three lines in the Gazette had brought misery enough to the inmates of the house in Grosvenor Square. How paltry to them now seemed the household cares and little money arrangements that had occupied their morning consultation. What was there to arrange for now? What signified it how things went? He would never return to enjoy the fruits of their care. What mattered it who had the house, and the fortune, and the plate, and the personalities, and all the paltry dross, which now showed its real value?—to-morrow it will begin again to resume its fictitious appearance, for grief passes as surely as does the cloud. But to-day, the General and Blanche are almost stupefied, and can think of nothing but Charlie—dear, *dear*, lost Charlie. The old man sits rocking to and fro, in violent paroxysms, frightful in one of his age—who would have thought he had so much feeling left in him?—and Blanche is exhausted with weeping, and lies with her face buried, and her long golden hair trailing over the sofa cushions, incapable of thought or exertion. Mary alone retains her presence of mind; Mary alone vindicates her noble nature in the hour of trial; Mary alone is fit to command; and Mary alone resolves upon what is best to be done, and proceeds at once to put her schemes into execution. There is but one person to apply to for advice and assistance: there is but one friend in whom the bereaved family can confide; who should it be but kind, generous, bold-hearted Frank Hardingstone? Mary puts on her bonnet and shawl: out of the confused mass in the hall she selects Mr. Hardingstone's card, ascertains his address, and without saying a word about her intentions, sallies forth to seek him out, primed with the eloquence of a woman's hopeless, unselfish love.

Frank has lingered on in London, he scarce knows why. He is training his strong, masculine mind to bear the loss of Blanche—for he feels that Blanche is lost to him—just as he would train to make any other effort, or endure any other suffering. His mornings are spent in close and severe study; his afternoons in those athletic exercises at which he is so proficient; and in the evening he goes into *men's* society, as gentlemen do when they are sore about the other sex, and tries to be amused, and to enter into the frivolities and pastimes of his associates, and succeeds sometimes indifferently badly, sometimes not at all. Strange visitors are admitted to Frank's morning-room at the hotel where he puts up—the waiter cannot make him but at all. Now, an engineer, in his Sunday clothes, but with a rough chin and grimy hands, is closeted with him all the morning, and the waiter overhears casual expressions, such as "power," and "gradients," and "angles," and "the motive," and "the bite," and "the catch," which, on the principle of *omne ignotum pro terribili*, make his hair stand on end. Then, just as he had made up his mind that Mr. Hardingstone is *professional*, and not a *real* gent after all, some live Duke or magnificent Marquis comes in with his hat on, and says, "Frank, my dear fellow, how goes it?" and the waiter's conclusions are again completely upset. Then an archæologian, with smooth white neckcloth and well-brushed beaver, steps gravely up-stairs, and remains for hours discussing the probable site of some problematic edifice which there is reason to suppose *might* have been pulled down by the Confessor; and on this interesting topic they lavish a store of knowledge, penetration, and research rather disproportioned to the result arrived at, till the archæologian stays to have luncheon, and shows no small energy even at that. The waiter begins to think Mr. Hardingstone is a gent connected with the British Museum (for which institution he entertains a superstitious reverence), and possibly a fellow-labourer with Layard and Rawlinson. But again, twice a week, an individual is admitted whose general appearance is so much the reverse of the respectable, sleek archæologian, that the waiter finds it impossible to reconcile the contradiction of Mr. Hardingstone's being, as he terms it, "*in* with both." This latter visitor is of athletic frame, and remarkably forbidding countenance, none the less so from an originally snub nose having been smashed into a sort of plaster over the adjoining territory. His hair is cut as short as is consistent with the use of scissors, and his arms, in very tight sleeves, hang down his sides as if they were in the last stage of powerless fatigue. He dresses as though he kept a horse, yet is his gait that of a man who is continually on his legs, active as a cat, and of no mean pedestrian powers. He remains with Mr. Hardingstone about an hour, during which time much shuffling of feet is heard, and much hard breathing, with occasional expectoration on the part of the visitor. The windows are invariably thrown wide open during the interview; and at its conclusion, the stranger being supplied with beer, for which fluid he entertains a remarkable predilection, wipes his mouth on his sleeve, and expresses his satisfaction at the hospitality of his entertainer, and the warmth of his reception, by stating, in reprehensibly strong language, that he has had "a—something—good bellyful." This too is a professor, and a scientific man; but his profession is that of pugilism, his science the noble one of self-defence. So the waiter is again all abroad: but when Mary Delaval puts up her veil, and taking out a plain card with her name written thereon, requests the astonished functionary to "take it up to Mr. Hardingstone, and tell him a lady wishes to see him," even a waiter's self-command is overcome, and he can only relieve his feelings by the execution of an infinity of winks for his own benefit, and the frequent repetition of "Well, this beats cock-fighting!" as he ushers the lady up the hotel stairs, and points out to her the rooms occupied by the mysterious guest.

Most people would have considered Frank hardly prepared to receive visits from a lady, both in respect of his costume and the general arrangement of his apartment. He was sitting in his shirt-sleeves, unbraced, and with his neck bare; his large loose frame curled up on a short, uncomfortable sofa, in anything but a graceful position, and his broad manly countenance gathered into an expression of intense, almost painful attention. A short pipe between his strong white teeth filled the room with odours only preferable to that of *stale* tobacco-smoke, with which its atmosphere was generally laden; and the book on his knee was a ponderous quarto, to the full as heavy as it looked, and fit for even Frank's large intellect to grapple with. The furniture was simple enough; most of that which belonged to the hotel had been put away, and a set of boxing-gloves, two or three foils, a small black leather portmanteau, and a few books of the same stamp as that on the owner's knee, comprised almost the only objects in the apartment. The morning paper was lying unopened on the window-sill. When he saw who it was, Frank started up with a blush, snatched the short pipe out of his mouth, set a chair for his visitor, and sitting bolt upright on the short sofa, stared at her with a ludicrous expression of mingled shyness and surprise. He was glad to see her, too—for why?—she belonged in some sort to Blanche.

"Have you seen the morning paper?" began Mary, in her low, measured tones, though her voice shook more than usual. "Have you seen those disastrous tidings from the Cape? Oh, Mr. Hardingstone, we are all in despair! Charles Kettering has, in all probability, been"—she could not bring herself to say it—"at least he is missing—missing, gracious Heaven! in that fearful country!—and we have only heard of it this morning. The General is incapable of acting; he is completely paralysed by the blow; and I have come—forgive me, Mr. Hardingstone—I have come to you as our only friend, to ask your advice and assistance; to entreat you to—to——" Poor Mary broke down, and went into a passionate fit of weeping, all the more violent from having been so long restrained.

Frank was horrified at the intelligence; he made a grasp at the paper, and there, sure enough, his worst fears were confirmed. But this was no time for the indulgence of helpless regret; and when Mary was sufficiently composed, he asked her with a strange, meaning anxiety, "How Blanche bore the fatal tidings?" Heart of man! what depths of selfishness are there in thy chambers! At the back of all his sorrow for his more than brother, at the back of all his anxiety and horror, he hated himself to know that there was a vague feeling of relief as if a load had been taken off, an obstacle removed. He would have laid down his life for Charlie; had he been with him in the bush, he would have shed the last drop of his blood to defend him; yet now that his fate was ascertained, he shuddered to find that his grief was not totally unqualified; he loathed himself when he felt that through the dark there was a gleam somewhere that had a reflection of joy.

"Blanche's feelings you may imagine," replied Mary, now strangely, almost sternly composed; "she has lost a more than brother" (Frank winced); "but of feelings it is not the time to talk. You may think me mad to say so, but something tells me there may still be a hope. He is not reported killed, or even wounded; he is 'missing'; there is a chance yet that he may be saved. These savages do not always kill their prisoners" (she shuddered as she spoke); "there is yet a possibility that he may have been taken and carried off to the mountains. An energetic man on the spot might even now be the means of preserving him from a hideous fate. These people must surely be amenable to bribes, like the rest of mankind. Oh, it is possible—in God's mercy it is possible—and we may get him back amongst us, like one from the dead."

Frank grasped at her meaning in an instant; and even while he did so, he could not help remarking how beautiful she was—her commanding sorrow borne with such dignity and yet such resignation. He drew down his brows, set his teeth firm, and the old expression came over his face which poor Charlie used to admire so much—an expression of grim, unblenching resolve.

"You're right, Mrs. Delaval, it might be done," he said, slowly and deliberately. "How long has the mail taken to come to England—twenty-eight days?—the same going out. It is a desperate chance!—yet would it be a satisfaction to know the worst. Poor boy!—poor Charlie!—game to the last, I see, in the general order. What think ye, Mrs. Delaval; would it be any use?"

"If I was a man," replied Mary, "I should be in the train for Southampton at this moment."

Frank rang the bell; the waiter appeared with an alacrity that looked as if he had been listening at the keyhole. "Bring my bill," said Frank to that astonished functionary, "and have a cab at the door in twenty minutes."

"You are going, Mr. Hardingstone?" said Mary, clasping her hands; "God bless you for it!"

"I am going," replied Frank, putting the short pipe carefully away, and pulling out the small black portmanteau.

"You will start to-day?" asked Mary, with an expression of admiration on her sorrowing countenance for a decision of character so in accordance with her own nature.

"In twenty minutes," replied Frank, still packing for hard life; and he was as good as his word. His things were ready; his bill paid; his servant furnished with the necessary directions during his master's absence; and himself in the cab, on his way to his bankers, and from thence to the railway station, in exactly twenty minutes from the moment of his making up his mind to go.

"Tell Blanche I'll bring him back safe and sound," said he, as he shook hands with Mary on the hotel steps; "and—and—tell her," he added, with a deeper tint on his bronzed, manly cheek, "tell her that I—I had no time to wish her good-bye."

We question whether this was exactly the message Frank intended to give; but this bold fellow, who could resolve at a moment's notice to undertake a long, tedious voyage, to penetrate to the seat of war in a savage country, and, if need were, to risk his life at every step for the sake of his friend, had not courage to send a single word of commonplace gallantry to a timid, tender girl. So it is—Hercules is but a cripple in sight of Omphale—Samson turns faint-hearted in the lap of Delilah—nor are these heroes of antiquity the only champions who have wittingly placed their brawny necks beneath a small white foot, and been surprised to find it could spurn so fiercely, and tread so heavily. Mary should have loved such a man as Frank, and *vice versâ*—here was the *beau idéal* that each had formed of the opposite sex. Frank was never tired of crying up a woman of energy and courage, one who could dare and suffer, and still preserve the queenly dignity which he chose to esteem woman's chiefest attraction; and so he neglected the gem, and set his great, strong heart upon the flower. Well, we have often seen it so; we *admire* the diamond, but we *love* the rose. As for Mary, she was, if possible, more inconsistent still. As she walked back to Grosvenor Square she thought over the heroic qualities of Mr. Hardingstone, and wondered how it was possible he should yet remain unmarried. "Such a man as that," thought Mary, revolving in her own mind his manifold good qualities, "so strong, so handsome, so clever, so high-minded, he has all the necessary ingredients that make up a great man; how simple in his habits, and how frank and unaffected in his manner; a woman might acknowledge *him* as a superior indeed! Mind to reflect; head to plan; and energy to execute! She would be *proud* to love him, to cling to him, and look up to him, and worship him. And Blanche has known him from a child, and never seen all this!" and a pang smote Mary's heart, as she recollected *why*, in all probability, Blanche had been so blind to Frank Hardingstone's attractions; and how *she*, of all people, could not blame her for her preference of another: and then the fair young face and the golden curls rose before her mind's eye like a phantom, and she turned sick as she thought it might even now be mouldering in the earth. Then Mary pulled a letter from her pocket, and looked at it almost with loathing, as the past came back to her like the shade of a magic-lantern. She saw the gardens at Bishops'-Baffler; the officers in undress uniform, and the grey charger; the evening walks; the quiet summer twilight; the steeple-chase at Guyville; and her eyes filled with tears, and she softened to another's miseries as she reflected on her own. "Selfish, unprincipled as he is," thought Mary, "he must love me, or he never would make such an offer as this. And what am I, that I should spurn the devotion of any human being? Have not I, too, been selfish and unprincipled, in allowing my mind to dwell alone on him who in reality belonged to another? Have I not cherished and encouraged the poison?—have I not yielded to the temptation?—do I wish even now that it was otherwise?—and am I not rightly punished?—have I not suffered less than I deserve?—and yet how miserable I am—how lonely and how despairing!—there is not another being on earth as miserable as I am!"

"By your leave, ma'am," said a rough, coarse voice; and Mary stepped aside to make way on the pavement for a little mournful procession that was winding gloomily along, in strange, chilling contrast to the bustle and liveliness of the street. It was a little child's funeral. The short black coffin, carried so easily on one man's shoulder, seemed almost like a plaything for Death. It was touching to think what a tiny body was covered by that scanty pall—how the little thing, once so full of life and laughter, all play and merriment and motion, could be lying stiff and stark in death! It seemed such a contradiction to the whole course of nature—a streamlet turning back towards its source—a rosebud nipped by the frost. Had the grim Reaper no other harvest whitening for his sickle? Was there not age, with its aches and pains and burdens, almost asking for release? Was there not manhood, full of years and honours, its appointed task done on earth, its guerdon fairly earned, itself waiting for the reward? Was there not crime, tainting the atmosphere around it, that to take away would be a mercy to its fellow-men, and a deserved punishment to its own hardened obstinacy, having neglected and set aside every opportunity of repentance and amendment? Was there not virtue willing to go, and misery imploring to be set free? And must he leave all these, and cut off the little creeping tendril that had wound and twisted itself round its mother's heart? There was the mother first in the slow procession—who had so good a right to be chief mourner as that poor, broken woman? Who can estimate the aching void that shall never be quite filled up in that sobbing, weary breast? She is not thinking of the funeral, nor the passers-by, nor the crape, nor the mourning; she does not hear rough condolences from neighbours, and well-meant injunctions "to keep up," and "not to give way so," from those who "are mothers themselves, and know what a mother's feelings *is*." She is thinking of her child—her child shut down in that deal box—yet still hers—she has got it still—not till it is consigned to the earth, and the dull clods rattle heavily on the lid, will she feel that she has lost it altogether, when there will come a fearful reaction, and paroxysms of grief that deaden themselves by their own violence; and then the wound will cicatrise, and she will clean her house, and get her husband's dinner, and sit down to her stitching, and neighbours will think that she has "got over her trouble," and she will seem contented, and even happy. But the little one will not be forgotten. When the flowers are blooming in the spring—when the voices of children are ringing in the street—when the strain of music comes plaintively up the noisy alley—when the sun is bright in heaven—when the fire is crackling on the hearth—then will her lost cherub stretch its little arms in Paradise, and call its mother home.

As Mary made way for the poor afflicted woman, who for an instant withdrew from her mouth the coarse handkerchief that could not stifle her sobs, she recognised Blanche's former maid, poor Gingham. Yes, it was Mrs. Blacke, following her only child, her only treasure, her only consolation, to the grave. Poor thing! her sin had been too heavy for her to bear; with her husband's example daily before her eyes, what wonder that she strove to stifle her conscience in intoxication? Then came "from bad to worse, from worse to worst of all"; the child was neglected, and a rickety, sickly infant at all times, soon pined away, and sickened and died. The mother was well-nigh maddened with the thought that it *might* have been saved. Never will she forgive herself for that one night when she left it alone for two hours, and coming back, found the fever had taken it. Never will she drive from her mind the little convulsed limbs, and the rolling eyes that looked upward, ever upward, and never recognised her again. And now her home is desolate, her husband is raving in the hospital, and her child is in that pauper-coffin which she is following to the grave. Mary Delaval, do you still think you are the most miserable being on the face of the earth?

CHAPTER XX
DAWN IN THE EAST

"'Gad, I thought the Major was very crusty this morning," remarked Cornet Capon, as he removed a large cigar from his lips, and watched its fragrant volume curling away into the summer air. "How he gave it you, Clank, about leading the column so fast, and about riding that old trooper instead of your own charger! I can't help thinking D'Orville's altered somehow; used to be such a cheery fellow."

"*You* needn't talk, my boy," retorted Captain Clank to his subaltern; "I heard him tell you that if you would attend a little more to your *covering*, and less to your *overalls*, you would be quite as ornamental, and a good deal more useful to the regiment; but I agree with you—he *is* altered. He's like all the rest of 'em—a capital fellow till you get him in command, and then he's crotchety and cantankerous and devilish disagreeable. Give us another weed."

These young officers were not very busy; they were occupied in, perhaps, the most wearisome of all the duties that devolve on the dragoon, and their task consisted of lounging about a troop-stable, attired in undress uniform, to watch the men cleaning and "doing up" their respective horses. They could but smoke, and talk over the morning's field-day to while away the time. Neither of them was encumbered with an undue proportion of brains—neither of them could have engaged in a much deeper discussion than that which they now carried on; yet they did their duty scrupulously, they loved the regiment as a home, and looked upon the B Troop as their family; and although their thoughts ran a little too much on dress, fox-hunting, driving, and other less harmless vanities, they were, after all, good comrades and tolerably harmless members of society. Cornet Capon's ideas oozed out slowly, and only under great pressure, so he smoked half a cigar in solemn silence ere he resumed, with a wise look—

"There's something at the bottom of all this about the Major, Clank. Did you notice where he halted us after the charge—all amongst that broken ground at the back of the Heath? We shall have half the horses in the troop lame to-morrow."

"Old 'Trumpeter' was lame to-day," returned Clank, with a grim smile, "and that's why D'Orville was so savage with me for riding him. You're right, Capon. The Major's amiss—there's a screw loose somewhere, I'm sure of it, and I'm sorry for it."

"He lost 'a cracker' at Newmarket last week, I *know*," said Capon, thoughtfully; "I shouldn't wonder if he was obliged to go—let me see— Lipstrap'll get the majority, and I shall get my lieutenancy. Well, I shall be sorry to lose him, though he *does* blow me up."

"Pooh! man, it's not *that*," rejoined Clank, who was a man of sentimental turn of mind, and kept Tommy Moore in his barrack-room. "You young ones are always thinking about racing. I've known D'Orville hit a deal harder than that, and never wince. Why, I recollect he played a civilian, at Calcutta, for his commission and appointments against the other's race-horses and a bungalow he had up in the hills. 'Gad, sir, he won the stud and the crib too—and not only that, but I landed a hundred gold mohurs by backing his new lot for the Governor-General's Cup, and went and stayed a fortnight with him at his country-house besides—best billet I ever had—furniture and fittings and fixings all just as t'other fellow left them. No—D'Orville's as game as a pebble about money—it isn't *that*."

Cornet Capon opened his eyes, smoked sedulously for about five minutes, and then asked Clank, "What the devil there was to bother a fellow, if it wasn't money?"

"Women!" replied the Captain, looking steadily at his companion; "women, my boy. I've watched the thing working now ever since I was a cornet, and I never knew a good fellow thoroughly broke down that there wasn't a woman at the bottom of it. Now, look at Lacquers; when Lacquers came to us, there wasn't such another cheery fellow in the Hussar Brigade— it did me good to see Lacquers drink that '34 we finished in Dublin—and as for riding, there wasn't another heavy-weight in that country could see *the way he went*—and now look what he's arrived at. Never dines at mess— horses gone to Tattersall's—sits and mopes in his barrack-room, or else off to London at a moment's notice—and closeted all day with agents and men-of-business—and what is it that's brought him to this pass? Why, that girl he wants to marry, who won't have anything to say to him—and why she won't is more than I can tell, unless she's got a richer chap in tow somewhere else. Capon, my boy, you're younger than me, and you've got most of your troubles to come. Take my advice, and stick to the regiment, and horses and hunting and that; but keep clear of women; they're all alike—only the top-sawyers are the most mischievous—you keep clear of 'em all, for if you don't you'll be sorry for it—mark my words if you're not."

This was a long speech for the Captain, and he was quite out of breath at its conclusion; but the Cornet did not entirely agree with him. He had got a *tendresse* down in the West—a saucy blue-eyed cousin, whose image often came before the lad's eyes in his barrack-room and his revelry and his boyish dissipation; so he contented himself with remarking profoundly that "Women were so different, it was impossible to lay down any general rule about them any more than horses;" and expressing his conviction that, whatever might be the secret grief preying upon the Major's spirits, it could have nothing to do with the fair sex, "for you know, Clank, D'Orville's a devilish *old* fellow—why, he must be forty if he's a day."

So the pair jingled into the mess-room to have some luncheon, and ordered their buggy, to drive up to London afterwards, and spend the rest of the day in the delights of the metropolis—since this it is which makes Hounslow such a favourite quarter with these light-hearted sons of the sword.

The Major was altered certainly, not only in temper, but even in appearance. He had got to look quite aged in the last few weeks. How strange it is that time, so gradual in its effects on the rest of creation, should make its ravages on man by fits and starts, by sudden assaults, so to speak, and *coups-de-main*, instead of the orderly and graduated process of blockade! We see a "wonderfully young-looking man"—we watch him year by year, still as fresh in colour, still as upright in figure and as buoyant in spirits as we recollect him when we were boys—we admire his vigour—we envy him his constitution, and we make minute inquiries as to his daily habits and mode of life—"he never drank anything but sherry," perhaps, and forthwith we resolve that sherry is the true *elixir vitæ*. All at once something happens—he loses one that he loves—or he has a dangerous illness—or, perhaps, only meets with severe pecuniary losses and disappointments. When we see him again, lo! a few weeks have done the work of years. The ruddy cheek has turned yellow and wrinkled—the merry eye is dim—the strong frame bent and wasted—the man is old in despite of the sherry; and Youth, when once she spreads her wings, comes back no more to light upon the withered branch.

Hair has turned grey in a single night. We ourselves can recall an instance of a young girl whose mother died suddenly, and under circumstances of touching pathos. Her daughter, who was devotedly attached to her, was completely stupefied by the blow. All night long she sat with her head resting on her hand, and her long black tresses falling neglected over the arm that supported her throbbing temples. When the day dawned she moved and withdrew her hand. One lock of hair that had remained pressed between her unconscious fingers had turned as *white as snow*. That single lock never recovered its natural hue. Like the Eastern virgins, it mourned in white for a mother.

Well, the Major looked old and worn as he sat in his lonely barrack-room, surrounded by many a trophy of war-like triumph or sporting success. Here was the sabre he had taken from the body of that Sikh chief whom he cut down at the critical moment when, six horses' length ahead of the squadron he was leading, he had been forced to hew his way single-handed through his swarming foes. There, spread out on a rocking-chair, was the royal tiger-skin perforated by a single bullet, that vouched for the cool hand and steady eye which had stretched the grim brute on the earth as he crouched for his fatal bound. On the chimney-piece those enormous tusks recalled many a stirring burst over the arid plains of the Deccan, when the boldest riders in India thought it no shame to yield the "first spear" to the "Flying Captain," as they nicknamed our daring hussar. Nor were these exploits confined to the East alone. On the verdant plains of merry England had not Sanspareil, ridden by his owner, distanced the cream of Leicestershire in a steeple-chase, never to be forgotten whilst the Whissendine runs down from its source; and did not that spirited likeness of the gallant animal hang worthily above the cup that commemorated his fame? Yes, the Major had earned his share of the every-day laurels men covet so earnestly, and truly it was only opportunity that was wanting to twine an undying leaf or two amongst the wreath. Yet did he look haggard, and *old*, and unhappy. His hair and moustaches had become almost grey now, and as he sat leaning his head upon his hand, with an open letter on his knee, the strong fingers would clench themselves, and the firm jaw gnash ever and anon, as though the thoughts within were goading him more than he could bear. Like some gallant horse that feels the armed heel stirring his mettle the while he champs and frets against the light pressure of the restraining bit, a touch too yielding for him to face, too maddening for him to overcome, so the Major chafed and struggled, and while he scorned himself for his weakness, submitted to the power that was stronger than he; and though he strove and sneered, and bore it with a grim, sardonic smile, was forced to own the pang that ate into his very heart.

"And this is what you have come to at last," he said, almost aloud, as he rose and paced the narrow room, and halted opposite the looking-glass that seemed to reflect the image of his bitterest enemy; "this is what you have come to at last. Fool—and worse than fool! After chances such as no man ever so threw away—after twenty years of soldiering, not without a certain share of distinction—with talents better than nine-tenths of the comrades who have far outstripped you in the race—with a brilliant start in life, and wind and tide for years in your favour—with luck, opportunities, courage, and above all, experience, what have you done? and what have you arrived at? Three words in a dispatch which is forgotten—a flash or two of the spurious, ephemeral fame that gilds a daring action or a sporting feat—the reputation of being a moderately good drill in the field—and a chance word of approbation from fools, whom you know that you despise. Truly a fair exchange—a most equal barter. This proud position you have purchased with a lifetime of energy spent in vain, and that thorough self-contempt which is now your bitterest punishment. Money, too; what sums you have wasted, lavished upon worse than trifles!—but let that pass. Had you the same fortune and the same temptations you would spend it all again. The dross is not to be regretted; but oh! the time—the time—the buoyancy of youth, the vigour of manhood that shall never come again. Fool! fool!" and the Major groaned aloud. "And what have I lived for?" he added, as he sat himself down and leaned his head once more upon his hand, looking into his past life as the exile looks down from a hill upon the lights and shades of the cherished landscape he shall see no more. "I have lived for self, and I have my reward. Have I ever done one single action for a fellow-creature, save to indulge my own feelings? have I not schemed and flattered, and worked and dared all for self? and this is the upshot. The first time I try to do a disinterested action—the first time I strive to break from the fetters of a lifetime, to be free, to be *a man*, I am foiled, and scouted, and spurned. Refused!—refused! by a poor governess—ha! ha!—it is, indeed, too good a joke. Gaston D'Orville on his knees, at forty, a grey old fool—on his knees to a wretched, dependent governess, and she refuses him. By all the demons in hell—if there *is* a hell—it serves him right. Laugh! who can help laughing? And yet what a woman to lose—a woman who could write such a letter as this—a woman who knows me better, far better, than I know myself; she would have shared with me every dream of ambition—she would have appreciated and encouraged the few efforts I have ever made to be good— she would have understood me, and with her I could have been happy even in a cottage—but no! forsooth. Her mightiness, doubtless, thinks the poor major of hussars, pretty nearly ruined by this time, no such great catch. And is she not right? What am I, after all, that I should expect any human being to give up everything for *me*? Broken-down, old, worn-out, if not in body, at least utterly out-wearied and used-up in mind, why should I cumber the earth? Gaston, my boy, you have played out your part—you have got to the end of your tether—'tis time for the curtain to drop—'tis time to lie down and go to sleep—there is not much to regret here—you have seen everything this dull world has to show. Now for 'fresh fields and pastures new'—at all events the waking will be glorious excitement—to find out the grand secret at last—where will it be, and how? I might know in ten minutes—many an old friend is there now—not badly off for company at any rate—there was poor Harry, the night before we were engaged at Chillianwallah he thought he was *there*. How well I remember him, as he told me his dream just before we went into action! He thought he was disembodied—floating, floating away through the blue night sky—hovering over the sea—bathing in the moonlight—flitting amongst the stars, and ever he got lighter and lighter, and ever he rose higher and higher, till he reached a cool, quiet garden, without a breeze or a sound, and there he saw his mother walking, as he remembered her before she died, when he was yet a child. And she placed her hand upon his brow, and the thin transparent hand clove through him—for he, too, was a spirit—till it struck chill like ice around his heart, and he awoke. Poor Harry, I saw him go down with a musket-shot through his temples; and he knows all about it, too, now. Pain! the pain is nothing. A dislocated ankle is far more acute agony than it would take to kill an elephant—'tis but a touch to a trigger, and the thing's done."

D'Orville got up coolly, and calmly walked across the room, took a certain oblong mahogany box from under his writing-table, and quietly unlocking it, drew his hand along the smooth, shining barrel of a pistol. He examined it well, pricked the touch-hole, shook the powder well up into the nipple, and then, having wiped the weapon almost caressingly, laid it down on the table at his elbow, and pursued his reflections, more at ease now that he had prepared everything for his escape.

"Well, it can be done in a moment, so there need be no hurry about it. In the meantime, let me see—I should like to leave some remembrances to the fellows in the regiment. There's that sabre—how game the old white-bearded chief died!—I almost wish I hadn't cut him down. 'Faith, I shall see him too. I expect he won't give me so warm a welcome as Harry—it's a pity I can't take him his sword back again. Well, Lacquers always admired it, and I'll leave it him. Poor Lacquers, he's a good fellow, though a fool. I'll leave a note, too, asking him to take care of the white horse, and shoot him when he's done with him: let him follow his master, poor old fellow! Yes; there's very little to arrange—one advantage in having got through a good property. I don't think there'll be much quarrelling over *my* will. And now, to consider the journey. I must have been very near it often before; and yet, somehow, I never looked at it in that light. 'Tis a different thing in action, with the excitement of duty, and watching the enemy, and keeping the men in hand, and that confounded smoke preventing one from seeing what is going on. No, I've never been *quite* so near as now; but I must some day, even if I should put it off—I *must* go at last—and why not now? What matter whether at forty or seventy? Time is not to be reckoned by years. I am old, and fit for nothing else. When the fruit is ripe, it had better be plucked; why should people let it hang and rot, till it drops off the tree, all spoilt and decayed? How do I know I may not want some of my manly energy where I am going? *Going*—how strange it sounds! Well, now to ticket the sabre, and write a line to poor Lacquers"—(D'Orville indited a few words in his firm, bold hand; if anything, firmer and bolder than usual)—"and now for 'a leap in the dark'—face the Styx, if there be such a place, just like any other *yawner*; and so, steady, steady!"

His hand was on the pistol—the lock clicked sharp and true up to the cock—one touch of the trigger, and where would Gaston D'Orville have been?—when his eye chanced to light upon the seal of Mary's letter. It was a casual seal, accidentally selected from a number of others, but the device was somewhat uncommon, and now struck D'Orville with a strange, painful distinctness that surprised him. It was but an eye, surrounded by an obliterated motto; yet it served for an instant to divert his attention; and—on such trifles turns the destiny of man—he laid down the pistol, and took up the letter to examine it more closely. The eye seemed to fascinate him. Turn which way he would, that eye seemed to watch him; steadily, unremittingly, an eye that never closes or slumbers seemed to be above him, around him, all about him; he rose from his chair, and still the eye followed him; he walked to the window, and the eye watched him steadily from out the blue summer sky. A trumpet-note pealed from the rear of the building; it was one of those merry stable-calls so dear to every cavalry soldier's heart. The familiar strain brought D'Orville to himself; the tension of his brain relaxed. As the excitement subsided, the visionary disappeared, and the real resumed its sway over strong nerves and a powerful intellect. Mechanically he put the pistols away, and carefully locked them in their case. Still the eye seemed to be watching him; and a vague feeling of shame began to take possession of him, as the suspicion rose in his mind that there was *cowardice* at the bottom of the resolution which he had made, as he thought so boldly, a few minutes ago.

D'Orville was a naturally brave man, and the force of habit and education had taught him to scorn anything in the shape of fear as the vilest of all degradation. To betray a woman in his code might be venial enough; but to shrink from aught in earth, or heaven, or hell, was a stain upon his honour *not* to be thought of. In his career of active service he had seen the advantage of courage too often, had discovered too frequently how much more rare a quality it is than is generally supposed, not to appreciate its value and worship it as an idol, although conscious of possessing it himself. It now dawned upon him that suicide was after all but a desperate method of running away—that the sentry had no right to desert his post until regularly relieved. By the by, in Mary's letter was there not something about warfare as compared to religion?—some parallel drawn between the Christian and the soldier? Again he perused that letter carefully, attentively, word for word: but the bitterness was past; the writer was no longer the poor governess, spurning a suitor whom she ought to have been proud to accept, but the high-minded, pure-hearted woman, feeling for his sorrows, appreciating his good qualities, and pointing out to him those consolations which for her could take the sting from earth's most envenomed shafts. One or two expressions reminded him of his mother—the mother he had loved and lost as a boy. Again he seemed to see that gentle lady bending her graceful head over him, as she spoke of other worlds, and other duties, and other pleasures totally unconnected with this lower earth. He remembered the very gown she wore; he seemed to hear her low, sweet, serious tones, as she called him "my darling boy," and insisted on those miraculous stories which she was herself fully persuaded were truths, and which the boy drank in, childlike, nothing doubting. Ah! what if they should be true after all? What if the whole history should be something more than a legend of priestcraft, an old woman's fable? D'Orville had thought but little on such matters; he had heard them discussed by clever men of opposite opinions, and it never struck him that either side could demonstrate very satisfactorily the futility of the adversary's arguments; but he was wise enough to know that the boasted human intellect has but a narrow horizon, that "the two-foot dwarf" sees little beyond the garden-wall, and that "there are more things in heaven and earth than are dreamt of in our philosophy." Here were the only two beings he had ever *respected* in the world, shaping their whole conduct, as they formed all their opinions, upon circumstances which they seemed to believe facts, as firmly as they believed in their own identity. Well, what of that? These might be facts or they might not. But stay: was there not something wanting in the whole scheme and constitution of life, as he had tried it? Could any man have had better chances of being happy here than he had had? Was he happy? Was he satisfied? Was there not always a shadow somewhere athwart the sunlight? Was there not always a craving for something more? As a boy, he longed to be an officer; no sooner was that distinction gained than he longed for fame, first in the boyish arena of mere field-sports, then in the daring exploits of real war. Had he not for a time drunk his fill of both? and was his thirst quenched? Could he sit down, "*uti conviva satur*," and say "Enough"? No, no, he knew it too well. Then came the daily craving for excitement—that longing for something unattainable, which, more than all besides, argues the inferiority of our present state—the necessity for a *to-morrow*, even when the sun of to-day has for us set its last. Well, had he not wooed excitement in all her haunts? Had he not gambled and raced and speculated, and shone in the world of fashion, and sunned himself in the smiles of Beauty? And had not the goddess ever fleeted away when just within his grasp? Was not his heart still empty, his desire unslaked? Even had he not endured this disappointment—had the only woman he really loved consented to be his—did he not feel in his innermost soul, was he not forced to confess to himself, that still there would have been a want?—still would to-morrow have been the goal, still to-day but the journey. Yes, disguise it how he might, deaden his sensations with what opiates he would, he could not but own that hitherto his world had been "stale, flat, and unprofitable." Had he not been so weary of life, that he had voluntarily, even now, been within the wag of a finger of laying it down, to go he cared not whither, so as it was anywhere but here?

Then if there was nothing in the present that could satisfy his soul, might he not presume that there was a future for which it was specially created and intended? Yes, there might be something to live for after all—there might be a career in which to win more than fame and more than honour—which at any rate should satisfy those longings and aspirations here, and might be the portal to such a glorious hereafter as he could not even picture to his world-wearied imagination—and if so, what scheme so probable, what religion so well supported by historical proof and logical deduction, as that which he had learnt at his mother's knee? One by one, thoughts came back to him that had lain dormant for more than thirty years; one by one he recalled the miraculous facts, the touching sufferings that had awed his boyish imagination and moved his boyish heart. For the first time for more than thirty years, he thought as a reality of the Great Example who never quailed nor flinched, nor shrank one jot from His superhuman task. Did he admire courage? There was One who had faced the legions of hell, unaided and alone, with but human limbs and a human heart to support Him through the dread encounter. Did he admire constancy? There was One who voluntarily endured the obloquy of the world, the agonies of the most painful death, and moved not an eyelash in complaint or reproach. Did he admire self-denial—that most heroic of all heroism? What had that One given up to walk afoot through this miserable world, with such a prospect as the close of His earthly career!—and for whom?—even for him amongst the rest—for him who till this very moment had never thanked Him, never acknowledged Him, never so much as thought of Him. The strong man's heart was touched, the well was unsealed in the desert, and, as the tears gushed from his unaccustomed eyes, Gaston D'Orville bent the knees that had not bent for half a lifetime; and can we doubt that he was forgiven?

In four-and-twenty hours D'Orville was laid upon his small camp-bedstead in a brain fever. The excitement of his late life; the reaction consequent on his abandonment of his awful resolution; the strong revulsion of feeling, into which we have no right to pry, had been too much for a constitution already shaken by years of dissipation and hard service beneath an Indian sun; and for days together life and death trembled in the balance so evenly that it seemed a single grain might turn the scale. And of all his comrades, who was it that watched at his bedside with the attention, almost the tenderness, of a woman—sitting up by him at night, giving him his medicine, smoothing his pillow, and tending him with a brother's love?—who but Lacquers! the unmeaning, empty dandy—the fellow with but two ideas, his dress and his horses—the ignorant, grown-up schoolboy that could scarcely write his own name; but, for all that, the staunch, unflinching comrade, the true-hearted, generous friend. When the lamp, after flickering and fading, and well-nigh dying out altogether, began once more to flame up pretty steadily, and the Major, gaunt and grim, with nearly white moustaches, and a black skull-cap, and haggard hollow cheeks, began to experience the superhuman appetite of convalescence, and the wonderful longing for open air and country scenery, and such simple natural pleasures, which invariably comes over those who have been near the confines of Life and Death, as though they brought back with them from that mysterious borderland the earlier instincts of childhood; when, in short, the Major was getting better, and could sit at his window and see the white charger go to exercise, or the regiment get under arms below, many and long were the conversations between him and Lacquers on the thoughts and feelings which almost insensibly had sprung up in each of them. Lacquers did not conceal his disappointment as regarded Blanche. Poor fellow, he had made her an honest, disinterested offer, and it had not entered into his calculations that he might be repulsed.

"I know I'm not good enough for her, D'Orville," the humbled dandy would sigh, as he poured his griefs into his friend's ear. "I'm not very 'blue,' and that sort of thing, though I suppose I've got natural talents just like other fellows; but I stood by her when all the rest gave way, and I was the only one amongst 'em that really liked her for herself and not for her money. Why, you yourself, D'Orville" (the Major winced), "you yourself never made up to her after you heard of the smash, nor Mount Helicon, nor Uppy, nor any of 'em; to be sure she had refused Uppy; do you remember how glum he looked that night at 'The Peace'? but I don't believe he'd have proposed to her ten days later. She might have liked me much better when she came to know me—mightn't she? and I would have read history and grammar, and Latin and Greek, and that, and made myself a scholar for her sake. I can't help feeling it, Major, and that's the truth. She's the only woman I ever really cared for; and what have I to live for now?"

Then it was that D'Orville showed himself an altered man—then it was that the thoughts which had first flashed across him when he contemplated self-destruction, and had since been progressively developing themselves on a bed of sickness, bore their fruit, as such thoughts will sooner or later where a man has a heart to feel or a brain to reason. He explained to Lacquers the views he now entertained of life, its duties, and its charms— how different from those on which he had hitherto acted! He pointed out to him the utter insufficiency of everything on earth to constitute happiness, when unconnected with a grand object and a future state of being. He talked well, for he was in earnest; and he reasoned closely, for his was a penetrating intellect, ever ready to strip at a moment's notice the illusive from the real. He had all his life been an acute man—saw through a fallacy in an instant, and, to do him justice, never hesitated to expose it:

"Called knavery, knavery—and a lie, a lie."

Such a mind, when convinced of truth, is doubly strong; and Lacquers listened, much admiring, though, it must be confessed, not always quite understanding the deductions of his mentor. Yet was he too, ere long, stirred with a noble ambition, a desire to fulfil his destiny in life with some credit to himself and benefit to his fellow-creatures—a longing to be useful in his generation—to feel that he was part of the great scheme, and, however humble might be his task, yet that its fulfilment was a fair condition of his very existence, and was conducive to the well-being of the whole.

"But what can I do, however willing I am?" he would say. "An officer of hussars cannot be a Methodist preacher, or even a moral philosopher, without doing more harm than good. If I thought I had talents for it, and eloquence and learning, I'd sell out to-morrow, and go to South Africa as a missionary, or anywhere else—Gold Coast, Sierra Leone—anything rather than be a useless drone cumbering the earth in a life without an aim."

"Not the least occasion for that," replied D'Orville. "Fortune— accident—call it rather Providence—has placed you in a certain station, and it is fit for you to fulfil the duties of that station without repining or restlessness, because, forsooth, it does not happen to square exactly with some vague notions of your own. You may do a deal of good, though you *are* an officer of hussars. Why should a soldier be necessarily an irreligious or an immoral man? It is not his profession that should bear the blame, however convenient it may be to make the red coat a scapegoat. We must have troops. We cannot be secure from war. Do you suppose a man leading a squadron gallantly against an enemy, doing the best he can for all—cool, confident, and daring—is not fulfilling his duty every whit as well as he who is on his knees in the rear praying for his success the while? Our calling bids us look death in the face oftener than other men, and that very fact should give us trust in Him on whom alone we can depend at the last gasp.

We are always nearer His presence than those who are not so exposed: and, for my part, I think it a proud and honourable privilege. Then, in barracks, may you not improve the *morale* of all about you in a thousand ways? You may look to the bodily well-being of your troop. Why?—first, because it's your duty; and secondly, because it's a pleasure to you, and a credit to have them smart and clean and well-disciplined! Why should you totally neglect their minds? They, too, have a future as well as a present. The one is not less a reality than the other. Ay, it's startling enough, because people slur it over, and don't talk of it, or allow themselves to think of it; but it's none the less true for all that. You may shut your own eyes as close as you please, but you won't prevent the sun from shining just the same. I grant you that the task is a difficult one. So much the more credit in fulfilling it, by an effort that does require some sacrifice and some self-denial. I have lived forty years in this world for *myself*—the careless, thoughtless life that a tolerably sagacious dog might have led—and I have never been really happy. Come what may, I hope to do so no more. I have found out the true secret that turns everything to gold, and I don't grudge a share of my good fortune to my friends."

"You're right, D'Orville," said Lacquers, shaking the Major by the hand; "you're right, though I never looked at it in that light before. I see that I have an object in life—that I have a task to perform; and I see—no, I don't see my way quite through it; but I trust I shall have courage and patience to do the best I can. D'Orville, I feel happier than I did. I'm not much of a book-worm, and I can't quite express what I feel; but, old fellow, you talked of exchanging, and going to India; well, I'll go too—we'll get appointed into the same corps—I'm good enough to be broiled in that country, at any rate—and I'll never leave you, old boy, for you're the best friend I ever had!" Little Blanche Kettering might have done worse than take poor, ignorant, good-looking, blundering, warm-hearted Lacquers.

CHAPTER XXI
HOSPITAL

We left Cousin Charlie, some chapters back, in a sufficiently unpleasant predicament. His arm broken by a bullet, a Kaffir's assagai through his shoulder, stunned moreover by a crushing blow from the butt-end of a musket (Birmingham-made, and sold in the gross at nineteen shillings apiece), not to mention a roll of some fifty feet down an almost perpendicular ravine, the boy lay senseless, and to all appearance dead. The tide of war rolled far away from the *kloof* that had been defended so fiercely, and won with such loss of life; and ere the young lancer had recovered his senses, an outlying band of the enemy, driven from their fastnesses far on the right, wound stealthily through this very ravine in full retreat. Fortunately they had that day got such a taste of English discipline as made them loth to improve any further acquaintance with "Brown Bess"; and although they stripped the lad from head to foot, believing him to be stone-dead, they had no time to stay and practise those horrid mutilations with which these demons signalise their triumph over a fallen foe. Not a shred of clothing, however, did they leave on the body; even his boots, the most useless articles conceivable to a Kaffir, were carried off as the spoils of war. For aught we know, to this day Charlie's smart jacket forms the ceremonial dress of some burly chief. Very tight, and worn with long, black legs, *au naturel*, it is doubtless a most imposing costume. Be that how it may, the white man was left naked and weltering in his wounds, whilst the routed party, who had wasted but little time in stripping him, made the best of their way to a more respectful distance from the British posts. Charlie never stirred for hours. The moon rose, and bathed in her cold light the crisp, rugged scenery and the ghastly accessories of that fatal glen. Here, a stunted jagged bush threw its smoke-blackened twigs athwart the clear night sky, and beneath it, bleached by the moonlight, lay some grinning corpse that had dragged itself there to die, whilst a clean musket-barrel shining in those pale beams showed it had been a British soldier when morning dawned. There, hurled in a fantastic heap, lay the swarthy bodies of some half-dozen Kaffirs, one balanced on the verge of a blank bare cliff, his arms and head dangling, limp and helpless, over the brink—his comrades piled above him, as they fell in their desperate efforts to escape. Yonder, where the moonbeams glimmered through the twinkling foliage, frosting the leaves with silver, and shedding peace and beauty over the unholy scene, a Fingoe auxiliary stirred and groaned in his last mortal agony, his dusky skin welling forth its very life-drops on the trampled sward. Shout and curse and clanging blow, all the riot and confusion of the strife, had long since died away. The writhing Fingoe groaned out his soul with a last gasping sigh, and save for the short yelp of a famished jackal in the adjoining thicket, silence slept upon the glen, and Night shared with Death her dominion over that blood-stained, devastated spot. Charlie came to himself—not that he knew where he lay, or was conscious of aught save a numbed sense of pain, and a confused stupefied idea, first that he was in bed, then that he was on the deck of a ship, heaving and plunging over the rolling waters. As sensation gradually returned, an intolerable thirst, so fierce as to amount to positive agony, began to rage in his dry, choking throat; then, with that unaccountable instinct to rise which is the first impulse of a man who is knocked down, he made a sort of abortive, staggering effort to get to his feet, it is needless to say in vain. The blood welled freshly from his wounds, the branches overhead spun round him, and he was again insensible. But the effort saved his life: the slight movement was seen, and in another instant a dark Fingoe girl was kneeling over him, with her hand upon his heart. The poor young savage had been stealing distractedly through the glen, looking for the body of her lover. She had missed him from his hut at nightfall. She knew there had been a severe engagement, and, like a very woman, faithful even unto death, she had glided away in the darkness to seek him out, succour him if wounded, and mourn over him if succour should come too late. It was a woman that alone recognised the body of the last of the Saxon kings, on the fatal field of Hastings. When earl and thane and liegeman saw but a mangled, mutilated corpse, Edith the swan-necked knew her lover and her lord. Keen was the eye, unerring was the instinct of affection, and Edith's fame lives in history and song; but our poor Fingoe girl was but a nameless savage, a wretched, ignorant heathen, debased almost to the level of the brute; yet she, too, had a woman's heart, and cherished a woman's love—she, too, recognised her barbarian lover, gashed and defaced by assagai and war-club, and it was whilst she wept and moaned over his mangled remains that her eye caught the stir of Charlie's white body, and her heart, softened by grief, bid her, woman-like, again come to the assistance of the suffering and the helpless. She threw a *kaross* over his naked body. Light-footed as an antelope, she darted to a neighbouring spring, shuddering the while—for that, too, was polluted with blood—and returned with a skin of the clear, cold water. She bathed his brow and temples—she poured the grateful drops between his blackened lips—and as he groaned and stirred once more, she knew there was life in him yet. The huts of her countrymen (half-armed auxiliaries to the British force) were at no great distance, and, savage as she was, the maiden would not leave a fellow-creature, particularly such a good-looking one as Charlie, to die like a dog without assistance. Her shapely limbs bore her rapidly back to her people. Alas! there was scarce a family amongst them that had not lost a member, and she soon returned with four stalwart Fingoes, who carried Charlie's senseless frame to their encampment, where they tended him with such knowledge of surgery as they possessed, far more efficient, despite of sundry charms and superstitions, than our College of Surgeons at home would easily believe. There were other wounded soldiers in the encampment, and Charlie, though not recognised, was judged to be an officer, and met with all the attention from these poor fellows that they could spare from their own sufferings. But it was to the Fingoe girl that, under Providence, he owed his life. Night and day she tended him like a child, and when at length a convoy arrived from head-quarters with a train of waggons to carry off all the sick to Fort Beaufort, it was with difficulty the poor savage maiden was dissuaded from accompanying him even into the distant settlements, and long and wistfully she gazed after the waggon that bore her white charge out of her sight. Charlie had not yet recovered his consciousness, and had scarcely spoken; and when he did, muttered but a few incoherent words; yet the girl had saved his life, and nursed him in his agony, and it was hard to give him up!

When our hapless lancer really came to himself he was lying on a comfortable bed, with all the necessary appliances and alleviations for sickness, nowhere so efficient as in an English military hospital. His first sensation was one of pleasing languor, almost of luxury, in the new feeling of complete repose; for, in the Fingoe hut, and yet more in the jolting, slow-moving waggon, his powerless limbs had never been able to dispose themselves in *real* rest, and the change was positive delight. He was too weak to take any note of time or place—he was conscious of but one feeling, that of bodily ease; and he could no more undergo the mental exertion of recalling past events, or judging from present circumstances, than he could play the physical one of getting out of bed. He knew he was bandaged—he knew he had not strength to stir a finger were it to save his life, nor did he wish to do so—he knew he was lying between clean sheets, in a bed, somewhere; it seemed strange, for he had not been in a bed for so long, and he was quite satisfied to take things as they were, and gaze drowsily upon the wall, and hear a stealthy footfall in the room, far too languid to turn his head, and so drop off to sleep again quite contentedly. And when the surgeon of the Light-Bobs—a gallant fellow, whose only fault was that he never would keep his confounded lint and bandages and tourniquet far enough in the rear—saw his patient in this second slumber, and listened to his soft breathing, and placed his finger on the fluttering, scarce-perceptible pulse, he stroked his chin with a self-satisfied air, and smiled, and muttered to himself, "He'll do now, *I think*—not above twenty—young constitution—never drank, I'll be bound. It's been touch-and-go; but I believe now he'll pull through."

So Charlie got over the crisis, and slept, and struggling hard with the ebbing tide, little by little gained ground and footing, and inch by inch, as it were, reached the shore.

As consciousness returned with returning strength, memory began to unravel its tangled skein of dim fantastic recollections, and by degrees the march, the engagement, the last brilliant charge, separated themselves from the ghastly moonlight glen, the dark phantom-shape that had saved him, the strange huts of the savages, and above all those excruciating sufferings in that jolting waggon. But with convalescence came the weary longing to be well, the restlessness of protracted confinement, the loathing of those tedious, monotonous days—their only event that unvarying meal—their only amusement to gaze upon the sunlight brightening that white-washed wall. How Charlie pined to feel the free, fresh breeze of out-of-doors; how horse and hound and field-day, the bounding charger, the jovial march, the cheerful mess, seemed to mock him with their phantom-like delights, as his body lay pinioned and helpless on that loathed couch, and his mind went soaring away in vision after vision of waving woods and rugged hills, and, above all, the glorious summer air, that he would fain have bathed in like a lark—have drunk into his very being as the true *elixir vitæ*!

Of serious thoughts as to his late proximity to another world, of gratitude for his narrow escape from death, we fear we must confess our patient was altogether innocent. The sick-bed is the last place in the world to promote such grave reflections: and those who trust to an illness as a means of making them better and wiser men, will generally find that they have leant upon a broken reed. The exhaustion of physical pain acts little more upon the body than the mind. The latter partakes of the languor which pervades its tenement, and has generally but strength to pine in helpless inactivity, and gaze idly on the balance of life and death, with scarce a wish even to turn the scale. If a man never reflects when well, still less can he expect to have power to do so when sick; and many a death-bed, we fear, has owned its tranquillity to the mere prostration, intellectual as well as physical, which quiets the departing sufferer. 'Tis an uncomfortable notion; but we hold it too true, nevertheless. Charlie had an instance in his very next neighbour, a gallant private of the Light-Bobs, who occupied the adjoining bed to our young lancer. He, too, had been shot down in the fatal ravine, had been nursed in the Fingoe huts, and forwarded to Fort Beaufort in the waggon-train. For a time his wounds went on favourably enough, and he seemed to have a far better chance of recovery than poor Charlie. But he had been a drunkard in early life; his constitution was sapped with strong liquor; something unintelligible "supervened," as the medical officer said; and the man was doomed—doomed, as surely as if he had been sentenced to death by court-martial.

In the earliest stages of his own recovery, Charlie would lie and listen to the poor fellow's ravings, till he shuddered at the wild imaginings of that delirious brain. Now the man would fancy himself back in England, amongst the low haunts of vice and debauchery which seemed most familiar to his mind. He would shout out ribald toasts and drinking-songs, and roar fierce oaths of mingled pain and exultation, till he roused every pale inmate of the ward. Then would a frightful reaction take place, and he would lie still as a corpse, hand and foot, but mutter and roll his eyes and gnash his teeth, like one possessed. He peopled the place, too, with frightful apparitions; amongst which a pale girl, with her throat cut from ear to ear, and the enemy of mankind, seemed, by his expressions, to be the most frequent visitors. With these he would hold long conversations, ludicrous even through their horrors, and would display much ingenuity in their imaginary questions, to which he poured forth voluble answers of abuse and blasphemy. Of his satanic disputant he generally seemed to get the better, by his own account; but the mutilated girl always brought on a fit of trembling that was frightful to behold. Once, after a visit from this spectre, which he detailed at considerable length, he tore all the bandages from his wounds, and was obliged to be pinioned in a strait-waistcoat. After this he got quieter, not so much from the restraint as the weakness and loss of blood consequent on his paroxysm. He would listen with marked attention to the chaplain, who visited him daily; and when the good man was gone, would mumble out incoherent words of repentance and amendment; but could never fix his mind upon their meaning for two seconds at a time. Then he would give it up in despair, and would shout and sing again more boisterously than ever. At length it became evident, even to Charlie's enfeebled perceptions, that he was sinking fast; and as the sand of life ebbed more and more rapidly, the dying man became more and more composed and tranquil, till he promised to make as peaceful an ending as ever did glorified saint in Popish calendar. The eye lost its unnatural glitter, the pain ceased entirely, and the pulse became quiet and regular—but oh, so weak for that active, muscular frame! The youngest tyro would not have been deceived by the change; it was obvious that his very hours were numbered; yet now, for the first time, he seemed to recognise place and people—called Charlie by his name, and asked Mr. Kettering after "the reg'ment," and whether the old major was shot dead when he forced the river so smartly, and the colour-sergeant (he never could abide that colour-sergeant) lost his life in the very middle of the stream; then he remembered how Charlie had led the assault, and from that time he seemed to confide in him, and whispered to him his plans, and his little spites against his comrades, and his longing for his old life; for he made no doubt of getting well. And so he slept for a few hours (the doctor came in and looked at him asleep, and shook his head), and woke about noon, and asked for something to drink; but his lips were quite black, and Charlie saw that he was somehow changed even before the man told him he was conscious of it himself.

"It's all up, Mr. Kettering," said he, in a husky whisper, "it's all up with me this turn. What's the time o' day now? Twelve o'clock? I shall be a dead man at sundown;" and then he told Charlie how he had received a warning, and he knew there was no hope "*here* nor yet *yonder*," he said, with a ghastly smile; for he had dreamt that he was standing sentry on a rampart over against the ocean, and the sun was setting in a golden haze, and the waters gleamed like molten gold; and he laid his firelock down, and rested and gazed with delight upon the scene; but a girl rose from the waves, far off between him and the sunset, and wrung the water from her long black hair, and pressed it with both hands to her throat, and seemed to staunch a ghastly wound that gaped at him even at that distance, and ever the blood flowed and flowed, and the sea became crimson, and the sun went down in blood-red streaks, and the sky darkened to the colour of blood, and everywhere there was blood, blood, nothing but blood; and the girl screamed to him in agony, saying, "Pray! pray!" and he knew that if he could speak a prayer before the sun went down he might be saved; and he strove and gasped, but he was choked; and still the sun dipped and dipped, and a fiery rim only was left above the sea, and still he could not speak; and it went down too; and the girl tossed up her arms with a shriek, and all was dark; and then with a convulsive effort he cried aloud, and his mouth was full of blood—and so he awoke. "And I shall never stand sentry nor carry a firelock again," he said; and from that time he spoke no more, but folded his hands and lay quiet, as if asleep. The afternoon shadows lengthened on the hospital-wall—the evening drew near—at half-past six the dying man muttered a request for drink—at seven the sun went down, and he was dead!—peacefully, quietly he parted, like a child going to its rest. Charlie never knew it was all over till the doctor came; and they took him away and buried him, and there was a vacant place by Charlie's bedside; and so Her Majesty lost a soldier, and a recruit was enlisted and sent to the *dépôt* at home, and his place in the ranks was filled, and he was forgotten, just as peers, poets, conquerors, sovereigns, and sages are forgotten, only a little sooner—for the grim Reaper makes no distinction, and the monarch oak of the forest perishes as surely as the weed by the wayside.

Week after week Charlie lay in that weary bed. One by one patients became convalescents, and convalescents went back to their duty, and still he was not allowed to move. A fresh action was fought, and more wounded were brought in, and yet Charlie was unfit for duty—in fact, was unable to rise. The doctor was hopeful and good-humoured, as doctors generally are, not being invalids themselves, and told him "he was going on most satisfactorily, and all that was wanted was a little time, and patience and quiet;" but at length even he hinted at sick-leave, and talked of a return to England, and the necessity of care and avoidance of exposure to weather, even after the wounds were healed; and Charlie's dearest hopes of rejoining his regiment, and tasting once more the excitement of warfare, were dashed to the ground. The kind doctor had written to his patient's friends in England, and assured them of his safety—on the rejoicings thereby created at Newton-Hollows we need not now enlarge—so that all anxiety on that score had passed away, and there was nothing to do now but to get well and embark for home. What a tedious process that same getting well was! Charlie began to pine, and grow dispirited and nervous. He had no friends, no one to speak to but the doctor; and the gallant boy, who would have faced a whole tribe of Kaffirs single-handed and never moved an eyelash, was now so completely weakened and broken down that he would lie and weep for hours, like a girl, he knew not why. At last he began to give way to despondency altogether. One day in particular, when the ward was again emptied of its recovered inmates, and the boy was left quite alone in that long, dull room, he lost heart entirely. "I shall never get well now," he said aloud in his despair; "I shall never see the bright blue sky again, nor the regiment, nor Blanche, nor Mrs. Delaval, nor any of them—sinking, sinking, day by day, and scarcely twenty! 'Tis a hard lot to die like a dog, in such a hole as this. Ah! Frank always talked of death as the ever-present certainty, and the next world will be a happier one than this, I do believe, though this has been a happy one to me. I used to think I shouldn't mind dying the least—no more I should, in the free, open air, leading a squadron, with the men hurraing behind me; or falling neck and crop into a grass-field with 'Haphazard,' alongside the leading hounds." (Charlie was barely twenty, and to him the hunting-field was just such an arena of glory as was the tilt-yard to a knight of the olden time.) "No, I could die like a man at home, but to rot away here in a hospital, thousands of miles from merry England, without a friend near me, it's hard to bear it pluckily, as it ought to be borne. Frank! Frank! I want some of your dogged resolution now. If I could see your dear old face once more, and shake you by the hand, I should be a different fellow. Ah! it's too late now; I shall never see you again, and you will hardly know what became of me. But you won't forget me, old boy, will you?" and poor Charlie gave way once more, and turned his wet cheek down upon his pillow, as he heard the doctor's step along the passage; for he was ashamed of his weakness, though he knew it was but the effect of his wounds. Hark! there is some one with him; the doctor is bringing a visitor to see him. He knows that firm, heavy tread. Is it one of his brother-officers?—how kind of them! No, that is no dragoon's step: it is familiar, too, and yet he cannot remember where he has heard it. Is he dreaming? Over the doctor's shoulder peers a well-known face, embrowned with travel, but with the old kind, frank expression beaming through those manly features. In another instant Charlie is clasping Frank Hardingstone's strong hand in his own two emaciated ones, and after an abortive "How are ye, old fellow?" and a vain effort to laugh off his emotion, is sobbing once more like a woman or a child.

"So you came out all the way from England on purpose to look after me," said he, when the first burst of feeling had subsided; "how like you, old Frank—how kind of you!—and what did they say about me at home? and wasn't Blanche sorry for me when she thought I was killed? and did Uncle Baldwin and—and Mrs. Delaval read the dispatch? and where are they all now? You know I'm to have sick-leave, and we'll go back together. When does the doctor think I shall be able to sail? Frank, he's a shocking muff; I've been in this bed for thirteen weeks, but I shall get up to-day—of course he'll let me get up to-day;" and so Charlie ran on, and Frank was soon forcibly withdrawn from the patient, whose over-excitement was likely to be as prejudicial as his late despondency; but the maligned doctor whispered to him as he went out, "Your arrival, sir, has done more for my patient than the whole pharmacopœia: he'll be well now in a fortnight."

The doctor was right. From that day Charlie began to mend. Many a long hour Frank sat by his bedside, and talked to him of home, and of his prospects, and of his cousin (honest Frank), and settled over and over again their plans of departure, to which Charlie was never tired of listening; and after every one of these visits the boy's appetite was better and his sleep sounder, and in a few days he got out of bed, and then he was moved into the hospital-sergeant's room, who readily vacated his apartment for the young officer; and then he got out on Frank's arm into the summer air, for which he had so pined—pleasant it was, but yet not *so* pleasant as he thought it would be, when he lay in that dull ward; and then his voracity became something ridiculous, and at the end of about three weeks Frank helped him up the companion-way of the *Phlegethon*, 200 horse-power, homeward-bound; and although wasted to a skeleton, his large eyes looked bright and clear, and now that he was really on his way to England he was well.

CHAPTER XXII
THE WIDOW

"My dear Mount, I think, after all, I shall spend the winter at Bubbleton," said Lady Mount Helicon to her hopeful son, as they sat one sunny afternoon in her well-furnished drawing-room. London was emptying fast; a few of the lingerers still contrived to keep up a semblance of gaiety, and those who stayed on, like Lady Mount Helicon, because they had no country-houses to go to, voted it *so* much pleasanter now the crush and hurry of the season was over. But even these could not conceal from themselves that they were but "the last roses of summer," that "all the world" was rushing out of town, and they had no business here any longer. The water-carts were getting very slack, and the dust unbearable; the Ride and the ring were fitting haunts for a hermit, and the Serpentine was gloomy as the Styx. Dinadam was inhaling appetite in his deer-forest—Long-Acre was tempting Providence in his yacht—Mrs. Blacklamb was breaking hearts at Cowes—ministers had celebrated their many defeats during the session by their annual fish-dinner at Greenwich—and grouse were advertised at five shillings a brace in Leadenhall Market. Yes, the season was over, and Mount would not have been here instead of in Perthshire had it not been for the absolute necessity of his writing his autograph in person for the ulterior disappointment of a Hebrew, and his own immediate benefit. He was an excellent son when he had nothing better to do, and now sat for hours with his mother and talked over his own plans and hers with the most perfect open-heartedness.

"Bubbleton," said he, "mother, and why Bubbleton?"

"Can't you see, Mount?" replied her ladyship; "Bubbleton is within visiting distance of Newton-Hollows."

"What then?" rejoined her son; "I thought you had made up your mind to drop them when you found they were of no use."

"So I should, my dear," confessed the diplomatic lady, "if things had turned out as I expected; but don't you see that the game is not yet half played out? That unfortunate boy who went off to the Cape has been severely wounded; you know they put on mourning for him, thinking he was dead; and it is quite on the cards that he may not recover; he never looked strong; then our little friend is as great an heiress as ever; and I am sure, with *your* eloquence, you could easily persuade her that it was jealousy, or pique, or something equally flattering, that made you so remiss for a time, and it would be all *on* again. Besides, I have been making a good many inquiries lately in a roundabout way, and I find that, even if the 'beau cousin' should return safe and sound, there will be a large sum of ready money to which the girl will be entitled when she comes of age. You want money, Mount, I fancy?"

"Not a doubt of it, my dear mother," replied he; "this has been my worst year for a long time, and you know I never holloa before I'm hurt. Goodwood *ought* to have pulled me through, if 'Sennacherib' hadn't failed at the last stride. I am afraid to say, and I can believe you had rather not hear, what that odd six inches cost me. No, mother, I can't go on much longer; I don't see my way a bit. If a general election comes I shall have to bolt."

"Listen to me, Mount," said her ladyship. "I have a plan that may save us all yet. I shall take a house at Bubbleton for the winter, and wherever I have a roof over my head you know I am too happy to give you a home. You can send down two or three horses, and hunt quietly in the neighbourhood, instead of going off to Melton with eight or ten, and losing a fortune at whist; and of all places I know, Bubbleton is the most likely for something to *turn up*—then *if* we should arrange matters with Miss Kettering, everything will go smoothly; but there is one thing I must beg of you, my dear Mount, and that is to give up the turf. It is all I ask," said her ladyship, with tears in her eyes—"all I ask in return for my devotion to your interests is to sell those horrid race-horses, and give the thing up altogether."

Mount made a wry face—"Sennacherib," notwithstanding his defeat, which, as usual, was from no lack of speed or stamina, but entirely in consequence of *the way the race was run*—"Sennacherib" was the very darling of his heart; and he had, besides, amongst his yearlings, *such* a filly, that promised, as far as babies of that age can promise, to have the speed of the wind. Must these treasures go to Tattersall's? Must the hopes of Olympic triumphs and future mines of wealth be all knocked down to the highest bidder, as the stud of a nobleman declining racing? It was a bitter pill; but he knew his mother was a strong-minded woman—he knew that if she insisted on the sacrifice being made a part of the bargain, nothing would induce her to fulfil her share unless he fulfilled his. He recollected how, in his father's time, crabbed as that respectable nobleman undoubtedly was, my lady always got her own way in the long-run, and he determined to make a virtue of necessity and give in, consoling himself with the reflection that, when all was arranged, he could easily buy some more horses with his wife's money. So he promised with a good grace, and his mother kissed him, and called him "her own dear boy"; and the pair separated—my lord to get upon "Trictrac" and ride down to Richmond, whither there is no occasion for us to follow him—my lady to write sundry little notes to her friends, to consult with her agent about letting her house in London—and then, with a good book upon her knee, to indulge in dreamy castle-building schemes for upholding the integrity of the house of Mount Helicon, not unmixed with rosier visions as regarded her own prospects for the future.

This pair, whatever might be their failings as regarded the rest of the world, seemed at all events blamelessly to fulfil their duties each towards the other. Yet behind this apparent sincerity and affection each was playing a separate game, totally irrespective of aught but self; each was actuated solely by motives of interest; each had a separate path to pursue, a separate object to attain. Mount Helicon came readily into his mother's views for the best of all reasons. Everything that could save the disbursement of a shilling was now of paramount importance to him. After a problematic trip to Norway in Long-Acre's yacht he would literally not have a roof to cover him. It was all very well to make a great merit of giving up Melton, and to dwell on the sacrifice he made on his mother's account in foregoing the delights of that very charming place; but Mount had now neither hunters nor the means of getting them, and a man at Melton without money or horses is like a fish out of water, or a teetotaller at an Irish wake. Everything had failed with him lately. Successful as were his literary schemes, their profits were but a drop in the ocean compared with his necessities. Goodwood had nearly finished him, and he hardly dared think of Doncaster, so unfortunate were his investments on the coming St. Leger. He could see only one way out of his difficulties—to sell himself and his title to some wealthy young lady, and he rather fancied giving Blanche the opportunity of becoming a purchaser; that which he would have considered a mere pittance some six months ago he now looked upon as a very fair competence; and the chance of young Kettering's death, with the reversion of that large property, was a contingency by no means to be despised; so he submitted, with as good a grace as he could, to selling his race-horses, and spending the winter at Bubbleton with his mother, inwardly resolving that when he had secured his object he would break out again into fresh extravagances, and shine with redoubled splendour.

Lady Mount Helicon, too, had her own ends to further in her affectionate and hospitable invitation to her son. She had found out that his agreeable qualities, his large acquaintance, and his brilliant reputation, always succeeded in filling her house with those whom she was pleased to term "the best men," fastidious individuals who never condescended to dine with her when Mount and she kept separate establishments. Now my lady calculated that with her title, her cook, and her celebrated son, she would create a prodigious sensation at Bubbleton, where neither rank, talent, nor faultless cutlets are as common as in London; and that with these attractions in her house, she would have an opportunity of seeing all the male eligibles whom that salubrious locality might bring together. And she could thus judge of them at her leisure, and pick and choose at her caprice. That was the end in view. The idea of entering once more into the holy bonds of matrimony had long been present to her ladyship's mind; and when she consulted her looking-glass, and saw reflected her large, comely form, her still healthy complexion, and her well-arranged hair, by courtesy called auburn, but sufficiently red to lose little of its youthful appearance from an occasional silver line, she grudged more and more that all these charms should be wasted on a widow's lonely lot, and resolved that when the time came, and the *man*, it would be no fault of hers if she did not stand again at the altar in the coloured robes of a bride who adds the advantage of experience to the ripe maturity of autumnal beauty. Bubbleton, then, was the very place from which to select the fortunate man. Its frequenters were many of them steady-going, respectable gentlemen of middle age, and like all unmarried middle-aged men, unless completely ruined, sufficiently well-to-do in the world. Such are by no means ineligible matches for a widow; and then, should none of these be found willing to aspire to such happiness, might not General Bounce surrender at discretion, if properly invested—more particularly should the other matrimonial scheme progress favourably, and the relationship thus created afford opportunities for surprises, *coups-de-main*, or the tardier but no less fatal advances of a regular blockade? He certainly had paid her attention in London; he was a stout, soldier-like man for his years; above all, he had a charming place at Newton-Hollows, and a good fortune of his own. Yes, *faute de mieux*, the General would do very well; and then the two families might live together, and if Blanche *did* succeed to everything, what a piece of luck it would be for them all! And her ladyship, with all her knowledge of the world, actually deluded herself into the idea that the two establishments could keep the peace for an hour together in the same house, or that Mount, after he had got all he could, and had no further use for his mother, would hear of such an arrangement for one single moment. So Lady Mount Helicon rose and smoothed her hair in the mirror over the chimney-piece, and looked at a miniature of herself, done before she married, and lying on the drawing-room table; and persuaded herself she was wonderfully little altered since then, and returned in haste to her good book and her seat with her back to the light, you may be sure, as a knock at the door announced an arrival, and her well-powdered figure-footman ushered in Lady Phœbe Featherhead.

CHAPTER XXIII
"STOP HER"

In these days of steam and perpetual locomotion everybody has been a voyage of some sort over the seas; and one of these uncomfortable expeditions is so like another, that it is needless to describe the transit of Frank Hardingstone and Cousin Charlie from the Cape home. There were but few passengers on board the *Phlegethon,* and those were as much bored with the length and monotony of their voyage as passengers usually are; they ate, drank, smoked, walked the deck, pestered the professionals with perpetual questions as to when they should make the Needles, and otherwise comported themselves so as to lengthen as much as possible the apparent duration of their imprisonment. Charlie was as idle and impatient as the rest. Frank alone seemed an exception to the general rule; when not reading hard in his cabin he was sure to be found studying steam in the engine-room, "shooting the sun" with the captain, or learning navigation with the mate. "There's a good man spoilt in making that chap a gentleman," was the constant remark of these worthies, who contracted an immense love and admiration for Frank. Yet of late he had maintained a grim reserve very foreign to his usual open demeanour, and more especially in the society of Cousin Charlie. He did not shun him, nor did that careless and good-humoured young gentleman perceive any difference in his friend's manner; but Frank could not conceal from himself that he was not thoroughly at ease with the boy for whom he had endured so much. He felt that he had given up his dearest hopes for his young *protégé*—that he had sacrificed to him the inestimable treasure of Blanche Kettering's love; he had on one or two occasions even done such violence to his feelings as to touch upon the subject of their approaching marriage in his conversations with her cousin, and had been surprised and disgusted at the coldness with which so engrossing a topic was received by the young gentleman most concerned. Frank could have borne it better, he thought, had Charlie been worthy of the blessing in store for him—had he appreciated the unspeakable bliss which others would have given all on earth to enjoy; but to yield her to one who scarce seemed willing to stretch out his hand to receive her—to resign all that made life valuable to another, and to find that other appreciated the object as little as the sacrifice—this was indeed a hard task; but Frank thought it his duty so to act, and resolved, with his usual determination and forgetfulness of self, that he would lose no opportunity of forcing upon Charlie the absolute necessity of marrying the only woman he had himself ever loved. Thus the voyage drew to a close. Contrary winds were baffled by the power of steam; the good ship stemmed the mountain waves of the Bay of Biscay, and at length the coast of England was hailed; and, though labouring in a heavy gale of wind and a cross-pitching sea, they were steaming steadily up the Channel, and congratulating themselves that to-morrow they would once more set foot on English ground. Frank and Charlie were on deck, enjoying the broken gleams of an afternoon's sun, that shone fitfully through the mists and storm-rack driving fast overhead; and their conversation naturally enough turned upon their own plans and intentions when they should get ashore. Charlie was full of his horses and his anticipations of sport in game-preserve and hunting-field, with sundry speculations as to the state of "Haphazard's" legs, much damaged by the never-to-be-forgotten steeple-chase; and it was with difficulty Frank could command his attention whilst he made a final effort to impress upon him the absolute necessity of his making up his mind and marrying his pretty cousin forthwith.

"It's not fair upon any one," said Frank, holding manfully on to the mizen-topmast stay, "it's not doing as you'd be done by, to keep a thing of this sort off and on; it's not fair upon your family; it's not fair upon your uncle; and, above all, it's not fair upon Miss Kettering herself. I conceive that you are bound, as a gentleman, to make all necessary arrangements, so that the business may be concluded within a month of your arrival at Newton-Hollows."

Charlie looked rather aghast. "Well, but," said he, "I should have to leave the regiment. You wouldn't have me bring Blanche out to Kaffirland— poor little Blanche, she'd be frightened to death, and I know I should have to sell out—Frank, I couldn't bear to leave the regiment. I like soldiering better than anything."

"We can't help that," rejoined his friend. "You've a duty to perform in life, and you must go through with it. You're not to live for yourself alone; and look how many people are interested in this question. In the first place, there's your cousin. In consequence of this will they've found, you have been the innocent cause of robbing her of a princely inheritance; this is the only method by which you can replace her in her former advantageous position. It was evidently intended all through by your uncle and your poor aunt that this marriage should take place, and their wishes ought to be your law. Then the General has set his heart upon it, I *know*, and you are both under great obligations to that kind old man. But all these considerations are as nothing compared with the feelings of Blanche herself. Charlie, would you begin by supplanting her in her birthright, and finish by breaking her heart?"

Charlie looked wofully disconcerted. This was altogether a new light, and he stammered out, "Of course I should like to do what's right, but I don't want to give up the army;—and—and—I'm very fond of Blanche, you know, and all that, but I don't think I quite like her well enough to marry her."

"Not like her!" exclaimed Hardingstone, to whom this latter reason was totally incomprehensible, "not like such a girl as that—the loveliest, the sweetest, the most angelic, the most ladylike creature on the face of the earth—I've never seen anything the least to be compared to her in *my* experience; and you talk of not liking her!"

"Hang it, Frank!" interposed the lad, "I wish you'd marry her yourself. I'll go shares with her in fortune; there's more than enough for us both, and you're much fitter to be a respectable man than I am."

The shaft went deep into his heart, but the strong man never winced or failed for a moment. "What right have you," he broke in, almost fiercely, "what right have you to talk of giving her money, and laying her under obligations? Like Falstaff," he added, relapsing into his usual manner, "you owe her yourself and the money too. For Heaven's sake, Charlie, don't tamper with the happiness of a lifetime—honour, duty, expediency, all point one way—do not, for a mere whim, neglect that which, left undone, you will repent ever afterwards. Promise me, *now* promise me, Charlie, that you will marry your cousin before you again leave Newton-Hollows."

Charlie bit his lip, stroked his moustaches, looked first one way, and then another; and finally, blushing crimson over his wasted face, exclaimed, "Never, Frank—if you must know it, you had better know it now—never, I tell you, and for the best of all reasons; of course it goes no farther, but the fact is, I—I like somebody else much better."

"And do you think you are the only person that has to sacrifice inclination—nay, happiness, existence itself—to duty? Do you think you are to be exempt from the common lot of man—to receive everything and give up nothing? Do you owe no duty to your cousin? Are you not all-in-all to her? And are you to destroy all the hopes of her lifetime, to break her young heart, as you have destroyed her prospects, for your own selfish gratification? Trust me, Charlie, she loves you, and whether you care for her or not, unless your word is irrevocably pledged to another, it is your duty to marry her, and marry her you must!"

"You're wrong, Frank," said Charlie, with a roguish smile; "you're wrong—you're a sharp fellow generally, but you're out of your reckoning here. Blanche has exactly the same regard for me that a sister has for a brother—but love, as you and I understand the word, bless you, she hasn't a notion of it, as far as I am concerned; but I'll tell you whom I think she *does* love, Frank—ah! you may wince and turn pale, but you ought to know, and I'll tell you. Frank, do you remember the Guyville ball?—why! you're not pale now—I should never have mentioned it if you hadn't driven me into a corner, but now out it shall come. Do you remember when you came up and turned away without asking her to dance, while we were waltzing together? Well, when Blanche looked up, her eyes were full of tears, and she said to me, 'What's the matter with Mr. Hardingstone? I'm afraid he's offended with us.' And I said, 'Blanche, you little flirt, he thinks you've jilted him.' And she blushed over her face and neck and shoulders—ay, redder than you are now, old boy; and she followed you with such a loving, piteous look—and I saw it all in a moment. Yes, Frank, Blanche is over head and ears in love with you, and I'm glad of it, for there's no other man in the world that's worthy of her; and *you* shall marry her, Frank, and *I* won't, and I'll get drunk at the wedding—but let's go below now. These cold evenings make me cough, and I suppose the steward will manage some supper for us, though it *is* blowing so hard;" with which gastronomic aspiration hungry Charlie disappeared down the hatchway, and left an altered man behind him, to pace the deck in a confused state of tumultuous, almost delirious happiness.

Frank was anything but a vain man; he always considered himself as possessing no attractions for the other sex; and that such a girl as Blanche Kettering should look upon him favourably was a happiness he had scarcely allowed himself to picture in his dreams; but now that it was suggested by another, now that it appeared to impartial eyes neither an impossibility nor an absurdity, a thousand trifling circumstances rose in his recollection—a thousand little lights and shades of looks, and tones, and expressions, came back to him distinct and vivid, with a meaning and a colouring they had never possessed before, and he could hardly restrain the happiness that gushed up in his bosom and sparkled in his eye, as after a few minutes of delicious solitude on deck, he joined the party at supper in the cabin, and one and all remarked that now the voyage was nearly over, the grave Mr. Hardingstone appeared to be quite a different man. To their questions as to the weather, he stated that it was "a beautiful night"; which caused the captain to look at him as an undoubted lunatic, inasmuch as the sea was getting up rapidly, and a thick mist was driving over the face of the waters. With the passengers he joked and laughed, and played *vingt-et-un*, and made himself so universally popular and agreeable, that those very persons who had all along voted him an odd, reserved, uncomfortable sort of fellow, now almost regretted that they should so soon be parted from such a rand of good-humour and merriment as they discovered, all too late, in their fellow-passenger.

The night grew blacker as the mist increased with the somewhat moderating gale, and a long, heaving swell came rolling up from the Atlantic, each succeeding sea appearing to rear its gigantic volume higher, farther, fiercer than its predecessor, and still the good ship steamed on through the darkness. A light at her foretop, and an indistinct glimmer at the binnacle, only made the surrounding obscurity appear more palpable, and through the dense fog, which seemed to pervade the very deck, and to hang around the spars and tackle, it was difficult to distinguish the two phantom figures at the wheel and the look-out man in the bows. The captain ever and anon dived to his cabin to consult his chart, and re-appearing on the wet, slippery deck, cast an anxious eye at the ship's compass, and the course she was lying—then glanced to windward, where some huge wave flung its crest of foam into the light, and sporting with that powerful steamer as with a plaything, dashed its beating spray, in wantonness of strength, high over the protecting bulwarks, till the very yards dripped and streamed with brine. A few gruff words, unintelligible to the landsmen, were addressed to the struggling steersmen, and again the captain glanced anxiously at the compass, and knit his brows and seemed ill at ease. Between the decks, confiding passengers snored in their berths and dreamt of home. Little thought they of darkness and fog and driving seas. They had paid their passage-money, and they were to be delivered safe at their destination—was it not in the bond? They were, besides, in the Channel; and the ladies on board derived unspeakable relief and consolation from the knowledge that they were once more in soundings—and they, too, slept the sleep of innocence and security. So midnight passed, and still the good ship held steadily on.

But the captain grew more restless and disturbed, and he ordered the steam to be slackened, and a sailor to be slung over the side, and to heave the lead; and these were wise and seamanlike precautions, but they were a few minutes too late. As the words left his mouth, a shock that made that huge fabric shake again brought him to the deck. True to his seaman nature, he shouted to "back the engines," even as he fell; but she was aground, and it was too late. Ere he recovered his legs he knew too well what had happened. Sea after sea came pouring over the deck; one of the men at the wheel was washed overboard, the other barely saved as he clung for dear life to the helm: everything that was not secured went at once by the board, and the dashing waves plunging heavily into the engine-room, put out the fires, and reduced that triumph of man's ingenuity to a mere helpless log upon the waters. The seamen came tumbling up to the forecastle, every man as he had slept, half-dressed, and even now scarce awake; yet such is the force of habit, that confusion prevailed more than alarm, and here and there even a jest arose to lips which in a few hours might probably be silenced for ever. But if not sole mistress on deck, Fear could boast of undivided dominion below. Shrieks and sobs and wailing prayers burst from the affrighted passengers, as they rushed tumultuously from their respective berths into the saloon, and asked wildly what had happened, and inquired with white lips if there was any danger; one said, "Is there any hope?" and the panic increased as it spread, and wives clung upon their husbands' breasts, and pressed their children to their sides, and screamed in an unbearable agony of fear; and one, a strong, stout man, shouted for help as though terror had turned his brain, and raved of his wife and his little ones at home—that home, on firm dry land, that he had never known how to prize before; then a white-haired minister, one of honest John Wesley's followers, proposed in a calm, steady voice that each and all should kneel down and pray; but the affrighted mass, now wavering and struggling to the hatchway, paid no attention to the good man's suggestion; for each strove to reach the deck as though it were a haven of safety, each instinctively shrank from the idea of perishing in that dark, dreadful cabin, and the selfishness of man came out and developed itself even in that maddened crowd as they pushed each other aside and struggled who should be first to reach the door.

"Charlie! where are you?" exclaimed Frank Hardingstone's unshaken voice, as he emerged already dressed from his cabin into the seething confusion of the saloon.

"Here!" said Charlie, struggling to free himself from the embraces of a stout old Frenchwoman, who, wild with terror, was choking the lad as she clung round his neck and implored him to be her preserver—"Here! Frank, we're aground, I think; I want to get on deck and make myself useful, if this old woman would let me go!"

Charlie freed himself from the venerable dame's embrace, but she clung hard to his garments, and he was forced to slip out of the dressing-gown which he had put on at the first moment of alarm, and leaving it in her grasp, to make his escape clad only in his shirt and trousers. When he reached the deck he found Frank already there, having put himself under the captain's orders, and now lending his assistance to restore discipline as far as possible, and to clear the wreck. The huge ship heaved and shivered in her throes, as wave after wave washed her farther on to the shoal; the fog, too, added to the confusion of the scene, and as it became doubtful whether her timbers could stand against the violence of these successive shocks, even the sturdy seamen began to hint at her going to pieces—and the cry, though none knew whence it first arose, thrilled from stem to stern, "The boats! the boats! Launch the boats!"

"By Him that made me! I'll strike the first man dead that stirs without orders," cried the captain, heaving a broad axe above his head, his voice rising through the confusion of the crew and the dash of the leaping waves.

"Can the boats live in such a sea?" whispered Frank, as he stood by the captain's side, prepared to lend him any assistance he might require.

"Undoubtedly, sir!" was the reply; "it's our only chance. We'll get the women and children in first. Mr. Hardingstone, you're a *man*! take charge of the larboard boat—let no man into it without orders—we may save them all yet!" and the captain sprang to the starboard boat, laid hold of the "davits," and sang out, "Lower away, men, easy!" whilst Frank, in a hurried whisper, gave his orders to Charlie, who was as cool as a cucumber throughout.

"Charlie, keep the hatchway with the steward—he's a bold fellow—don't let a single man up till the women and children are all on deck. If any fellow runs rusty, *knock him down*!"

By this time order was to a certain degree restored—the passengers were indeed in a frightful state below, when they found their egress barred, as they thought, so arbitrarily, from all hopes of safety; but on deck every man had his own duty to perform, and the magic power of discipline, assisted by the dawn, which was now struggling into light, bid fair to give them every chance of safety that knowledge and experience could suggest. But one man was mutinous. A strong, black-bearded fellow, with a dogged, lowering countenance, who had been most assiduous in helping Hardingstone to lower away the larboard boat, no sooner found it launched than he made a rush for the side, to place himself, as he hoped, in safety, regardless of the helpless and the weak.

"Stand back!" said Frank, in a voice of thunder; "wait for your turn."

"Turn be — —," growled the man; "who made *you* skipper? D'ye think I'd lose my life for a land-lubber like you?"

"I warn you!" said Frank, clenching his fist, and looking dangerous. The man advanced as though to push him aside. Frank drew himself together and struck out. He knocked him clean off his legs on to the deck, where he lay stunned and bleeding.

"Serve him right," cried Charlie from the hatchway—an observation which was echoed by the crew; and Frank had no further difficulty in preserving discipline at the station of which he had taken the command. One by one, pale trembling women, and bewildered little children, pattering on the deck with bare feet, and enveloped in shawls, petticoats, anything that had been first caught up in the hurry of the moment, were handed through the hatchway, and lowered carefully over the side into the heaving boats. There they clung together, shivering and drenched with spray, some of the women with scarce any other covering than their white night-dresses, their long wet hair hanging about their shoulders; but even in that extremity thinking only of their children, and regardless of their own sufferings and danger. Poor things! how scared they were by the first minute-gun that boomed from the wreck! for the captain, assisted by Frank Hardingstone's coolness, and now equal to any emergency, had not neglected the precaution of making every possible signal of distress. Then the male passengers were drafted singly, and handed over the side by the dauntless seamen. Some behaved gallantly enough, and offered to stand by the ship and the captain to the last; some trembled and cowered, submissively obeying every order given them, and apparently rendered totally helpless by fear. One sturdy little boy, of some ten or eleven years, clung manfully to a toy, the property of his infant sister; and when compelled to lay hold of the guiding-rope with both hands, seized the bauble between his teeth, and so reached his mother in the boat. The rough sailors gave him a cheer.

At length the passengers were disposed of; a few cloaks and pea-jackets were thrown in to cover the women; the ship's compass was placed in one of the boats; a crew of seamen were told off, and seized the oars; the mate took the command; strict injunctions were given for the boats to keep together; and they shoved off into that heaving sea. It was now broad daylight, and the rain falling heavily.

"Thank God, sir," said the captain, with a sigh of relief, "we've disposed of the passengers. The wind's falling now, with this wet, and they'll make the land in three or four hours. I trust in Providence every hair of their heads will be saved; and we've nothing to think of but ourselves."

"There's a dozen of us left," said Frank, looking round on the dripping group, who were clinging to the different parts of the wreck, consisting of one or two subordinate officers, the boatswain, and a few old, weather-beaten seamen; "that boat will hold us all, if she will swim; but she's rather a cockle-shell for such a sea as this," he observed, pointing to a small, shallow skiff that hung at the stern, and which had not yet been lowered.

"It's our best chance," said the captain, looking very grave, as another rolling sea made the wreck heave and quiver and strain, as if she must go to pieces; "but she'll never hold us all. I'll stand by the ship to the last; and you two gentlemen, to whose coolness, under Providence, the passengers owe their lives, will bear witness I did my duty. God bless you! Lower away, men; cheerily, oh!" So the boat was lowered, and as she touched the water she filled and sank, and appeared again, bottom uppermost, some fifty yards away; and so the last chance of escape was cut off. The little party looked at each other in blank dismay; even Frank's bold heart tightened itself for an instant in the pressure of despair. Only the gruff boatswain found words to say, "That bit plug, that didn't ought to have been neglected, 's worth exactly twelve men's lives. This here's a stopper over all, blessed if it ain't." There was nothing to be done now but to wait manfully for death. Poor Charlie was already half-dead with cold; but Frank took off his own pea-jacket and wrapped it round the lad, and lashed him to the foremast; for though the weather had moderated considerably, a sea came every now and then driving over the deck, and carrying everything before it. The wreck was by this time filling fast, and sinking gradually: already she had settled by the stern, and only her bows and a part of the forecastle remained above water. On this the sufferers were congregated, and few words did they interchange, for consolation or hope there was none in this world. Their powder was exhausted—true, there was plenty below, in the powder-magazine, but that was long ago swamped, so that their very cries for help must be silenced—that iron voice, their sole chance of rescue, must be dumb. The fog, too, began to clear away, and a bright gleam of sunshine ever and anon shone out upon the yellow, foam-crested waves, and glistened on the white wings of the dipping sea-gulls. By degrees the blue sky peered overhead, and the gap widened and widened, and the mists rising in wreaths from the waters, now heaving and subsiding into rest, floated lazily away, and the discoloured sea became bright and blue, and the sun burst forth into a glorious autumn day, and the warmth of his rays almost comforted those poor wet wretches, clinging hopelessly to the wreck. It seemed hard to die on such a day, but exhaustion was beginning to tell upon some of the sufferers, and the lassitude of despair was creeping over them with its drowsy influence, and the reason of more than one began to give way. So they waited and spoke not, and some strove to pray, and some shut their eyes as if in sleep; and noon came, and the day was bright and hot, and the sea-birds screamed and soared, and everything was full of joy and life, and only that little circle of twelve were doomed to die. Frank and Charlie were together, and every now and then each pressed the other's hand, but neither spoke. The captain, who was nearest them, seemed stupefied with despair; and he, too, spoke not. They were a silent company. The day crept on: every minute was precious, yet the minutes dragged on like lead. Once the captain stirred, and Frank, glancing eagerly at his face, was aware of a strange light upon it, and a gleam in his fixed eye that was almost unearthly. Was it insanity? Could it be hope? Frank's breath stopped as he followed the direction of the captain's gaze, but he could see nothing, save the glancing waters and the hopeless sky-line. But still the captain stared, and the old boatswain, too, was looking eagerly in the same direction, and another seaman seemed to wake from his stupor, and Frank strained his eyes, and at last he was aware of a black speck on the horizon, and, ere he could trust his sight, the stout old captain burst into tears, and a feeble cheer rose from the exhausted seamen, a cheer that thrilled through Frank's very marrow, for he knew that they were saved.

"What is it?" said Charlie, faintly, opening his heavy eyes.

"It's a boat," was the reply—"a boat; the bitterness of death is past, thank God! thank God!"

Then came the painful suspense, the agony of hope and fear; it might after all be but a spar, or a black fish, or anything save what they wished. No—it was a boat, a real boat; but her crew might not see them—they might be fishing—they might never think of the wreck; then the poor exhausted fellows strained their throats in a feeble hail, or rather a hoarse, desperate shriek. But the boat is bearing down upon them—she nears them. "Wreck ahoy! hilli-ho!" Never was music like to this on mortal ear. Her sharp nose comes dancing and dipping over the waves, the glance of her oars flashes in the sun; now they can distinguish the forms of the rowers—now the cheery voices of their countrymen gladden their very heart's core—and now she is alongside; and despair is over—suspense and misery are forgotten—and the past is like a dream.

The steamer had struck far nearer the shore than her reckoning had given the captain reason to suppose, and her guns had at length been heard by some fishermen on the beach at St. Swithin's. There was a heavy sea running; but the lifeboat was soon manned, and our old friend Hairblower himself took the stroke-oar, and manfully those gallant fellows pulled till they reached the wreck. They had fallen in with the ship's boats about half-way from the shore, and now brought the welcome news of their almost undoubted safety.

"To think of you and Master Charles being aboard, sir," said Hairblower, who seemed to consider the whole matter of the wreck as an every-day occurrence. "This is, indeed, what may well be called 'a circumstance,' if ever there was 'a circumstance' hereaway;" and he settled his two friends comfortably in the stern of the lifeboat, ere he busied himself to place the rest of the rescued seamen where they would least interfere with the efforts of the oarsmen. They were soon safely disposed, and by sundown, wet, weary, and exhausted, they stood once more upon that shore which they had scarcely dared to hope they should ever see again.

When Charlie woke the following morning in a comfortable room at the Royal Hotel, the first person that greeted his opening eyes was honest Hairblower. That worthy had taken entire possession of his former *protégé*, and now made his appearance with a steaming glass of hot brandy-and-water, the only orthodox breakfast, in his opinion, for a man who had been wrecked the day before; though rather disgusted at Charlie's obstinacy in refusing this specific, he was extremely anxious to assist him through his toilet, and was only to be got rid of by an assurance that his young favourite would be down to breakfast, where he would answer all his questions, and listen to all his protestations, in an incredibly short space of time. Hairblower accordingly drank the brandy-and-water himself, and waited patiently during what appeared to him an unreasonably long period to spend in the process of adornment.

When Frank and Charlie met in the coffee-room, the sailor too made his appearance, and, with much circumlocution, managed to deliver himself of a request which had evidently been all the morning brewing in his mind.

"If it was not a liberty, Master Charles, and you, too, Mr. Hardingstone, I should make bold to ask of you both to let me join company in a cruise. I conclude as you're bound to London this afternoon at the latest—soon as ever you've got rigged out decent and presentable. Well, gentlemen, you see I've a little business, too, in London town. I haven't been there not since, Mr. Hardingstone, you lent me a hand so kind, and I've got to be there, sooner or later, about the fishing business; for, you see, my mates, they wish me to be spokesman like with our governor, and he can't leave London—so, in course, I must go to him. Now, if it wasn't too great a liberty, I should be proud if you gentlemen would let me wait upon you, just for the voyage like. I can't bear to part with you so soon: and though you've no luggage, seeing all your traps is still aboard, and spoilt by now, and I can't be useful to you, I should like just to see you and Master Charlie safe into London town, and shake you both by the hand there afore we part."

Need we say the permission was joyfully granted, and that the afternoon train bore the trio in company to the metropolis, whence Charlie and Frank were to start next day together for Newton-Hollows?

CHAPTER XXIV
KING CRACK

"Sweet are the uses of adversity" to some malleable natures, which, bending to the storm, rise from it softened and refreshed as from an April shower; but there are desperate and rebellious spirits on whom grief and misfortune seem to have an exactly opposite effect. Such are more prone to kindle into resistance or smoulder in despair, and whilst the humbled penitent kneels meekly to kiss the rod, the hardened offender gnashes his teeth in impotent fury, and glories in his mad career as he forces himself from bad to worse, even to the very threshold of destruction—"game," as the poor fool calls it, "game to the last."

Such was the disposition of Tom Blacke. When his child died, the whole of his better nature seemed to have followed the infant to the grave. He had nothing now to care for in the world; and it is needless to enlarge upon the danger of such a state. His wife's misconduct—for she, poor woman, maddened by despair, had but followed her husband's example, in drowning sorrow with drunkenness—added fuel to the flames; and Tom was descending, just as gradually and as surely as one who walks step by step into a cellar, down into the lowest abyss of infamy and crime. The gradations are imperceptible, there are many windings in the path, but it never fails to terminate in the black gulf. At first the wayfarer may be easily checked and turned aside; but every onward step increases his velocity and his helplessness (the laws of gravitation are no less true in the moral than the physical world), and though a gossamer might have held him at starting, a chain of iron shall not break his fall as he nears the bottom. The beginning, too, is as insidious as it is effectual. The cheerful glass, the harbinger of good fellowship and kindliness, who would be such a churl as to deny a man the harmless pleasure of indulging in moderation with a friend? But one cheerful glass creates a craving for another, and ere long the liquor begins to have a charm of its own independent of the company. Then the dose must be increased, or it loses its power, and nightly indulgence begins to be followed by daily reaction; so a trifling stimulant is taken in the morning, just to steady the nerves and keep the cold out—a salutary precaution in this damp climate! Then the pleasure becomes a necessity, and partial intoxication begins to be the normal condition of the man. Meanwhile the habit is expensive, but who can doubt that the moral sense becomes blunted in so unnatural a state? and the drain on his means is supplied by the toper's application of his wages or other resources to his own brutal gratification. Self-indulgence soon destroys the sense of self-respect, and the temptation to procure money is irresistible, for without money how can he purchase drink? So the man first begins to lie, then to cheat, and lastly to steal. He has now arrived at the second stage in his downward journey. He has enlisted in a profession which has its rules, its customs, its triumphs—nay, to a certain extent, its pleasures—but from which there is no release. The drunkard is now a thief, and, to deaden the stings of conscience, no less a drunkard still. Then comes madness, for a state of habitual excitement can but be called madness, and visions of daring recklessness rise in the brandy-sodden brain—perhaps a sort of false ambition to triumph amongst his fellow-ruffians impels him to crimes of deeper dye than any he has yet contemplated, perhaps a vague longing for peril, perhaps a morbid thirst for blood. The wretch plots under the inspiration of brandy, and spurs himself to action with the same maddening stimulant. His nerves fail him at the critical moment, or the frenzy of despair dyes his hand with the ineffaceable stain of murder. In the one case a living death in the hulks separates him for ever from his fellow-men; in the other, the just retaliation of the law leaves his body quivering on the gallows, whilst his name becomes a byword and a curse in the mouths of generations yet unborn. This is the third and last stage of the downward journey; further we dare not follow the culprit; but few arrive at this awful ending without having gone regularly through all the previous gradations. Tom Blacke had only reached the second stage. He was now a professional thief and receiver of stolen goods. The lodgings in the Mews could now show curiosities and valuables that any one but a policeman would have been surprised to find in such a place. Gold watches, silks and shawls and trinkets, yards of brocade, ells of lace, and last, not least, a caldron always on the boil for the manufacture of that all-absorbing fluid which is called "white soup," and sold by the ounce, surrounded the once virtuous Gingham in her once respectable home. She, too, was on the downward track, and she drank to stupefy the sense of guilt, which she could not altogether stifle, and from which she had not energy to extricate herself. Mr. Blacke, however, as he began again to be called, allowed no conscientious scruples to interfere with business. He dressed well now, always had plenty of money at command, might be seen at many places of public resort, and though aware that the police had their eye on him—to use a common expression, that they were only giving him "rope enough to hang himself," and would undoubtedly "want" him ere long—he appeared resolved to live out his little hour with the usual blind recklessness and infatuation of his kind.

Blacke was a plotting villain, and he had been for some time meditating a daring sweep that should eclipse all his previous doings, *and, if not thwarted*, realise a share of booty that would place him above want for the rest of his life. In order to discover and frustrate his plans, we must take the liberty of overhearing a conversation carried on between him and his confederate, in a small snug parlour off the bar of that very public-house in which Hairblower had been so shamefully hocussed and robbed on his former visit to the metropolis—an excursion he was not likely soon to forget.

"Bring a quartern of gin," said Tom to the flaunting maid who waited on him, as he took his seat at the council-table, with a bloodshot eye and shaking hand, that showed such a stimulus was by no means unnecessary. "Shut the door, girl," he added, in a threatening voice, as the undiluted spirit was placed on the table between him and his companion; "this gentleman and me has matters of business to talk over; see that we're not disturbed— d'ye understand?" The girl gave a saucy smile of intelligence, and left the two worthies to their consultation.

"My service to you," said Tom, abruptly, as he lifted a brimming wine-glass full of gin to his shaking lips.

"Here's luck," laconically replied the gentleman addressed, wiping his mouth on the back of his hand, and turning his glass down upon the table to show how religiously he had drained every drop.

There was an ominous silence—Tom felt the moment had arrived to explain the whole of his plans, and he paused a little, like some skilful general, as he ran over in his mind how he should impart them in the clearest manner to his companion, a man of somewhat obtuse intellect, though strong and resolute in action, and who was indeed no other than Mr. Fibbes. That worthy's appearance had decidedly changed for the worse since we had the honour of making his acquaintance at the truly British game of skittles, or even since we last took leave of him in earnest conversation with his patron, Major D'Orville. He had sustained two domestic afflictions, from each of which he had suffered severely: the one in the loss of his little black-eyed wife, who had been suddenly taken from him, and who, although, as he himself said, she was a "rum 'un when she was raised," had certainly kept him out of a deal of mischief; the other, in the premature death of his pride and prime favourite, Jessie, whose sufferings during distemper and subsequent dissolution he averred would have moved "a 'eart of stone." Under the influence of these combined sorrows Mr. Fibbes had neglected his person, and taken more decidedly to drinking than formerly, and was now seldom or never in his right senses; a fact sufficiently attested by his bloated red face, his dull leaden eye, and general appearance of dissolute recklessness. He was indeed ripe for mischief, or, to use his own words, "up to anythink, from skinning a pig to smothering a Harchbishop," a frame of mind very likely to lead to dangerous consequences. Tom filled his glass once more, and opened the plan of his campaign.

"It must be done to-night, Mr. Fibbes," he remarked, with polite energy; "this is the last night we can manage it cleverly, on account of the moon. See now—I've been down in the neighbourhood to make sure. My missus, she knows the place as well as I know you. Bless you! she was bred and born there. But I wouldn't trust to that. I've been waiting down about there for a week. At last, the family they all goes out a hairin' in the phaeton or what not—I walks boldly up to the front door and rings the bell. Up comes the housekeeper, all in a fluster, settling of a clean cap—thinks I, the footman's gone with the carriage, and the butler's out shootin', and directly his back's turned, the under butler he's off courtin', and the boy when the coast's clear, he runs out to play cricket, so there's no one left but the women—trust me for managin' of *them*."

"Good," said Mr. Fibbes, approvingly, as he filled and emptied his glass.

"'Is the General at home?' says I, quite promiscuous, and looking up and down the portico like a harchitect.

"'No, sir,' says she, politely enough; 'did you wish to see him?'

"'It's of no consequence,' says I, pulling a bundle of prints and a measuring-line out of my pocket, 'merely a small matter of business; the General's confidential servant would do as well.' Ye see I knowed the butler was out, else he'd have answered the door.

"'Perhaps you'll leave a message, sir,' says she.

"'O ma'am,' says I, 'it's a matter of no importance, only I *am* going to town by the train to-night. Perhaps, ma'am, as you seem to be the governess, or a relative of the family, you might give me permission to do all I want.'

"'What is it?' says she, looking as pleased as Punch.

"'Well, ma'am,' says I, 'the fact is, I'm engaged in preparing a work for publication that shall comprise all the principal seats of the nobility and gentry in the Midland Counties; would you oblige me by glancing over the proofs? and if there are any that strike your fancy, pray favour me by acceptin' of them,' says I. 'Your noble family owns one of the finest residences we have yet surveyed, and we shall be proud to do justice to it.'"

"Good," again grunted Mr. Fibbes, who was beginning to weary of the detail, and wanted more gin to keep him awake.

"Well," resumed Tom, "with that she takes me into the hall, and shows me over the drawing-room, and the dining-room, and the conservatories; and she stops and pints out a statue—rank indecent, I calls it, without a rag of clothin' to bless itself—and the pictures, and what not; but I wasn't satisfied with this here; what I wanted was to know where the plunder was stowed, and though pictures may be very profitable to them as sells 'em, the plate-basket's more in my line of business than those shammy gold frames that make such a show, and isn't worth half-a-crown a yard. 'You'll excuse me, miss,' says I (they likes to be called miss when the bloom's off 'em a little), 'but I've always understood as the offices in this house is a perfect pattern as regards servants' accommodation and general arrangement. Now, my governor, he's building a country residence for the Earl of Aircastle, and if it wasn't takin' too great a liberty, I might ask to be allowed to inspect the basement; I could get a hint or two that would please his lordship, who's a very particular man—uncommon.' With that she hesitated a little, and looked hard at me, so I goes at her again: 'I wouldn't detain *you*, miss,' says I, 'but perhaps you'd be so good as to ring for any of the hupper servants, and they could do all I want.'

"'Oh,' says she, smiling again, 'I'll show you over the offices myself.' With that, blessed if she didn't take me down-stairs, and walk me through the sculleries, and the kitchen, and the pantry, and the servants' hall, and the back-kitchen, and the housemaid's closets—precious corners they was, too, for a game of hide-and-seek—and the butler's room, where he sleeps the nights he isn't off to Bubbleton on the sly; and I could put my hand on the plate-chest in the dark, and I know where the General keeps his money, and there's gold watches and such like in the drawing-room, that would make a matter of a hundred pounds directly they saw old Sharon's back-shop; and I kept my eyes open, as you may easily believe, and I've got it all in my head now, let alone a bit of a plan I've taken of the place just in the rough;" and with this Tom pulled a sheet of paper out of his pocket, and proposed with its aid to elucidate the manœuvres he proceeded to put in practice. "You and I can do it all," said Tom, "just the same as we stripped the old hall near Devizes. I don't relish more than two, not if a job's any way ticklish, and I do like to finish off my work neatly, I confess. Now, look ye here, Mr. Fibbes, this is how we'll act—the station's not ten minutes' walk from the house, and the mail-train stops there about 12.50. There's a luggage-train comes by about three in the mornin' that would bring us back quite handy, and we should have plenty of time to finish off handsome, and so be home to breakfast. Take another drain, Mr. Fibbes: talking's dry work."

Mr. Fibbes seemed to think the same of listening, and acquiesced with great good-will.

Tom Blacke got up, opened the door to see no one was eaves-dropping, peeped into the cupboard, and into a red-curtained snuggery off the bar, commanded by a small window in the room he now occupied; and having satisfied himself that both were empty, proceeded to unfold his plans.

"We'll leave the trap behind us this turn, Mr. Fibbes. We can carry all *we* shall want; there's my light valise and the blue bag will hold everything; we shan't take anything that's very hot, nor yet very heavy. You mind to put on the green spectacles, just for the journey, and I'll be the man with the prospectuses, the same as before, for the station-master's a smart chap, and maybe he'll know me again."

"I mustn't forget the jemmy," grunted Mr. Fibbes.

"The jemmy!" replied Tom, in a tone of injured feeling; "what's the use of the jemmy? This ain't a rough job, Mr. Fibbes; you seem to take no pride in your profession! No, no; you just put the centre-bit in your coat-pocket for a precaution, and leave the rest to me. The back-scullery's our place; it's got a regular sash window, and opens with a common hasp; there's a shutter, too, but I see a cobweb across it when I was there, and I think maybe they sometimes forget to fasten it. So you and me we alights at the station as though to walk into Bubbleton, then we come quietly up to the house, takes a bit of brown paper and treacle, and so breaks a pane in that scullery window without a chink of noise, then in goes a hand to unhasp it, and you and me, Mr. Fibbes, we walks in without a hinvitation. Now, look you here," and Tom produced his chart of the interior, "we goes quietly into the butler's room—he's safe to be at Bubbleton, because it's a theatre night—we takes a piece out of the cupboard with a centre-bit—none of your noisy jemmies—and we stows away the plate in the blue bag; then we creeps along the passage, and so up the back-stairs there" (pointing to the plan with his finger) "into the drawing-room; and here, Mr. Fibbes, I shall want your assistance, in case of haccidents. Ye see one of the ladies she sleeps above the drawing-room, and ladies is mostly light sleepers. Now, from what I've heard tell of this one—the governess she was—she's as likely as not to come down if she hears any disturbance. She might know *me*, for she's seen me along of my missus in Grosvenor Square. If she should walk in—. Take another drain, Mr. Fibbes—what's that noise?" broke off Tom, abruptly, his white face beaded with perspiration, and his lip working in guilty trepidation.

"Noise? there's no noise," replied his confederate, looking doggedly up to him, though a strange light shone too in his bloodshot eyes; "if she *should* walk in, what then?"

"Why, run the long knife into her," hissed out the less daring villain; "it makes no noise, and she'll tell no tales."

"Share and share alike, and it's a bargain," said Mr. Fibbes, dashing his great hand heavily down on the table. "D—n me, Tom, you're a deep 'un; you put me in front in that last job, and so help me I didn't clear five pounds. I'll have none of these games this turn, and if I *have* to whip out the 'bread-winner,' I'll be allowed something handsome over and above, see if I won't."

"Of course, Mr. Fibbes," replied Tom, "honour amongst gentlemen. You understand the plan now, I think, or would you like me to go over it once more?"

"Bother the plan," remarked Mr. Fibbes, who was a man of action rather than a man of science; "let's have another quartern and be off—why, it's getting dark now."

"Easy," said Tom, "we'll just call at my place for the instruments, and so walk on to the station. It's a nice fresh night for a jaunt into the country; but what a thing it is when gentlemen can combine business with pleasure!"

Mr. Fibbes grunted a hoarse laugh of approbation, and, having finished their gin, these two worthy members of society walked off, arm-in-arm, on their nefarious expedition. It is needless to say that Newton-Hollows was the house for which they were bound. General Bounce and his unconscious family, resting peacefully and securely as usual, were to be robbed, and, if any resistance arose, were to be murdered before daylight, and this because Tom Blacke, being, as he said, connected with them by marriage, and having received many acts of kindness from the warm-hearted old General, had obtained a sufficient knowledge of the inside of his dwelling and the habits of his household to make a descent upon his property with every prospect of success. After a vehement discussion with Mr. Fibbes, who was extremely anxious to travel first class, and whose aristocratic prejudices were so shocked when he found his confederate would by no means consent to this imprudent arrangement, that he nearly threw up the job altogether, the worthy couple stowed themselves away in a roomy compartment of the second class, and were soon steaming along from the lights of London, into the dark, broken masses of the cool, fresh country.

Though, in this instance, the power of steam seemed friendly to the purpose of these two finished ruffians, they could not divest themselves of certain superstitious misgivings, which probably they would not have entertained had they been bounding along on two free-going horses, like the gentlemen highwaymen of the olden time, or even bowling merrily down the road in the light spring-cart, and behind the "varmint" bay mare that made the pride of a cracksman in the early part of the present century. But the rail! there was a deal of insecurity about the rail. That electric telegraph, too, was the devil. At every station they almost expected to see the face of some too well-known detective glaring in behind the station-master's lamp, and to hear the unwelcome though civil greeting with which he would request the favour of their company. Then might he not be even now in the next carriage, separated from them by that half-inch of woodwork? Mr. Fibbes scowled as he contemplated the possibility of such proximity, and clutched more than once at the long knife. Still they sped on, uninterrupted; half the journey was already satisfactorily performed. A succession of respectable good-humoured second-class passengers got in and out, and handed their bundles and pattens and umbrellas across the two housebreakers, and entered into conversation with them, and thought the dark smaller man a vastly accommodating person, and his morose companion a stout well-to-do grazier coming home from Smithfield, judging of them just as we cannot help judging of our temporary companions, particularly when travelling, and making probably no worse shots than we all do in these fancy biographies *à la minute*. But there was a man in the next carriage to the two professionals who puzzled everybody. A stout fellow he was, with a shiny hat, but no power on earth could get him to utter a syllable. Some thought he was dumb, and some made sure he was drunk.

CHAPTER XXV
"DULCE DOMUM"

We must return to Newton-Hollows, now mellowing in the last tints of fading autumn, its dahlias already cut off by the morning frosts, its well-kept gravel-walks, despite the gardener and his staff, strewed here and there with the withered leaves of the declining year. A light mist, rising in smoke-wreaths from the sward, anticipates the early twilight of the shortening day, and the fire burning brightly in the library is none the less acceptable for its contrast to the gathering shades of out-of-doors, which seem to stalk nearer and nearer to the unshuttered windows.

Blanche has just come in, fresh and blooming, from an errand of mercy amongst the poor in the adjoining village. Her bonnet is even now hanging on her arm, and her long clustering hair is damp and limp with the dews of evening. Is that a tear clinging to her eyelashes? or is it only the moisture of heaven caught as it fell, and prisoned in those silken meshes? Blanche is often in tears now, and loves to be alone. She and Mary ride and walk together as usual, but the unreserved confidence that used to exist between them is gone. It has been dying a natural death ever since the former paid her memorable visit at Frank Hardingstone's hotel; and though it has flickered up again with an expiring flash or two, it is now finally extinct. Our young lady has aged much since her thoughtless days of only last spring. Pique, disappointment, anxiety, and self-communing have been doing their work silently and surely, shading the fair young brow, indeed, but at the same time tempering and mellowing the careless, buoyant heart. Blanche has begun to find that life is not all *couleur de rose*, even for the young, and the lesson has not been without its usual salutary effect. Though no longer the wealthy heiress—and, to do her justice, she seldom dwells upon that as a misfortune—she is beginning to feel that she too has a part to act on the stage of life, or rather that, no longer acting the vain part of every-day frivolity, she has a *reality* to fulfil. So she is never so happy now as when busying herself about her poor people, her decrepit old women, and her little ragged children, to whom she does acts of unassuming kindness, in the performance of which she forgets her own annoyances and heart-burnings, though her woman nature is as yet but half-trained, and she has occasional fits of despondency and bursts of reactionary sorrow, which make her very unhappy for the time. Blanche has had a fresh grievance, too, for the last few days, connected, of all things in the world, with Cousin Charlie's return—that return which was to have been such a jubilee of rejoicing, and which she now almost dreads to look forward to. The girl feels as if she had lost her self-respect, and turn which way she will, the sting ever rankles in her breast, ever reminds her of what she chooses to consider her degradation. The fact is, she has sustained an interview with Uncle Baldwin in the formidable study; and the General, who is not given to beat about the bush when he has an object in view, has developed to her, in as few words as possible, his projects for her future welfare, and proposed to her, point blank, that on her cousin's return from abroad she should marry him forthwith. Blanche, as in nature bound, made sundry hesitating objections, all of which her uncle chose to consider as mere maiden modesty, *de rigueur* on such an occasion; and as Blanche could not say she *didn't like him*, and as Uncle Baldwin had always been so kind, in fact, a second father to her, and made such a point of it, and it would prevent Charlie going back to those horrid Kaffirs, and was to make them all so happy, and, above all, had been her dearest mother's wish—why, the girl gave in, as girls often do on the most important topic of their lives, paralysed, as it would seem, by the amount of the stake at issue, and yielded a sort of conditional half-promise, which, notwithstanding the bursts of applause that it met with from the General, the instant it passed her lips, she would have given worlds to be able to recall. But there was another consideration, buried deep in Blanche's little heart, which, although she would have been very angry to be told so, although she would not allow it even to herself, had far more weight in inducing her to listen favourably to these advances on the part of her unconscious cousin, than all the General's skilful sophistry and affectionate eloquence; and this was a feeling which, as it is the usual accompaniment of love, resembles that epidemic in so far that, where it rages most fiercely, it is invariably most stoutly denied. Men take it freely enough, and when under its influence commit sundry absurdities, which, if they make "angels weep," certainly make their fellow-mortals laugh, and of which they have generally the grace to be heartily ashamed; but with women, as we believe its seeds are never altogether dormant in those gentle beings, so its virulence, when unchecked, pervades their whole system, and one of its commonest and least startling effects is that species of moral suicide which is best described by the vulgar adage of "cutting off one's nose to spite one's face," and which produces that most incomprehensible of all vagaries termed "marrying out of pique."

Now we need hardly say, that we have written in vain "for that dull elf who cannot picture to himself" how Blanche Kettering, from her very pinafore days, had been over head and ears in love with Frank Hardingstone: not a very sufficient reason, it may be said, for consenting to marry some one else; but yet a natural consequence of that inverted state of feelings we have described above, which under the name of jealousy is capable of more extravagant feats than this. And of whom was pretty Blanche jealous? Why, of her own fast friend and dearest associate, the peerless Mary Delaval! The more she thought over the characters of the two, so suited to each other in every possible way—which very similarity Blanche was not philosopher enough to perceive was an insuperable obstacle to any tenderer feeling than respect—the more she considered their corresponding strength of mind and hardihood of spirit, their equally high standard of worth and elevation of sentiment—the more she reflected on the opinions she had heard each of them express (the bass notes of that moral duet had sunk deep into her heart)—the more she thought over that memorable day, when, at a word from Mary, and at a moment's notice, Frank had started for South Africa, without so much as coming to wish her (Blanche) good-bye—the more her heart sank within her as she linked those two commanding figures in the halo of love, blurred even to her mental vision by the tears which filled her eyes as she contemplated the bare idea of such a union. Blanche had long struggled against this feeling; she had hoped against hope, as she firmly believed, rather than give Frank Hardingstone up; but now she would deceive herself no more; he was actually corresponding with Mrs. Delaval, which, to say the least of it, she must confess was very indelicate. This was the second letter Mary had received from him. Why had he written to Mary from the Cape? It was surely very strange; and Mary had never offered to show her either of the letters—of course she would rather die than *ask* to see them. Poor Blanche! little do you guess the cause of your friend's unusual reserve as regarded these important missives. Mary Delaval, quickened by her own experience of a hopeless love, saw it all—saw that her high-minded, manly correspondent was devoted heart and soul to Blanche; and she pitied him, even as she pitied herself, for a misplaced attachment. But it was not for *her*, of all people, to do aught that might shake Blanche's affection for Cousin Charlie—*she* could not be so selfish, so traitorous, as to lend her assistance to anything, however slight, that might in the most remote manner wean Blanche from her cousin, and leave him free. So Mary, treasuring the letter, as containing oft-repeated mention of the beloved name, placed it in her bosom, but did not volunteer to show a single line of it to a living soul. Therefore is Blanche desponding and unhappy; therefore, as gloomy thoughts sweep like shadows across her mind, the tears gather in her eyes, as she leans her head upon the marble chimney-piece, and sorrows all alone in the deepening twilight.

"And this is the day I thought I was to have been so happy," thinks poor Blanche—"the day I have been looking forward to ever since we heard Charlie was coming home. Ah! I wish I could meet him now as I used to do in the happy days when we knew nothing about marrying and money and family arrangements. And poor Charlie, after all his sufferings!—Uncle Baldwin says it will break his heart if I don't marry him. And dear mamma, if she had lived, she would have been so glad to see it all settled! And so I suppose it *must* be; and then Mr. Hardingstone will very likely marry *her*, and everybody will be happy and contented but *me*. Ah! well, there must always be some one sacrificed; and I suppose I must be the victim this time; but it *is* hard to give up all my hope, all my sunshine—to have no future any more. Yes; I hear the autumn wind sighing round the house. I am not yet twenty; and it will be all autumn to me for the rest of my life. Oh, it *is* hard—very hard!" and Blanche pressed her brow against the chimney-piece and wept bitterly.

"Blanche, dearest Blanche, what is it?" whispered a gentle voice close beside her, and she felt Mary Delaval's arm passed caressingly round her waist. Blanche started up, and checked her tears. She could have borne anything but this. She could not endure to be consoled by her triumphant rival. "Nothing," she replied, withdrawing herself almost rudely from the encircling arm—"nothing; I'm only tired and nervous, waiting for these people. I think I'll go and dress, for it's getting late; and—I think—I think I'll go by myself, Mrs. Delaval," said Blanche; and she hurried away, leaving Mary surprised and hurt at the first unkind words she had ever heard from Blanche's lips. "Anything but that," said the girl as she walked up-stairs, swelling with indignation; "anything but that *she* should come and *triumph* over me." And she banged her door angrily; and Mary, in the drawing-room, heard it, and was grieved.

Triumph, indeed!—was that poor pale face one of *triumph*? Were those deep eyes, hollowing day by day; that sad brow, on which care seemed visibly to rest, as a cloud rests upon the hill, and softens even while it darkens—were these the outward signs of satisfied affection and *triumphant* love? Blanche, Blanche, you think yourself very unhappy; but little do you know the struggle going on in the bosom of that faithful friend with whom you are now so unjustly at variance. Little do you guess that she has torn the one only image, the fulfilment of the ideal of a lifetime, from her heart, and vowed to worship it no more; and prayed that the very thought which made the sunshine of her existence might pass away; and all for you. So it is in life: we make a sacrifice which costs us nothing; we give that which perhaps we are all well satisfied to get rid of; and the world says, "How noble! how generous! how disinterested!" or we yield up the one dear hope that has cheered us all our journey; we consent to travel the rest of the way in darkness and dreariness and listless despair, and the world thinks us only stupid and disagreeable; those who look below the surface perhaps suggest that we are bilious; and the one for whom we have made all this ruin, for whose well-being and security we are stretched helpless, exhausted, bleeding by the way, thanks us blandly at the most, and takes it much as a matter of course, and passes by, very likely, on the other side.

But "fight who will and die who may," the outward world goes on much the same notwithstanding. The clock goes round, and dinner-time arrives; and whatever may be the sorrow brooded over and locked up in the inner life, we dress for dinner when the time comes, and look in the glass and dry our eyes, and have a glass of sherry after our soup; and the tyrant Custom, and the motley jester Society, bid us sit between them; and this woos from us a vapid smile, and that lays his iron hand upon our brow and dares us to stir; and we are all the better for the hypocrisy and the restraint.

Thus, although the ringing of the door-bell that announced the long-expected arrival of the guests from Africa vibrated through the very hearts of the ladies in their dressing-rooms, even as it vibrated through the ground-floors and offices of Newton-Hollows, we are not to suppose that it crumpled a fold of muslin or moved a single ringlet out of its place with its agitating summons. Below-stairs, indeed, the old butler settled himself hastily into his coat, and rushed to the door with as hearty a welcome for the travellers as if it had been his own house; whilst from a gallery that overlooked the hall divers lighted candles might be seen glancing, and pretty faces looking down from beneath smart caps, all eager to get a glimpse at Cousin Charlie, whose wounds and exploits had made him a second Roland in the estimation of these admiring damsels; while sundry exclamations might have been overheard, as, "Which is him?" "That's Master Charles, him in the pea-jacket." "Lor', how thin he's growed!" and, "Well, he's a genteel figure, let alone those 'orrid moustaches," from the upper housemaid, who was a new acquisition since Charlie's departure, and having once been engaged to a journeyman glazier, thought herself a judge of young men. But the General had rushed from his den in the meantime, half-dressed as he was, and had pulled Charlie into the well-lighted drawing-room, and had shaken Frank Hardingstone a hundred times by the hand, and was never tired of reiterating his welcome, and his delight at seeing them both once more.

"God bless you, Frank!" exclaimed the General for the twelfth time, as he fidgeted about the room in braces and shirt-sleeves. "What! you've brought him back safe and well? D—n me, sir (God forgive me for swearing), I tell you I'll *never* forget it. Zounds, don't tell me! Brought him back, sir, like a resurrectionist! I never thought to see this day, sir—I tell ye—Gratitude! how d'ye mean? And you, Charlie, my trump of a boy—thanked in Orders—General Orders, by all the gods of war! Ah, I hadn't lectured you over the old port for nothing. You took 'em in flank, the rascals. *In flank*, or I'll eat 'em. Don't tell *me*; couldn't be done otherwise. Lads! lads! it's too much: you make me feel like a child again. What?" and the old General's eyes began to overflow with the fulness at his heart; so he relapsed into a state of unusual gruffness, and stirred the fire fiercely to conceal his emotion; and finally hurried them off to dress. "None of your licentious camp habits here, Charlie. Dine to a minute, you dog! I trust you'll find your room comfortable, Frank, my boy. I saw to the fire myself not half-an-hour ago. What? Ring for what you *want*, and my servants will bring you what they *have*." So the old gentleman toddled off to finish his own personal adornment, and the guests, with beating hearts, well concealed from each other, proceeded to dispatch theirs as quickly as might be.

If ever there was a banquet that to all appearance should have been one of triumphant hilarity, it was the sumptuous dinner to which our party sat down that day in the bright, warm, cheerful dining-room at Newton-Hollows. Notwithstanding Lady Mount Helicon's sneers, no man understood better than the General that process which is conventionally called "doing things well." The servants glided about noiselessly as if shod with velvet—the doors were never left open, still less closed with a bang—no bumps and thumps of tray-corners against projecting wood-work disturbed the conversation, to irritate the host while they alarmed his guests. Nor as the different courses made their appearance, did a gush of cold air accompany them from below-stairs, tainted but not warmed by the odours borne with it from the kitchen. The soup was as hot as the plates, the champagne iced to a turn, even as the haunch was roasted. Glasses were filled noiselessly by the butler, as a matter of course (by the way, an immense pull for the ladies), and everything was handed to everybody at the instant it was wanted, and this, to our humble ideas, is no mean auxiliary to the general success of an entertainment. The old Roman *bon vivant* evidently knew a thing or two about dinner-giving (he called them suppers), or he would not have so dilated on the necessity of attention to trifles, *vilibus in scopis, in mappis*, etc. The General, too, understood these details thoroughly, and therefore it was disrespectful youth voted *nem. con.* that Newton-Hollows was "a rare shop at feeding time," and that "old Bounce, if he was rather a bore out hunting, was nevertheless the boy to dine with, and no mistake!"

"The boy," however, on this occasion seemed to have all the hilarity of the meeting to himself. Of the four individuals that constituted his party, each was acting a part, each had set a guard upon his and her lips, and was originating broken, disjointed sentences, vainly endeavouring to form a matter-of-course unrestrained conversation. The ladies were even more reserved than the gentlemen. Blanche was thinking how brown and handsome Frank looked after his voyage—so much more manly than her cousin—and wondering why he should say so little to *her*, and yet pay no attention whatever to Mary. That lady again was full of tender alarms and anxieties about Cousin Charlie, his wasted figure, and his frequent cough, and gulping down the tears she could scarcely repress, as she glanced ever and anon at his glittering eye and emaciated face. "Perhaps," she thought, "he will never live after all to be Blanche's husband." A thrill shot through her at the thought that then he would indeed be all her own: but if this was joy, good faith! it was a joy near akin to tears. As for Frank, he was more in love than ever. Nor indeed is this to be wondered at. If a gentleman having voluntarily surrendered himself to that epidemic, which, like the measles, we must all go through sooner or later, and which, like that indisposition of childhood, is prone to cure itself by its own progress—if a gentleman, then, having undergone a favourable eruption, and, at the very crisis of his disorder, shall voluntarily absent himself from his charmer, to return from a sea-voyage amongst rough companions, and contemplate her for the first time, attired in all the brilliancy of dinner costume, and further embellished by the favourable disposition of light, which sets off such entertainments, and which is generally considered highly conducive to female beauty, he need not be surprised to find that he is less a rational being than ever, or that the disease for which absence is considered so unfailing a cure should come out with redoubled virulence under such an interruption of that salutary course. But Frank, though in love, was also disappointed. His hopes had risen most unreasonably since Charlie's disclosures on the evening preceding their memorable shipwreck. He had indulged in such day-dreams as, for a sensible man—which, to do him justice, he generally was—were the acme of absurdity; and now because Blanche had neither thrown herself into his arms when they met—a feat, indeed, she could hardly have conveniently accomplished, "dinner" being announced at that interesting moment—nor had spoken to him more than she could possibly help—for which reserve she likewise had excellent reasons, the principal one being that she could by no means trust her voice—our philosophic gentleman was disappointed, forsooth, and consequently hurt, and the least thing sulky. Charlie, again, though more at ease in his mind than the others, was tired and exhausted: he was always tired now towards the evening; and although rejoiced to be once more at home, once more gazing his fill on the only face he had ever much cared to look at—an indulgence that partook, he knew not why, of the nature of a stolen pleasure—yet his satisfaction was of that inward kind which does not betray itself by outward signs of mirth, but which, more particularly in failing health, flows on in a deep silent current, that to the superficial observer has all the appearance of apathy and cold, selfish carelessness.

But the General was in his glory. Fond of eating and drinking himself, his delight was to see his friends eat and drink too; and as he urged on his guests the different good things for both purposes that smoked on the table or sparkled on the sideboard, he monopolised the conversation with the same zest that he demolished a considerable share of the entertainment.

"Charlie, you eat nothing, my boy," said the General: "that haunch was roasted a turn too much; let me give you a bit of the grouse. Zounds! we must fatten you up here—what? commissariat disgraceful at the Cape! 'Gad, sir, we wouldn't stand it in India. I broke three commissaries myself in the Deccan, because there was no soda-water in camp—fact, I pledge you my honour, Mrs. Delaval. I don't believe Charlie's had a morsel to eat since he went into training for the steeple-chase."

"You wouldn't have said so if you'd seen him getting well at Fort Beaufort," remarked Frank, rousing himself from his fit of abstraction; "his voracity was perfectly frightful! I wish you could have seen him, Miss Kettering, in a black skull-cap, as thin as a thread-paper, on crutches, asking every ten minutes what o'clock it was, dreading to die of starvation between two o'clock dinner and five o'clock tea; you never beheld anything so thin and so hungry."

Blanche laughed her old merry laugh; and Charlie, stealing a look at Mary Delaval, saw her eyes were full of tears. How his heart leapt within him, and how a chill seemed to gather round it the moment after, and curdle his very life-blood, as the possibility flashed across him, that even now it might be *too late*. Too late!—he was but twenty-one, yet something warned him that his was no secure tenure, that there might be truth in the startling suspicion that had of late obtruded itself like a death's head on his moments of enjoyment—that the world might be no world for him when autumn again shed her leaves, and the browning copses and cleared fields brought back the merry field-sports he loved so well. No more football—no more cricket—no more panting excitement and rosy out-of-doors exertion—no more sharp gun-shot ringing through the woodland, nor hound making music in the dale, nor airy steed careering after the pack, fleeting noiselessly o'er the upland. And though these were hard, bitter hard to leave, 'twas harder still to give up the opening dream of ambition, the budding promise of manhood; and harder, harder than all, the first glowing reality of woman's love. It is well to perish with trust unshaken in that glorious myth; to sleep before that too is discovered to be a dream. But Charlie shook off these moments of despondency with the elasticity of his age and character. In that bright, luxurious room, with those friendly faces around him, encircled by beauty, wealth, and refinement, death seemed *impossible*. Have we never felt thus wrapped in security ourselves; and when some "silver cord has been loosed—some golden bowl broken" from amongst our own immediate associates, have we not felt almost angry at the unmannerly visitor who intrudes thus without knocking, and pauses not to wipe his shoes for Turkey carpet more than sanded floor? "*Pauperum tabernas regumque turres*," he has the *entrée* of them all.

The General was a little disappointed with his guests, when, on the retirement of the ladies, a magnum of undeniable claret exhaled its aroma for their immediate benefit, and he found it did not by any means disappear with that military rapidity to which he was accustomed in his younger days. Charlie's cough was a sufficient excuse for his abstemiousness; and Frank Hardingstone, though he could drink a bucketful on occasion, would not open his lips on compulsion; so the General found himself in consequence obliged to grapple with the giant almost single-handed. This, to do him justice, he undertook with considerable *gusto*, and by the time he had got to the bottom of his measure, had arrived at that buoyant state in which gentlemen are more prone to broach such matters of business as they may think it expedient to undertake, than to explain clearly the method by which their desired ends can most readily be attained. Accordingly, when Frank and Charlie rose to join the ladies in the drawing-room, our old soldier called the latter back to the fire-place, and filling himself a large bumper of sherry as an orthodox conclusion to the whole, bid his nephew sit down again for five minutes, and have a little quiet conversation on a subject which should not be too long postponed. "Just three words, Charlie," said the General, sipping his sherry; "won't you have a whitewash, my boy? Three hundred and sixty-five more glasses in the year, you know. You won't? Well, Charlie, I'm right glad to see you back again. To-morrow I must go over everything with you as regards money matters. Frank has told you all about the will. What? Zounds! it was very singular—I confess I expected it all along." The General was one of those truest of prophets whose predictions are reserved until the fulfilment of events. Finding that Charlie took this extraordinary instance of foresight very coolly, he proceeded, as he thought, to beat about the bush in a most skilful manner.

"Well, Charlie, and how d'ye think we're all looking, eh? Wear well and struggle on, don't we? I've taken pretty good care of your cousin for you, my boy, during your absence. How d'ye think she's looking, eh?"

Charlie, who had not thought about it at all, answered, "Very well."

And the General filled himself another glass of sherry and went on—"By Jove, Charlie, I congratulate you on *that*, eh? Shake hands, my lad. Zounds! we'll drink Blanche's health. Now I've put everything *en train*. We can have the lawyers down at a moment's notice. Blanche's *things*, to be sure, will have to be got; women can't do without such a quantity of clothes. Why, when Rummagee Bang's widow was burnt—however, that's neither here nor there. Now tell me, Charlie, when do you think it ought to come off?"

"My dear uncle, I can't think what you're talking about," replied Charlie, trying to look as if he didn't understand; "I don't see what I've got to do with Blanche's things."

"Talking of?" resumed the General, "why, the wedding, to be sure. What else should I be talking of? You're quite prepared, I suppose. I've arranged it all with Blanche; she cried and all that, but *I* know the sex, Charlie, and *I* could see—zounds, sir! she's *de*-lighted. Never was such an arrangement—keeps all the money together, fulfils everyone's intentions. What?—and then it's been such a long attachment, ever since you were both children, corals and long petticoats. Petticoats! How d'ye mean?"

"But, Uncle Baldwin," pleaded Charlie, with some difficulty getting in a word edgeways, "don't you think all this is somewhat premature?"

"Premature! what the devil?" replied the General—"zounds, sir! not at all premature; quite the contrary, been put off too long, in fact. Never mind, better late than never. These things should be done out of hand. Why, sir, when I was at Cheltenham in '25, the very year of that claret, by the way," pointing to the empty magnum, "there was a handsome widow wanted to marry me at twelve hours' notice. Did I ever tell you how I got off, Charlie? 'Gad, sir, Mulligatawney, of the Civil Service, got me out of the town in a return hearse; but even death couldn't part us, my boy—zounds! she followed me to Bath, and I was laid up on the second-floor of the York House with the scarlet fever—*the scarlet fever!* and I was as well as you are—till we starved her out; and when they said I was disfigured for life she gave in." The General chuckled till the tears came into his eyes; then, recollecting his moral was somewhat anti-matrimonial, checked himself into supernatural gravity, and resumed on the other tack. "But marriage is a respectable state, Charlie; there's nothing like it, so Mulligatawney tells me, to sober a man. Marriage, Charlie," said the General, oracularly, with a solemn shake of the head, "marriage is like that empty decanter. It comes in sparkling and blushing, like sunrise on a May morning. What?—You draw the cork, and the first glass is heaven upon earth—that's the honeymoon; then you fill another—same flavour, but not quite equal to the first. Never mind, try again; so you keep sipping and sipping, to analyse, if you can, the real taste of the beverage, and before you satisfy yourself you come to the end of the bottle; then, sir, when you get to the bottom you can see through it, and you find how empty it is! Not that I mean exactly that," said the General, again catching himself up, as he found that his metaphor, having taken a wrong turn, had led to a somewhat unexpected conclusion. "But we can't stop here all night," added he; "so tell me, my boy, when I may begin to send out invitations for the breakfast."

Charlie blushed up all over his emaciated face, as he replied, pulling vehemently at his moustaches, "Why, uncle, it's best to be explicit, and I like to be straightforward about everything, so I may as well tell you at once, I—I'm hardly prepared to marry—in fact, I'm rather adverse to it—in short," said Charlie, gaining courage as he went on, "I've no immediate idea of marrying at all, and, with all my respect and brotherly affection for her, certainly not Blanche."

"*Certainly not Blanche!*" repeated the General, in something between a shriek and a moan. "*Certainly not Blanche!*—and why, in the name of all that's de—de—disgusting? *Certainly not Blanche!* Zounds! I see it all now; you've got a *black wife*—don't deny it!—a black wife and a swarm of piebald picaninnies. Oh dear! oh dear! that I should live to see this day—I shall never get over it—it's killing me now;— —, I feel it here, sir, in the pit of my stomach! I'll go to bed," he vociferated, untying his neckcloth on the spot; "I'll go to bed this instant, and never get up again!" With which lugubrious threat the General, regardless of Charlie's protestations and remonstrances, did in effect stump furiously off to his den, whence his dressing-room bell was forthwith heard pealing with alarming violence; nor did he appear any more that evening, leaving the gentlemen to drag out a weary sitting, still at cross purposes, each in the society of her he loved best in the world.

CHAPTER XXVI
"EUDÆMON"

It was a soft dark night—such a night as is peculiar to our temperate climate towards the close of autumn. There was no moon, and not a star to be seen, yet was it not *pitch* dark, save under the gigantic trees or in the close shrubberies that surrounded Newton-Hollows. A man could see about ten yards before him, and one bound on an evil errand, by cat-like vigilance and circumspection, might have made out the figure of an honest man at that distance, and remained himself unseen. The night-wind sighed gently through the half-stripped hedges; and the fragrance of the few remaining autumnal flowers floated lightly on the breeze. It was a beautiful night for the purpose. "Quite providential," Mr. Fibbes said, as, clad in a long great-coat, he stumbled up the dark lane that led from Newton station to General Bounce's residence. His companion made no answer; Tom Blacke was pre-occupied and nervous. It may be that the stillness of the hour, the soothing tendency of all around him, brought back too painfully the innocent days of the past—it may be that he contemplated with some misgivings the hazardous undertaking of the immediate future. Mr. Fibbes, however, allowed no such gloomy reflections to influence his spirits, and the pair proceeded in silence, save where the latter, stumbling in some unseen rut, anathematised the slovenly finish of "these here country roads," and sighed for the gas-lit pavement of his beloved London. Once Tom halted, grasping his comrade's arm with a low "Hush!" and whispering in his ear, "that there was a step behind them, walking when they walked, and stopping when they stopped."

"Hecho," replied Mr. Fibbes, accounting for the phenomenon by natural causes, but prefixing a superfluous aspirate to the name of the invisible nymph. "Hecho," said he; "I've often knowed it so—'specially at night. But, Tom, what's up, man? blessed if you ain't a-shakin' all over,—have a drain, man, have a drain!" and the never-failing remedy was forthwith produced in a goodly case-bottle from the great-coat pocket. Nor did the doctor neglect his own prescription, and much refreshed the twain proceeded on their way. A slight difficulty occurred in scaling the park-railings, Mr. Fibbes affirming with many oaths that nothing but his weight and the age of his nether garments saved him from being impaled there for life; and the tremendous disturbance occasioned by a panic-stricken cock-pheasant compelled a halt of several minutes' duration, lest the inmates of the Hall should have been aroused by the vociferous rooster. All was at length still— the church clock at Guyville chimed the half-hour after one. The night grew more cloudy, and the wind died away into a low, moaning whisper. The pair stole across the lawn, like two foul shades returning to the nether world. A heavy foot-mark crushed Blanche's last pet geranium into the mould. Tom shook like an aspen leaf, much to the covert indignation of Mr. Fibbes, and they reached the scullery window unheard and unsuspected.

"Gently, now!" Why does Tom shake so, and even Mr. Fibbes, with his bull strength and iron nerves, feel so ill at ease, so willing even now to go back a guiltless trespasser, and leave the job undone? But no—it has been boasted of in anticipation at their flash resorts; what would the professionals think? Why, the very detectives would sneer to learn that "Leary Tom" and "the Battersea Big 'un" had been frightened at their own shadows, and after a long journey into the country had returned bootyless to London, the sleepers undisturbed—the "crib uncracked." "Gently, again!"—a jackdaw on the roof brings their hearts into their mouths; were it not for the case-bottle they would "drop it" even now. Another pause, and Mr. Fibbes, summoning all his energies, proceeds to act. Gently and stealthily he produces the brown paper, and the treacle with which it is to be smeared. Lightly he applies it to the selected pane, Tom turning the dark-lantern deftly on the job. How ghastly the white face on which a chance ray happens to gleam! Warily—gradually—the heavy hand presses harder, harder still, and the glass gives way; but the faithful treacle absorbs every stray fragment, and not a particle reaches the ground either without or within. Fortune favours the rogues; the shutters have not been put up. They are in for it now, and both gather confidence, Mr. Fibbes assuming the initiative. A large dirty hand gropes through the broken pane, and the hasp of the window is moved cautiously back; but with all their care it gives a slight click, and again they pause and listen with beating hearts. "The grease," whispers Mr. Fibbes to his confederate, and the sashes being plentifully smeared with that application, the window opens noiselessly to the top. Admittance thus gained to the body of the place, our housebreakers are now fairly embarked on their enterprise. Their shoes are pulled off and stowed away in their pockets. The centre-bit is got in readiness, and Mr. Fibbes feels the edge of his long knife with a grim sense of dogged, bloodthirsty resolution. All is, however, in their favour. The scullery door is left open, and they reach the passage on the ground-floor without the slightest noise or hindrance. And here we may remark for the benefit of those who are affected by nervous apprehensions of their houses being "burglariously entered and their property feloniously abstracted," to use the beautiful language of the law—that there is no precautionary measure better worth observing than that of carefully locking *on the outside* the door of every room on the ground-floor, and leaving the key in the lock. There are three things, it is said, of which the housebreaker has a professional horror—a little dog loose, an infant unweaned, and a sick person *in extremis*. The first is an abomination seldom permitted where there is anything worth stealing; the second, a misfortune which Nature kindly suffers only to exist at considerable intervals; the third, a calamity to which we may hope not to be subjected *very* often in a lifetime. In the absence, then, of these unwelcome defences, every door secured as above makes an additional fortification against the enemy. The thief having perhaps effected a skilful and elaborate entrance into your dining-room, where he finds no booty but an extinguished lamp and a volume of family prayers, must commit a fresh burglary before he can reach your study, or wherever you keep your small stock of ready money for household expenses; and though he came in at the window, reversing the usual order of things with an unwelcome visitor, he finds it no easy matter to get out at the door. The probability is he will hardly work through three solid inches of mahogany, for he cannot conveniently pick the lock, if the key is left in it, without some little noise. Thus (although to the damage of your upholstery) you get an additional chance of being aroused, and a few minutes more time to betake yourself to your weapons, whether they consist of an unloaded blunderbuss, a twelve-barrelled revolver (out of order), or a hand-candlestick and a short brass poker. In the meantime, your *placens uxor*, uttering piercing shrieks out at the window, alarms the country for miles round, and, what is more to the purpose, frightens the robber out of his wits, who decamps incontinently, leaving no further marks of his visit than a window-frame spoilt, an inkstand or a jar of curry-powder upset, and a small box of lucifer-matches, his own property, and seized on by you as the *spolia opima* of this bloodless victory.

Stealthily, noiselessly, like the tiger on his velvet footfall, our two ruffians glide along the passage towards the butler's sleeping-room, where the plate is kept. Small need have they of the dark lantern, so accurately have they studied the plan of the house, so apt are they in their nefarious trade. But they have reckoned without their host upon that official's absence at Bubbleton; the late arrivals from Africa have kept him at home. However, he has been celebrating their return so cordially that, as far as being aroused and making an alarm goes, he might as well be a hundred miles off. They pass the lantern twice or thrice across his sleeping, open-mouthed face, and Fibbes feels the edge of his knife once more, with devilish ferocity, ere the centre-bit is brought into play, and a hole bored in the plate-cupboard, which soon makes the robbers masters of its contents. That receptacle is emptied, and its treasures transferred to the blue bag, with astonishing silence and celerity. The adepts, growing bold with impunity, almost regret the deep slumbers of the inmates, sufficiently attested by the prolonged snores resounding from that portion of the basement where the other male servants repose, and arguing that the jollifications of the evening have not been confined to the somnolent butler alone: had the garrison been more on the alert, think the invaders, there would have been more satisfaction in foiling them, and it would have been a "more creditable job" altogether. Hush! is that a footfall along the passage? They stop and listen intently. The kitchen clock ticks loudly throughout the darkness, but other sound is there none. They resume their labours. By this time the plate is packed; the great object of the foray has been attained—melted silver tells no tales—and there is nothing further to be done than to strip the drawing-room of such portable articles as are worth the carrying, and so decamp in triumph. Up the back-stairs they steal. The General hates a door to *slam*, in which aversion we cordially agree with him; and the green-baize one communicating with the offices revolves noiselessly on its hinges. So they glide through without hindrance, and on past that statue the nudity of which had shocked Tom's sense of propriety on a previous occasion. Mr. Fibbes, who is of a facetious humour when under excitement, seizes the dark-lantern, and turns its glare full upon this work of art, with a high-seasoned joke. They reach the drawing-room door; for the space of a minute they listen intently; prolonged snores from the direction of the General's apartment pervade the house; other sounds there are none. Cautiously the lock is turned, and the door thrown quickly open, that no creaking hinge may betray them by its moan. A gleam of light well-nigh blinds them, accustomed to the darkness of the passages through which they have been groping; and Mr. Fibbes, who enters first, starts back, paralysed for a moment by the unexpected apparition of a female figure robed in white, and shining like some unearthly being in the strong light of his lantern turned full upon the place she occupies. The figure starts up, and utters a long piercing shriek. There is no time for deliberation; Tom hisses a frightful oath into his confederate's ear, and the big ruffian gripes Blanche's white throat in one hand, whilst the other gropes in his dress for the long knife. Already the blade quivers aloft in the candle-light. Crash!—a terrific blow levels the villain to the floor. Tom, turning madly to escape, finds himself in the powerful grasp of Frank Hardingstone, who shakes him as a terrier would shake a rat—Frank's extremely airy costume being highly favourable to such muscular exertions. Bells peal all over the house; lights are seen glancing along the passages; female voices rise shrill and high, in scream and sob and voluble inquiry. Charlie and Mary Delaval meet on the stairs, and he only exclaims, "What is it? Thank God, *you* are safe!" The General rushes tumultuously down in a scanty cotton garment, disclosing the greater portion of a pair of extremely sturdy supporters, and in which, crowned with a red nightcap, and armed moreover with a short brass poker, he presents the appearance of some ancient Roman of "the baser sort," inciting his brother-plebeians to an agrarian tumult. "Guard, turn out!" shouts the General, in a voice of thunder. "Murder, thieves! Let me get at 'em; *only let me get at 'em!*" And he bursts into the drawing-room, where he beholds Frank still shaking Tom Blacke, who is by this time nearly strangled; Blanche in a "dead faint" on the sofa; Mr. Fibbes' huge body extended senseless on the floor, and standing over him, apparently ready to knock him to shivers again the very instant he should show the slightest symptom of vitality, our old friend, rough, honest, undaunted Hairblower!

"Drum-head court-martial!" exclaimed the General, as he struggled hastily into a somewhat warmer costume than that which he had worn during the brunt of the action—"drum-head court-martial at three in the morning. Zounds! I only wish I was in India, I'd have 'em hanged in front of the house before breakfast-time. Frank—hollo!—march the prisoners into my study, under escort, my boy, and be d——d to them. No, I will *not* swear," and the General took his place at his study-table, with all the pomp and circumstance of a district court-martial, as the hapless housebreakers, with their arms pinioned behind them, and guarded by the whole male strength of the establishment, were paraded before him, Hairblower bringing up the rear, and keeping his eye steadily fixed on Mr. Fibbes, as if only watching his opportunity for an insubordinate movement on the part of that individual to knock him down again. Mr. Fibbes maintained a dogged silence throughout; save once, when he muttered a complimentary remark, containing the figurative expression, "white-livered son of a ----," supposed to be explanatory of the state of prostration in which he saw his fellow-prisoner. Tom Blacke was utterly unnerved; he cried, and shook, and staggered like a man with the palsy, and would have gone down on his knees to the General, had he not been forcibly held up by the two tall footmen, who seemed to mistrust even the slightest movement as preparatory to a fresh outbreak of ferocity. "This once," pleaded the wretched coward, "forgive me this once, General, for the sake of my poor wife—Miss Blanche's maid she was, sir—only this once, and I'll confess all—the forgery and everything—you might transport me for life, but you won't be hard upon me, General—this job wasn't my doing, 'twas him that set me on it; 'twas his plan, I'll swear," pointing to Mr. Fibbes, whose countenance was expressive of intense contempt and disgust. "Well," muttered that gentleman, as if this was indeed a climax, "well, I am ——," something which he certainly was *not*, however much the mode of life he affected might eventually lead to such a consummation. "Forgery!" exclaimed the General, "what? Zounds! here's something of importance! swear him—no, he's on his trial—take his words down in writing—forgery indeed!—here's a pretty discovery!" As Blacke became more composed, out it all came—how his wife had forged Mrs. Kettering's name, and obtained the legacy, and got the will proved, through that knowledge of the law which he was always ready to turn to evil account—the whole confession, which was indeed full and satisfactory, for he was frightened into telling the truth, closing with another earnest appeal for mercy, and another denunciation of his dogged confederate.

The General was in raptures—Blanche was an heiress once more—even Charlie's contumacious refusal to be married against his will was now a matter of secondary importance. In his delight he would have let both the rogues go, and pledged himself not to prosecute them, had Frank Hardingstone not reminded him that the duty he owed to civilised society would hardly admit of such injudicious lenity; so the prisoners were marched off, still under a numerous and voluble escort, and carefully locked into a coal-house, whence, it is needless to observe, they made an easy escape within two hours, when their temporary gaolers, after beer all round, returned to their repose—nor should we omit to mention that they were retaken by the London police within five days, and eventually transported—Mr. Fibbes for fourteen years, and Tom Blacke, in consideration of divers little matters that came up against him, for the term of his natural life.

But in the meantime, the General, his guests, and servants, returned to their respective couches. Blanche, after the administration of such restoratives as ladies alone understand, was put to bed by Mary Delaval, who would not leave her till she saw her sink into a quiet refreshing slumber—then the governess too sought her room, and oh! what a happy heart she carried with her to her rest. "Thank God, *you* are safe!" It was but five words—yet what depths of joy and hope and tenderness that short sentence opened up—what a different world it was now—true, they were far apart as ever in reality, but she felt that in the bright realms of fancy they were linked in a bond that could never be forgotten—"yes, he loved her." 'Twas *his cousin's* scream that had disturbed him in his chamber; 'twas *his cousin*, his betrothed wife, as she had once thought, who was in peril and distress; yet in all the hurry and confusion of the moment, *she*, the poor governess, was uppermost in his thoughts. "Thank God!" he said, "*you* are safe!"—yes, he loved her, he loved her, and he was hers for evermore. They would never be united in the material world; other duties, other affections would supplant her in his outer life, his every-day existence—but when the cloud of sorrow overshadowed him—when joy more than common flooded him in its golden light—when a strain of music, or a gleam of sunshine, or the song of a bird, or the ripple of a stream touched his higher nature—whenever the springs of feeling gushed up in his inmost heart, then would her image rise to vindicate its sovereignty over its spiritual being—then would she claim him and possess him as her own, her *very* own. First love is a fatal illusion—the plant may never come into full bloom—it may blossom but to be cut down—it may be nipped by bitter frosts or rent by the blustering gale—it may be trodden into the dirt by rude feet, and covered by grass mould, or spotted by the slime of trailing reptiles. For years it may be buried and forgotten, yet when the south wind breathes its fragrance over earth, when the gentle rain descends from heaven, its fibres will again put forth their leaves; from its burial-place the meek plant will again raise its head above the surface, and its perfume will steal over the senses like a sigh from Paradise. So thought Mary with regard to that superstition. To do them justice, women in general cling with wonderful tenacity to this article of their faith. Poor things! they seldom have it in their power to observe it practically, but their adoration in theory for the holiness and inviolability of first love is all the more disinterested and edifying. So Mary lay awake for hours in an ecstasy of happiness, and when she did close her eyes what wonder that her dreams, take whatever shape they would at first, invariably resolved themselves into a circle of merry-makers, and in the middle a figure on its knees before her, with fair, upturned face, and tender, smiling lips, whispering, "Thank God, *you* are safe!"

It is now high time that we should explain by what fortunate train of circumstances Hairblower and Blanche should have met at that critical moment, when the astonished girl found herself in the grasp of a ruffian, who but for the timely intervention of the seaman's arm, would in all probability have murdered her on the spot. Her champion's own account of his proceeding was so intermixed with professional terms and peculiar phrases, which in his vocabulary possessed an entirely different meaning from that which is found attached to them in Johnson's Dictionary, or any other standard authority on the English language, that we prefer giving it in our own words, merely observing that the whole robbery and rescue was a proceeding which he designated "special," and should, indeed, be considered, so he said, "a circumstance from beginning to end." Hairblower, then, having transacted his fishing affairs with his "governor," as he called him, in which interview, we have since been informed, the "governor," a shrewd, hard-headed man of business, got very much the better of the seaman; and having failed in his intention of making a ceremonious call on his foreign friends, "the True-blues," who were then making a tour of the provinces, was irresistibly impelled by a species of morbid curiosity to revisit the scene of his former misfortunes. So he actually turned into the very public-house where he had been robbed on his previous visit to London; and finding no one there but the bar-maid (a late acquisition), very quietly had his dinner and drank his beer in the small snuggery of the bar, which we have mentioned as being lighted by a window from the identical room in which Tom Blacke and Mr. Fibbes were in the habit of holding their nefarious consultations. The seaman had paid for his liquor, and was in the act of departing—in fact, the girl thought he had already gone, when the two housebreakers entered the door, and Hairblower, resisting his first impulse, which was to do battle on the spot with the twain, "one down, t'other come on," shrank back unobserved into the little room he had been occupying, and taking off his shoes, concealed himself behind an old-fashioned chest that stood against the wall. His first idea was to remain in hiding till the two worthies should have arrived at the height of their jollification, and then, bursting in upon their banquet, to administer to each what he termed "his allowance." The conversation, however, which he overheard was of such a nature as to modify considerably this desire for immediate blows, and when the horrid method of silencing the alarm likely to be raised by some female watcher was discussed in cold blood as a matter of regular business, the listener's hair stood on end as he resolved, come what might, to prevent this deliberate and inhuman murder.

But Hairblower was completely in the dark still as to the "where" and the "when" of the intended burglary. He could not therefore warn the inmates, nor had he time to inform the police. He could but watch the plotters, lie still, and listen. Little thought Tom Blacke, when he looked outside the door and peeped through the red-curtained window, as he imagined to make all safe, that the avenger in the shape of his old sailor friend was within five yards of him; little thought Mr. Fibbes, in his acoustic speculations about "Hecho," that in this instance hers was a substantial frame dogging his every footstep, a strong heavy arm ready and willing to strike him to the earth. They thought they were secure at least of all *outside* the house, and they took their measures accordingly.

But honest Hairblower enjoyed one of those enviable organisations to which fear seems positively unknown, and when he reflected that, in his ignorance of where they were bound and when their plot was to be ripe, his only chance was never to let the ruffians out of his sight till he could place them in safe custody, it seemed to him the most natural thing in the world, alone and unarmed, to dog the footsteps of two desperate men, one of whom was an acknowledged murderer. He followed them accordingly from the house; he waited on the opposite side of the street whilst they got their implements from Tom's lodgings; he arrived at the station twenty yards behind them, stole up and heard them take tickets to "Newton," took a similar one himself, and sat down in the very next carriage to them, with the collar of his pea-jacket pulled high over his face, and a guard placed upon his lips, lest his old acquaintance should by any means overhear and recognise his voice. As he journeyed down, he thought over every possible plan by which he could frustrate the robbery. If he gave them into custody with the railway people, he could prove nothing; they were two to one; they would not hesitate to swear black was white, and they might easily turn the tables upon him, and perhaps succeed in transferring him to durance vile instead of themselves. If he asked for assistance from a fellow-passenger (and there was one stout-made countryman in whom Hairblower was sorely tempted to confide) he would probably not be believed, or at any rate the explanation and consequent watching would be very likely to place the ruffians on their guard. No, he would do it all himself. He could rely on his own stout heart and powerful frame; he would hunt them to the world's end. At Newton station great caution was necessary. He remained in the train till they had left the platform, then nimbly jumped out as it was on the point of starting, and delivering up his ticket, got clear of the building in time to distinguish their footsteps stealing up the lane not fifty yards ahead of him. This distance he cautiously diminished. Like most sailors, he could see pretty well in the dark, and was used to going barefoot, so taking his shoes off once more, he had no difficulty in keeping within earshot of the chase. At last they reached the house; Hairblower no more knew whose it was than the man in the moon; but he had determined, as soon as they were all safe inside, to make a dash at Tom Blacke, knock him senseless, close with Fibbes, and alarm the inmates; thus, he thought, they will be taken in the fact. Had he known his dear Miss Blanche was in jeopardy, perhaps he might not have been so cool. Fortunately, sailors are so used to every sort of difficulty that it is next to impossible to put one wrong, and Hairblower managed to creep through the scullery window nearly as deftly as either of the professionals, with whom proficiency in such exercises is a necessary part of their trade. Whilst they robbed the butler's pantry he stood behind the door; but the moment, he thought, had not yet arrived. In that small room, he calculated, he had hardly space to "tackle" with them properly, and with admirable coolness waited a better opportunity, and followed them up-stairs. As they entered the drawing-room he was close upon them; and had it not been that he was as much startled as Fibbes himself at the apparition of "Miss Blanche," his arm would have been raised an instant sooner, and might perhaps have saved that young lady a fainting-fit, as it did save her life. As he turned to seize Tom Blacke he beheld him in the grasp of Mr. Hardingstone, and then Hairblower felt indeed that he could have encountered a host; but by this time the house was alarmed, and further violence unnecessary.

Now, although we are aware that it is not customary for well-nurtured damsels to sit with lighted candles in drawing-rooms at an hour when the rest of the family have retired to rest, yet allowances must be made for such as have the misfortune to be in love. This was Blanche's case, and being unable to sleep, she wisely slipped on her dressing-gown, and stole down-stairs for the purpose of getting the last new novel, then lying on the drawing-room table, and administering it as the never-failing soporific. When there, she found the room so much more comfortable than her own, that she lit the candles and sat quietly down to read, till disturbed by what she thought at the moment a frightful apparition. Her delight at recognising Hairblower when she came to her senses was only equalled by the enthusiasm of that formidable auxiliary himself, who with difficulty refrained from embracing her on the spot, a mode of worship in which Frank Hardingstone would willingly have joined. That gentleman, we have reason to think, was in love too; at least, on the night in question he was restless and fidgety, and courted slumber in vain. Then he heard a door open, and got up and put on a few clothes, and then he fancied he distinguished a stealthy footfall in the passage below; so he too left his room, and arrived on the scene of action in the nick of time. How the disturbance of that night influenced the destiny of several of the party it is not now necessary to state, nor can we tell what Frank saw, heard, or felt, to induce him the following morning to send to Bubbleton for his horses, and to make such arrangements as argued his intention of protracting his visit at Newton-Hollows during some considerable portion of the hunting-season. We are satisfied, however, although she did not say so, that this arrangement was by no means unwelcome to Blanche Kettering.

CHAPTER XXVII
FLOOD AND FIELD

It was the last day of the Old Year, and he seemed to have resolved on making a peaceful ending, such as the thirty-first of December seldom vouchsafes in any climate but our own. Thoroughly English, too, was the party assembled round the breakfast-table at Newton-Hollows, from the red face of the old butler struggling in with the hissing urn, to the corresponding colour of Frank Hardingstone's coat, betokening that he meant to enjoy our national sport of fox-hunting. Blanche was already down, looking charming in a riding-habit, as all pretty women do; and Mary's quiet face showed more animation than usual, perhaps in consequence of an arrangement which was broached, apparently not for the first time.

"I am *so* glad we persuaded him not to ride," observed Blanche, appealing as usual to Mr. Hardingstone; "he will *not* take care of that cough—men are such bad patients! Now with Mary to drive him in the pony-carriage, he can keep himself well wrapped up, and the air will do him good."

"Undoubtedly," replied Frank, "Mrs. Delaval must take good care of her patient" (Mary looked as if she *rather* thought she would); "and I shall be completely at your service, Miss Kettering; you know I am *not* an enthusiast about hunting, like Charlie."

"Oh, I shall do very well with old Thomas and Uncle Baldwin, if he can only keep up with me," replied Blanche; "so I won't ask you to stay with *me*."

Frank seemed to think this would be no great sacrifice; but, as she spoke, the subject of their conversation entered the breakfast-room, and took his place as usual at Mrs. Delaval's side. Poor Charlie! he looked thinner than ever, and the cough, though not so violent, was every day more and more frequent. To be sure his eye was bright, and his colour at times brilliant; everybody seemed to think he was better, save the Bubbleton doctors, and they never would give an opinion one way or the other.

"So Haphazard is to be disappointed of his gallop again," complained Charlie, as he stretched his wasted hand for his tea-cup. "I have had quite enough of being nursed, Blanche, even by you. I really think I might ride him, just to see them find. I could get off if I felt tired, you know."

"Get off when the hounds are running!" replied Blanche, "not you. Now be a good boy just this once, Charlie. Mary has promised to drive you in my pony-carriage with Scrub: she says you shall see everything if you'll only trust yourself with her; and nobody will take such care of you as Mary, I know," added she, rather mischievously. Charlie made no further objections, and Mrs. Delaval kept her eyes immovably fixed on the pattern of her tea-cup.

"Late, of course—servants always are late, except for dinner. Charlie, my boy, how are ye this morning? You've got no breakfast. Zounds! why is everything cold? Blanche, my sweet girl, ring all the bells, and kick that old fool into next week, if he don't bring hot mutton-chops instanter. I can't stay a moment. I must be off to Snaffles, or he'll make some cursed mistake. It's very singular that nobody ever understands my directions," said the General, bustling into the room in a state of more than usual ferment, as is generally the case with occasional sportsmen on a hunting-morning. The General had been up since daybreak, but had not yet succeeded in snatching a quiet five minutes for his own breakfast; and even now, as he fussed about in a short green coat and high Napoleon boots, it seemed doubtful whether he would settle down to his meal, or be off on another visit to the stables, for the further confusion of the unfortunate Snaffles. Hunger carried it for the moment, but the trampling of hoofs and grinding of wheels on the sweep at the front-door soon drew our party to the window, from which Blanche's eyes were delighted by the appearance of her favourite Water King, his fine coat glistening in the morning sun, his long thin tail whisking about as usual, and his rounded form seen in all its beauty under the unmounted side-saddle. "Isn't he a darling?" exclaimed Blanche from the window, as the horse stepped proudly round to the door, pointing his small ears and glancing in every direction as though looking for his mistress. Old Thomas on a steady brown; Frank's two hunters, well-bred, weight-carrying animals; the General's black cob, and the little pony-carriage, completed the cavalcade, which was at length got into marching order, not without much difficulty and the issue of several contradictory orders from Uncle Baldwin, who, what with his anxiety about Blanche's mounting and his care that Charlie should be properly wrapped up, to say nothing of his directions to every one concerning that undiscoverable passage, "the shortest way," was already in a white heat, and altogether in a state quite the reverse of what we should suppose anticipatory of a day's *pleasure*.

However, Blanche was in the saddle at last, and pacing quietly on with Frank by her side. The General, too, was mounted, but by no means as yet under way—so much had to be impressed on the butler in case of the Field stopping to luncheon; so much on Snaffles, who remained at home, about sundry brood mares in the paddocks, all in an interesting situation; so much on the keepers, who neglected the earth-stopping generally; and so *very* much on the bailiff, who invariably appeared at the last moment, that had it not been for the determination evinced by the black cob, his master would have remained at the front-door till dinner-time; that animal, however, a resolute Roman-nosed conveyance, seeing his stable companions rapidly deserting him, and rejoicing moreover in a stiff neck and perfectly callous mouth, made no more ado, but took the bit between his teeth, and lowering his head to the well-known angle of insubordination, rushed doggedly to the front, bearing the General rapidly past the pony-carriage in a manner more ludicrous than dignified. Charlie was in fits. Even quiet Mrs. Delaval laughed outright; and this simple incident, perhaps, made their drive far more lively—we will not say more agreeable—than it would otherwise have been, inasmuch as they had started in solemn silence; and, like all couples who feel that they are more to each other than either dares to confess, they might have remained unwillingly mute during the precious hours, from sheer inability to talk upon any topic but one, and a nervous dread of entering on that one lest an explanation should at once dispel the dream that had been the happiness of their lives. Now, however, they chatted gaily enough; and certainly if ever there was a situation calculated to raise the spirits of mortals, it was that in which our young lancer and his lady-love found themselves, on their way to Crop Hill, that thirty-first of December—a drive never afterwards to be effaced from the memory of the gentle charioteer. It was one of those beautiful balmy mornings that (when we get them) make an English winter more delightful than that of any other country in the world. It can only be described by the expression which it brought to every one's lips, "What a hunting morning!" There had been heavy rain in the night, and the freshened pastures seemed actually to smile in the sun, as ever and anon he shone out with chastened beams over copse and meadow and upland; the very hedges, leafless though they were, seemed to breathe the fragrance of spring; mid-winter as it was, Nature seemed to be not dead, but sweetly sleeping; the robin hopped merrily from twig to twig; the magpie jerked and chattered, and flew before the pony-carriage, lighting now on this side of the lane, now on that, now disturbing its mate, now soaring away over the high thick hedge towards the distant wood. As they emerged into a line of fair open pastures from which their view, unchecked by fence on either side, swept over a rich green vale, dotted with cattle and clothed with hedge-row trees, they caught sight of their mounted friends cantering merrily along the grass ahead of them, Blanche's habit fluttering in the soft, light breeze, her cavalier's red coat and shining stirrup-irons glistening in the sun, and the General bumping steadily behind them on the high-stepping black cob, who, albeit usually an animal of imperturbable sobriety, had contracted a fatal passion for the chase, which on occasions like the present put him into a state of rebellious excitement that lasted throughout the day, and produced a sad reaction in the stable on the morrow.

"That's the best fellow in England," said Charlie, as he pointed out his friend to his companion. "I shall be glad when it's settled, Mrs. Delaval, as *I* know it soon will be." Mary thought they were on tender ground, and applied herself diligently to her driving without producing any great increase of pace on the part of philosophical Scrub. "Ah!" said Charlie, and his voice trembled as he spoke, "I've envied Frank all my life, and I envy him more than ever now."

"You *do*?" replied Mary, glancing quickly at him, while her heart for the moment seemed to stand still.

"Not his bride, Mrs. Delaval," replied Charlie, "for his bride you'll see she will be. No, no; I'm very fond of Blanche, but not in that way." Mary was blushing crimson, and it was surprising what a deal of driving that little pony required as Charlie proceeded. "But I envy him all he has that I can never have again—health, strength, all that makes life enjoyable—all that was once mine, but that I feel I have now lost for ever."

"Don't say so," replied Mary, though her rising tears almost choked her utterance, "don't say so. With care and good advice, and all of *us* to nurse you, oh, you must, you *shall* get well;" but even as she spoke she felt a sad foreboding at her heart. Charlie caught her glance, though it was almost instantly averted, and he proceeded as if half to himself—

"I could bear it well enough if I was like Frank in one respect, if I knew my life was bound to another's, and that other the one I cared most for in the world. I could struggle on for *her* sake; but no, I shall leave none such behind *me*, and perhaps it is better."

"Do you think we are so heartless?" she burst forth; "do you think we can part with you without a murmur? With *you*, for whom we have watched and prayed and longed all those dreary months; dreary indeed whilst you were——" Mary stopped short. She felt she had said too much, but it was Charlie's turn to blush now. His breath came quick and short; the boy dared not look the woman in the face, but he put his hand into his bosom and drew out a glove—a white kid glove it was formerly, now sadly soiled and discoloured, for a gallant heart had been beating against it many a long month—but with a rim of velvet round the wrist; there was no doubt of its identity, nor of the fair hand it once had fitted. Charlie drew it out and pressed it to his lips. She turned on him one swimming glance. They understood each other; the moment had at length arrived when—

"*Gently*, Ravager! back, hounds, back!"—and the loud crack of a hunting-whip disturbed their romantic *tête-à-tête* at this critical moment, and announced the proximity of that well-known pack denominated the Harkholloa Hounds, trotting gently on towards the place of meeting, and rapidly overtaking the pony-carriage and its pre-occupied inmates. The noble impulse of equine emulation, usually dormant in the shaggy form of Scrub, was now aroused by the inspiring influence of the passing pageant, and the clean, dainty-looking, motley-coloured pack; the neat, well-appointed servants in their bright scarlet coats and glossy velvet caps; the well-bred, well-groomed, hunting-looking horses they bestrode stepping airily along, jingling their bits, and snorting to the morning breeze. All these objects raised the mettle of Blanche's quiet pony, and Mary had now enough to do in earnest, as he tugged at the reins and drew them rapidly on in rear of the pack towards a slight elevation in the distance crowned by a windmill, and rejoicing in the dignified title of Crop Hill. A renewal of the tender subject was impossible, for as they neared the trysting-place the plot thickened rapidly, and sportsman after sportsman cantering by on his covert-hack had a bow for Mrs. Delaval, and a word to exchange with Charlie; now congratulating him on his return, now condoling with him for his inability to ride, now cordially hoping that he will soon be in the saddle, with an inquiry after the welfare of the celebrated Haphazard. Charlie's spirits rose as they proceeded, and ere they reached the windmill he was a boy again.

"Yoi, over there!" holloaed the huntsman, standing in his stirrups and waving the willing pack into the cover, a patch of sunny gorse lying on the south side of the hill, and commanding a vale of large green pastures that to contemplate alone brought the light into Charlie's eye.

"This way," said the General, sidling and piaffing and coming tail first towards the pony-carriage, for the double purpose of placing it in a favourable position for viewing the proceedings, and of exhibiting his own horsemanship before the eyes of Mrs. Delaval. The General was under the impression that if there was one thing in which more than another he excelled, it was the art of *manège* equitation, and perhaps on an animal less self-willed than the black cob he might have been a very Bellerophon, but certainly at the present juncture he jerked, and fumed, and kicked, and wiped his brows in anything but a graceful mode of progression.

"This way," said he, after a violent effort which brought the cob broadside on across Scrub, whose recognition, however, his excited friend disdained to acknowledge.

"From the brow of this hill you can see for miles. If we don't find here—how d'ye mean, *don't* find here? If there's no fox in the gorse I'll eat this hunting-whip!" eyeing his own iron-handled one as he spoke. "If you keep along the—(Stand *still*, you brute!)—if you keep along the brow, Mrs. Delaval—(Zounds! *will* you stand still?)—you'll be able to—Tally-ho! he's away, d'ye see him, yonder by the oak! now they have it. Forward! forward!!" Charlie could not resist a prolonged screech of delight, though he coughed for five minutes afterwards, and the General went off at score, as eager for a start as if he had been riding the best horse in England, and bumped, and thumped, and scuttled, and slid down the hill, towards a friendly hand-gate, as only an elderly gentleman can, who has survived all his passions save this one alone! What a scurry there was over the vale below! Immediately in the foreground a group of foot-people, a keeper in velveteen, and a labourer with a terrier in his arms, laughed and gazed and vociferated, and made sundry uncomplimentary remarks on the sportsmen whose prowess they could so effectually overlook. Lower down careful grooms on second horses, a steady-going dark-coated array, had diverged nearly at right angles to the line of chase, and keeping studiously together, seemed to be holding perseveringly for some point of their own, well down-wind. At the bottom of the hill, a horse-breaker, on a four-year-old rearing straight on end, was endeavouring to make the passage of a white gate that had slammed to, unpropitiously, just in front of him. As the man had dropped his whip and did not dare get off, he was likely to remain there some little time longer. Just in front of him again came the Field, a motley mass of colours, red predominating—streaming like a flight of wild-fowl, as they crossed the enclosures, but huddling confusedly together as often as they reached the fence, under the mistaken notion that there is safety in numbers.

Amongst them were men of all sorts and ages, ranks, weights, and sizes—some plying elbows and legs as they shot occasionally to the front, only to drop back to their native obscurity when the fatal necessity of jumping should arrive—some holding steadily on, satisfied to be in good company, with no more idea of where the hounds were than if they had been in the next county—discreet spirits breaking the hearts of valorous horses by keeping them back—eager enthusiasts rapidly finishing their too sorry steeds by urging them forward—but still one and all convinced that they were distinguishing themselves by their prowess, and prepared to swear over their wine that they had been all day in the front rank. To the right of these might be seen the General in a line of his own, leading him through a deep ridge and furrow field, in which he laboured like a boat in a heavy sea—already its inequalities had brought him to a slack rein, and even at that distance the rider's heels could be plainly distinguished in convulsive persuasion.

Five minutes more at that pace would unquestionably reduce the black cob to a walk. A field farther forward than these, and released from the turmoil and confusion in their rear, struggled a devoted band, the forlorn hope of the chase—those adventurous spirits who "mean riding," but "don't know how"—though small in number, great in hairbreadth 'scapes and thrilling casualties. There a rood and a half of fence was seen tumbling into a field with a crash like the falling of a house, followed by a headlong biped describing a parabola in the air, and closely attended by a huge dark object which resolved itself into a rolling steed. Farther on again a crashing of rails was heard, and a reckless pair seen balanced across a strong piece of field-upholstery, only to subside dully into a fatal ditch gaping to receive them, not in vain—

"*Rider and horse in one red burial blent.*"

A wisp of scarlet lying motionless on the greensward, and a loose horse galloping furiously to the front, completed this ill-fated portion of the panorama, and carried the eye forward to where some half-dozen detached cavaliers were gradually diminishing till they looked like red balls bouncing over a billiard-table, as independent and nearly abreast each sped his own line across the distant fields. These were indeed the "chosen few"—the deacons of the craft, quick, quiet, wary, and resolute—they had surmounted all the obstacles of the commencement, all the struggle for a start, and were now enjoying their reward. Each man as he took his horse well by the head settled himself in his saddle, and scanning his ground with keen and practised eye, crashed through the impervious bullfinch or faced the uncompromising timber, enjoying a deep thrilling ecstasy totally incomprehensible to the rational portion of mankind. A Frenchman once remarked to us, anent this particular form of lunacy, "Monsieur, nous ne cherchons pas nos émotions, nous Français, à nous casser le cou." But deep and stirring were the *émotions* of our English enthusiasts as they strained after the fleeting pack, now diminished to a few white, scattered dots, glancing over the green surface a field ahead even of these.

"Happy fellows!" exclaimed Charlie, watching the first flight, where his own place should have been, with straining eyes. "It looks uncommonly like a run!—but where's Frank? he ought to be forward with the hounds. Oh! he's philandering there on the right with Blanche;" and Charlie's mouth drew itself down into an expression of intense disgust—although in love himself, he could not understand Venus being allowed to interfere with Diana. "If we keep down this lane," exclaimed he, still bending his gaze on the disappearing pack, "we shall come in upon them again, to a certainty, with this wind. Wilmington Copse is his point, I'll lay my life. Go along, Scrub!" and the pony-carriage was again set in motion, not without flagellation of Blanche's favourite, bumping and swaying down an extremely bad road at the best speed it could muster. Ever and anon the drivers cast a look over the vale at the fast-disappearing chase, but the excitement was rapidly subsiding. All the reds had by this time vanished, save one extremely cautious sportsman in a lane; the more sober colours were gradually fading into the distance. The horse-breaker was gone, the keeper in velveteen shouldered his gun, the labourer put down his terrier, and the pedestrians were lounging home to dinner. After two miles or so of severe exertion the panting Scrub was again pulled up at Stoney Cross, a place where four byroads met, commanding an extensive view of the surrounding country. Mary was almost as keen about the run as her companion, so catching is excitement, particularly hunting excitement. "Listen," said she, intently eyeing the distance, "can you hear anything?"

"Nothing but Scrub blowing," replied Charlie; "no, they're having an *extraordinary* run—we shall never see them again!"

Both strained their eyes till they watered. Profound silence reigned over the landscape, save when the wintry wind moaned softly through the boughs of some leafless poplars overhead. The sun had disappeared; a dark grey haze was creeping over the distance; even Nature seemed to be suffering a reaction after the excitement of the last half-hour, and Charlie too felt despondent and melancholy; the air was moist and chill, the sky dark and lowering; it was the last day of the year—would he ever see another? Must he leave this pleasant world, pleasant even in the subdued melancholy of winter's russet garb, and lie in the damp, cold earth, whilst his friends and comrades were full of life and hope and energy? The last time—was this indeed the *last time* for him of the sport he loved so passionately? No more to back his gallant steeds, and feel his life-blood thrill as they bounded beneath him in the real ecstasy of motion; no more to join the jovial scarlet throng, with bit and bridle ringing round him, and laugh and jest and cordial greeting passing from lip to lip in that merriest of merry meetings at the covert side; no more to stand in the deep fragrant woodland and cheer that chiming music to the echo, sweeter to him than the very symphony of heaven; and when silence, startling from its suddenness, succeeded to those maddening sounds, and warned him they were *away!* others would race with the racing pack, and revel in the whirlwind of *pace*, glancing over pastures like hawks upon the wing, but his place would be vacant in the front rank, and he—where would he be? Hard! hard! now that life was so sweet and sparkling, now that the cup was crowned with that last drop that bid it brim with happiness—the consciousness of love. And must it be put untasted by? Hard—hard, yet perhaps better so!

"I hear them, I'm certain," said Mary, raising her taper hand in the air; "that must be the horn. We shall see the finish after all!"

"Not yet," cried Charlie, all his melancholy reflections dispelled on the instant. "See, they've checked on the plough yonder. Now they acknowledge it. Well hunted, my beauties! Look! look! did you see him?—there, in the middle of that large field, beyond the spinney!"

Mary looked and looked, and at length made out a dark speck stealing away in the distance too slowly for a crow, too smoothly for a dog; had she not been told she never would have suspected that minute object was the fox.

"He's not killed yet," observed Charlie; "there'll be some *grief* before he's in hand! See, he's pointing straight for the forest—by Jove! they'll have to swim the Gushe. What a capital fox!" And now, once more, the pageant passed in full view of the pony-carriage; but oh! how altered! Despite the check there were but two men near the hounds, and even these were a full field behind them (after dinner they acknowledged to twenty yards); then came one solitary individual in a cap, who was indeed the huntsman, and who was now riding in the combined enjoyment of a horse completely exhausted, and a morbid dread lest the more fortunate twain in his front should press too much on his treasures—a needless fear, could he but have seen the mode in which these treasures were increasing the distance between themselves and their pursuers. Behind him again was a gentleman (clerical) standing by his horse, apparently investigating his stirrup-irons with minute interest. He never could be got to explain clearly why he had stopped at this exciting moment. Gaining gradually upon the latter came another red-coat, making the most of an extremely slow canter; and not a soul besides was to be seen on the line of the hounds. What had become of them all? Where was the Field? Why, pounding down the very lane in which the pony-carriage had drawn up, pulling and hustling, and grinning and clattering—coat-tails flying, neck-cloths streaming, the leaders' faces bathed in perspiration, the rearward horsemen plastered with mud, all riding like grim Death, all frantic with hurry and excitement—the General and his black cob not the least furious of the throng. Few noticed the carriage, all were intent on some object in the extreme distance, possibly the bridge at Deep-ford, inasmuch as the hounds were now pointing straight for the Gushe.

It was quite a relief to watch Frank Hardingstone's unmoved face as he cantered quietly by, and smiled and spoke to them, without, however, relaxing in his vigilant care of Blanche. That young lady looked prettier than ever—her violet eyes dancing with excitement, and her long fair curls floating over her riding-habit.

"He's going to *have* it," screamed Charlie, in a state of tumultuous excitement, as they watched Frank turn away from his charge, and leaping the fence out of the lane, take a direct line for the calm, deep, silent river, and consequently for the hounds, who were already struggling in the stream, throwing their tongues occasionally as they were swept along by its force, to land considerably lower down than they had calculated. One of the foremost sportsmen went gallantly in with them, but his horse was already exhausted, and, after sinking twice, rider and steed emerged separately on the hither side, glad to get off with a ducking.

"Blanche, you foolish girl, stop! I desire you to stop!" exclaimed the General, foaming with excitement, and himself with difficulty pulling the black cob across the road. But Blanche either would not or could not stop: Water King's mettle was excited; he had been following Frank Hardingstone's horse all day, and true to his name, he was not to be deterred by the perils of a swim. Taking the bit between his teeth, he bounded out of the lane at the spot where his leader had jumped the fence, and tore away over the level water-meadows, regardless of the volley of imprecations which the General sent after him as of the feeble grasp which strove to check him in vain.

Frank meanwhile, all unconscious, sped steadily down to the stream. Already his cool resolute eye had marked the safest place at which to land. "If I can only get *out*," thought Frank, "there's never much difficulty about getting *in*." Already had he gathered his horse well up on his haunches, turned his stirrup-irons over his saddle-bow, knotted the thong of his whip to his rein in case of dissolving partnership on emergency, and sliding quietly down the bank, was immersed in deep water, laying his weight as much as possible along his horse's neck, when a faint scream, a rushing sound close behind him, and a tremendous splash by his side, made him turn wildly round and well-nigh pull his unfortunate steed over him in the water. How shall we describe his sensations at what he saw? Water King plunging and rearing himself above the surface; Blanche clinging helplessly to her horse's neck, her white face glancing on him for an instant with an expression of ghastly terror; another furious plunge, a faint, bubbling scream, and the limp skirt of a riding-habit disappearing beneath the whirling wave. The horror-stricken sportsmen in the lane saw a lady's hat floating on the stream some fifty yards lower down. But assistance was near at hand; twenty men were soon gathered on the bank. People never know how these things are done. Frank was away from his horse in an instant; he believes he dived for her twice; but two minutes had scarcely elapsed before he was hanging over her exhausted form on the bank, regardless of the surrounding crowd, regardless of his usual self-command and reserved demeanour, pouring forth the torrent of his feelings, so long dammed up, in words that were but little short of madness.

It was fortunate, indeed, that Scrub's fatigue had prevented the pony-carriage from going any farther on the line of the crowd, who were by this time blocking up the narrow passage of Deep-ford Bridge, as Blanche, despite her wet clothes, was too much exhausted to attempt riding home, and was accordingly placed by Mary in her own little equipage. The pony made small difficulty about retracing his steps towards his stable, and the cavalcade proceeded rapidly to Newton-Hollows; Frank riding alongside in his dripping garments, with an expression of unspeakable joy on his manly features never seen there before or since; Mary praying inwardly with heart-felt gratitude, and the General sobbing like a child. As they turned in at the gates, Charlie was the only one of the party who retained his composure sufficiently to observe, with an expression of deep interest, "I wish we knew whether they've killed their fox."

CHAPTER XXVIII
"THE SAD SEA WAVE"

And of all places in the world, where did they choose to spend their honeymoon? Why, at St. Swithin's; there they had first met—there the girl had first seen her young ideal of manly perfection—there Frank had first surrendered the self-control he held so dear. When at the end of a twenty-seventh chapter the gentleman saves from drowning the lady after whom he has been hankering through the previous twenty-six, it is needless to specify how "bride-cake must be the issue." "Hot water" after cold is a fair conclusion; so the dressmaker in Old Bond Street was written to—and the man-of-business came down from Lincoln's Inn—and there was a gathering of friends and relatives—a breakfast to the grandees—a dinner to the tenants—a ball to the labourers—and the bells of Newton ringing almost without cessation for eight-and-forty hours—the bridesmaids smiled and sparkled—the bride wept and trembled—the bridegroom looked like a fool—everything was strictly orthodox, save the interference of the General, who wanted to set the clergyman right during the sacred ceremony, and very properly received a rap over the knuckles from that dignitary, which was no less than he deserved—the county paper devoted a column and a half to its description of the ceremony—the *Morning Post* dismissed it in three lines under the head of "Fashionable Intelligence"; and so the knot was tied, and Frank Hardingstone, M., took Blanche Kettering, N., and they became man and wife.

We must now shift the scene to where we first introduced the characters of our somewhat lengthened narrative; nor will we, after the fashion of sundry eminent divines, prolong our "in conclusion" to an indefinite abusing of the listener's patience and the Queen's English. The honeymoon is over—they never last more than a week now-a-days—and the relatives of the principal performers have broken up the *tête-à-tête*, and joined the happy pair at St. Swithin's. It is a mild sunny afternoon about the middle of February. At the sea-side, where there are no bare trees and leafless hedges to destroy the illusion, it might be midsummer, so soft and balmy is the air, so bright the beams glinting on the Channel, so hushed and peaceful the ripple of the ebbing tide; the fishing-boats seem asleep upon the waters;

a large square-rigged vessel looms almost motionless in the offing; and a group of five persons are congregated about an invalid's couch on the beach. As Mary Delaval moves round it to place a cushion more comfortably at his back, we recognise the delicate features and waving moustaches of our young lancer. It is indeed the wasted face of Cousin Charlie, attenuated to an unearthly beauty, and wearing the calm, gentle expression of those who are ere long to be summoned home.

"Outward-bound," says a stout seaman-like man, shutting up the glass with which he has been diligently conning the distant ship. "Outward-bound, and an Indiaman, as I make her, Miss Blanche; I beg your pardon." Hairblower never can call her by her matronly title.

"If that's an Indiaman, I'll eat her," exclaims the General; "don't tell me—I should know something of that class of ship at any rate. Look at her spars! She's bound for the Baltic; I can take my oath. Indiaman!—if she's not a Dutchman, *I am*."

The General's appearance indeed gave weight to this assertion. His stout, short frame enveloped in a jacket and trousers—for, out of compliment to the locality, he thought it necessary to appear in nautical costume— possessed that well-filled appearance which custom has chosen to consider indigenous to the Hollander. The General's love-making did not progress very rapidly, but he had still a hankering to stand well in the opinion of Mrs. Delaval; and when he considered the care and attention with which she tended poor Charlie, administering to all his wants and fancies as only a woman can, he thought that such a wife would indeed be a treasure for an elderly gentleman who was beginning to experience sundry twinges at the extremities, reminding him most unpleasantly of good things long since consumed, and claret bottles emptied in life's thirsty noon.

"What do *you* think, darling?" says Blanche, sidling up to her husband, and placing her arm confidingly within his. Like all newly-married women she is a little *gauche*, and wears her happiness with too demonstrative an air, appealing on all occasions to her lord, and hanging on his every word and look as if there were no one else in the universe. To do the sex justice, however, this is a fault of which they are invariably cured in less than a twelvemonth, and radically too—we cannot call to mind a single instance of a relapse.

"How should I know, my dear?" replies Frank, awaking from deep thought; "yet stay, may it not be the very ship in which your old friend D'Orville was to sail?" with a malicious glance at Blanche, who looked up at him with such an open smile as showed how little impression the handsome

Major's attentions had ever made on *her* young heart. "Let me see, what day was he to start? I've got his letter in my pocket."

"Pocket!—letter!—what? read it!" exclaimed the General—"that will prove the thing at once—you'll see she's a Dutchman."

Blanche glanced at Mary; and even that grave face brightened into a smile—while Frank, seating himself on the shingle, drew a letter from his pocket and began to read.

"Cannot resist—hem—congratulations—hem—blessings in store—hem—leaving this country for a long absence." ("Ah! here it is.") "As I am going out in command of troops, I shall have the pleasure of once more rubbing up my seamanship by a voyage round the Cape. We embark at Gravesend on the —th, and shall probably sail when the tide suits the following day." ("'Gad—I believe it is the Indiaman!") "Lacquers accompanies me, having got the majority in my corps, and has become a *great* soldier—perhaps thanks to your success in the attack on which I now write to congratulate you." ("Here's a long story about *you*, Blanche—shall I read it?") Blanche passed her little hand over his mouth, and Frank proceeded. "As I shall probably not have another opportunity of writing to my English friends for four or five months, I will not apologise for the length of my present epistle, but give you all the news I can to enliven your honeymoon—a piece of presumption which, I conclude, is like refining refined gold or painting the lily. London is not very full, although Parliament has brought its regular quantum of members who stand in awe of their constituents—no small number in these reformed and reforming days. *I* recollect, my dear Frank, though *you* don't, when all the electors for a county met in the Justices' room, and returned the Lord-Lieutenant's nominee with as little discussion as my orderly-sergeant will make this afternoon when he reports 'the officers' baggage gone on board.' However, they won't stand that kind of thing now. Talking of Parliament, you read Mount Helicon's speech on the Tallow question, of course. It quite took the House by storm. Honourable members expected *something* from the author of 'Broadsides from the Baltic,' and they were not disappointed. Not a word, however, taken from that exceedingly clear and voluminous pamphlet; and where he can have picked up such an additional store of information is a mystery to every one. The speech, however, has floored his party. Its whole tone, every sentiment it breathed, was so diametrically opposite to their policy, that they found themselves at its conclusion without a leg to stand on. Having selected him for their mouthpiece, they were furious, and no wonder. What can he be at? We soldiers are plain-dealing men, and cannot understand all this mining and counter-mining. His lady-mother, I understand, is still at Bubbleton. You must have seen something of her in the winter, unless you had only eyes and ears for one—particularly as I hear she gives out everywhere that she has refused General Bounce. If your abrupt uncle is the man I take him for, she never had an opportunity." (Frank was here obliged to pause, the General's delight at this portion of the letter venting itself in a series of chuckles that threatened to choke him. It was with difficulty he restrained himself from relating the whole story of the widow at Cheltenham, as a narrative bearing irresistibly on the case in point. He swallowed it, however, and Frank proceeded.) "We never thought her ladyship a great beauty, but they tell me now she is dreadfully altered—disappointed about her son—disappointed in her winter campaign—dreadfully sore at the slights she fancies she has received from the Dinadams, who passing through Bubbleton on their way to Wassailworth, had no time to return the visit she paid them at their hotel—and conscious of growing old, without having done the slightest good in her generation. No wonder the worn-out fine lady is sick of her wretched world, such as it is—no wonder she is startled to discover that she has spent a lifetime of illusions, and never found out the *real* world after all. You will smile, my dear Frank, at my moralities, but I do begin to see things a little clearer than I used; and if I have reason so bitterly to regret the forty years I have spent in selfish uselessness, what must be the feelings of threescore years and odd, with the world slipping from under its feet, the waking moment rapidly approaching, and the feverish dream leaving not one solid reality behind it—not one satisfactory reflection to gild the past—not one well-grounded hope to hold a beacon through the dark cold voyage of the future?"

"Frank ... drew a letter from his pocket, and began to read."

Hairblower, who had been listening attentively with a puzzled expression of countenance, brightened up considerably at a metaphor which had reference to his own daily occupations, and muttered something about "ballast aboard," and the "anchor apeak"; whilst Mrs. Delaval stole a longing, lingering look at poor Charlie, who had closed his eyes as if wearied out and half asleep. Frank read on.

"Tell young Kettering I have many inquiries after his health from his friends here, amongst others an old fellow-campaigner in Kaffirland whose tent he shared, and who is full of Kettering's famous attack in support of the Rifles. He says it was one of the most dashing things of the war, and the service can ill afford to lose so gallant an officer. He sends his own and his terrier's kindest remembrances."

Charlie's eyes opened wide; he did not seem drowsy now. The long wasted fingers of his right hand closed as if upon the handle of his sword, and a light stole over his countenance as if the sun had just gleamed athwart it—the soldier-spirit was stirring in that powerless frame. He looked handsomer than ever, poor boy, poor boy!

"His admiring well-wisher," the letter went on to say, "who, by the way, is one of the best-looking fellows in London, got his promotion in that very action, and is now on leave, making up for past privations by every kind of dissipation which the village affords. I do not see much of him; but dining last night at the 'Peace and Plenty,' he told me that our mutual friend, Sir Ascot, was going to be married. Mrs. Hardingstone will be amused to hear this. The fortunate lady is a Miss Deeper, who threw over young Cashley, as in duty bound, for the baronet. Laurel, too, has carried off pretty Kate Carmine at last; they are the poorest couple in Christendom, and the happiest. I met Sir Bloomer Buttercup yesterday at the 'Godiva.' He and Mulligatawney were, as usual, discussing the matrimonial question; the latter more 'Malthusian' than ever, since Mrs. M. has taken up the Rapping theory. Sir Bloomer thinks that now he can only pretend to a widow, but is still determined to marry as soon as his affairs can be put 'on a footing.' We are all of opinion if he waits till then he will die a bachelor. You are aware I have got my promotion, and am going out to take the command of one of the smartest regiments in the service. I trust it will not deteriorate in any way whilst in my hands. Lacquers unites with me in congratulations and cordial good wishes to the whole of your party. If Mrs. Delaval is with you, remember me most kindly to her, and believe me," etc.

"Well done the Colonel," said Frank, folding up his letter and putting it in his pocket. "I never saw a man so changed and so improved. Blanche, don't you regret now?—eh?" Blanche laughed, and called him "a goose";

but Mary applied herself more assiduously than ever to the invalid's cushions; and whatever may have been her thoughts, she kept them most carefully to herself. We can guess, however, that notwithstanding the many good qualities developing themselves in her old admirer, she never for an instant thought of comparing him with that poor helpless boy whom they were now obliged to carry into the house, lest even the soft evening breeze should strike too chill upon his lacerated lungs. Next to Mary, however, perhaps none tended the sufferer with such patience and gentleness as Hairblower—that worthy's view of the malady and its cause was peculiar to himself, and he clung to it with heroic obstinacy. "It all came of making him a soger," said the seaman, with a tear running down his weather-beaten cheek; "goin' about half-dressed in them monkey-jackets and sleepin' out o' nights without a dry thread to bless theirselves—it's enough to kill a cat, let alone a gentleman. Now, if he'd had a dry plank above and below, and a hammock to swing in, and watches to keep all regular and ship-shape, he'd have lived to be an admiral—see if he wouldn't. But he's better, is Master Charlie, much better, now the *salt's* gettin' into him. Oh, he'll be well in no time now, will Master Charlie—not a doubt of it!"

"Not a doubt of it," echoed the General, the illness of whose favourite was a sad cause of grief and anxiety, which vented themselves in a more than customary abruptness and irritation. "Better? How d'ye mean? Zounds, sir, don't talk to me of doctors! I tell ye the lad's rallying—rallying, sir. What? If that boy's not a-horseback in June, I'll——" And here the warm-hearted old General's courage invariably gave way, and as he thought of the alternative he would burst into tears, and stump hastily off to hide his emotion.

There never was such a February as that. Even inland people congratulated themselves on enjoying at last a *really* mild winter; and in such a sheltered, sunshiny situation as St Swithin's, the weather would have borne comparison with any boasted climate of the warm Mediterranean. Like some poor, draggled, pining bird, the invalid seemed to drink in health and strength from the very sunbeams; and as he lay full-length upon his couch, drawn as near the waves as the tide would allow, and basked in the warmth, and inhaled the soft fresh breezes of the Channel, he looked so composed, so happy—and the cough, though frequent, became so much less violent, that all agreed there never was "anything so providential as bringing him down to St. Swithin's"—"these illnesses are only fatal when not taken in time"—"positively it was the very saving of the boy's life." But Mary looked very pale, and shook her head. She seldom spoke much now.

One evening, just at sundown, Charlie begged to speak to Uncle Baldwin alone. He was lying as usual close to the open window, and as the breeze fanned his cheek he seemed to drink in its fragrance with a keener zest than he had shown for days. He felt better and stronger, too; he was able to sit up, and his voice was steadier and fuller than it had been since he came home. He spoke almost jestingly of his present state; but the words of hope which he thought it right to affect, in consideration of his uncle's feelings, were belied by the topic on which he sought an interview.

"Uncle," said he, "you've been a father to me, and I've never been strong enough to thank you till to-day."

"Stronger, my boy—to be sure you are—virtually, you're quite well. Don't tell——" There was something in Charlie's smile that checked the General, and the boy went on—

"Life's very uncertain, uncle, and if—you know I only say *if*—I should not get over this business, I want you to arrange two or three little matters for me. This is a beautiful world, uncle, and a pleasant one; but I sometimes think I'd rather *not* live now. I—I don't mind going. No, I don't seem as if I belonged so much to this earth—I can't tell why, but I *feel* it, I'm sure I do. Well, dear Uncle Baldwin, when I'm *gone*, I want you to give as much of my money to poor Gingham as will enable her to go out and join her husband in Australia. I know she wishes it, and I think it would come better from me than any one. If I get well, I mean to do it myself; but I like to make sure; and—and—uncle"—a deep blush spread over Charlie's face—"all the rest I wish to go to Mrs. Delaval; but don't let her find out it's from me. Promise me, dear Uncle Baldwin—promise me this."

The General started. He began to see what he now thought himself very blind not to have seen long ago, but he promised faithfully enough; and Charlie, lying back as if a weight had been taken off his mind, added, with a placid smile, "One thing more, uncle, and I will not trouble you any more—take care of poor Haphazard, and never let him run in a steeple-chase again." The General's heart was in his eyes, but he concealed his feelings from the invalid; and this too he promised, much to Cousin Charlie's satisfaction, who talked on so cheerfully, and avowed himself to feel so much better, that when at last Uncle Baldwin left him he joined the rest of the party more sanguine than any of them of his ultimate recovery, and vowed "he could not have believed what the sea-air would do." "You may sigh, Mrs. Delaval, and shake your head, but he's as strong to-day as ever he was in his life. Lungs!—his lungs are as good as mine. What?—he's only outgrown his strength—don't tell me, the lad's six feet high. Why, I saw Globus this very day, and he assures me confidently that he thinks Charlie will be quite well by the spring."

Spring bloomed into summer and summer faded into autumn. When London became empty—that is to say, when some thousand or two of its millions took their departure from the swarm—we went, as is our custom, to court health and sea-breezes at St. Swithin's. Though we follow blindly the example of our kind, rushing tumultuously to crowded resorts and overflowing watering-places, yet do we love solitude in the abstract as do most men who have outlived their digestions, and consequently we were not disappointed to find the day after our arrival so gusty, gloomy, and disagreeable, that the fair-weather visitors were compelled to remain indoors, and we had the beach pretty well to ourselves. There was a thick haze over the Channel, and a small drizzling rain beat in our face. We may be peculiar, but we confess we have no objection to a fog, and rather like a drizzling rain; so we breasted the breeze, and walked boldly on till we got clear of the town, and keeping steadily along "high-water mark," could enjoy our humour of sulking undisturbed.

But one figure shared our solitude—a tall, handsome woman, dressed in the deepest mourning, short of widow's weeds, that we ever saw. As we passed her, she was gazing steadily to seaward, and we caught but one glimpse of her countenance; yet that face we never have forgotten. Care had hollowed the eyes and wasted the pale cheek, and streaked the masses of dark hair with many a silver line, but the deep expression of holy beauty that sat on those marble features was that of an angel—some spirit sorrowing for the spirit-band from which it was parted, and yearning for its home. She was listening intently to the regular and monotonous gush of the Channel waves as they poured in their steady measured music, like a requiem for the dead. A well-beloved voice spoke to her on the sighing breeze, an old familiar strain was borne upon the rolling waters: she was communing with another world, and we left her, but not alone.

Mary Delaval has never quitted St. Swithin's. Marble, wrought to warlike trophies, blazons in a lengthened inscription the blighted fame and early death of a blooming warrior, who dragged his sinking frame hither to gaze upon the shining waters, and so to die. But it is not in the stately aisle or over the speechless stone that Mary weeps for her lost hopes, and mourns her buried love. No, she had rather wander by the lonely shore and listen to the "sad sea waves," as they murmur their mournful tale of the unforgotten Past. Day by day, ay, night by night, she glides about amongst the poor, ever on errands of mercy—ever eager but for one thing on earth—to do good—to fulfil her destiny—to die *here* where *he* died—and so to go to *him*. By the bed of sickness, in the abode of misery—ay, in the very den of vice, if it be but hallowed by grief, that pale sad face is as well known as the High Church curate's or the parish doctor's; but the poor respect her sorrows; and the rough fishermen, the busy artisans, the very careless romping children will turn out of the path, and forbear to intrude upon the presence of the "dark lady," as she sits looking wistfully to seaward, or wanders dejectedly along the beach. They seem to feel that she is *with* them, but not *of* them—a sojourner here, but not for long.

We love to gaze on the blooming merry faces of the young—we can admire the bright, hopeful girl—the contented, happy matron—childhood—prime—and old age. All have their beauties, all reflect more or less vividly the image of their Creator; but never in mortal features have we seen such a heavenly expression as that borne by Mary Delaval with her aching heart; deeper than hope, holier than joy, it hallows those alone whose every tie to lower earth is torn asunder, whose treasure is not here, whose home is beyond the grave—of whom Infinite Mercy has said, "Blessed are those that mourn, for they shall be comforted."